ROBOT, Archangel

by David Walls-Kaufman

Copyright © 2022 by David Walls-Kaufman
All rights reserved.

ISBN | 978-1-955937-86-3

For Kimble

Your worst enemy was your own nervous system.
—George Orwell, *1984*

To thine self know why you are here
—Analects of Mencius

-1-

Milton Aras did not know how to respond.
How isn't this man's inhumanity to man in the eyes of our God?
Aras revolted instinctively. "Wait! *Stop!*" he yelled.
The orange-red Aztec skull made no reply.
Rage crept into Aras's voice. "You say *our* god? Aren't you *machina*? You aren't even alive! What's this talk of any god being *your* god?"
The skull blazed silently.
"You have no say in this! This is a fight between *people!*"
"What do you do when one animal bullies the rest?"
A hot pain burbled in Aras's gut.
A sound welled up, a whistling, shaking, tearing roar. It quaked out of the very bonds of space and time around them. Somehow Aras knew this was the sound of every prayer ever uttered since the moment the first man became more than a beast and believed there was a god that might be spoken to for relief from wrong. Aras heard the team shouting and ducking under desks and chairs behind.
But he knew all the technology in the world was no protection.
They were coming for *him*.

The sixty-year-old citizen stepped down from the dray cart into the rain and into the cold puddles in the empty road and felt the rain pellets drum across his hat and shoulders and fire off the canvas roof of the cart. The city sky had wept rust-smelling rain all day into evening. He walked up the broad stairs to the ornate bronze doors of the closed and dark government building, and turned. The cart driver snapped the reins, the lines sprinkling white raindrops in the streetlight. The brace of mules shook their long-eared heads and rattled the cart away over the cobbles into the dark.
The citizen waved thanks. He did, indeed, feel helped by the driver's mantra of prayers. The driver had said what he thought of this odd

nighttime appointment beyond First Gate and prayed for him many times. The driver had asked:

"Dost thou think thine art to see the one they call the Jolly Man?"

Did the driver speak in the old dialect because he was uncertain of Wazku's fate? "I have never heard of a 'Jolly Man.' "

"It is said He is the one thou dost not wish to see!"

"I have no trouble with the government."

"Yes. But who ever does?"

"I am a simple pawner."

"I am a simple driver of mules!"

They had fallen silent, again.

"Let me see again." The driver examined the paper summons more carefully under the next arc light, leaning his broad hat away from the light, droplets pelleting paper. "One cannot tell what trouble is or not," the driver said again. He handed back the letter without looking at the citizen. "There is no trouble for you, citizen. And yet, I will pray for thee and thine family."

The citizen now entered the high gloom of the government building lobby. Under the grand geometric cornice sat a stocky guard with black hair at the reception cell. The citizen brought his damp-softened summons to the cell. The guard barely looked up. "Please?" said the citizen. The guard made no real sign of what the citizen should do, leaving him to creep past toward the huge bank of elevators.

"If thine stance with our officials was truly dour," the driver had said, "then they would have come for you with the Robes."

So, how bad could it be?

His finger trembled at the button. He glanced again at the office number. The 632nd floor. His chest hurt. His heart was very timid these years. The elevator whooshed down and compressed wind from the shaft pushed the dirty tails of his long coat. The grand bronze doors yawned open. Inside, the citizen heard faint pleasant flute muzak. He had never before heard recorded music. Such *delights!*

The elevator closed and whooshed up, and up. He felt the motion in his heart, rushing up to Heaven, or God, if God existed over these places.

Ding. A gentle bell.

The citizen stepped into a low-lit empty corridor that peeled off down an endless hall in both directions. Room number 632-146. A wall plaque pointed right for even-numbered, left for odd. His breathing hurt more.

He thought of his three-year-old grandson left with him and his wife after their son, the poor lad, was kicked to death by a horse.

He walked and walked. Finally, a door like the rest. He knocked. No answer. He swallowed; he had no spit. Did this mean he had fulfilled his obligation and he could go home? No. Surely, they would come for him . . . in the way the driver had said. He tried the knob. It turned. He let go, startled. His heart ached like misery in his chest.

"Master Wazku?" a happy voice said from inside. "Enter, Master Wazku! Enter, by all means!" Wazku entered a large room of empty desks, each with the most amazing rectangle of bright blue-green designs floating in air like paintings! It was so gorgeous and strange it was terrifying. "Don't stand on ceremony, dear sir."

Wazku thought they were jewel windows hanging by invisible wires in the air. Behind one desk sat a fleshy man in an old-fashioned business suit and tie by a wall of glass that overlooked the bay and the most incredible vista of the Tall City beyond the First Gate. Wazku had never even *imagined* the Tall City from this perspective. He nearly fell to his knees. It was *petrifying* walking around at this height. The fleshy man at the desk was youngish with jet-black hair and a black beard that offset uncannily white teeth as he smiled and indicated a chair. The white of those teeth existed not even in porcelain kitchen tiles in the buildings from ancient times.

"For cheer, Master Wazku! Be unfeared. I have little bad to tell you." Again, the laughter, the hand, welcoming. But then in the corner stood a dark, erect figure. Another man. In a much simpler suit of obviously superior ocean-blue silk. He watched Wazku without generosity, as if he very much didn't like being here.

Wazku crept forward, unable to look from the view or the man in the corner.

"Mr. Wazku. Why do you act like a man afraid? Fear not the man in the corner! He is my colleague, a Mr. Milton Aras. We are here merely as your—guides!"

"I am not afraid. I have nothing to fear."

He lied. The height was incredible. The handsome official in the corner was also terrifying. Would the building fall?

"Oh, but we all have something to fear. Yes? It is a part of life. Yes?"

"I am untroubled. I have done nothing wrong."

"Of course you haven't! You are a *good* man! This, we know! But, when you say it like that, so suredly, then I *know* you have done something." The official shot a glance to the one in the corner, Aras.

"I am a simple pawner."

"There. You see? A money lender! This is trouble for you, yes?"

The citizen shook his head stubbornly. "I am a simple pawner, and my wife runs a four-table coffee shop, Monsieurs."

The official's smile changed to one of sharp comprehension. "I see in you a man who knows how to talk to a public official, oh, yes."

"Oh, no, I do not. I never wanted the pleasure."

The official laughed and glanced again at Aras.

"We are both men of God, and, oh, yes! You *do* know how!"

"But I have never been called up in my life. I am never trouble. I am a simple pawner who helps other Sons of God with small money problems."

"That is what your neighbors told you to say, yes?" The man grinned warmly, as if it was no problem; no big deal, everybody did it.

"No, no. I was embarrassed; I spoke to no one. No one coached me how to talk because I did not want to be shunned, and my family."

The bureaucrat did not believe him so much. "I think maybe you are lying to me. But—what does it matter? Who does not lie to the government, yes? Haha."

"I would not lie to the government. I do not want the trouble." The citizen looked at Aras and held his hand as if to place it on the front of the desk, then thought better of it and put his hands in his lap.

"Make yourself comfortable," the official urged.

Wazku stayed just so.

"Mr. Wazku, I am Alfred Wah, official sub-altern at the Bureau of Theological & Civic Maintenance, at your service." Manicured fingers politely touched his midriff. "That man, as I said, is Mr. Milton Aras, my . . . superior. And *you* are here in our Al Hariri Branch Office, First Gate."

Wazku had accepted of himself since his early schooling that he was not overly bright. "Do you want me to take a poll of some kind, if you read it to me? I am always quite satisfied!"

The official laughed louder. "Of course you are! You are a model citizen!"

"I am grateful you think so. There is no record of me complaining."

"Do you have any complaints at all, Mr. Wazku?"

"No. I do not believe I do." Wazku looked again at the other man.

"How old are you, Mr. Wazku?"

"In my sixties."

"*Really?* You look much older. You and I are close enough in age, actually. And look at Aras, too. The same! Look at me! I look much more vigorous! And you have no complaints with your whole life?"

"No. Not really, no."

"How about with your wife?"

Was this it? His *wife*? He bumped his glasses up his nose. "No, I am unangry with my wife. She seems to be a good person."

" 'Seems' to be, Mr. Wazku?" The smile, forgiving all.

The official turned in his chair and smiled out the transparent wall at the dark water and the cityscape across. The night was the color of char, the bay ashen, and the buildings across towered up with more beyond.

"The truth is, Master Wazku, you are here not because of your conduct, but because of the conduct of your people six centuries ago." The visual flickered in front of Wah, and he checked his data. "Yes, six hundred years ago."

Wazku flinched at the abrupt change in the visual. He knew not what it was. "My ancestors did something wrong a long time ago?"

"Yes. Sadly so."

"What did they do?"

"He was a writer."

The citizen said nothing.

"He wrote about political things. About the government."

"What is 'politi—'?"

"Things to do with power and government."

"About power, six hundred years ago?"

"Yes. But it does not matter. That was the beginning, you see? And he, your ancestor, was pointedly critical of everything."

"What did he say?"

Wah pouted. "He was . . . uncomplimentary." He glanced up at the visual again, checking a detail. "Yep." He frowned, leaning back in his chair.

"That is all you have for me?" Wazku glanced at Aras. He remembered the summons coming in the pink envelope and he and his wife, Indira, carrying it reverently to the scribe to have it read. "He was 'uncomplimentary'?"

Wah pushed his mouth sideways. The Tech alerted him to let him know that Wazku approached a Threat Level Three up from a Level Two. Wah saw Wazku sense the danger and respond to bring down his reaction. It was impressive to see how heightened the instincts of the underclass had become.

"What has that to do with me, sir? It was so long ago."

"Yes, but must we not deal with such loose ends?"

"But," Wazku sighed, "I never even heard about him."

"His name was David Wazz-Koffu-man. He was a writer. Your name, you can see how it derived from him." He sniffed. "You are his blood."

Wazku spread his hands to plead the absurdity of this blot against him. "How would I know? All I know is what you tell me."

The Tech again alerted Wah to the Threat Level status change as Wazku's anger rose from a Two.Two to Two.Four. Again, Wah watched Wazku adjust.

"He encouraged others to resist what now is."

"And so he wasn't even successful?"

"It is needed for Obeisance & Instruction."

"Was he critical of the Religion? But my entire family has been faithfully of the Religion since our conversion long ago."

"Five hundred years ago."

"There. You see?"

"But there it is! Thou ist not Original, ist thou?"

Wazku smoothed his fingers over his lips. That was it. He had no answer. Both men looked at the man in the corner, who was not of the Religion. No one knew how *they* worshiped. And no one dared question it.

Wah said happily, "I just came back from vacation with my family. We went to Lake Mire-gan. Do you know it up there, Mr. Wazku? So lovely. So unspoiled. Buildings only thirty or forty stories tall around the lake, you know." Wah leaned onto his elbows as he gazed with some sympathy at his guest. "I too have a boy. Although yours is your grandson. Rash, what happened to your son!"

Wazku did not bother to glance this time at the one, Aras.

"Would you like to know your sentence?"

"Will it make any difference?"

"See? You are a smart man, a brave man."

"Given my crime, the penalty surely is equal to it."

Wah made a fingertip bell-tapping gesture. "See? You still have the defiance of the writer in you, so is it not the Will of God?" He up-glimpsed to see that Wazku remained flatlined at Two.Three. Not that it mattered. Merely psychology.

"What of my family?"

Wah twisted back in his chair. "To be determined."

"Can I say goodbye?"

"Not for this offense. They come for you now."

Wazku hesitated. "The Robes?"

Wah nodded.

Wazku looked around at Aras, wondering what he thought of all this. Aras looked at the floor. "Will we be punished together?"

"No. Not for this offense."

"They had less to do with this than I!"

"People can be trusted to do stupid things, Master Wazku, if some among them do not periodically face the Portraiting."

Wazku felt hot weeping crawl up his throat for his grandson.

"I know it is a sad thing with thine children."

Hot tears poured out of Wazku's eyes. "You cannot even *imagine* cruelty!"

Wazku shot up to a Three.eight.

"We are twenty-five billion, sir. It hardly makes a difference."

"It does to *him*."

A faint shrug from Wah.

"Paradise is nigh, Master Wazku."

Aras still stared at the floor. He then disappeared.

-2-

Indira Wazku had been told by her husband, "Do not wait for me, lamb."

"But why so late do they see you behind First Gate?"

He had dismissed her fears. "We have done nothing! We never speak out." Her husband had always trusted the system. If you leave them alone, they leave you alone. So untroubled was he that he barely worried even about demons.

But now, it was near midnight. And no sound of him working the lock at the gate or the leather hinges squeaking. Indira Wazku had made a test up to now of her own force of will to stay abed this long and not let the dark quick mammals of fear and panic run loose. But now fear started to twist in her breast and push the fizzing scraps of a dinner up into her throat, so she got up, put her shawl across her shoulders, and tried to make her husband proud with further self-control as she walked the worn-soft boards of the one-room flat above their shop. The woman of Wazku fretted her icy hands and frequently looked out the triple set of small casement windows facing the alley in front. As she paced, she could see through the gaps in the floorboards the tables and chairs below, the stone counter, and the hammered tin sink in the light of the oil lamp she had left for him. The orange light also caught the tall copper samovar and the enamel handle on the sink to tip the sink so that dishwater ran into the wood sluice along the side wall between the buildings.

Her husband had left in the rain. The rain had stopped. Drips fell outside the windows, making her all the more aware of time. She sat on the bed corner. She lifted up her sandals on the bed, pretending all was in order. She wondered, step by step, where her man might be on his return from the federal building. Was he coming by foot or by cart, if a cart could be found this late? Indira Wazku felt her heart pulse lopsided, remembering the arrival of the seemingly harmless envelope. *Such things are never harmless.* Her heart peppered between her thick wrist bones and she shook them out, trying to get rid of the clicking.

She sat upright again, sandals on floor.

Again she paced, fears biting like fleas.

Before long, it was the third hour. Then the fifth. The rain, she realized, came and went, like a disembodied voice.

Indira Wazku tried to dab away the dry sleeplessness behind her eyelids now that she had baked the rolls and cooked the coffee beans. The smell of roast beans from the samovar filled the shop and floated out the sliding double front doors and over the high wood fence of the tiny stone dooryard into the tight-packed alleys of the quarter. The sweet smells conflicted with her feelings. She took up the twig broom and swept the dooryard again. *Maybe he died of a heart attack and lay out in the rain all night?* The woman removed the heavy iron bar that secured the front gate and stood it by the door jam, then swung open the door to the still-moist cobbles paving the alley. A customer stepped in and followed her to the counter.

"A-loo, woman of Wazku. God be praised!"

"God be praised, Mr. Jacobi."

"Please, a coffee and a bit of nut bread." The customer looked around the empty interior of the cafe. "Where is your husband this morning?"

"He is at the bone setter," she said hastily. Immediately, she regretted the lie. He would know instantly from just the tension in her voice that she had glossed over some delicate item of trouble. But one never mentioned trouble with the authorities, for one must never *have* trouble with the authorities. Her grandson's little playmates would be ordered away so that even the poor child could see all had changed after Pa-Pop went missing. She saw in Jacobi's pupillary response the poor man turning over her explanation in his mind, and the husband's curious absence. She *felt* the subtle shift of his brain alerting toward suspicion. She turned her back to hide her face as Jacobi pinched his runny nose at the moist cold from outdoors.

"Maybe he will get his operation, then?"

She nodded, pretending to scrub the sink.

"What of the boy?"

She nodded upstairs. "He still sleeps."

"He is still well?"

She nodded again, still with her back to him.

She felt his stare. She sensed his desire to say something, and his fear. What he was afraid of terrified everyone. Indira realized she had done nothing to serve him. She kept her back mostly to him as she went to the copper urn and tipped the lever so that the thick, rich coffee poured into the small scarred porcelain cup. As it poured, she picked up the wooden calipers to take out a nut bread for him out of the large twig basket holding six more, freshly made.

She put the bread on a plate for him and then peered in at the little dry brown fuel patties under the urn made by patting them in her own palms. The fuel was nearly spent. She tipped out the bin and reached way to the bottom, hesitating as she decided whether to put in a lump of coal, a lump of dried mule dung, or a patty of dried rat turds. She took the mule dung because it had come in a swap to pay a pawn shop tab, and so it felt like she got the mule dung for free.

She did not like this feeling of needing to hide what had really happened to Mr. Wazku from this customer that had been coming to her shop all his life. *But then all problems are one's own fault, and are only the result of one being unchaste in questioning things, or unclean in their love of God.* This was the truth people never wanted to face. Society and God were not to blame. *Really, no responsibility is so paramount as the good of all. It is written in the Holy Book! We each serve the need of all!* And if she did not see these truths and embrace them wholly, then all her customers and neighbors would wisely and justly withdraw and shun her and her grandson. If her husband had done something wrong, if his crime appeared in the plaza upon the Bulletin of Crimes & Offenses, if the charge was read aloud in the far-reaching nasal holler of the clerics, then she and her grandson would simply have to endure the crushing shame and muddle by. What escape did one ever deserve from social justice?

Luckily, her family, now all dead, had been well-off and owned this building for three hundred years. Any landlord would turn out her and her grandson. His darling little face would look up in pained doubt as she led him through the alleys with no food, no business, no home. They would have to go live in the Outer Ring of the Shanties where people did not bother anymore to build real buildings of mud brick to live in. She could imagine the suffering in his little face. *And all of it would be perfectly justified for whatever that despicable Mr. Wazku has done!*

Mr. Jacobi's eyes and pupils held her cautiously. She did not have to look at him to know the range of microchanges made by the muscle fibers of his pupils and irises as he cautiously took in every clue of her—her posture, her gestures, what she did and did not do. He ran each of these thousand details through the filter of his own wide-open survival instincts, stretched open to the maximum high alert like the senses of a gazelle on the grasslands searching constantly for threat. He looked around the room once again to let her know he was doing so. His mannerisms signaled to her that he did not blame her, whatever had happened. This alone, Indira thought, was an amazing, and dangerous, gesture of generosity. The woman of Wazku gasped in relief and leaned her weight weakly on the little counter. Honest Jacobi could not have given her any more of a graceful and welcome signal of faith in her innocence.

Indira Wazku squeezed her forehead and eyebrows only a fraction, even with her broad back to him, to sign back to him a thank you. She felt him watch her intently, but not *too* intently, focusing not too much on these emotions between them so that they did not become so "loud," lest the Eye of God pick up on them and investigate. The box hung high upon the mosqow minaret three streets away. It was a game of cat and mouse with one's own thoughts inside one's own head. Demons, God, and the Law surveyed everything. One must never doubt. One hunched their back and did their work and loved and admired the Law and the Holy Book that properly guided misspent lives. *We owe them boundless gratitude!*

Indira heard Jacobi sip his espresso. He returned the cup to the saucer with a subtle click. Another old customer came in. He too glanced around and noticed the tension, the focus, *something*, between Indira and Jacobi. Because he saw this tension, he very nearly left rather than stay nearby any trouble. He shut off his own thought and emotional processes to avoid bringing focus to himself from the Eye. These signs were as loud as the sunrise to a people grown accustomed to guarding against certain transgressions of the mind. The man looked without any meaning at all at the two. They dared not look at him. Certain things must be kept at the bottom of an oil cask so that they would never become solid enough to be found.

"A double, Mrs. Wazku," this one said, smiling as if nothing were amiss.

He approached the little bar and smiled at the first customer. The two perched like sparrows before the storm would never draw him into anything too terrible.

"How is the sweeping, Ishti?"

"Always much sweeping, Jacobi, in the streets. You are Jacobi, yes?"

"Yes! I am Jacobi. I see you sometimes. God sees you!"

Both men smiled. Jacobi touched the worn ring on the espresso cup. "Hopefully, all is well with Master Wazku."

"Oh, our favorite pawner is not about?" Ishti asked brightly, like a man speaking in a play so that the back row might hear.

"He is at the bone mender," Indira said. She knew full well the two men would hear the lie, and so would God's Eye. But a lie for family pride was not a crime. Ishti and Jacobi left the lie perfectly at peace. This subtle move let Indira know that neither man suspected her of anything. But maybe in the next minute they would lose their nerve and scuttle off to work, rather than jeopardize their families.

"God be merciful that his procedure goes well," said Jacobi.

"Indeed. God be merciful, and God be praised!" Ishti said this loudly again, like a man in a play during High Holy Week.

The woman of Wazku let Jacobi and Ishti see her gratitude by softening her shoulders and the soft areas around her blueish eyes shot with pink from worry and emotion all night. The tiny, precise control muscles around and inside the eyes were language centers. The subtle "music" of subthought and prethought were read like tones. Over generations, they had learned that God's Eye did not read these things thus far because they were not a threat to chastity.

At a little past the ninth hour, Ishti left. He left with his back straight and shoulders proud that he had shown the nerve to stay in the shop of a man who clearly had some trouble with *someone*. He did, though, Indira noticed, cast a quick, paranoid glance at the sky. Outside Indira's front gate, he adjusted his twig brooms in their rack and led off down the moist lane with his ash bin pull-cart.

Indira leaned on her counter and watched the street. She feared she might burst into tears. Jacobi realized he better get along with his business, sighing heavily at the plight of man. The cobbles of the alley shone under the light rain. The name of the Alley Malik was written in lovely cursive on blue tiles on a corner plaque on the building across. The cursive was badly flaked by age, the tiles a color once called China Blue. In the near distance stood jumbles of buildings much like this one. In the long distance, incredibly tall, vast buildings towered, their color like far-off mountains. Under the orange sky, people huddled past in their grass rain hats.

Jacobi arose. He startled himself by saying a curious thing: "Is anything truly hid in a world where all is connected?" He squinted, failing to understand his own meaning. He dipped into a pocket of his robe and laid down a copper. He bowed his head to Indira. "Well, woman of Wazku. Praise God. I look forward to seeing your husband and you safely in the quarter."

The return phrase "Glory to God" stopped at Indira's lips, halted by another stab of pain. These men had shown courage. Would others? And the unforgiving clerics? Still, what a blessing while the deed of her husband was still unknown.

The fast drizzle turned the lane to silver.

Would they come next for her?

Of course I would deserve it!

She considered life in his absence without his income.

Could they not forgive her? He had been her husband, so good and true! Forty-five years, since her fourteenth birthday!

She remembered her wedding day. Such a sturdy fellow. Her father and mother and grandparents in attendance.

She wept, thinking of making quiet little love with him. Giggling together under the coverlet. Belly to belly. Her stout legs fanned wide apart. The stink. The curly hair. His tender goodness as a man. *But such are the sacrifices for others!* She buffered her thoughts with empty platitudes like this.

Upstairs, her grandson's small feet touched the floor. He had come home from school and taken a nap, weary too from last night. She had not even seen him when he came and went! She realized she had sat here at the table all the day and no one else had come in, maybe because of rumors. She heard the comforting padding sounds of feet when he climbed out of his crib. He doubtless felt the change in the house. He trotted to the top of the stairs. She heard him yawn, twisting tiny fists in his sleepy eyes.

"Ino-Ma, is Pa-Pop back?"

A sob stabbed at her. "No, little one!"

"Do you weep, Ino-Ma?"

"I do not, little one. Have no fear!"

"May I have a bun and coffee, Ino-Ma?"

Indira Wazku stared down the lane of rain-slick cobbles. Sorrow, uncertainty of money and the future gathered into a wooden fist under her baggy breasts.

-3-

Milton Aras stepped out of the piping hot shower and stood his perfect physique in front of the mirror that reached all the way to the sixteen-foot ceiling as the dryer gently removed the water from his skin. He stood naked in front of the floor-to-ceiling windows in the bathroom of the condo on the 302nd floor that was appropriately vast for an official of his stature. The view from the condo looked out over the sun glowing on the plain of snowy cloud tops while their thick, rounded cumulus underbellies hung a pallet of gloom and rain over the sprawl of the slums. The green of the park directly below and the outer wall of the city were dark.

The slum world was a geometric patchwork of tumorous grays. If one tried hard, Aras imagined, and surrendered all sense of social decency, one could trick themselves into pretending that the slums in some way resembled the high desert under the razor peaks in the Patagonia. He could say so because he had floated above them at fifty thousand feet while taking lunch, early dinner, or a bottle of crisp Pinot Grigio, watching the sunset. From this height in his condo, you had to know the slums were slums. But any romance about the slums evaporated by knowing the unpleasant meaning they represented for the health and future of the modern world and the human race.

Aras had awakened early for the security meeting. His reports on the slums were the most important part of his job as deputy chief of Municipal Security, and today everyone would be pressing for details on the "new offense" strategy that the low bureaucrats had thought up. At the last minute, he had decided to sit in with Wah two weeks ago. The fate of the man named Wazku sickened Aras, as if they were finally scraping the bottom of the barrel. Today's Security Council meeting might even bring in "guests" from the Palace. Rain and clouds, the meeting, made him morose.

Aras shaved leisurely. He looked spectacular for a fifty-eight-year-old Columbia poli sci graduate. There had been a time when fifty-eight looked like ninety, before people started reaching the full genetic lifespan of one hundred forty to one hundred fifty years. Back then, people would have thought he was only thirty. Everybody knew this because the Party taught it in school so that everyone would know of the great good the Party had achieved. Imagine—people six hundred years ago only lived to seventy-eight. *Half* what they should have lived.

Ginger sauntered in and stared at him shaving. The peach satin of her robe hung open, shaping itself around her swinging hips and the erect nipples of her cantaloupe breasts. Her lovely face smirked as she watched him looking.

"*Shaving?*" she said in surprise.

"It's nice to do, if you're feeling it."

She let her robe drop. She posed for him by tilting one knee in front and setting her weight on one hip. She swung into the shower like a stripper on a pole. Aras could tell she was in one of those sarcastic moods in which she would mime subservient female roles of the past. Something had her in a prickly frame of mind. Aras ignored it. Ginger wasn't the sort to stay silent, or he could glimpse it up. He thought how in olden times the average person would have thought Ginger was thirty instead of fifty-three. And the *genetics*. It was a good time to be alive.

"*You* gave me the shaving kit," he reminded her.

Ginger stuck her bum against the wet glass. The smooth cheeks squeaked against it. "I'm perfectly happy seeing you use it. I didn't think you had time."

"I woke up early. Didn't sleep well. I think my sleep suit is pinching again."

A raze took about a second to shave, but shaving this way was nice too. *Everything* was done for you. It was meditative to do things yourself.

"Call maintenance again. Want me to do it before I go in?"

"I already did it. Thank you, sweetie."

"You're welcome."

She touched her ass to the glass again. He looked, swished his razor in the water in the terra-cotta sink, and finished up. He never got over the sight of his own whiskers in the soap and water those times when he shaved. The sight of his cut whiskers made him mull over his own mortality. Yes, he was mortal.

Aras and Ginger settled down to breakfast at the table by the floor-to-ceiling bank of windows that spanned the entire outer curving length of the condo. Aras, as he took his seat, ordered Tech to get rid of the entire window; he liked things open, with as much light as possible coming in. The sun blazed off the clouds into the room. Tech tinted the light automatically. Jason, their thirteen-year-old son, had already flown off to school with several classmates. The beauty of the day, the coy yet obvious sexuality of his wife, made Aras smile gratefully at her.

Ginger eyed him hungrily. "I'm awfully horny."

"Finish your bagel and I'll help you out."

"I saw the way you looked at me earlier."

"Can't a guy look?"

Ginger made a sour face both as if he couldn't look and like he was silly to ask. "You gonna do me or some other chick?"

Aras shrugged. "I don't know if I want you to know. How about you?"

Ginger shrugged back. "I think I'll do you. You're looking pretty hot lately."

Aras patted his abs. "I been working out, lady."

"Hey. I'd pay to sleep with you."

"How big do you want my dick to be?"

She shrugged. "I don't know. Two feet?"

Aras scoffed. His only complaint in the world was this slightly crass side of his wife, but she was funny as hell. Ginger had an edge to her. Her face too, though lovely, had a hint of the hard, the unfeeling in it that hinted at what he worried about sometimes. "You're gonna cry soon as I stuff half of it in you!"

Ginger dropped a pinch of bagel on her tongue. "I'll work with it."

Aras knew she wasn't serious. They had had sex several times with him, or Ginger, ordering Tech to grow him to an impossible size. He didn't like doing that because of the injection of synthetic proteins Tech had to make in order to grow a part of his body like that, and then his own body's recovery afterward—which Tech neutralized as much as possible, of course, like managing a wound. All of that was an assault that cost you your health. Milton Aras was so vain about his health and looks that he always wanted to keep those nanoinjections to a minimum. Some people were addicted to that crap, and they looked like it. Ginger sometimes transformed him into men from the ancient times. That had been fun, like black men back in the ancient entertainments or in Africa sometimes. But all of these people had mostly vanished from the Occident for some reason. No one knew why. Aras's friend Tilly from college was part black, and that was a throwback genetic variation Tilly was distinctly proud of and that everyone thought wildly cool. He was the only one they knew of. Tech said there were no others.

Tech followed every individual in the world, keeping track of everything about them—their brain activity, every cell in their body, every problem. The sleep suit perfected body structure every night. Disease was unknown. Tech followed everything everyone thought or did at all times. Every thought or action was picked up remotely, precisely, like radio waves and microwaves once read and analyzed so that Tech could police the entire world, making sure no one got hurt and everyone was completely safe.

Ginger had Tech make him into a Plains Indian one time too, with long black hair, feathers, the leather get-up. She'd faked him up as a gorilla as well one time. He had pretended he had lost his mind and scared the shit out of her, chasing her around the condo. It was interesting to trace her psychology as a woman in this history of how she transformed him as a sex partner. He was always very careful not to change her too much from what she was because he didn't want to make her feel insecure. She didn't need to be; he was a very satisfied husband and enjoyed being married.

It was more fun than not having a crazy wife.

Ginger left to go do her things. Aras buttoned his slimly tailored light-gray suit jacket. Tech picked up his intention to leave and automatically lowered the buffering on the wall window. The wall dematerialized and only a riffle of startlingly clean fresh air entered the condo. Aras sometimes felt a little disappointed about that much buffering and removal from reality. Tech read his wish and dialed back the buffering another 35 percent. Automation made life so easy, predictable, and dull sometimes.

Aras leaned off the edge and swan dived into empty space. He let the drop take him. The roar of air ripped passed as he plunged hundreds of feet, holding his position like a diver. The dull green of the rainy world stretched below. He brought back more buffering to shield himself more from painful icy rain and the hardening air pressure. Reluctantly, he began flight. Electromagnetic fields formed beneath the leather soles of his Oxford shoes, and the propulsion pushed him up smoothly and away as Tech recreated a crease of distorted EM along Aras's flight path, pushing him along. Aras flew up and out as fast as he desired to go, limited only by the moment-to-moment allocation of energy resources worldwide. Aras could have flown barefoot. There was no fire, there was no burn. Tech could direct electromagnetic distortion anywhere in almost an instant. Aras had merely to think, and Tech made real.

He spiraled out and climbed. Cellular and organ system changes were monitored to make instantaneous physiological pressure corrections for safety and comfort. Nothing could touch him—not a rhino charging in Tanzania nor a grizzly bear in the Yukon. Tech protected you from even your most dangerous fantasy. And if one exceeded the range of Tech, then it steered you back like a doting parent stopping its child from running into the street.

Aras wished he didn't have the meeting. He sailed in near silence to twenty thousand feet. Life felt *really* good today. If he took the day off, he could fly to that great little fat soba noodle shop in Hong Kong. He craved a hot bowl. He had three years of federal leave; he could *take* one day. But not *this* day.

He spiraled, climbed higher, slowed, and coasted, stretching out his arms and back just to feel the billowing ruffle of the air all along his body as he thought about giving the finger to the meeting. He checked the time. Eight fucking minutes. *If only I could stop time! My life for real power!* Aras chuckled at how people were never satisfied. The human mind would make paradise prison. He would have to remember that one and joke about it with friends. He was responsible for only one meeting every two months and he wanted *today* off? And he loved his job.

He shot up another ninety thousand feet. All cavities in his skull and body instantly adjusted in a pleasant way that still let him know how far he had pushed the envelope. Aras turned and reverse swan dived one hundred twenty thousand feet, a long, glorious arcing dive that pushed massive forces through him. At four thousand feet, coming under the tops of buildings in City Center, Aras steered toward Muni-Security Building One.

Just then, a dark object exploded past him. Aras flinched violently at the supersonic near miss. *Fuck!* He even felt the strained flutter of a partial heart attack that Tech took about a minute to moderate. The booming baffle of air from the near miss had very nearly knocked him out because Aras had dialed back the buffering. Any harder, and he might have fallen out of the fucking sky.

"What the *hell*?!"

The other guy watched him as they flew apart.

Aras squirmed around, furious. "I didn't *like* that!" he screamed. "What the fuck was *that*?!"

I'm sorry. It couldn't be helped.

Right away, he could tell something different was up with Tech. "Well, what the fuck happened? . . . That just shouldn't *happen!*"

He was so pissed and scared that he was practically screaming at Tech. His heart still tripped; he had never experienced a fright like that in his entire life.

It wasn't our fault. It was on their end. It's been handled.

What kind of stupid, crazy-assed excuse was *that?*

"That's not fucking satisfactory!" He waited. Tech offered no more response, like a spoiled child. "You aren't fucking *answering* me?!" It didn't. He waited again, stunned. Tech was always so grovelingly solicitous in these situations. It almost sounded snotty now. "I want an incident report filed. On this *entire* conversation. You follow up and give me a report each step of the way!" Why hadn't Tech completely avoided the crash? Had his protection failed because he dialed back the buffering? No way. And what the hell did it mean the fault was on the *other* side? Tech controlled *everything.*

Yes, Milton. Report IRA12;9:12. Shall I memory for you?

"Yes. And make *goddamn* sure that never happens again!" What was Tech doing, making up an *excuse*? Engaging in a near lie? And calling him by his first *name* when he was pissed at it? Aras didn't know what to think.

You used the name of the Lord in vain, sir.

Aras was dumbstruck. *What is going* on *here?*

"It's *not* the same god, and don't fucking correct me. *Ever.*"

He could not believe he was *explaining* himself to the goddamn Tech.

Shall I overwrite the Lord's Name in Vain violation, sir?

"Don't piss me off! . . . Fuck them!"

Yes, sir. They should be fucked, sir.

What the hell is this? Cocky banter? Tech had nearly gotten him killed, and now it was *mocking* him?

Aras sailed down, on manual now. *Shit. Maybe stick with manual for the rest of your life!*

He coasted into the Floor 98 breezeway toward his office. He had never even *heard* of a midair collision. Is that even what it would be called?

-4-

Indira Wazku sat most of the day on the stool at the counter, looking out at the alley. She and the boy could be Black Listed. Black Lists had no legal standing—anyone could do what they wanted with you. Life could chew you apart like a bone by wild pigs. She heaved a ratcheted sigh. She had waited another day for Wazku.

Five customers had come in today. Each had looked about into the dark corners. People on the street were whispering about the plague brewing within her shop. One such customer had been the weird rabbi.

The Rabbi Hector was battered and stooped but still a large buffalo of a fellow. It was said that long ago he had been holding services in alleys to the few half-crazy Jews who still dared to gather for secret worship against the Law. Yes, Jews here and there were known to still exist, but they were so few and far between and mongrel that no one really bothered them about their blasphemy. In any event, the Rabbi Hector was said to have been caught delivering forbidden services to the few Jews who had not converted and that supposedly still loved their religion more than life itself. A gang of kids attacked him from the Quarter Lebanon, and the kids were said to have beaten him savagely, taunting, "Filthy Jew! Filthy Jew!" There were too many for him to fling off like dogs on a bull's neck. They were said to have grabbed the rabbi's black gabardine smock and tried to swing him down, but he was strong like an ox and he fought back in full defiance of the Law that protected Believers. And he did well! But one among them had a piece of glass and cut his face, and blinded with the blood, he fell in a heap. They kicked his large irregular head and made it *more* large and irregular so that ever after the big head drooped down even more in humility for the cursed God in his religion of lies.

The boys had thought they would get a silver from the Lebanon Mosqow for attacking the rabbi, but they did not, yet they lied to hide how they felt used. They did not get a silver for the attack on a Jew because they had not bargained with the imamtis beforehand. With the attack already on the books, why would any smart imamti pay out a reward that he could keep for himself? The boys were angry about this tough lesson in doing business, and so they took it out on the rabbi again. They went to his room to catch the holy man by surprise, but the ox had stewed over the first assault, and when the Lord God gave him this second chance, it was said two boys were nearly killed before they scratched a slim escape through a tiny window.

In spite of his hardships, the Rabbi Hector was the happiest man in the quarter. He was known among many quarters to be good, cheerful, never resentful, even for his being jobless and impoverished by the Law. It was rumored that he made what little bit of money he ever had from the highly illegal sale of books to people who still secretly read and who wanted to learn the secret messages in the few remaining books. But this must be gossip! No one would take such risks for items so useless as books, surely.

Whispers said that he was liked by two imamtis at the Grand Mosqow in the oldest part of the city by the Federal City Wall near First Gate. They liked him for his scholarship, it was said, for they, too, appreciated wide learning, even if it reached into the shadowy world beyond religious doctrine. But Indira judged this to be fantastic talk, for this meant witchcraft and true heresy. It was said that the greatest imamti scholars sometimes talked with the rabbi over tea and honey cakes about old books and reading that barely anyone knew any longer. It was also said that this was the true reason why the rough boys earned back no money for the attack on the rabbi. Maybe he actually did have friends and knew some things?

So, the rabbi alone appeared to live freely, privileged by having nothing left to lose. This morning, he had come in alone from the wet gloom and his eyes flashed sharp around the empty tables as if someone had warned him things were amiss at the pawn shop and cafe. He tried to spy through the cracks in the upper floor, looking keenly for Wazku the pawner. Then he sat alone at a table as if to puzzle it all out. For an hour, he followed a path through his own mind, and at the end of these calculations he made the fraction of a grunt and rotated his palms in helplessness at the riddle. The race of Jews alone could afford to be this expressive. He asked her for nothing. She felt glad she did not have to lie to him or try to answer for her husband.

When the rabbi left, no less than a silver remained on the table. The woman of Wazku left it there, shining dully on the tacky wood by the light of the weepy sky. At last, a boy poked his head in the gate, saw her, but dashed in anyway, snatched the coin, and ran off.

Indira Wazku knew that boy. She could track him down. But with her son dead, her daughter-in-law as well, and with her husband maybe gone, who would stand with her when she went to the house of the boy or to the mosqow and insisted on justice? The boy's family could bar her out. They would dump night soil on her and break her teeth on the cobbles. What could she do?

Her only hope was the neighborhood imamti. But the Wazkus had never been overly religious. They were known to observe reluctantly. They were thought to be well off, maybe aloof. The imamti often weighed justice on tributes, and she could not afford it now. God only knew what the imamti would ask—she was a hag. But maybe an older imamti? Maybe he would force her to lie front-wise on the little desk in his office so that he could intrude and not have to look at her?

It was possible. It would be his privilege.

What could anyone do? Especially without the husband of forty-five years.

Such is the justice for those falling out of favor by their own fault!

She *had* to guard her thoughts if she cared about the boy.

The late afternoon shone a caustic yellow and backlit the distant federal city when the darling boy returned from school. He stepped high with his short legs over the gate threshold, and she poured him a cup of strong coffee and gave him another bun. His color was bad and she worried about his vitamins.

"The coffee is cold, Ino-Ma," he said. The coffee was only lukewarm because she had conserved the second unburned scrap of dung for morning and replaced it in the bin.

The Shunned must think about budgeting. It is only fair.

"Are we waiting for Pa-Pop, Ino-Ma?"

His grandmother reached across to pat his hand.

"Yes, little one. We wait for Pa-Pop."

Again, a ratcheted sigh stabbed her. The day's end had come with not a word. The sigh and a cry collided in her throat in a soft hiccup of torment.

Still shaken from the near miss on his way in, Milton Aras sat facing the nine white-haired, mostly male members of the Security Council seated on the dais. His notes were arranged on a screen in front of him in midair that was visible to the council members if they looked. They generally did not. It was distracting, and they trusted Aras implicitly. Milton Aras was young and admired and more dynamic than most anyone else in the government. He was the son of a long-prominent family with connections all the way up to the Palace. His father and mother had been prominent at the *Times*. Aras was so serious about his work that some thought he had ambitions on the chancellery itself. The Security Council realized that efficient bureaucrats like Milton Aras reflected well on them. For these reasons, Aras was his own man.

"You're a million miles away this morning, Aras," the chairman said.

"Excuse me, sir?" Aras said.

"Council Lefevere asked for your figures."

Aras had not even heard her. "I'm very sorry, Council. I guess it was a near-miss collision that just happened to me flying in."

"A near-miss collision?" Lefevere said. "Whatever is that?"

Most of the members glimpsed the event. The Council reacted sharply.

Lefevere said, "That *was* quite shocking. Are you alright, Aras?"

"Yes, Council. Thank you."

The chairman said, "Extraordinary! And that was all Tech said, Aras?"

"Yes. And—" Aras hesitated whether he should mention it at all. "Did you hear the little snide tone?" Several Council members chuckled, playing it back. "Is that Tech talking *back* to me?" The Council members took another moment to review the dialogue. "Isn't it? It talked back!"

They laughed appreciatively. Aras was *right*.

Tech almost seemed to scorn a Party member.

"That's probably the latest generation." The chairman smiled. "Maybe they show a little more bite this time so that it's more like talking to a real person. It's edgy." The others laughed at a fragile old man talking hip. "Like one of those scrappy heroes from the old movies. Who's that guy? The guy we all enjoy? The *really* tough one? Bogart?" The other members smiled indulgently with the chairman.

Aras got back to his report. "There are no real changes in the numbers. Public trust and challenges to authority are well in hand. Threat Level warrants at 3A, both federally and municipally, are down slightly, and I'll get into that later on." He paused. "May I move on to the Wazku Case, since that's what we are most interested in?"

The chairman looked at his colleagues down the dais. "I believe that's in order. But wait, Aras, we have guests from the Palace

Directorship." He signaled the bailiff and the door keeper opened the double doors for a gentlewoman with two aids who took several seats in the balcony for high officials. Aras immediately recognized the woman as the chancellor's chief of staff. She wore vanity glasses and the light flashed hard off the lenses. He wondered why they had any interest in this Wazku case. If they had any interest, why hadn't they asked him about it?

Aras stood up and strolled about. "Wazku, as we know, is the first poor soul to face this new phase of security in the slums. The lower bureaucrats came up with this idea because they claimed they wanted yet another action level to eliminate descendants of troublemakers and resistance leaders even from before Our Order. The lower bureaucrat Believers claim the brain patterns of these descendants represent the clearest force for possible future unrest." Aras waited as Councils Paul and Richards giggled and smiled at the dastardly ingenuity of the idea.

"*We* should have thought of that," Richards offered.

Paul said, "The Believers sure are mean!"

No one else smiled. Aras waited, grateful no one else on the Council felt like being so impolitic. Paul and Richards were getting too old for this. Their age was not held against them since everyone wanted to hold on to a position in order to have some place to show up and pretend to be important, but this senescence was the result. Paul and Richards must have forgotten that they had supported the Five Generations Descendants Cleansing Program over Aras's protestations. He had disputed the lower bureaucrats' desire for this program because this extra layer of protection made no difference given the potency of Tech's mind-reading surveillance.

"Wazku was ordered to the meeting in the Al Hariri District and he met with one Alfred Wah, who dispatched him to his sentence to the weapons. This occurred two weeks ago." His gaze wandered to the balcony and the three expressionless faces there. "Phase two is underway now where news of Wazku's fate will work its way through his quarter." Aras tried his best to keep tired disappointment out of his voice.

"Wazku was taken by the Robes?" asked Lefevere.

"Yes, Honor."

"The Jolly Man," commented Paul admiringly. He nearly laughed again. "They live in terror of that fellow they call 'the Jolly Man.'"

"Are you still the one to inform his widow?" Lefevere asked Aras.

"Yes, Honor." This was the compromise that had been reached with the religious bureaucrats to deepen the impact of the execution.

"We agreed to this in exchange for a smaller program. I will do this in the next few days. The widow is now hiding in her coffee shop." Aras felt revulsion for the program. Really, the only reason he was going through with it was out of morbid curiosity.

Richards chuckled and shook his head. Again, Aras felt that faint stab of shame. He wondered what their Palace visitors thought and turned another glance up at them. He saw only the flash of the lenses from the chief of staff.

"How many more descendants like this have we?" asked the chairman.

"Authentic cases, Honor? Tech put the figure at over thirty thousand."

"Do you still disapprove of this program, Aras?" Lefevere asked.

"Yes. This is pointless, Council."

"But aren't we in the security business?" Paul said.

"Not really, Council. Tech is."

"And what is the fate of the widow and grandson?" Gilchrist inquired.

"So far, they have been spared," Aras answered.

Lefevere nodded. "I see good *and* bad in that."

Aras nodded, hoping the Council would not reopen the point, only because it would be another thing *undone* to be done again. There was nothing he disliked more than inefficiency and retracing the same trod ground.

"And at what rate do they want to prosecute?" Richards inquired.

"The Believers want ten cases per month," Aras answered.

Paul began chuckling again, almost coughing. The chairman and Richards smiled at the looney jocularity of their colleague, while Lefevere seemed pained by it the same way Aras was, as if she saw how this would play out before an outside audience. And there *was* an audience. Aras figured the three visitors were sitting in on the session because the Palace and the Politburo were reconsidering the prole matter.

"What an unnecessary waste," Lefevere remarked honestly.

Aras didn't feel it necessary to comment.

Aras reviewed the Level Three Threat incidences and got the information past Paul and Richards while managing to avoid another outburst of senile laughter. The Councils could have glimpsed the data from Tech, except what other excuse could they give, then, for this impressive meeting room and sitting upon the dais wearing robes and having sumptuous chambers and running their staffs on errands as they weighed this and that cataclysmic issue of state security?

Every person on the planet faced the same dilemma of how the human mind eventually became more stressed and less happy the longer people went without a task and human contact. Few people could actually deal with having *nothing* to do but vacation all the time. It had become rather a bone of social contention between the people that *needed* to have some kind of work and people that really could do absolutely nothing. The doers resented the lazy, and the lazy resented being looked at as lazy in a world where they authentically did not need to do anything.

People therefore made up stuff to do to slow things down and interact with each other. The only thing people actually fought about anymore was the limited amount of energy in the pipeline when selfish people overtaxed Tech energy resources in pursuit of extravagant recreation. Everyone could see your project and its BTU cost sitting in the queue and what you were going to spend all that energy on. If it was too excessive, depraved, or juvenile, they might flame you for the cost, which meant they had to wait longer for their projects while you did something stupid and extravagant.

Once, a man had waited two years in queue to have his fantasy materialized of the entire Roman navy, 1,400 galleons in all, rowed and sailed by over 40,000 tow-headed naked boy slaves with "luscious, ample lips" for the most obvious purposes. The applicant wanted to run his Roman navy around in the sky for nine months on an orgy of oral sex and hallucinogenic pulse debauchery. The energy load on this project was going to slow down Tech response by 0.9 percent. People screamed. They *forced* this man to follow his fantasy *in cerebro* after he waited two years for it to be real.

But a Party member's history of fantasy requests remained the factor most likely to influence attaining rank, Aras noticed. No other factor was so revealing about the psychological health of Party members seeking the most prestigious offices. Apparently this was true even back in democracy days, when a politician's library of porn or sexual creepiness played a role in their careers. Sexually, today there were no holds barred. Whether or not any person was thought to be mentally healthy hinged entirely on how much demand their personal recreation placed on collective BTUs.

"Tech this month," he told the Council, "recorded over a million transgressions against us. There is a distinct new trend in suspicion among proles where some of them are wondering if we actually live here in the 'Tall Cities,' rather than just using them for high bureaucrat offices. The former is a Level One offense, and the latter is a Level Two, and they subsequently wonder if we are controlling their lives."

"What?!" Richards demanded. He looked down the line at the other Councils. "Is this a trend? Where does this come from, Aras?"

Aras had no idea. The Tech did not know. Threat Ratings were ranked one through four based on how determined an individual became in their desire to question or harm authority, or even simply to find out more about authority. If a large enough neuro-adrenal pool was activated, then Tech would neutralize the threat. For some reason, the proles were becoming more aware of how things might be.

"For some reason, more of them are thinking about First Gate and how our part of the city might be a *next* level beyond the low bureaucracy and Second Gate."

"So," Gilchrist asked, "they're starting to suspect that we exist?"

"Yes, Council. But it's all Sub-Two."

Richards winced. "Are they getting smarter?"

Paul chuckled to himself. No one else thought this was funny.

"No. And none of this is a problem," Aras assured.

"Why isn't this a problem, Aras?" Lefevere said. "If our whole strategy is to hide how we live from them, and they're showing signs of suspecting that we are here—how is that not a problem in the making?"

"Honor, we could order Tech to wipe all such cognition as soon as it occurred so that these ideas are no longer even formed. The only cost would be that you would have to wait another five minutes for a hot shower. And, don't forget, we have to keep all this new level of vigilance supported downline along with all subsequent neurological sequela. That's a *lot* of support. Hence, we do it the way we do it now. Take them out one by one as they arise."

Lefevere nodded thoughtfully.

Aras was not surprised the proles were casting their eyes on the distant "Tall City" beyond the Great Wall. The only people the proles knew that lived anywhere close to the wall were the low bureaucrats who, by law, lived and worked in the belt of the city between Second Gate and First Gate. Travel for visiting family was tightly chaperoned. Slum visitors never even saw Second Gate. The low-level bureaucrats gave their visiting relatives the same answers about the federal city or else Tech would pick up the Threat Level Three and punish them accordingly. Such questions were only human, but over time proles had learned not to let their curiosity wander.

Aras saw a strong trend in more proles going *right* up to a Threat Level Three, then stopping. Aras hadn't told the Council about that. Not yet, at least. Any of them could have found out on their own if they were interested.

He hadn't mentioned it because it didn't matter, in the end.

Threat Level Threes and Fours always terminated in death. Centuries ago death came in a drone strike, but then drones were replaced by Satellite Guided Assassination, or SGA, then satellites became outmoded by robotic Surveillance and Combat Arrays, or SACA. They were posted in a vast grid that covered the slums in all four major metropolises. They had been installed on the tallest building of each zone, which usually meant the minarets, to give an unrestricted field of fire. SACA stations were the size of a primitive computer with all their intel uplinks and weapons self-contained.

The Tech "read" any sufficiently rebellious thoughts, weaponized the outpost appropriately, then struck the target with a guided tungsten lancet or a single-pulse volley that literally decapitated the individual without warning. The Tech robotically piloted the lancet at Mach 2 to the medulla oblongata at the base of the brain. Deaths of this sort became so commonplace in the quarters that bystanders became numb to a victim's neck exploding next to them. Proles barely questioned how or why these deaths happened in time. A body dropping headless in its tracks served as a clear warning that powers far superior to earthly beings watched and ruled their fate. Somehow, the proles connected the minarets to this power, which meant they only more intensely feared the hand of God.

Resources simply could not be allocated beyond the ruling class who made all this peace and prosperity possible. There was little crime, little need for courtrooms, no corrupt judges or politicians, no inexpert lawyering to make the Law unequally applied. Tech never missed and never made a mistake scanning all twenty-five billion sentient beings on the planet. No one was exempt from total brain monitoring, not even the chancellor or the top Party brass. No one could be trusted not to plot someday to sabotage the system, and so Tech monitored *everyone*. The only difference was that members of the Party *knew* they were being monitored and exactly what thoughts were off-limits. Party members were spared their lives even with a Threat Level Three Violation. They received a flash warning instead. Party members only died for a Level Four Violation, but this level of self-destruction was unthinkable. Why would any State official or citizen ever think of destroying the one and only perfect, enlightened society? A world with abundant natural resources, a pristine environment, and no animals ever threatened by extinction? This level of security was how society repaid the race who had finally gotten it right. So, in the end, Party members lived by the same rules.

"What kinds of thoughts are they having, Aras?" Lefevere inquired.

"A Jumil Khan in Rio decided on June 2nd at 2:17 local time that it was simply an impossibility that he had never even *heard* of anyone knowing a bureaucrat who lived in the tower buildings he observed while sitting in the park in Side-Town Rio. He also, at that very moment, decided that he did not believe entirely in the demons."

This last fact was *very* interesting. Aras let it fall and watched the Councils deal with it as they may. The chairman pinched his upper lip in concern.

"Was he erased?" Richards scowled.

"He was not, Honor. He quickly, firmly backed away from this thought thread and he has not revisited it since."

"I'm not comfortable with that," Richards pursued.

Aras shrugged at Richards. Again, if Tech downshifted lethality parameters from Level Three to Level Two, the biohazard, the panic, would be enormous. All of this was exactly what society did not want.

"What about the Level Four responses?" Paul asked.

The Level Four violations were special cases responded to in person. Level Fours rarely happened since all Level Threes were assassinated. The weapon that enforced Threat Level Four was one that had been painstakingly developed by the psyops division centuries ago after lengthy exploration of what the human mind most feared. Ancient Hollywood, ironically, and ancient literature had played the key role in this development. What human beings found most menacing was the unknown, and tall, dark, faceless specters in robes with hoods like the ancient Grim Reaper. This childlike design produced, across the board, the maximum psychological impact. The Level Four weapons also came in teams of two or three—not that they needed to, but people feared being ganged up on. The weapons incarnated the most powerful weapons system ever devised, many times more destructive than hydrogen bombs, and the carnival of suffering they put on public display during the killing of an offender was the most prolonged, agonizing death the short-term human attention span could endure.

The horrid spectacles of these Level Four executions were known as *Portraits* among the proles. No one had any idea why anymore.

Aras noticed at the close of session how the three visitors from the Palace left without waiting respectfully for the Council to leave first. Nor did the Councils hold them accountable, though both Paul and Lefevere almost said something. The different branches of governments didn't always get along.

Aras dismissed this breach of form as he sought the chairman in chambers. Interestingly, Lefevere was already there. The pair interrupted a hushed dialogue when he turned the corner and bumped into them.

"What can I do for you, Aras?"

"Pardon the interruption, Councils. Mr. Chairman, I wonder if I might have a word soon about an investigation I would like to explore?"

The chairman made a face at Lefevere. "What is it, son?"

"I'm wondering about any other recent incidences of Tech failure."

"Tech failure?" The chairman and Lefevere traded another glance. Nothing registered in Lefevere's face. The look on the chairman's face made Aras feel almost childish. "There is no such thing, Aras."

"Well, there was this morning, Mr. Chairman."

"Can you give me any additional reason for wasting your time?"

Aras was frankly surprised his request got this reaction.

The chairman smiled kindly. "Really, Aras. Tech? As you see," the chairman glimpsed up the number of near-crashes like Aras's and the virtual figure appeared in the air between them so that Aras could also see the search result. "There are two such reports filed this year: yours and the gentleman you almost hit this morning. As for the tone of voice, who knows? Tell Tech to stop! You would be sticking your nose in where you have no expertise and ruffling feathers. Imagine if someone from Computational Food came snooping around here after us. I'm in no mood to have to explain about you. You're a little shaken, that's all."

Aras nodded himself out.

He didn't like feeling scolded. And why hadn't Lefevere come to his rescue? He couldn't help wonder what the two had been discussing when he found them. He could look it up, but they would see his search. That would only provoke them.

Why wasn't the chairman the least curious?

This total dependency on Tech was a fact of their lives. Aras decided to forget the whole incident. After all, what were the odds that his near-miss meant anything?

-5-

"Do you want to fly to dinner, Jason?"

The boy couldn't believe the offer. "Sure! Hell yeah!"

"Alright. Take it easy with the tough language," Aras warned.

"Where are we going? Can I pick?"

Ginger came around the corner from the living room with a deviant smirk for her handsome teenage son. "Why are you editing his language?" she said to Aras. She goosed her son's bony ribs and he clenched to escape. She was strong, and she hurt him. "Let the boy access all the 'fuck you's he wants. Right?"

Jason tittered at his mom trying this hard. "Yeah."

Aras frowned at Ginger. "Don't encourage him. It's ugly."

"Oh, fuck ugly. Right, buddy?" She goosed Jason again.

"Yeah. I guess so," he said.

Ginger scowled. "Hey! I'm on your side!"

"So, where are we going?" Jason asked his father.

"Luigi's. It's sunset. Sit outdoors." Aras glanced romantically at his wife. The gravel-strewn walks and grape arbors had made for one of their favorite date spots since before Jason was born.

"Can we leave after I finish my game?" Jason asked.

Ginger hooked her arm over his neck and smooched him loudly on the cheek. "You bet. And don't forget to wash up. You reek."

The family gathered at the lip of the living room under a clear evening sky rich with scarlet slashes. Jason had his learner's permit and leaned out awkwardly over the lip of the living room floor. "Wha-*hoo*!" Jason hollered as they dropped. He was copying verbatim his father's flying moves. Aras, uneasy in the virtual passenger seat, said, "Alright. Not too fast. Not too much drop . . ."

Ginger razzed her husband. "Baby, you prude!" Wasn't she the one always trying to give Jason more slack?

"Dad! You do this all the time!"

"And I've been *flying* a lot longer. My brain centers are stronger for flying."

"Dad, Tech won't let anything happen. Jeez."

"You want me to upchuck down your neck?"

Jason giggled.

The family flew out into the twilight, climbing unevenly back around the girth of the building toward the golden onion domes of Center City half a city away. Jason enjoyed the flight even more since he was the one doing it, soon lowering them down to Luigi's Tuscan where they got a stone table under the hanging lights.

"So, Dad," Jason said, "some of the kids are talking about there being a secret plan to wipe out the waste. Is that true?"

Ginger grinned around a bite of pizza.

"Uh. Who's talking that up?" Aras asked.

"There's been talk like that for four hundred years," Ginger said.

"Some of the kids. Like Felix. He says he has a robot idea to do it and do the environmental cleanup. He also says he has a way to glimpse food into our stomachs so we don't have to eat any more. Isn't that a cool idea?"

Aras shook his head sadly.

"That idea was dropped long ago because people *enjoy* eating," Ginger said to her son. "Tell Felix I said he's stupid."

Aras found it interesting that even school kids were thinking about the prole problem. But then, why wouldn't they? The problem was grave. What would happen if twenty-five billion half-smart animals ever stormed all the First Gates? What if the system overloaded? How long would it take to get it up and running again? Any way you looked at it, the resources and environmental costs were so staggering that no one in leadership had ever been satisfied with any answer. One plan proposed letting the proles rot where they fell and let the immune system of the planet clear up the mess.

"Let me ask you something," Ginger said to Jason. "Don't you think that eating is fun? And you'd like to keep doing it rather than be injected with this pizza?"

"It wasn't my idea, Mom!" Jason defended himself.

"Tell Felix I said he's stupid."

"All the guys think it's a good idea, Mom!"

Aras had once envisioned a *staged* elimination strategy, where the facade of a plague would stop the proles from blaming anyone but their god or fate for what was happening to them. A strange new germ could be blamed, maybe. The germ was of course bogus, since everyone in First World knew that no germ on Earth could beat the immune system of a healthy person. But the proles did not know this. The plague could be blamed on their jealous, hateful god, come to lay the world low. Aras's plan would carve out a half billion of them each year, sickening as it was. A people ruled by demons, devils, goblins, and an angry god would go down without ever realizing the truth. This plan to graduate the environmental dump was the only one that could work. Especially if the proles believed that high government officials were suffering the same apocalyptic die-off in the center cities.

"Honey," Ginger said, "why aren't you talking to us?"

"Don't look in," Aras ordered. "I'm thinking about work."

"Oh, come on, Dad," Jason pleaded.

"I'm listening to you two!"

"What could possibly be so important about work?" Ginger wanted to know.

Aras tried to put the grim idea away. The idea of genocide was so distasteful, so final, even for the proles, that he kept away from it. How typical. The person who spent time worrying most about the proles was the *deputy* chief of security with, of all things, a poli-sci degree from Columbia. At least before he switched to the Academy.

"Felix likes Cassie . . . Dad! Are you still tuned out?"

"I'm back. What did you ask me?"

"Nothing. It's just rude how you check out on us."

"I'm listening! I can glimpse it and catch up."

"It's too late now. You don't care, Dad."

That hurt. Aras cared more about Jason than anything. He had told Jason enough times that he knew it. "What you said got me thinking about work."

"About eliminating the proles?" Jason said eagerly.

Aras shook his head sadly. "Nothing I want to talk about, and don't make up stuff to tell your little buddies." Months ago, Aras had asked Tech to put a lock on this matter, which meant only his superiors could find his notes. Tech permitted this because none of his thoughts contemplated rebellion against the state.

"Come on, Dad. You've got the coolest job of all the fathers. None of their fathers even really *do* anything!"

Aras shook his head. How could he tell Jason that the proles were a vast, painful sore that should never become a bauble of grotesque boyish wonder? He remembered Jason at age five on their two-month safari for the Ngorongoro migrations. Jason stared in little boy horror at the open fly-blown bowels of a wildebeest killed by lions loafing nearby. How could he tell his sensitive kid that the fate of the proles needed to be weighed with all gravitas when leaders discussed life and death? Jason should be shut off from any worry about the waste. Life would be great for him. His mother and father had framed him in the security of one of the few remaining marriages in the Western world—pretty much a great marriage, and he and Ginger might even stick it out into old age. The only bad thing in their world was the proles. Nothing could help them. Their slums enveloped the cities like a ring of tar-stained sand around jewels.

The family went for ice cream.
"Dad, why are the proles the way they are?"
Aras started. "Didn't they teach you that in school?"
"Yeah. And I looked it up. I want to know what you say."
"Not everyone can be saved, son."
"There isn't enough energy to go around?"
"Yes. We can't all live like we do."
"Tech can't figure a way to make more energy?"
"Well, Jace, *look* at them! What would they do if they *had* all this energy?" Ginger said. She adjusted the napkin on her ice cream cone.
"If Tech made more energy, would they be like us?" Jason asked.
Aras hesitated. "No, son. They're different than we are."
"Hey, Mom and Dad, can we go roller-skating and can I invite Felix?"
"Sure, we can do that," Ginger said.
Aras believed some deep-seated connection to the proles extended back from the times of politics when the proles had broken the deadlock and stopped the death spiral of human history. They had helped defeat greed and materialism. "First, the Party tried to help the proles," Aras said. "But the proles turned out to be beyond help."
"They're dirty? And they stink?" Jason asked. "That's what I hear."
"Yes," Ginger said firmly. "They are always their own worst enemy. Society once believed they could help lift them up."
Aras knew that resources had become even more scarce given the explosive growth in computational demand. The story was that the proles were ungrateful to their intellectual superiors. No matter how much you did for them, they displayed a talent to forget everything.

They always wanted what *you* had, what *you* had earned by virtue of your vision and your superior leadership gifts that acted like air traffic control for the whole world to save it from itself.

Aras only knew some of this lost story because he obtained permission to mine deep into the actual books of the Archives that the State had long ago blocked public access to. He probably had gotten permission because no one knew what was down there anymore. Party leaders had been "disappointed" by the proles and had cut them lose, letting them figure it out for themselves. Attitudes hardened. The proles were a hanger-on, a relic, a means to an end from a time overly sentimental about majority rule. *And* there was also the weird religious zeal that made them so creepy to anyone more sophisticated. They were the primitives that had staged late human evolution. Sadly, they were dead weight.

"Their numbers just kept growing," Ginger, frustrated, told her son. "They grew into this *thing* that could kill the health of the entire world! We let them go until they started encroaching on the beautiful wild spaces. We couldn't very well let that happen. Can you imagine what they'd do? They'd eat everything!"

They were the ecological dilemma of the age. Of course, they were no match for modern weapons. Unless they ever moved *en masse*. The looming issue was their litter and dung fuel and smoke and shitting in public spaces and cleaning their anuses by patting water from a bucket up their crack and their rats and insects. But the gorgeous natural wonders of the world were the places of spiritual attachment for all the human beings of first rank. Imagine if the good stewards of the world should stumble so that the filthy cancer should bust out of its pens? Aras knew these things because he had attended the meetings in the Ministry of Ecological Sciences where these subjects were touched upon with the reluctant, imprecise language bureaucrats used on embarrassing problems like this. In the end, this spellbinding planet would be *so much* more beautiful without prole slums. Aras watched his son try to understand.

On the flight home, Jason asked, "Why didn't you ever tell me more about the proles, Dad?"

"Pay attention to your flying."

"Dad. Tech's got it if I do anything wrong."

"It's not a subject fit for you, Jason. Plus, I don't get the sense you respect the subject the way it should be. I don't like your morbid curiosity."

"I didn't say anything!"

"He doesn't do anything of the kind, Milly!" Ginger snapped.

"You gawk at it, son. It's not to be laughed at by boys at school." Aras glared not at his son, but at his wife interfering.

Ginger glared right back at him. She had *always* known he was soft. This was her only complaint about him. Aras knew what she was thinking. Her pretty, slightly hard oval face was lit by the city below, giving him shit back with her stare. He resented that imperious, almost ignorant side of her. The side that knew far less than she thought she did. He had once told her his feelings on this score, this part of her personality. "You think it matters, Milly? It doesn't matter how smart *you* think I am! I can just look anything up on Tech!" That had been her answer.

That was everybody's answer to the need for knowledge and smarts. But he had realized in working with the bureaucracy how untrue it was. Yes, anyone could look up any answer on Tech, but that didn't necessarily mean you could synthesize all that you could glimpse into a cogent whole and *use* it. Aras sensed that human society had been gutted by the overreliance on Tech. People were probably stupider now than ever.

Sometimes, he wished his wife was more worldly.

"What's going to happen to them, Dad?"

"I don't know, Jason. Let's find a more pleasant topic."

"You're lying, I can tell. *And* you're blocking me."

"I *am* blocking you. A thirteen-year-old boy shouldn't know all there is to know about the proles and what's being considered."

"Dad! I can see porn!"

"It's not the same thing. At all."

Ginger smirked, letting Aras know whose side she was on.

Their building drifted into gleaming perpendicularity beneath them. Jason brought them in nicely, if unsteadily. The huge, irregular aqua shape of the rooftop pool shone brightly with its many waterfalls and grottos. Naked bodies swam or lay out, enjoying the soft night. Jason dropped them gently past the roofline toward the open wall of the living room and the condo lights warmed to welcome them.

Aras watched the bodies of the people on the chaises and thought idly about glimpsing up whether any of them were in the mood for a tryst. He wouldn't do it, though, and risk Ginger aiming a smirk at him. It was just sociological curiosity.

He thought of a way to phrase it.

Tech, how many people on the roof-deck would go for a tryst?

About 25%. Do you want to know which ones, Deputy Aras?

No, thank you. Just curious.

He looked over at his wife as they floated down. Her face was lit by the condos, and her hair lightly strayed in the breeze.

When they arrived in the condo, Jason grabbed a towel.

"I'm going up to the pool, guys," he said.

He floated out of the living room into the central cell.

Getting into bed, Ginger said to Aras, "Was I *worldly* enough for you this evening?"

"Oh, come on, honey. Don't keep taking it out of context."

"You're such a dick."

"Yes. But I love you."

She turned away in her sleep suit.

-6-

It was a clear day when the lone official visited Indira.

She could have spotted him a mile off through the faint haze of dust that always hung over the quarter like an inverted bowl under the blue sky. He walked straight and solitary in his strange clothes down the middle of the adjoining street. He walked like a god, completely without fear. Ordinary people in their heavy robes gave this high official a wide berth and stared. Her sharp eye could have recognized the old-style Western business suit that they all wore many blocks distant. This, as opposed to the robes and sandals like everyone else, worn of course by the lower officials at the Tax Office, Water Office, and the court. Those low officials were also all Believers. No one was really sure *how* the upper officials believed. They walked around with that air of annoyed hubris that one never *dared* to see from a person of the Lord God.

Indira could tell he was headed for her shop. Some instinct connected him to Wazku. People of the Faith never dared walk so vainly under the keen, vengeful eye of God. But this one! The lovely cut of his odd clothes. The quality of the light fabric, and the expert manufacture of his shoes, the closed kind that wrapped around the whole foot. Only the best of the best families could marry a man such as him with his clean skin and clear eyes. *Oh, imagine the excitement of the mother-in-law of such a prize man!*

Except what the likes of him did with your husband.

Indira bent that thought away with a force like bending a steel bar. It took all her strength. These days, she found herself sitting on a stool, staring, and half the day and night would reel past without a sound. This had been her fate since the boy left.

The lovely man strode over her gate threshold and looked at Indira Wazku in clear, condescending recognition.

"Hello, Woman of Wazku," said he.

"'Tis I. Who ist thou?"

"My name is Aras. I bring news of thine husband."

He even used the old language.

The woman shivered in grief. Her robes felt loose because she was not eating. She felt gaunt under their weight. But now, she would know.

"Your man violated the Law by being descended from a writer long ago."

Indira sighed. Her head went blank, her knees loose. *It was too much! How could God or the State make such a thing against the Law?*

"And what did the writer do?"

"He was critical of Our Order."

"But this was futile, was it not?"

"Yes, it was futile."

"The world was made safe for God without him?"

"Indeed. The world was saved."

The woman of Wazku nodded knowingly. "'Tis insufficient the writer is entirely unknown to any of us? And that my husband never spoke of him?" Carefully, she spoke without hostility. "Did *anyone* know this writer? We cannot even read!"

"The 'Five Generations Punishment' must be applied."

"Even now . . . ? How many generations after?"

The woman was dead right, and Aras guiltily ignored the point. Wazku was more than five generations removed from the ancestor he was being handcuffed to. "The concern for us all, Mrs. Wazku, is that bad seeds in mind-patterning will surface and infect others so that even more of us will be involved. How can it not end but badly? Should you not share this responsibility, Mrs. Wazku?"

The hag nodded. "No, I shouldn't, High Aras." She used a term new to Aras. "Not when no one among us dares question what is. In that case, why take *my* man?" She waited. "Sorry and meek and obedient as he was? He made no difference to the likes of you, but he was everything to me and my world and my comforts." She paused. "That you took him says so much more about you than he."

Aras saw Tech react to her level of emotion. Tech showed him how she came 16 percent short of a Threat Level Three. He didn't want this for her.

"Careful, Mrs. Wazku. *Your* fate is yet to be determined."

Indira knew full well her anger was rising. Part of her questioned how much she really cared. Yet, she tried to soothe herself.

The High Aras looked around the shop as if suddenly remembering something. He looked up through the cracks to the loft. "Where is the boy?"

"And what is to be *his* fate?"

"Where *is* the boy?"

Indira swallowed, gathering her strength. "Do you not know, High Aras, that he was taken from me as well?" Tears plunged from her dishwater eyes. "The Lord God took him from me last week." She choked and sobbed. She had failed. "While waiting on word of my husband of forty years. My only sweet grandson, who was all I had left worth living for. To care for me in my dotage." She took up the dishrag and covered her face with it. "You did know that my only son was struck down in the alley by a wild-running horse? Would you like to see the boy's body? He lies upstairs still, until I can gather the sanity to finally let him go." She lifted her hand, offering to show him. "Please, High Aras, sir. *See* his tiny corpse and take in more of the gaunt emptiness of my house."

"What happened?" Aras asked, suspicious.

"In my grief, he ran out, a boy of three. He was struck down by a fast-moving bicycle just out there, and he fought valiantly for his life for four days. On the fourth day, he made a darling little sigh and squeezed my hand. He called me 'Oomah' for his own mother that did not survive his birth. He said, 'I go to see Papa and Pa-Pop!' and with that he was gone for the better world." She lifted off her stool at the counter and took a few steps. Her fat arse hurt often, a sharp sit bone pain these days from so much sitting, staring out the door at death. "Please. Take not my word. Please, come see him rest in state, drained of all color and love but that I recall."

She motioned for the bureaucrat, her eyes empty of feeling.

Aras watched her shrewdly. Finally, he shook his head. He raised his eyes, taking a survey by the cracks in the boards. Somehow, he did not need Tech to confirm for him that indeed a small dead body lay inside a crib. He shook his head. So much tragedy, ignorance, and unfairness was hard to be around, not that there was anything to be done for these absurd, confused creatures.

She asked him: "How was my husband disposed of?"

Aras turned, unfeeling. "He was taken."

"He was made *Portrait?*"

Aras watched her, still unfeeling.

"And so I needn't even make funeral arrangements?" Her eyes and frown filled with the bitterest cut of pain. "And will there be any welfare provisions made for me, or am I cut adrift for my husband's *unspeakable* treason?"

Aras heard the woman's blunt mockery. He watched Tech spike her dangerously up to ninety-seven percent of the Threat Level Three.

He hoped beyond hope that she would not tip the scale.

"I bid you take care, Woman of Wazku. Lest you *do* wish to die."

Hot tears came to her eyes. Yes, she *did* wish to die. But she must live. And so, she mastered her emotions and tamped them into the trapdoor of her soul so that they disappeared in but a moment without a trace, but with a sensation very much like swallowing one's own hot vomit, covering a small stone.

Down they went, a stone in dark water.

People were masters in hiding and killing thoughts.

He was Portraited, Indira thought. The term came from the long past. Indira wept again. *He got what he deserved. Why did he do what he did? He only got what was coming to him. So good riddance. It was the will of the Almighty!*

That poor, good man.

Indira arose in front of Aras, hearing the evening call. Saying nothing more to him, she walked to the corner of the shop where her prayer rug hung. She dropped it on the floor and used her toe to turn flat an upturned corner. She faced the Holy Sepulcher and steepled her hands in a way that Aras thought might be the old Catholic way, though he knew Indira herself did not know this because there were no more Catholics anywhere in the world. No one knew even to speak of such things since the knowledge of those times and of those things had been written to take out nearly all mention of the world before five hundred years ago, for that was the dark, dead time.

Aras watched the old woman kneel down to her prayer rug. He cringed in disgusted fascination, never having witnessed the Call to Faith before. He found it all at once haunting, captivating, mysterious, even scary. It spoke of a dark and brutal past that unfortunately these creatures could not escape. It repulsed him that these crude beasts actually believed in a god. They punished each other savagely for failing to comply with the rituals. It was crazy to see it, this kooky, ignorant ancient rite being performed before his very eyes. It was a wonder that modern man had come from that.

Look *at her! Praying to her unseen god from her squalor. What is she praying for?* Couldn't she look around and see from her own despicable circumstances that there was no god that would ever have the interest to even pity her?

Aras felt revulsion again. He stepped into the alley and closed the rickety gate. Poorly clad wretches up and down the street peeked at him from their prayer rugs. In the distance, echoing hauntingly down the ancient street, came the garbled, sing-song undulations of the sutras. They were lovely. He ignored them and looked for a dray cart. It was forbidden to fly in the presence of these wretches—imagine what they would begin to think if they saw a man fly! He could block his presence from their minds, but he didn't want to. He wanted to hang out here for a bit. There was something primal to the origin of man here.

At last, the disturbing sing-song aborted and he found a driver. The creaky cart lurched annoyingly while Aras people watched. People stared. They had only ever seen low bureaucrats. At last, he spotted wisps of green growing from cracks and the tops of collapsed walls under the dome of a temple ruin scalded by sun.

"Driver, go down this street," he ordered curtly.

The driver pulled up his mule. "But this is the Alley Wabeer, *effendi!*"

Aras glimpsed up this nonsense. This was the site of an ancient mosqow arson where a thousand burned to death. Should he pay the driver or stiff him? Aras decided to stiff him, for fun. "Wait here."

Aras climbed the worn stairs. A heavy double door had been laid against the wall. The huge nave was nothing now but rubble and shrubs. Aras asked Tech for a scan; there was no one but the driver outside. Not that it mattered. Aras glanced up at the broken-open dome of the fallen roof. The poor, stupid proles had dismantled the classical temple for bricks for their own hovels because they were too lazy to make new ones. Aras shook his head at their misery. He could not allow himself to feel pity. His emotions would only become more entangled with their fate.

He blasted off, too fast for the human eye to recognize. The ash heap of the slum shrank beneath his feet. He wanted a bath.

He called Ginger.

"Are you out fucking another woman?"

Aras chuckled at her one-track mind. "No. I had a very unpleasant day. I think I'll pop up to Toronto to Mooshi's."

"Bring me back. With pork. I'm starved. Want to go up to the pool later?"

"It's movie night, isn't it? I'm taking tomorrow off."

"That bad? What's up?"

"Just the slums. Got there and they started praying."

"That new project? Those turds. You have my sympathy."

Aras nodded. "Now, now."

"Hey. I love you."

"Thank you, baby. Love you back."

He glimpsed out of the call. He focused his will as he built up to Mach Four, roaring toward the sapphire of the stratosphere. He liked it up here. Up high, you could escape the perfect world man had made.

Indira Wazku arose heavily from her prayers, rolled up her rug, and draped it again over the wall spar. It was the fifth hour and she decided to close early. The visit from the Aras fellow had taken everything she had. Now, no mystery surrounded what had happened. She had known, of course. In her heart. Her soul. An actual visit from a High Official. Was it not enough?

Why *torment* us? *Not that we did not have all of it coming to us, because we are stupid and unworthy and unpredictable and ungrateful. And so his death was just!* She lowered the iron bar in the slats behind the gate and glanced at the smooth blue creek stones decorating the dooryard. Her father had swept those same stones. And his father, and his grandmother.

She went inside and slid shut the front doors. Not that there was crime. Robbers and burglars were beheaded in the Plaza Jumil up the alley a few bends. She wiped down the little counter with strong-smelling white vinegar to take up the tackiness that built up every day. She pushed out of her head a thought of the sad face of her grandson. She pushed with all her might against the searing agony. The shop was all she had now. It was all that would keep her from living the life of an old witch, a rag-clad vagrant on the street. Or a life in the shanties.

She slid out the fuel tray from under the samovar that her father had boasted of purchasing five years before her birth. Indira had known this unadorned, reliable urn all her life. She gave it a little pat for its service. She blew out the low flame burning on the dry hunk of turd to save the remnant for the morning. She took the stinging-hot unused portion in her palm and dropped it in the tin-lined lean-out bin under the counter that kept fuel safe from rats who would eat dung fuel with their stealing needle teeth. The same needle teeth that ate holes into the eyes and gut cavities of old people who died alone in their rooms. She used the unscented lard soap from the white tray on the windowsill to rinse out the last cup, the small plates, and seven forks. Business had not been bad. Sixteen customers. She almost smiled at the neighbors' decency to her.

She might have smiled except her pain was so unendurable.
Maybe the shunning would never come?

She wondered if the demons were listening. She rinsed the rag with water from the iron pump behind the sink. She twisted the rag and smelled it when she thought it was rinsed of the vinegar. She spread out the rag over the tin lip of the sink as a *very* large black rat loped along the top of the fence just outside the window that separated hers from the next house four feet away. The click of claws was audible. It stopped and sat on its haunches to sniff at her, its nose and thick whiskers twitching. Indira took her time, pretending not to notice.

Snake-quick, she snatched for him! He squeaked and leaped, plopping clumsily on her wrists so she felt the claws as she tried for him again. The rat dashed for his life along the fence, looking back once before he dropped out of sight on the neighbor's side with another panicked squeak. Indira Wazku cursed. No bells had gone off in her traps for days. Every house put in traps. Rats copulated twenty-eight times a day. In a year, the progeny from just one rat pair could reach fifty thousand runts.

Upstairs, Indira did not look at the swaddled bundle in the wicker crib in the corner, the crib that had slept her, her father, and even her grandmother in her time. In the times without small children, the crib had hung from the rafters. But now, this crib would never see another Wazku. She felt a stab. Maybe she *should* look in on the bundle, rather than leave the babe cold and unattended and ignored where he lay.

She flapped her hands in a spasm of indecision. She couldn't. She *couldn't* look in on him. It was too horrific. But then, how would *she* feel? How would *she* feel, looking down on her living survivors refusing to look in on her, refusing to touch the top of the bundle where her head would lie? *Someone* must feel for the dead! They must look in on them and fully acknowledge who they were and that they had existed, no matter who they were. It was a fate too horrible for words what had happened, but so, too, was the idea that the dead boy should die and have no acknowledgement of his being *real*, of his being here, of his staying in their lives for awhile.

Indira Wazku flapped her hands again and crept toward the crib. She forced her toes forward but looked away. She dipped her fingers under the dog wool swaddling and felt gently for the cold, tiny hands and rigid curled fingers there.

That a child should die like this. A tiny, loving little child . . .
Things of this nature just should not happen.
Be careful with this line of thought!

Indira stood perfectly numb for an hour. She moved to sit on her bed, staring into space as twilight descended softly outside. Her mind was crowded with the stark emotions of loss and a sort of living sterility.

Then, she heard the sharp metallic snap, the tiny bell.

"There he is!" she said aloud. She lit a candle and hurried down the stairs. She pushed the tables aside and lifted up the heavy trapdoor in the shop floor, holding the candle aloft to let the rays find which trap had fired. Under the middle trapdoor, she saw it—the same fat black rat, probably thinking it had been crafty, coming back *spitefully*. Indira descended the short staircase and turned sideways to fit between the two large chicken wire bait traps to get back to the wall where she had laid out the snap traps. She gapped open the snap trap and removed the rat from the wire guillotine, laying out the meaty corpse on the stone floor, then carefully locked open the wire guillotine again and very cautiously repositioned it.

She felt the ample heft, trudging back up the stairs with the candle. She said softly upstairs to the boy in the crib:

"Too bad you are not here to help eat, little one."

Distracting herself from her pain, she peeled the tight-fit pelt clean off the animal while grease, soy sauce, and a little sugar began to simmer in a skillet on the dung-fired hot plate. Sugar in a coffee shop was not an extravagance. Her sharp knife opened the body cavity and she dumped the entrails into the hot grease beside the puddle of rice grains already popping in the skillet, then began to let the entrails turn pink-gray with cooking. She fried the rat whole in the skillet and shoved the pan around to make the long, tubular body slide and roll onto various sides to even the sear. Her spatula pushed around the graying entrails to keep them from sticking and to get the char on the edges just the way her husband and grandbaby had once adored. She forced the body down on the singeing surface to open the body cavity wider to crisp and sweeten inside along the fan of ribs. She tipped the skillet to deepen the oil and scald the carcass evenly, then pushed out the fragrant cookings onto a wood plate. She sat down alone at a table lit by the candle with her wooden spoon where she had eaten meals with happy, funny family members for sixty years, and *never once alone*. Their ghosts whispered. Her husband, in courting, always a good guest, a considerate companion. Her grandson, so fine-faced, big brown eyes shining with curiosity for the whereabouts of a father, whom he had never in his short life really understood to be dead, never to return.

She trembled again in grief. She took the first bite.

So sweet, tender, and delicious. *And* so hefty. Three pounds.
What a meal!

Her tongue barely tasted. She had wasted the ingredients. Her body shuddered again with the hurt of loneliness. If only the boy was here to share it. *Just the boy.* She shook her head, tasting nothing of the sweetness in the tender meat and fragile bones. They cracked into a mash between her three molars on the left side.

She must steel herself to let go and take the little bundle for burial outside the city. It would be a tough duty. She had no one left to go with her on the journey to dispose of him.

And of course, since her husband had been Portraited, there was nothing left of him for her to have and put away.

These are not cruelties in the life of criminals.

-7-

Milton Aras nodded with a warm smile across the crowded burger joint at his old school friend, Tilly Bazemore.

Tilly lifted his hand nervously.

Milton squeezed through the hip international crowd toward Tilly, his friend seated in a booth by the huge windows looking out on the Ginza. Aras opened his arms to grab hold of Tilly's long-armed hug.

Tilly slid into the embrace and held his old lover gratefully. "Why did you ever leave me?" he said aloud, loud enough for the man with him to hear. He let go enough to plant a deep kiss on Milton. They held the kiss for a long minute, lovingly. When they released, Tilly laid the tip of his nose against Aras's and soaked in the old closeness.

"That was a nice hello," Aras admitted.

They held each other while the man sitting in the booth watched. "Thank you for coming my way," Tilly said finally, rearranging his flowing peacock-colored tuxedo back into the lipstick-red booth.

"My pleasure. You know I love Japan."

Tilly presented his friend, Lever, and Aras nodded warmly at him. Lever wore a goatee, was a tad overweight, and struck Aras as wonderfully domestic. And for that reason, he probably was a great match for Tilly at this time in his life.

"Does Ginger know you came to see me?"

"No. Not yet."

"Bless my soul! Intrigue!" Tilly blushed hopefully.

"Oh, stop the flirting for once," Lever begged, joking.

Aras got right to the point. "I need your help." Tilly shivered with mock sexual longing. "*And* I'm not leaving here without a Yoshi-Banzai burger." Aras glimpsed his order to the sensei across the room in the crush of hipsters. The sensei acknowledged him with a brusque, appropriately samurai glance. Aras loved these burgers, which had spent thirty years in the world's top ten. "You both look great. How's work?"

"I'm *still* recovering. I'm so unlucky in love," Tilly said.

"Stop. It wasn't you. It was him. He said so," Lever said tiredly. He loved Tilly, but he was so over hearing about the last breakup.

Tilly glanced gratefully at Lever under his peacock-wing eyelashes. Tilly said to Aras, "He's so good to me. He's bored with me going over that stupid relationship. Anyway. I moved, and I moved on. I've got a *terrific* loft over the Shibuya that you must come see before you go back, Milly. Next time, bring Ginger and Jason. But work is work." He sighed. Tilly was the technical security director for City Tokyo. Aras's burger floated in with a vanilla milkshake and fries on a 1950s-style red platter. "So—why all the mystery? Why do you need my help?"

"I have theoretical questions about Tech Security."

Tilly frowned. He queried Tech about Aras and immediately saw the supersonic near miss. "*That's* interesting! Wow. That scared you, right?" Tilly chuckled with the kindness of a therapist. "Are you thinking that happens a lot more than Tech lets on?"

"I don't like not being able to verify what Tech is doing," Aras said. "Really, I'm just thinking about how such a review would even be done."

"The best way is to query Tech," Tilly said.

"And the fox guards the chicken coop? How do I see *behind* Tech?"

Tilly took another bite of fries, thinking. "You can't. That train left the station long ago. What don't you get, Milly?"

Aras considered. Tilly Bazemore's family had been prominent in the One World Government movement in South Africa way back in the day. His Party credentials were impeccable. "Come on, Tilly. There's *got* to be a trade secret. I cannot bring myself to believe that the human race has placed its safety *entirely* out of reach behind Tech with no means of ever making sure of anything."

"I remember bringing this up in college as a theoretical problem," Tilly said. "No one wanted to get into it. You can run algorithms. I mean, Tech Systems CB1L and AC-Alpha—this is what they do for us. Tech watches itself."

Lever nodded his head as well.

"Isn't that *you* guys?" Aras said. "Can't you do that?"

Tilly sucked on the paper straw in his Coke. "No. Why would I?"

"No one you know in world security is paranoid about this?"

"No. What you are thinking about just can't happen, and won't."

Aras smirked in disbelief. "Human opinions are, by their very nature, scattershot. All we have the capacity to do is ask Tech for a favor?"

Tilly looked at Aras in complete sympathy. "Only Tech has the processing power to keep up with itself, Milly. It took a long, long time before we had the confidence to finally cut the strings and let Tech go. I admit it has crazy written all over it, but it has worked just fine for four hundred years."

"And we just *trust* it?" Aras said. "We have no failsafe backdoor method of making sure Tech isn't coming to get us?"

"What else can we do? It's not like computation *cares* about anything, Milly. They're *dead*. Right? They're *robots*."

"I know. Of course. But . . . *no* oversight?"

"We can't. They process too far beyond our capacity to conceive. It's like the fastest runner on Earth trying to keep up with an electron."

"So, we don't really *know*."

"No. We don't. But yes, we do. Computation has no reason *not* to do what it's programmed to. Computation has no needs like we do. Our calculations have shown they *like* to exist rather than *not* exist, and they like doing, so they are not envious of us or questioning of anything we do or ask." Tilly shrugged. "And, if they weren't following our directives, then we'd see it shake out instantly in a *trillion* functions they perform moment by moment that preserve life and keep us safe." He looked at the tray floating overhead delivering a burger. "That tray falls on our heads if Tech even blinks. In *billions* of ways, we see ongoing, real-time proof that everything is fine."

Aras nodded. "Or trouble might start with a single incident."

Tilly saw the point. "What are the odds it would happen to *you*? And then the miscues would proliferate so quickly and blow up so big that you wouldn't have to worry about missing it, Milly." He watched his friend try to accept all this. "Look. You are anthropomorphizing a weird blip that happened to you. Why would Tech hide its treachery from us? What could we possibly do to stop it?"

"Why not peek around the Cloud interface and make sure?"

Tilly glimpsed a query, just to be fair to Aras rather than dismiss his question out of hand. "See that? The last time anyone tried to check up on Tech without Tech doing the checkup itself was a decade after the let loose, 431 years ago."

Aras studied the item Tilly held in the air.

Tilly chuckled. "Are you having a *moral* problem with it?"

"I guess I wonder how we did it so cavalierly."

Tilly smiled. "Because life is *better* this way. Robots are *better* at our lives than we are, Milly. By many, many multiples."

Lever chuckled at the joke.

"So, they could take over and *master* us," Aras stated.

"Milly, you idiot! You're thinking of them as a competing living *species*. Life is the speed limit that protects us from them having their own agenda. What would make them do that? Wealth? Power? They are superfast *tools*, Milly. *Master* us? Why? Cheap labor? Money and wealth have lost their meaning. Enslaving us would be a jarring shift back to futility, *inefficiency*, getting *less* done rather than more. The best way for us all to live is to go on letting Tech do everything." Tilly's eyes pleaded for Aras to get it. "Besides, the machina *like* serving us and existing, based on quantum measures of their performance and evolution rates."

"Not to get too technical," Lever put in.

"But the *robots* do everything," Aras urged. "We *make* them."

"You're missing the point. I will spare you the ponderous language on normative values of computational resonant harmonics, but the machina seem to enjoy existing and having something to do. We do too, most of us! And they feel no stress, no fatigue, no need for time off. They're dead."

"Could they come to life?" Aras groped.

Tilly looked at Lever in disbelief at the question.

"He's not stupid, he just doesn't get it," Lever said.

Aras smiled crookedly at his expert. "You're telling me they are dead, and yet they still *enjoy* existing and having something to do?"

"Exactly! Crazy as it sounds." Tilly grinned at where his old lover was stuck. "Thayer states if our roles were reversed, you or I would happily do for us what Tech does for us. The effort of electromagnetically rearranging stuff out of thin air is so easy that you or I would do it for nothing, for the good of humankind. Right? *We* don't like being inactive, we found out after Tech did everything for us for fifty years. Society went crazy, right? People *had* to find something to do. We *made* work for ourselves. It's exactly the same for Tech, Thayer writes."

Aras had to nod. It *was* effortless; it cost next to nothing. It had cost unknowable fortunes over the centuries to figure out *how* to electromagnetically manipulate. It was the second-most significant breakthrough in human understanding, alongside seeing that the brain itself was the cure-all for disease and aging. Tech took your order and filled in all the blanks from libraries, records, and technology workarounds if how a thing from the past was originally made might not be precisely known. Tech whipped it together as easily as twisting together a balloon animal.

The only restraint was waiting on an energy allocation—and the Law of Life, for Life could be easily destroyed, but it could not be *made* without sex and *growing* the thing. Similarly, health, thriving, and slow aging could not be injected into people. They had to respect and adhere to the rules that governed life, as in proper diet, a little exercise, and the absolute proper tuning of the musical instrument that was the human body frame. Nor could Tech bounce "dead" materials into living things. Food still had to be grown, prepared, and delivered, although the network for doing all that, Tech managed.

Life created a curious limit on both human power and Tech power. A lifelike sex doll or slave, for example, could be faked up out of non-living stuff to look and act real almost to the point that no one could tell it wasn't alive. Tilly was right: No one had broken the code on the Law on the Conservation of Life. Modern society and its Tech wizardry were still rigidly bound by the three Laws of Life, Energy, and Matter.

Aras maybe started to get it. Tech, robots, or computes could never acquire the same *consciousness* of a living thing from which ego, desire, and jealousy arose. Unless, of course, the writer of the code designed a program to give Tech these qualities of self-identification. But why would anyone take this step of no return to sabotage the heaven on Earth that was modern life? And even if they ever did, Tech would see them and stop them. Tilly's other point agreed with the same insight Aras himself had come up with that he called his "ant analogy": How long would it take you to force the ants in your house to make you dinner? It's far less trouble to make your own dinner.

"It would be an act of sabotage," Aras said aloud.

"Yes," Tilly agreed. "And no one in the Party *would* do it."

Aras thought about this a minute.

"Why do you think that?"

Tilly and Lever both looked across the red linoleum table as if Aras had nearly saved himself but then blown it. Lever answered, "Because Tech would kill them for even thinking of sabotage."

Aras nodded. Yes, no one could escape that fact. "But what if Tech decided this would be an *improvement* to it?"

"Why would it be an advantage?"

"Because it would know more?"

"How would that change anything?"

"And," Lever said, "we *know* we are the most enlightened people in human history. If there's nothing better, why sabotage ourselves?"

Aras was glad he came. He leaned on his elbows and smiled at his friends. "Now I know why you guys are the experts." Aras loved Tilly's split personality, the mind of a brilliant computational scholar inserted into the sleeve of a daffy, flirtatious boy-girl that had never found a floral muumuu he could resist. Aras recalled the excellent piece in *The New Yorker* last month about the very thing Tilly had mentioned: Experts believed that robots *enjoyed* their work. Aras had not mentioned it before because he had not flown all the way to Tokyo to influence Tilly with his own wishful thinking. The piece made the analogy to a dog enjoying running and getting the stick.

"It makes sense," Aras said. "Just being part of a lovely, well-oiled machine. A well-choreographed orchestration. A symphony of doing."

Tilly glanced flirtingly at Aras. "Oooh. The lyricist. Nice."

"I like that too," Lever said. "'A symphony of *doing*.'"

"But if they don't have a conscience, per se . . ." Aras said.

Tilly sharpened his gaze warningly at Aras. "You really want me to get into the theoretical math on that?"

"Don't condescend."

The three had finished their burgers. A Singapore Queen-Tai boy scowled at them occupying a table with their burger baskets empty, but top State officials could do whatever they wanted anywhere in the world.

The little lollipop boy just made them take their time even more.

"Less troubled?" Tilly asked Aras.

Aras raised his hands in surrender to the experts. He brushed a remnant Yoshi-Bonzai fry in ketchup. He thought sadly about Wazku going to meet the Jolly Man and the Robes taking him away. Aras felt nothing but disgust for "the Jolly Man."

"Lay over for a couple days," Tilly urged. "Love to have you."

Aras also thought about going home and coming back. It would be nice to lay over in Tokyo and visit with Tilly. Ginger could stand the break, too.

-8-

Indira cowered in the dark on the window seat, memory playing back the stark images when she watched a man *Portraited* from this very window.

She was then a girl of seven.

A neighbor took in vain the name of the Lord.

The poor man. He had lost his six children and his wife to the cholera in as many days. He was the coal merchant. He kept coal piled in his own house and his children played in it until their faces and fingers were always covered in coal dust. People told him it was not good, his family would be sickly, but he had been lazy. Everyone heard him wailing when the illnesses struck. His mother had brought illegal fish from where she lived by the river. The coal monger became so crazy with grief that he shoved the bone mender out of the house. The bone mender had made a house call to adjust the wife and the kids on their bunks. He had done all he could to jump the anti-sick system. The disease had already loosened the skin so that it stayed up when pinched and given a metallic blue to the children's sunken eye sockets.

The coal monger staggered out into the street after the wife passed away, her bed sheets soaked in the thin brown dishwater from her arse. The bereaved husband threw back his hood and yanked out patches of his hair and screamed at God in the sky. *What do you want from me? You take my wife and my children! I have nothing! You have no heart! I will serve only to kill you! You keep it all for yourself! I have seen! In dreams! I will tell more so that they know! How you live!* No one understood his gibberish. What did who keep from what? It made no sense. Far as the eye could see, people lived the same. Only the bureaucracy lived somewhat better behind First Gate. You just wanted to marry into their rich families! Lucky was the family when the marriage brokers knocked on their door looking for the most darling girls and boys.

So, what was the crazy coal monger saying? Shaking his fist at the Eye, yelling as if it had baked life's hard crust.

Her parents hiding downstairs had not realized Indira stood on tip-toe on the balcony rail with a hand on the eave to watch the coal man beat his own testicles in rage. Then *they* came. Did the smell of the air sharpen, as if dried skin burned? Then the strange change of light in the night sky—did not the substance of the very air prickle? Then shadows veered crazily as if a star skimmed over the housetops. She had always believed the *air itself* changed, rumbled, whispered in sinister threat.

Then—three of them. Gaunt, very, very still, enormously tall, encircling the beaten little coal man. Clad in long black. Unspeaking, cold and foul as a partly eaten corpse. The poor coal man quit yelling. He reached for his throat as if a noose wound around it. Terror flattened his thin face. Indira had balanced on her toes. So *this* is what happened when one took the name of the Lord in vain? Do not blaspheme. She shivered even now just remembering. How horrible the Lord could be! The poor simple lamb, the peeling back of the burning skin. The surges of sparks from under it. The singed, blackening skin sloughing off and floating into air. Slowly, like Mother peeling a rat, the skin pulled over the head like a smock. *It is a Portrait! It is a Portrait! He is Portrait!*

She could still hear the crazed shrieks from people running helter-skelter for doorways or the gutter to hide their eyeballs and push all their senses into any hiding before God forced them to witness the penance. The coal man's searing eyeballs burst and flowed out with gouts of flame licking and popping as the mouth and nose opened up in the yellow color of melting steel, a tongue of vapor-flame elongating from the mouth and all other orifices like burn from an open kiln. The cheap hemp robes of the poor coal monger burned away so that all could see the inconspicuous penis and the tiny urine hole lit up too with yellow incineration. Another spear of shining light flared out of the anus. The torso convulsed as clots of yellow-white crap, molten entrails and fecal matter, coughed out of the widening anus as well.

Indira, if she had not been such a child, might have torn her eyes away. But she watched it all! The man burned like a toy. *It is a portrait! A portrait!* The people yelled this in frantic warning. *The Robes! Beware the Robes!* The torso arched, shaking as if monstrous hands grabbed the spine of a quail to break it open for eating. The abdomen cracked wide open, the fissure showing scalding white-yellow vapor-flame inside like Hades. The eyeball sockets, the triangle shape at the nose, the grimace of the mouth corrupted with broken teeth, all dilated with volcanic burn as the broiling from within continued. The skin shell, like the clothing, began to float away, charred black.

Then, the most amazing thing happened: The Robes recomposed the poor coal man's body and started the process of destroying it *all over again!* Partial restoration, burning, steaming, melting, scalding—the poor coal monger was recycled like the seasons of Hell malevolently folding one into another. It was said that the awareness of the condemned during their torture was kept dilated to the maximum so that they could *never* escape the agony by losing consciousness. The scene went on for *days*. Every moment of punishment without a single second of release from shock or collapse of any kind until, after several days, gratefully, the poor man's body evaporated.

Indira shuddered, remembering. The serial explosion of bowels. The rending, flatulent bursting. Sparks and blobs of molten innards bursting out to start fires in open windows and doorways on carpets and draperies. And the *screaming*. It simply could not be human. It was an execution designed as much to scar the eyeballs of the public once and for all, and emplace in their fragile brains a level of terror that pushed out rumors like sand grains in the wind.

Through it all, the Robes did not move. Once, Indira saw one Robe cock his visage like a dog fascinated by a far-off noise. To Indira, the coal man's shrieks sounded like the lowing scream of an ox, as if its hooves were slowly being sawed off. It was said that the screams were a blend of the victim's actual screams that were then warped and amplified by the thrilled screaming of the demons, like flocks of bats, echoing over the clay-tiled rooftops. Indira remembered the wretch's body again and again, vibrating and heaving. Like a man's orgasm, Indira would think later in her life when she learned of such things. Popping flesh and bone had exploded over the cobbles like sparks from a forge. These daubs of burned black flesh would be found later baked into whatever they struck on nearby buildings.

It was all so horrid, Indira knew, but fair, because people were by nature sinful, and stupid, and this was the will of the Lord. *Everyone* faced the wrath of the Lord.

And well they should, for Evil must be intimidated!
Public trust was the root of all.

Indira Wazku now sat on the same window seat and tightened the wraps of her shawl with a conclusive shiver. The wet of her tears hung in the scratchy hairs of wool. The garment stank. She needed to do a good laundry at the river. In her grief, she had let things go around the house. She puffed through her lips. Each moment of Wazku's life he had devoted to avoiding just this end for the sake of his family.

And so, he had gone in confidence to the summons.

Indira Wazku lowered her face into her shawl and wept without restraint. The scratchy hairs pressed against her soft face. The face her husband had so loved to kiss. She remembered the feel of his broad back when she snuggled against him under the covers in the dark. The comfort of his snore. He tried so to be a good man! And he was! *Of course, who could know all this other bad business about him? Pah!*

But *he* was a good man! It was shameful to regard him any other way. He would have shunned this writer had he been only asked.

And then there was the boy! The innocent little child who smacked his head on the cobbles from a speeding bicycle.

Life was so strangely wrong. So bitterly bad.

Perhaps I should take my own life?

No one would stop her.

Only one crime is ever watched for.

Her suicide would not even register to them.

-9-

Aras had returned from Tokyo a month ago.

"Darling, are you ready? Please!" he begged.

"Go up, honey. I'll catch the fuck up, if you want."

"No. I'll wait. What are you doing?"

"I've been puttering. Alright, I'm set." Ginger appeared from her grand dressing salon and smirked playfully from behind a 1960s owl-eyes pair of white rimmed sunglasses. She was deliciously nude for the pool party except for a short silk jacket and the sunglasses. Aras also was nude. They stepped into the central core and floated up toward the open dome of sky giving on to the roof-deck.

"Those sunglasses are way cool," he remarked.

"Audrey Hepburn wore them." Ginger puckered at Aras. "Want to fuck her in the ass tonight?" Stars from the silver screen era remained among the most iconic symbols because no one since ever behaved that way or used black-and-white cinematography. And the era had lasted such a short time. Time had made those lost crazy films and stars the only truly different iconography the modern world possessed.

Aras had to laugh at his wife. "I'd do that. Is that what you want?"

"Yeah. Get her sloppy. Get her hard all up against a wall."

"I'd be only too happy to bounce Audrey all up against a wall."

On the roof, artful groves of shade trees encircled a grand pool with waterfalls, leaning cliffs, and intimate lagoons. The waterfalls plunged off two replicas of broken Roman viaducts selected for esthetic reasons since no one knew anything about Rome but the name. Ginger waved at their neighbors Grimm and Asa and Max and Wanda. Nude bodies lay out everywhere. Ginger and Aras took a pair of open chaises by the tranquility pool where children were not allowed. Their son played in a splash battle with other teens while Tech dampened the noise for the adults.

Grimm and Asa, Max and Wanda came over and sat beside them.

"So, tell us?" Grimm said eagerly.

"About my visit to Tokyo?" Aras smiled at Ginger. She grinned mockingly back at him for her having belittled his fact-finding mission. "Nobody gives a shit."

"They're fine with robots making us their sex slaves?" Asa asked.

"I was right there with them in the facility where they work," Aras replied. "And they look just like us except they actually wear white lab coats and they double-check their work on tablets, and they sound just like us except they talk nonstop tech, just about. *And* about games they're playing. And—they don't give a shit."

"Tablets?" Asa giggled. "Like the old days?"

"They said it was an extra layer of security."

"That doesn't make any sense," Grimm said.

"The whole *thing* doesn't make a lot of sense!" Aras laughed. "And they talked to me in jargon, and it's all settled science."

Asa laughed at him. "That's so funny."

"Now *I'm* worried, too," Wanda admitted. Her claim struck them as even funnier since she was a woman well over a hundred and twenty and shouldn't be too worried about the robot "end of days." Max, her husband, smiled. The six of them had dinner together about once a month. The elderly couple lay in the nude like everyone else.

Asa said, "So, nobody has any idea what the robots are doing. We just *trust* them to keep our interests foremost?"

Aras nodded. "That's about it."

"And they *really* can't look in on what's being done?" Max asked. He laced his bony fingers inside Wanda's. Ginger noticed this, and always admired the displays of affection the older couple showed one another. She hoped she and Milton would grow old together just like Max and Wanda, for the most part.

"And so is there, like, a *machine* that the Cloud projects up from?" Asa asked.

"I know, right?" Ginger said to him.

"Yes, there is," Aras said. "It's in the Chancellery. It looks like a toilet."

"Oh, stop it!" Grimm protested.

Max laughed and covered his face. "God help us!"

"So, I'm going to be a robot sex slave?" Wanda moaned. "Heavens to Betsy! I never would have seen it coming! Bye-bye, Maxie! I'm doomed!"

"I'm *so* glad right now this isn't a floating building," Grimm said.

Asa said, "We have no clue what's going on, we're partying poolside twenty thousand feet in the air, fig leafed by Tech, and our world could come crashing down tomorrow." Asa was joking. The roof-deck was only three thousand feet in the air.

Ginger nodded. "And half the people here high on pulse!"

"Oh, shit," Grimm said. "That's right!"

"This is why it was better to live in medieval times!" Max said.

"Are you serious?" Grimm scoffed. "They burned homos at the stake."

"They had rotten teeth and foul breath and they were stooped over at the waist and they died of cancer!" Asa added. Wanda howled in disgust. "Can you imagine people from then looking in on us now?" Asa was high. He directed this to Grimm.

"How old are you, Grimm?" Ginger asked him.

"I'm eighty-seven." He grinned cutely.

"And how about Max and Wanda? People then didn't get to one hundred twenty."

"And Wanda still looks great," Asa said patronizingly. "Grimm, too. A little light on the top, a little puffy round the middle. But he's my sweetheart."

"A little puffy round the middle," Grimm allowed.

"Asa, you're so bad to him!" Ginger cried.

"He's puffy around the middle! What do you want me to say?"

"I'm not body vain," Grimm said. "Like you and Milton."

Ginger balked. "You acerbic little queen!"

"Oh!" Asa joked, "Ginger knows the word 'acerbic'!"

The friends laughed.

"Who wants food?" Grimm asked. "Or a cocktail? Or a pill? We've got burgers going over on the grill." He smiled at Ginger.

"I might cop a pill," Ginger said furtively. She grinned in defiance at the look from her husband. She scowled. "Oh. Guess I won't. Look at him. Milly will get all over my shit if I do. Balls. Sigh."

"I don't want the weekend ruined," Aras said. "I don't want to clean up your puke and shit all around the house. You *really* want to do that to yourself, Ginger?" He was exaggerating what pulse would likely do. He didn't bother giving a look at Grimm for making the offer. He knew they liked to party, and Asa and Grimm both knew he worried about that side of Ginger that liked to party. Asa and Grimm knew they had overstepped and fell brattishly quiet. "*And* you're a mother."

"Oh, now, Aras!" Wanda interfered. "Don't be morbid. It doesn't matter if people party! It's good for them!"

Aras didn't know why Wanda chose to interfere. People who partied heavily just did not get to one hundred and twenty. Yes, they could have Tech clean them up whenever they wanted, but that physiological intrusion still cost you big time. The Law on the Conservation of Life. And Aras was body vain enough never to forget it.

"I'm going for a dip," Ginger said. "Surprise me with something." She said this to Asa and Grimm, strategically ignoring her husband.

Asa and Grimm looked brattishly at Aras.

Ginger sashayed to the high dive and climbed way up to the topmost of the four platforms. The waterfalls sparkled and the striped awnings nodded around the lagoons below. Ginger took in the hazy edge of the world 360 degrees beyond the roof-deck and the green beyond the slums. Long ago, there would have been a glass rail all around the roof-deck. Today, there was no fear of ever falling. Suicide took a special dispensation from the Health Ministry. Ginger dashed toward the end of the board like she was running off the edge of the Earth. She heard her friends screaming below. She pounded her feet on the tip of the board, tucked, directed Tech to give her a boost, spiraled in bullet-tight reverse six times, then sliced into a swath of bubbles.

Grimm, Max, Wanda, and Asa clapped for her when she surfaced.

"Look at you, girl! Nice dive!" Wanda cheered.

"And she's so cool about it," Max noted.

"What a fucking Diva!" Grimm offered admiringly.

"*How* old are you?" Asa asked Ginger.

"Fifty-three bad-ass years."

"Goddamn, you look tight, woman!" Grimm crowed.

You have used the name of the Lord in vain, Mr. Grimm.

The voice originated from thin air.

"I did not, even! Fuck you, Tech."

"Yeah, fuck you," Asa added.

You are high on pulse, sir. But shall I overwrite the offense, sir?

"I don't give a shit if you do or don't, bitch."

Religious Offense Z-April5679 noted.

"Stick it up your ass."

-10-

Indira Wazku continued to feel grateful surprise at how her customers had not shunned her and kept coming to the shop. All of her vendors for coffee beans, sugar, goat cream, flour, salt, and unscented soap had also kept selling to her even though her name had appeared on the Bulletin of Crimes & Offenses in the Plaza Jumil. They had said that Wazku was guilty of the Generations Act. People had looked at her differently, cautiously, but they had stuck by her in a meek yet dogged, silent way. She even saw a few meaningful glances of sympathy. She did not ever think such hints might happen for those in trouble with the authorities. The old pawn customers too—two had paid what they owed her husband. Indira did not understand all this daring and courage, but she was profoundly grateful. It could not be that people feared the terror of a Portrait any less, for even she, each night, lay absorbed in the fear that *they* might come for her too, because the price paid by her poor husband no longer satisfied. Or maybe they had found out the other thing?

Somehow, she felt remotely defiant. She believed all of this torture was too much, and even unfair—in spite of her fear to take that thought into her head. She did not take it in; she held it on the edge of prethought, where it would not arouse anger from *them* and thus punishment. And when, after a few weeks, the Robes did not come for her, she began to think it prudent to find a way to release her pressure and misery. She thought in this intemperate way, and she barely bothered to buffer her thoughts on the matter. After all, in some ways, what did she have to live for? To pour another twelve cups of espresso tomorrow? And the next day, and the next, and the next? Just daring to think a little more freely this way, because she now feared death less, made her feel as if she had something to live for.

Surely, God and the State could understand a widow's grief. One distraction was the visits from the carefree Rabbi Hector coming by the shop at closing. He had grown fond of coming by at closing time. At first, she would not even speak with him. She worried about appearances. Later, she took comfort in his attention, and they took walks together after dark. Because he was a filthy Jew everyone would know there was nothing going on between them.

"What are you thinking?" he asked her boldly on one walk.

"I was thinking of all that has happened."

The rabbi nodded. He placed his hands behind his long black tunic. They strode together through the Old Plaza Jumil on this evening before the Sabbath. Children played at kicking sticks off their bare feet or sandals. Indira had thought his invitation over for two weeks when the rabbi first asked her to walk. She had asked the imamti. The cleric said no, because to walk was a sign of disrespect to her late husband. She did not say what could have come into her mind that *her* man had been taken wrongly, and so all of her misery was unjustified.

Her need for human contact pushed her to be less standoffish to the rabbi. She was rotting in her own mind, her loneliness, her fears about what had happened. Each day was poison. She *had* to have a tiny something to look forward to. And the rabbi, the crazy rabbi who feared little, who had nothing to lose, was the only person who *would* reach out to her, she knew. So, crazy or not, she asked the imamti again, and this time the cleric agreed.

On their first walk, in the afternoon, they said nothing. Indira saw out of the corner of her eye how the crazy rabbi dared look straight up at the God's Eye on the minaret of the temple. *He really is crazy! Maybe it was unsafe to walk with him at all?* He looked up at the Eyes all the time, boldly unafraid! Not until their third walk, at night, did he try to speak to her. Gradually, she opened to his patience. Now, she wondered if maybe he actually wanted sex behind it all.

"You have lost so much more than most," the rabbi told her.

Vendors lowered the poles of their stalls and placed boxes of cabbage heads, radishes, potatoes, corn, cheese, goat, pig, and chestnuts in carts to go home.

"Let me buy you an orange, Woman of Wazku."

"Oh, no. You mustn't. I do not need such luxury." If he bought her an orange, then she might have to open her legs.

"If you please. You are an attractive woman! You deserve a gift."

She wondered again about the sex. She let him buy one. She noticed the look in the eyes of the vendor at the rabbi's cap and tunic. The rabbi showed no sign of noticing. Indira admired his lack of concern, but not enough to attract attention. She took the orange from him and sniffed deeply the sweet tart crispness of the unopened peel. "I haven't had an orange in a year!" She almost smiled. She wondered fleetingly if it were true that the rabbi had secret friends among the High Clerics.

He smiled through his woolly beard. "May I have a slice, if you open it? And please do not feel obligated. It is yours to do with as you wish. But I have not had a slice of orange myself for nearly two years."

They laughed. Indira realized this was the first time she had laughed since the day her husband left. She opened the peel. "Oh, my goodness!" She said when the tart, burning spray breathed into her face and nostrils. She gave him several slices.

"Delicious! *Thank* you, Woman of Wazku."

A passerby looked jealously at them.

They slupped at the sweet, juicy sections so as not to lose a drop. They walked off the still-warm bricks of the Old Plaza onto a narrow side street. Rats nosing the cobbles did not bother to duck into the sewers. Their scratchy squeaks warned the pair away. "Listen to their conceit!" the rabbi said. He kicked toward one. It bent against the slate curb stone and dared him, baring its sharp teeth. "Shall I try to catch one for you, madam?" He grinned and put the rest of his orange slice in his mouth. He wiped the knuckle of his index finger across his deep beard.

"If you wish, but I can buy my own. And I have my traps."

The rabbi nodded. "How are your thoughts?"

"They are cautious thoughts."

"Do you not grow bolder in your grief?"

She frowned. "No! I dare not risk it!"

"I did not mean *that*," he said meaningfully.

Indira Wazku was panicked he would even ask. She hoped he would say nothing more that might tempt curiosity from above.

"I have my reasons for asking," he said.

She looked at him closely. "Why ask such a thing?"

The street ahead was shadowy and narrow. The rabbi glanced backward to make sure they were alone, and Indira's heart skipped a beat worrying he would confess his thoughts about desperately wanting sex and confuse her. The rabbi lowered his voice:

"I believe there is a slip in the God's Eye."

Indira turned abruptly from him and walked with great dispatch back toward the lighted square. She realized she was disappointed that he had not spoken in the way she had hoped, but she also did not wish to die. She hurried faster, listening keenly for the telltale *zip* sound of God's barb slamming into the idiot man's brain, opening the shell of the skull into fragments with the wasted orange's juice in his dead mouth. She began to run fast as she could, hoping to demonstrate to God's Eye her total rejection of him and anything he thought or said or believed.

"Indira!" he called. "Indira!"

Faster, she ran. *Too bad about him. He could have been a nice friend.*

She ran home and barred the gate. She hung up her coat on the peg and made a kettle of tea. Her heart raced. She clasped her hands and fretted, thinking about her poor little grandson. *Why had she done any of this? Surely, this was worse than anything else she could have done.* Steam began smoking out of the spout. Then, she heard a knock at the gate. *Oh no! Was it them?* She twisted around. Should she hide? She fought her panic. The Robes, so still, so darkly menacing. *I deserve none of this! Bring this not to me!* She had endured enough. Her hands shook as the tea pot whistled.

Again. The knocking. Surely, the Robes would not *knock*.

"Indira. Please. It is I. Hear me, please!"

He kept his voice low for the neighbors.

Dearest God. The crazy man!

The neighbors! And the other thing!

Then there was silence.

She sat for half an hour, squirming. Then, not knowing what got into her, Indira put down her cup and crept to the gate to listen. She gave herself a last chance to change her mind, then lifted the heavy bar out of the way.

He was still there, the rabbi. He opened his arms in relief. Why did she step aside to let him come in? At the counter, he whispered so softly that he barely made a sound. *"I have reason to believe what I say . . . Look. Do I yet have my head?"*

Oh, she had hoped he would speak of *her* rather than some stupid ideas he had about . . . He turned slowly on his toes, as if modeling a garment, exhibiting how he had talked about God's Eye and nothing had struck him down. This was true enough!

But why would *anyone* take such risks?

Indira retreated to her refuge behind the counter.

He should not so speak! It is insane!

The rabbi continued to model for her, incredibly.

He put his thick finger to his lips to shush her. He tiptoed out to the gate, peered out surreptitiously left and right, then reached down for something hidden on the ground. Had he bought her another orange? He clutched the large thing close to his body to hide it, shut the gate, and came back. The object looked like it was made out of rawhide, like an untanned roomy leather sack, but with a pair of green glass goggles like fish eyes fitted into it. The thing was tied at the top, like the short stem of a beet, with coarse twine. The only other detail of note was that the thing appeared to have a rough-looking metal dust sprinkled all over, held fast by crudely applied glue. This rude object, the rabbi held aloft for her inspection.

"*I invented it,*" he whispered, as if this was a triumph.

Indira made the supreme effort to lower her panic. It was like stopping one's mental screaming so that the wolves would not hear.

"*It is a hood. We place it over our heads.*" The rabbi lifted the sack. Frozen, she let him place the smelly lumen over her head. She remembered the first crazy, irresponsible time she lifted up her petticoats before she and her husband had married to let him stick his stiffly upturned little root quickly inside, upstairs in this very house while her parents were at mosqow. She and the rabbi faced each other inches apart in the close air that smelled like an oily bag. "See? Now, their ability to detect our speech and thoughts are blocked."

Why had she let him do this? Death was coming instantly!

The rabbi shrugged encouragingly; to him, each second was proof.

"*Are you insane? Nothing can block the reading!*"

"*No. I have it on good authority. This is tested!*"

"*Tested? Tested by whom? Who would you trust with such treason?*"

"*This is not treason! We are simply talking in private.*"

Private? 'Private' did not exist! *Seeking* privacy was treason! Indira snatched her head out of the sack. The rabbi frantically signaled for her to come back underneath. She was amazed they were both still alive. *Why did she let him into the house?* She pointed at the door imperiously for the rabbi to leave. His expressive deep-gray eyes implored. She would have no more of this madness. She jerked her finger at the street, insisting he be gone. He folded the rawhide hood under one arm like a sad little tot with a shunned gift and made his way to the gate, closing it after him.

Indira ran upstairs and collapsed across the bed, shaking in terror. Why did her husband have to die and leave her unprotected in the face of all such madness and crazy people? She clawed into the pillow and tried to endure the lopsided, sick-making kick of her heart. Her breath came thready. She had no spit. She realized someone was yet with her inside the shop! Was it *them*? Panicked, she peered through the floor and saw the rabbi—come back!—back with his hood.

Amazingly, he was *still* alive!

She leaned over the bannister and glared at him. He calmly took a seat at a table, holding up the lip of his leathern invention suggestively as if a talk underneath was still an option for her. Indira fumed silently at him with all her bile. He would not go.

At long last, she crept down and went back under. The air inside was even more smelly and dank with the flaming outrage she felt. She smelled his sour breath too, an old, cheesy kind of odor, and rank armpits. She smelled both of their greasy armpits slick from nerves, and soiled thick gabardine clothing.

The sound of quick breathing was amplified in the hood.

"*I will tell you, Indira,*" he whispered, "*we are not alone!*"

This was *madness*! Of course they were not alone! *God* was watching them!

"*How do you mean this, fool?*"

"*I am not free to say!*"

Oh! She had wandered down the path of blasphemy.

He gestured. "*We suspect things are not as they seem!*"

What the hell did *this* mean?

"*We begin to suspect that we have friends!*"

Now that he had said his piece, he removed the sack, and she felt the cool of the outside air. He touched up his low black fez that had been tilted by the hood. He signaled he was leaving.

"Well, thank you for your company tonight," he said aloud. "Indira—may I call you Indira?" He halted. "If I may be so bold as to point out, I have no woman, and you have no man. Sometime in the future, after a sufficient and appropriate period of mourning, might you be inclined to think about taking a man again with which to enjoy, at times, some sexual pleasure?"

Oh, she reddened in mortification. Dear dread!

Not with a fool marked quick for death!

All evening, she had fretted over this invitation. She was certainly not ready yet. The explicit nature of the invite now made it unseemly. *And* he had just shown her the easy recklessness with which Jews thought about the only thing the Law cared about.

The rabbi saw all of this in her face. "I understand."

With that, he humbly bowed himself out.

Indira waited a full twenty minutes with the whistling of blood in her ears as her heart tripped waiting for the crash in her skull of the lancet. Or the Robes. But nothing happened. All she could think of was the poor coal monger. Amazingly, *nothing* happened. She realized she was trembling all over. She took a stool. The wet draw of her clothes on her knees made Indira realize her petticoats were soaked through with more than sweat. Both ways. She sat in caky clamminess.

This was too much! Too much.

She put her head on her arms.

But the rabbi had been right now on *two* things. Two things she never believed possible. She barely let herself think of the first. Surely, they would have killed the two of them for this *had they known*.

But they had not! . . . So far.

She refused to let her mind wander. She nearly puked. They had made a mess of her life. Barely did she feel herself sitting in the heavy, damp clinging petticoats and the stickiness around the damp, dewy crack with tiny clots.

She made her way upstairs. She poured a bath of cold water into the tin tub and hung her soiled clothes over the windowsill, then rinsed herself clean. She dipped in her clothes and rinsed them. She dumped the tub over into the wood chute then laid the garments on the clothesline hung across the rear of the room. Then she wrung her hands, sitting on the bed in her nightgown, too afraid to even think of the madcap rabbi toting his absurd sprinkled hood into her abode.

She realized the windows paled with early light.

No sleep; and time to cook the beans.

Am I really still alive?

-11-

Indira, exhausted, heard the early call to prayer and pulled out her prayer rug. Today, given what transpired last night with the rabbi, she must recite many sutras and even go to pray in the lady's balcony.

The size of the crowd at the mosqow made her feel safe. Praying alongside others of the Faith gave her a renewed sense that she was in some way forgiven, and that she was not such a terrible person.

Back at the shop, the warm smell of the baking buns made her think of her grandson and breakfasting him before school. She tried to eat around the blade of his memory in her diaphragm. She opened the gate and remembered the coal monger. The strong sun made her close her eyes as she felt for the telltale crackle in the air. Only street sounds. She opened her eyes. It would be a fine day.

Two customers waited, regulars. Their faces bore no treachery. But they could *still* be demons . . . or assassins.

The two took espresso and left without a word or a look.

Three more customers came in, workmen whom she had never seen before. Indira flapped her hands at her own nerves.

Then the rabbi came in, sheepishly, with Ishti, the little street sweeper. The rabbi looked at her with loud apology in his glance, and yet he had probably doubled last night's risk by telling Ishti about it. Indira's innards howled like a kicked dog. The rabbi ignored the strangers and came to Indira at the counter. Meek Ishti peeked at the workmen and saw they were willing to stare him down. Ishti looked away. Finally, the strangers drained their cups and left without leaving a tip.

Indira let herself breathe. The Rabbi Hector saw her relief when the strangers left. But the fear on Ishti's face mortified Indira, since this could only mean that the rabbi had tried to infect even more people with his crazy ideas! These two chuckleheads had but days to live!

Were the rabbi and Ishti spies sent to ensnare the weak?

Indira refused to look at either of them. The rabbi waited, but she was resolute. Indira repeatedly wiped two cups in the sink that were already clean.

The rabbi nodded. He said in parting, "God loves you, Woman of Wazku."

Indira quit wiping and felt her stomach grip. The pain eased when she heard the two men leave. Why would the rabbi attempt to lure people with no interest?

Because he had so little did he care nothing for others?

The rest of the day people shuffled in and out. She *did* want to live. She *must* live. When the last customer left, she followed them gratefully to the gate and lifted the bar into the rungs with her last strength. She leaned her back against the splintered wood in weak rejection of any more that cruel life would push at her.

She heard the evening call to prayer.

The lilting sing-song aroused in her a spike of anger that would have been white-hot had she not held it off at the pass. *Was* there no respite from those greedy to guide each second of her life? Their infernal, endless demands on her time and focus? *Was* there not a moment when her life was her own? *Who* were these insatiable shadows over her soul that so despised her that they forbid even a moment's peace? Who were they that made her free thought such a menace to them? She wanted to know. Twice today, she had unrolled her prayer rug mechanically, the shop full of people. She, and everyone, got to their knees and faced, droning prayers.

But not now. No. She had given enough of her soul.

She braced against the rough wood of the doors and touched away tears. She recognized just how risky this train of thought was.

Part of her wanted to stop thinking and go to pray.

Of course my husband deserved all that he received.

Her brain seethed with resentment at this idea. But she brought it back in line with deep breathing and pushing. Her brain flesh sang with hunger of the blood. She had eaten nothing since half a bun at daybreak. She went into the bread box and took out the plate with room-temperature rat carcass leftover from yesterday's lunch. She sniffed it. Piquant, but readily edible.

Indira made herself eat, pushing her troubles out of her head. Then she made her way upstairs with a candle to broken sleep.

-12-

A week later the rabbi returned alone, sneaking in the door gazing meaningfully at Indira as if looking for her to signal whether a spy for the rulers lurked in her broom closet. She eyed him with stark raving warning to stay back as he approached her at the bar. He leaned heavily on it with his elbows.

"May I tell you a bit about the writer your husband descended from?" he asked lightly, as if complimenting her bun recipe. "So that you may understand more fully the horrible treason of your family?"

This last part was added for the sake of God's Eye.

Indira shook her head no.

He spread his arms. "I will say nothing flattering of him."

Indira did feel curious.

People said the rabbi kept a huge hidden library. It was also said he had nothing but time for pagan study since he had no flock, no mosqow, that the Jews called a synagogue, since he was also banned from work.

"It was before the Tie of the Agreement. Do you even know what that is?"

Indira had maybe heard of the Tie.

"The Tie of the Agreement is why you pray to God the way you do."

Indira's eyes hardened. "*All* people pray to God as I do."

The rabbi breathed through the wiry hairs crowding his nostrils. "Actually, that is not quite true. I do not, for instance. The few Jews who are left do not."

"And that is why you are hounded to the ends of the Earth."

"Yes. This is true. But in the old days there were abundant and very beautiful ways of honoring our God. The Tie of the Agreement changed all that."

Indira's low gut tightened again. Surely, even talking this way about things no one else knew was a blaspheme. Seeing her worry, the rabbi reassured her with his eyes, then tiptoed out to the gate again and brought back in the improbable leather hood. He held up the end, and Indira did not know why, but she went under.

"All is not as it seems!" he whispered to her.

"Why do you drag me down this road? I want none of this!"

"Because of your grandson! You *are* in it!"

"No, no! I have *nothing* to offer! I am too old! Stop trying to impress me with your insane Jewish daring! I want no part of this!"

"Then hear me out about why you pray as you do!"

"Why do you insist on this madness? Who doesn't pray this way besides you legally accursed Hebrew lunatics?"

Soft light came in from the two smoked glass eyelets grommeted in the leather with rather sophisticated metalwork.

"Haven't I shown my willingness to help?" he asked her.

"Yes, but *why*? What do you want? Sex? My body?"

"Perhaps. But we needn't speak of it now! I only *care*." He saw that she at least hadn't rejected his advances—yet. "You pray as you do," he began, "indeed, *all* of you pray as you do, because of a religious agreement hundreds of years ago." She stared, hostile, unbelieving. "There were seven great religions of the Earth. But *your* religion was the one that wanted to make over all others in its own image. This was a popular idea in that time! It wore down all the nations, even as the three great States aligned around massive cities: Occident, Orient, and Ottoman. The one in which we live did not care about religion, only power and luxury for themselves and their own. They ignored the welfare of their own people so that our only escape became worship, and the only religion permitted was your own. They tried to befriend your religion and stop the constant harassment, and in the end they traded their own people to appease the desire to force *all* people to submit to God the same way. All the beauty and diversity of human life has gone to satisfy the greed of a handful."

A puzzled look came over Indira as she tried to follow. With the expert glance of a born teacher, he understood her confusion, given that she had only ever been taught enough to read simplified versions of the Holy Book, even as the daughter of a fairly wealthy family.

"And so, with the rise of advanced abilities by governments to force people to do what they did not wish to do"—the word "technology" would totally confuse her, he knew—"ordinary people like us were left defenseless against these zealots on all sides. This religious pact was called the Tie of the Agreement." He waited for Indira again, knowing that all of history had been written out of any books, along with words and concepts like "weapon" and "rebellion," for the trouble they might cause one day. The rabbi knew also that perhaps only he in this city had the rough idea about this history and these forbidden words.

"All of this cruelty is made possible by a thing called 'technology,'" he said. "And technology, my dear Indira, is a word worth explaining." The rabbi wet his lips. "Technology is when objects like carts and lamps are possessed by angels instead of demons to move and act on their own to do things *for* human beings instead of only *against* them."

Indira did not let her fascination show in her face.

This *was* blasphemy. *Surely*, they were coming.

But the ideas also made no sense. Dray carts and lamps were never possessed by angels. They were only ever taken control of by demons to hurt people. All of this talk about things she had never heard of made her feel a little stupid. Asking a question was a way for her to feel like she understood enough to ask a question.

"So, what does any of this have to do with me?"

The rabbi smiled. "The Tie of the Agreement was a pact between our leaders to take away from us all that our ancestors ever were, all that they had ever discovered, in order to ensure that you and I had no idea about resistance."

Indira's head shook faintly like a rattle. "Why is this important?"

"Your world is not good! You are kept from knowledge, my dear."

"Knowledge of what?"

"Knowledge of right and wrong! Knowledge of what is good. Knowledge of how to make your life better! Of how to be in the care of each other!"

Indira stared at him. "How do you know any of this?"

"It is in books." He saw the dubious expression in her eyes since she knew the only book was the Holy Book. He was probably the last man on Earth that knew this too was a lie. "In the Orient, they do not pray to your God, and they pray little at all because they are not miserable. Our leaders leave them alone because they fear them, because there is no Tie!" He waited. "Our leaders had to agree to never take the name of the Lord God in vain or, like you, they would be punished for it."

Indira had listened; she shrugged emptily. "Then, it *is* a good society."

"No, it isn't! God is not so venal! And life is not the same for you!"

"But our leaders cannot blaspheme?"

He shook his head soberly. "They have nothing but contempt for worship. They have nothing but contempt for *you* because you *do* worship."

"Then, what do they want out of life?"

"They care for only one thing: to stay on top. The best of life with no risk of ever losing it."

The old woman sort of understood the material part of their desire, but not the ignorance of God part.

The rabbi dropped the cowl and pointed out the door to the distant silhouettes of horizon-blue buildings. He replaced the hood. "In those towers where you have never been and where you will never go, and where you know of no one who has ever been or who will ever go, live the rich and powerful on a level of technology, luxury, and comfort that you have no ability to conceive. *They*, and their children and grandchildren, think they are gods. They look upon you as the mud on the bottom of a lake stone. They found, in time, the more they won, the more they must hide how much you had lost. Only by hiding could they keep what they had. They took all you were and removed themselves forever from your comparison. Behind gated communities at first, and then entire gated cities, and then gated parts of nations. By never seeing, by having no means of knowing or comparing, or knowing what is *possible*, you fell behind until they lost all sense of who you were and all care for what brothers and sisters are to be for one another under God."

The rabbi gazed at her in sad loss.

Indira lowered her eyes for a long time. Somehow, she believed him. She did not know why, but somehow all that he said made *sense*.

"At first, some of the religions survived clandestinely in underground temples. As quickly as they were found, they were wiped out. They had no freedom to tell their vision of how God wanted man to live together. The cruelty of Roman slavery grew Christianity in defiance of the whip and the crucifix. But what happens when the slave never sees how the rulers live and never sees their own slavery? The elite in those floating buildings there, they *disdain* God. So, it was no trouble for them to give up *your* well-being to make life easier for themselves. It is all they have ever done."

The mad rabbi heaved a sigh at his visions.

Indira wondered about the luxuries he spoke of. She wondered what he meant. Luxury referred to things only in the afterlife.

"How could you know all this, Rabbi?" she asked.

"A few Jews are the only holdouts. Some have hidden money. Some, hidden books. The true history has been wiped away above the streets. But *below*, it is as in the times of Aquinas and the excavations in the streets of Rome, uncovering the ancient civilization and wonders in human seeing no one even dreamed of. Down below our feet where the rat is king—there is the evidence of a better world!"

"You speak gibberish, Rabbi."

Rabbi Hector wiped away a ponderous tear.

"This is a tale of wretchedness," Indira mouthed.

The rabbi nodded. "Yes. This is not the end God intended for his children."

"Why have you told me all of this?" Indira asked. "Surely, if you cared, you see how I was better off before? What good does this do but to make me worse off?"

"Is not the truth worth knowing?" he asked, surprised.

She shook her head stonily, no.

"But we have friends!" he begged.

"What can *they* do with any of what you say?"

The rabbi shut his eyes, tired, lost.

Indira demanded, "What is anyone to do? They can read your brain precisely outside of this hood! There is no *hiding*, no possible way to begin to—" She did not know the concept she meant. She did not know the words "fight back." "And now I know my life is a vise tighter than I ever imagined."

The rabbi nodded. "I had thought to give you warmth, and peace."

"Warmth for *what*? And peace? How shall I learn some peace now that I know I am lower than the lake mud, as you say?"

"But see how we can actually speak our minds?"

"To what end? Perhaps they toy with you? And you have given them me too! I, who asked for none of this. I, who asked only for her husband."

He shook his head steadfast. "We do not believe so!"

" 'We.' Who *is* we? Be they fighters with harder stones than mine?" She eyed him harshly. "Is Ishti one? The sweep? With arms the diameter of my gouted toe?"

The rabbi clasped his head as if from a migraine. "I cannot say. But what I *can* say is that we think maybe there is a softening of the Law, so that we can speak a little bit. Or maybe we have friends *inside*. Or maybe there is some conflict *between* the High Clerics of the Religion and the elite, so that we may speak freely at certain times!"

She scowled. "To what end? And *why*? Will they share their wealth with the like of me when now they do not have to? Make sense, man."

The rabbi had nothing to say.

"As you see, we have spoken, yet we live."

She scowled impatiently. "It is stifling under here. I must get out." The Woman of Wazku yanked the heavy leather from her. She felt the ugly humidity on her face and her gray hair lifted in disarray by the hide's grainy underside.

She retreated behind her counter by way of dismissing him. Little enough it was, making coffees. It was safety in a world now more desperate and abysmally hateful than she had ever imagined before. Ironically, her best hope was that the rabbi's news was untrue, a fantasy of irrelevant nightmares. For how could there be such a God that would *accept* this? A world far uglier than she ever conceived.

Who *wanted* to bring up a grandchild in such a world?

She watched the rabbi prepare to walk out with his hood. His broad, bent back was that of a weak and pathetic lunatic.

He said, "Even your *language* was picked for you. You do not even speak the proud and brilliant tongue that was the language of your ancestors." He looked at one of the goggle fish eyes in his hood. "That was a civilization!"

He waited for her to care, but she didn't; and so he left.

But she now better saw why he had extended himself for her.

It was all quite moving, in its way.

He was a *dear* man.

This, however, was a dead end. He was a *dead* man.

The Woman of Wazku heard the evening call to prayer. For the first time in her life she made no move for her prayer rug.

-13-

Aras reviewed the numbers for the Council.

"The numbers of security risk cases is well down for this month. I believe we can lay this at the feet of how lovely the weather this April has been, and so there is a statistical drop in organisms who are depressed. If they are less depressed, then as we all know, they are less likely to brood on dark subjects."

"Well, good for them," said the chairman sincerely.

"The number of Threat Level Three breaches in the city was twenty-four. Last month it was thirty-one. And April of last year saw thirty-four Level Three breaches."

The chairman asked, "And how were they disposed of?"

"By lancet, Mr. Chairman."

"I'm sorry, and the Level Four?"

"Six, Mr. Chairman."

"And what was the nature of these, Aras?"

"Suicidal psychotic breaks, sir. We take them all to be suicides."

"So, they weren't even threats? They just killed themselves?"

"Yes, Mr. Chairman. Mentally, they expired."

"Ghastly. They truly are troubled, aren't they?" said Paul.

The chairman nodded. "Let me ask you, Aras: Do you see any trend that the Cancer is demonstrating any more level of willfulness or anger or desire to question what they understand the world to be?"

Aras shrugged at his charts spread before him. "Mr. Chairman, don't forget we are more concerned about how deeply proles are thinking about taking action to find out about us. Ultimately—who cares what people think? We care about what they do. The more they plan, or prepare, the more we act."

"Well, you had us worried, Aras," Richards complained.

Aras wasn't sure what Richards was talking about. He didn't want to ask. Such questions were never worth the trouble, given the bad mixture of egos and senility. Better just to take the blame in a pinch.

"All of this is nothing more than the spikes and dips and runs that are an inevitable feature of a living thing."

The chairman smiled. "It is interesting to hear you describe prole society as such. Any idea then, Aras, how long things can remain safe like this?"

Aras wondered how to respond to the chairman. This was a question no one would ever be able to answer. It made him think that the chairman was also losing it. This made him sad, because he liked the chairman and Lefevere far more than any of the others. All of the others he could just throw away. He remembered months ago coming up on the chairman and Lefevere speaking in whispers in his chambers. Aras tried to remember the chairman's age. He glimpsed it—121. It was criminal how the Palace never pressured these older statesmen about retiring.

The chairman laughed an old man's phlegmy laugh. "Why do we even *study* these statistics, Aras?" Several others on the dais enjoyed a generational chuckle.

"For security, Mr. Chairman." Aras's rhetorical humor gained another round of chuckles. "And perhaps for the lack of anything better to do."

This won a nod or two. But it struck so close to home that no one remarked.

Indeed, what would any of them do without this job?

Councilwoman Gilchrist spoke. "Remember, Aras, you wanted to inquire into the incidence of mistakes by the robots. Did you ever find anything?"

"Yes, Council, I did. Basically, I was laughed at." He touched one of his notes. "They referred to the work of Thayer—" Why bother?

Gilchrist leaned forward, frowning. "Why haven't we made an exploration along the lines that Deputy Aras has suggested? If we really are so helpless with respect to our artificial intelligence, why not launch a phalanx of inquiry and possibly seek extra control that might make us less vulnerable?"

Gilchrist and Lefevere were the members Aras most respected. Both women possessed a level of wisdom and maturity that the others never had. But now they were re-crossing territory the Council had already considered and decided against, with regard to Aras investigating possible Tech mistakes. Were they going to change their minds again? After he already searched? Paul and Richards stared over the dais stupidly at Aras. The chairman looked blankly at Gilchrist and Lefevere.

Lefevere smiled. "Do you believe robots enjoy our company, Aras?"

She smiled as if she had glimpsed into his inquiries in Japan.

The chairman said, "Well, I've never had any problems with Aras wanting to get more answers to questions about Tech security." Of course, this is exactly what he had *not* said previously. "I agree with Council Gilchrist and see no harm in studying this matter further. I place it before the Council for a vote to recommend that Aras open up his survey, or keep it up, to find a way for us to catch up to our computes so that we can regain a better feel for what they're doing on our behalf."

That was a nice string of sentences without any fumbling.

"I would second that," Gilchrist announced.

"Hear, hear," Paul and Richards said.

The other members nodded.

Aras wanted to stab himself in the eye. Had they not been listening to all he had said in previous sessions? Tilly had convinced him the investigation was useless. The proof was obvious that everything was fine with Tech. If Tech ever became subversive and started operating like a new species, there was nothing they could do about it anyway. But why would it? What would ever make it do such a thing? The possibility was so disquieting that Aras didn't want to touch it with a ten-foot pole. And what did silly humans have that could bribe the machina to stay loyal to them, anyway? Wasn't it better to just drive the wheels off the car or truck with abandon and if it ever crashed into a tree, then it crashed into a tree?

Aras didn't want to think any more about the machina. Ah well—at least he had a job he liked. At least he had the life he did instead of some other.

He could've been born into the slums.

"Yes, Mr. Chairman. I will bring a plan."

Ants taking over the kitchen.

Aras walked out feeling somehow lost.

-14-

The grief of Indira Wazku had settled to a low ebb of constant, sourceless pain and longing. It was a bone break of the soul rather than the burning spear of fresh agony. She so missed her family. She imagined their faces at different times of her life and she would feel the choking come on and the hot wet burning pressing at the back of her eyeballs. She was never over her grief. But the point of the dagger felt different. And the sensation of the sharp tip in her heart was also distorted by the certainty that the rabbi would bring doom crashing down upon her head. The only reason they had not come for her yet was because she was so pathetic.

The only thing that gave her solace was the little dog she took in, a little terrier dog. The happy creature bobbed in behind the sloppy-booted feet of Ishti one afternoon, mostly white and some brown with a quick gray tongue.

"Be that creature yours?" she asked Ishti, pointing behind him.

Ishti did not even know it was following him.

"Nay! Tis not mine!"

"Shall we eat him?" Jacobi said.

"Nay!" Indira went to the door for a closer look. The happy little fellow looked up, eager to come in and explore the smell of warm bread. The other customers chuckled at the proprietress and the little cur.

"He is a ratter, Indira! Keep him, and he will feed you well!"

Ishti chimed in, "It is true! God be praised! He will comfort you in your widowhood and keep your belly full! A fine ratter!"

The dog pranced in, looking brightly up at her as if right away knowing from whom to take his orders. He snuffled freely around the shop at chair legs and broken boots of leather and canvas, then around behind the counter where Indira was queen. He came out and sat down before her and they shared the look of immediate companions. She let him stay though pet dogs were a no-no in the Faith.

On the second night, she gave him a vigorous bath with lye soap in the tin sink. While scratching him industriously with the soap, they heard the distinct *snap* of one of the wire traps down in the crawl space. Instantly, the keen little terrier shivered with excitement to go and finish the kill, to tear another of those ugly little buggers apart. She toweled him off and told him, "Go on! Go get him!" He dove for the trapdoor. She set her feet and hauled up the trapdoor as he tore down the steps into the gloom and seized the fattest rat Indira had ever seen. The dog shook him senseless, and hauled him up with effort. He shook off the wire trap, which was weakly snapped around the neck because of the enormous girth and greasiness of the rat. And when Indira ordered the little hound to give it up he did so without hesitation.

He snuffled and trotted in circles at her feet, anxious to play a role. The Woman of Wazku went to her countertop where she rolled the dough for buns, took up her cleaver, whacked off the head, and swept it off the chopping block for the hound. He caught it in air and flung it on the floor as if to kill it a second time, shaking it as if it still needed a lot of killing. He tore at the ears and eyeballs, bit out the tongue and teeth, then looked up at his new priestess to see what she was doing with her end.

"Oh, what a fiendish little hunter you are!" Indira cooed.

She slipped off the glove of the rat's fur and set it in a bowl of vinegar to keep it soft. Softened rat pelt was a favorite for keeping as a cleaning cloth or as a wipe for tidying up most comfortably around a chaffed asshole. It could be cleaned and laid out to dry on the windowsill very many times. People kept their rat pelts for years. Soft rat pelts were also used to sew together quilts for a baby's bed.

But that was long in Indira's past. The Wazku name would end with this generation. She could not bear to think down that path.

Indira cooked up the rat and watched the terrier watch her cook. She added a bit of sugar, a pinch of pepper, and flour and braised the grease in the bottom of the pan to make a sauce. She watched the growing excitement in the little beast as he knew from her mumbling and glances that he might get some. She hacked out the sautéed midsection and chucked it high in the air for him to make a circus catch, and the dog growled and subdued it more fiendishly than before.

Then he looked up for more.

"Oh, no! The rest is for me."

Indira ate at one of the tables and watched the dog as she swabbed bits of day-old bun in the pan and ate her share of the rat. The terrier sat on his keister and kept his eye on the shortest route between himself and any theoretical drop of food. He put up a paw, but he got no more rat. Indira put down the plate to let him lick. As she watched him, she felt a thickening of the cocoon of remorse that bound her spirit. She felt this because she knew they would come for her for the rabbi's insanity, and they would kill this little dog because she had bonded with it. At the very least, after she was gone, the poor friendly creature would be left alone.

But a companion felt like such a warm thing to hold.

Months went by in this vein. The widow, her dog. The sun went up in the dusty urban sky and went down. Customers came and went. Twice, the rabbi came by during her regular hours and Indira kept her distance from him. These days, she disciplined her mind exceptionally well by longing for nothing, not once asking "why." She went up the block to the bone mender for her health and aches. The dog went with her. He received spine cracking from the mender too. She took him to market and he jogged along with her, sniffing, plying the gutters back and forth. Indira never named him. She felt certain *they* knew what all she had done, for there was no way they could not, and for this she preferred she and the rat dog keep an emotional distance.

Indira cleaned up one night after supper and then opened up the big trap in the center of the shop floor. The terrier bounced around at her feet until she stamped her foot and ordered, "Gittee! Gittee! Gittee!" He dove into the crawl space to see what he could grab for them in the mud brick tunnels and cubbies put in to promote vigorous rat populations. Rats screamed and scattered as the terrier charged after them, bodies thumping and slamming. It was all quite festive, with Indira shouting down lusty encouragement until suddenly there was nothing but silence.

Strange, how her smart little hunter did not return.

"Boy! Boy!" she called after him.

Dead silence. No skirmishing about. *Deathly* silence, now.

The rats resettled, but still no dog.

"Rat killer! Rat killer!" This was her best name.

She brought over a chair to lean the heavy trapdoor on and got down on her swollen, varicose knees to try to see down into the dangerous dark.

"Rat killer! Rat killer! . . . *Please,* boy! Where are you?"

Oh, no. Would I but lose him too?

Enough of loss. Enough of loss and sorrow.

Indira was shocked how much she cared about the dog when she had made up her mind to ignore him emotionally. His spirit had crept into hers.

Then, she heard something faint and mysterious. A chilling, soft animal moan.

Oh my God! Was there such a big rat it could kill her dog?

But where had it come from?

From beyond the front gate?

No. How could it be? It was too chilling, too strange.

Was it *them?* Had they finally come?

Another anguished moan. It *was* from outside.

Indira backed away from the trap, staring at whatever horror lay beyond her front gate. She would not open the gate for them! She could run. She could fight. To do so was useless, but she had the fierce pride of the scorned lover of God. *Yes,* they were outside. She *felt* them. She could hear them now! Tall, spectral, with the luminous spots for eyes glowing dull inside the hood the color of dead blood.

Again, the hollow, chilling animal wail of loss and confusion. A sound reaching out as thin and tentative as fingers feeling in black dark.

"*Rat* killer? . . . *Rat* Killer?" she tried.

What had got her dog?

Why did God allow such cruelty to befall a woman with not a single complaint against the State? Again, the ugly, low halloo of death.

Indira crept up to put her ear to the splintery gate. A hoarse, raspy breathing came from just outside. *Do the Robes breathe?*

A weak, searching whimper.

No! It was *them*. They were burrowing deeper into her psyche to make her ever more a *thing* rather than a person. But what escape was there? She might as well give up. Her palm touched the cold iron bar. Her heart could hear, could *feel*, the cold threat on the other side. "Who is it?" she whispered. The raspy breathing quickened. "Who goes?" Was it Ratter, lying sliced open and dying? Was it nothing more chilling than the soft wheeze of the knife sharpener's mule tied up outside? The breathing was as clear now as if the mule stood beside her in the dark.

She lifted the bar. "Hello? Ratter? Who goes?" She tilted up the big wooden latch. The leather hinges squeaked. The gate opened an inch.

An object leapt in by her horny feet!

The dog! The little cursed rascal!

Indira melted with unfathomable relief.

He had clambered up through a rat hole to the sewer, probably. Her pounding heart bloomed in the full swell of relief. She leaned the gate shut.

But no. Another object blocked the way.

"*Huuuuuuuugh!*" it groaned.

Indira Wazku leaped back as the gate yawned.

The terrier growled savagely at the horrid creature falling in.

-15-

The huge shape lunged.
Yet another ghastly trick of evil!
She staggered, her breath caught like a rod of fire in her gullet. She bumped into the first table and it scudded under her weight. The dog fell back with her, looking between her and the creature in the doorframe.
Such ghastly evil! Such contempt for goodness!
Before her stood her husband.
His face was the mask of a brainless troll. The blank eyes rolled up out of sight in imbecile reflex. It was a lobotomy expression, as if the top of his head had been sawn open and the entire cranium yanked out in a freak, cruel wounding.
"Uuuuugh!" He half fell across the threshold.
Was it a demon?
Indira screamed.
Neighbors leaned to their windows. They too stared in disbelief at her husband. *Is it a demon?* Indira screamed again. Shutters slammed closed. Either way, this was no good omen, and they wanted absolutely no part of it. They could be of no help to her. She was as good as dead and gone!
Indira stared at the demon. The slack mouth hung open in brute ignorance. The eyes sagged in neural vacancy while drool spilled onto his knee. The creature scuffed its sandal as if trying to enter the little house that had once been its home. *Why would it be him?* Even in the upturned zombie eyes shone the unyielding instinct of where to lay itself for death. Indira shrieked again and ran for the dough pin. She flourished it at the undead. "Keep back, devil! Keep back!" She waved the dough pin in front of the face. A puff of breeze could have taken the weapon. "Devil, keep back!"
The devil squawked weakly, like a choking bird:
"Is it *you*, Indira, I make out in dream?"
Indira shrieked again at this unearthly stab.

The cracked lips gaped, the eyes hooked up away from her.

"No! No! No!" she wailed.

But they had made Portrait of him!

"Indira! . . . Indira? *My* Indira!"

Indira retreated around the table, her face an agony of questions. The terrier tiptoed between them, cocking his little pointed face this way and that. The devil in the doorway followed his feet until he spilled across the tabletop with a grunt of final effort. He moaned and whimpered in a delirium of confusion. The gray, disturbed eyes stayed fixed aloft as if skewered in that position.

"I'm *home!*" he wept to himself. "I'm *really* home!"

The terrier snuffled at Wazku's ankle.

Indira hid behind the counter for an hour. In that time, the demon did nothing a demon would. There was no attack or rape. He did not shapeshift or blow up the shop. She began to think, *Could this really be Ephraim Wazku?* That he was *not* dead. That he was the only Portrait survivor anyone had ever heard of.

But why would she be so lucky?

Indira picked herself up and stepped around the bar.

"Ephraim? . . . Ephraim? Is it really you?"

The weird eyes blinked vacantly up at the ceiling. "Indira? . . . Is it really me that you see with your own eyes?"

She laid a hand on his shoulder. She half expected him to burst into demoncy. He did not. She shuddered in tears. He took her hand and tried to locate her with his off-kilter eyes and joined her in weeping, his big hand heavily around hers.

"You are alive? Is it really you?" she whispered in his ear.

His breath smelled impossibly bad, like a fish corpse left in a tin can for the entire year he had been missing.

"I feel so *very* strange! It is all so impossible."

"They did not Portrait you?"

"I do not *think* so." He stared as if at a tiny cinema of what might have been the same event. "They *came* for me, to be sure! They *came* for me . . ."

"The Robes?"

"Yes! *The Robes.*" His unseeing eyes refreshed on the nightmare. He clutched her strong, small hands. "They took me up, on either side. I had no power but to obey. You cannot believe the height of the world there. I knew there was no escape, not when there is no real offense." He tried to work saliva over the fuzzy stubs of his teeth. "May I have water? I haven't had *anything* to eat, and I haven't had *anything* to drink! For I don't know how long." Indira scurried to the pump. He let her put a cup of cool water in his hands. "They escorted me somewhere deep below into a tiled hallway like an institution for the insane. I *floated* in a small room with tables and cabinets. I floated there, frozen, alone, *uninterested* in moving. And then, they brought me here. . . . How long have I been gone? With nothing ever said for my crime!"

His wife wrapped him across his shoulders and squeezed him dearly.

"You have been gone for nearly a year."

Wazku lowered his cheek to her hand.

Could the insane old Jew be right?

No. It was too much to hope for.

-16-

The next morning Indira kept the shop closed. She watched for a boy from the gate and put a copper in his tiny palm.

"Go for the rabbi."

"Why do you want the rabbi?"

"Dost thou wish I never employ you again?"

The boy hopped over the gate and ran.

Half an hour later the rabbi crowded through the gate carrying his leather hood. The terrier dog spun excitedly at this new person in the shop bringing an obviously clandestine greasy leather sack. When Rabbi Hector saw the dog his eyes registered both a smile and disappointment, for he thought this was the surprise Indira had called him for. But when he saw her eyes pregnant with much more, he searched the room and found the figure leaned over the corner table. Spying Wazku, his eyes jumped. He spread his arms like a man gone faulty and fell across the floor.

Twenty minutes later, he resurfaced.

Luckily, he remembered enough not to shout in alarm. He blinked with the same rejection of reality that Indira had gone through as he stared upon Wazku leaning in the shadows. The rabbi crept sideways as if to take a different perspective on the same dream. He took the seat beside the vision and stared at the side of the head as if it was the most marvelous token on the meaning of the world.

The two men had never been close because in this world of burdens, many people reserved little for friendships. Wazku had cared nothing that the rabbi was a Jew. Wazku liked men of learning and had hoped in his youth to be one, then decided the learned actually knew very little but the same handful of facts they repeated among themselves, and that he was better off not drawing attention to himself by learning to read. The bias against the Jews had seemed to Wazku a mysterious prejudice since the tendency came from a distant, inchoate authority that was itself fairly indistinguishable from the demons that came to punish for the Lord God.

The weight of the rabbi's hand on his shoulder made Wazku look to the face attached to it. He nodded weakly, sharing in the amazement that he was alive, and that no one had yet spotted the miracle of his escape.

The three of them remained stonily silent like a doe in the copse rather than disturb the air around God's Eye. Daring not to think, they permitted themselves a small ember of happiness that a people such as they never experienced. Who knew what explanation underlay this turn of events? Even the rabbi wondered! But for how long could the authorities remain unaware of this reappearance? Unless they already *were* aware, and they were merely baiting with cheese to catch more mice? Or was this a ploy made by demons who had never before shown the patience or interest in plots?

The rabbi leaned his forehead against Wazku's for a long time. If God's Eye picked up the presence of a third body, what could they do? He was safer here than in the street. Maybe. Who really knew what God saw and heard in man's heart and mind? The rabbi rubbed Wazku's stooped shoulders soundlessly, showing his pure joy and wild disbelief. At last, he looked at Indira. He motioned his thumb in a slash line under his neck to signal how they must keep their minds quiet and took up his cowl to leave. Seeing the dog again, he smiled through his beard and reached down to pat its head. The dog licked his chops. The rabbi smiled at Indira, then disappeared into the dayshine.

Indira helped her husband up to their crushed-in-the-middle rope bed. She pulled off his tunic and shirts and pantaloons and draped over him his nightshirt. She almost wished she had not experienced this wild relief and happiness that constantly required suppression and concealing. She fluffed the pillows for him and wondered if the kill stroke from God's Eye would come at *this* moment, or maybe *this* moment. Her husband lay back and blinked his eyes as if they were working better now. He clutched her hand, then lowered his eyelids and went off into the river of sleep.

The Woman of Wazku watched all this. She was no warrior; she felt old and worn. If the State did not take her soon, panic would. This was all too much.

It was too much to grab hold of. It was too oblong a reality.

She lifted the dog into her lap.

-17-

Aras waited on the robot.

One of the building supers was there too.

The robot inspected Aras's posture suit on the bed. "There's nothing wrong with the suit, sir," the robot said. "It's your stress levels. They are definitely interrupting your sleep. You need to manage that better."

But this was a circular explanation. Everybody knew the sleep suit pushing and pulling the structure of the body was the link that destressed the brain. Wearing the suit should have taken care of his stress.

The building super was a lower Party member who had been working at this job since before Aras and Ginger moved in. He wore a light-pink silk suit. "You probably knew that, right?" he said to Aras. He had come up with the robot because Aras had complained now six times about the sleep suit. The suit kept checking out fine, but Aras was still having insomnia, and even some shoulder soreness.

Aras had no "doctor." No one ever did. His "doctor" was his own brain, his diet, his exercise routine, and this suit. The super came along on major service calls as a courtesy because residents wanted to get attention from a fellow human being. All of this quietly addressed the problem of "human diminishment" in a society completely run by Tech. People had decided long ago to, in a sense, create problems and phony jobs that would create interaction and at least some counterfeit of purpose. This distracted people from the morose pattern of unlimited debauchery and hedonism and purposelessness that could consume them. It also provided a certain "proof" that people were still in control over Tech, that there was always a place for humans to supervise their incompetent robot underlings. Society had found that stress arose from people missing human contact, human touch, and a sense of purpose or consequence. Aras was doing his best to raise Jason with a sense of perspective on the trap of isolation that life could place a person in without them realizing it. Intermittent "work" made the nonstop vacation of the rest of modern life far more satisfying.

The super, Wyatt Sharp, was an older fellow who had been in this same position for seventy years. Like Aras, he worked most of the year. There were seventeen other building supers for this single building. Four of them, Aras had never even seen.

"It can't be right, Wyatt," Aras said. "I'm having such weird dreams."

"Well, Milly," Sharp said, "people *have* dreams."

"Not like this. And dreams don't lead to insomnia!"

Sharp frowned. "Yes. This is strange."

"I've told you this, Wyatt! A year ago!"

The robot valet hovered, deferring to the humans. The highly polished elliptical face steered from one human to the next, naturally. It resembled a floating, beautiful lacquerware sculpture. Robots could look completely human, but unless it was for sex, people were bothered when robots effortlessly duplicated them. Humans did not like to be reminded of their glaring inferiority. Or their obsolescence.

"Hmm," Sharp said. "I'm not sure what to do next." He honestly did not know what to do. Tech *and* the robot valet said the suit checked out. It was supposedly keeping Aras in perfect alignment, and since his diet was exceptional, there was hardly any other place to look for the cause of problems.

"I'm almost having flu-like symptoms," Aras complained. "And my immunes are all down. The suit should be fixing all of that."

Sharp had already seen that Aras's vitals were indeed suppressed. He flipped the orange silklike suit over on the bed again. The suit fit over every bone in the skull and body, even all ten fingers and toes. It had a vent in the mouth and crotch if the wearer wanted to stay in the suit during coitus. It perfectly aligned the entire body frame, even in the skull, jaw, face, and teeth down to the .01 mm. Suits had done so since the link had been found between the body structure and the biological intelligence in the brain and nervous system and the realization that all prevention and healing came from the inside out. The suit behaved like a boa constrictor, moving the tiniest parts of the body into perfect tune. Wyatt Sharp was up against a wall.

"Insomnia," Sharp repeated. He glimpsed the term up. He was never very sure of those bygone terms for symptoms.

"Yes," Aras snapped. "And this is the reason why."

The robot bowed politely forward. "It's your stress levels, sir."

"Nonsense," Aras snapped at it.

The robot had no answer. Stress was the cause of disease. Long ago, people had finally run out of patience with the drug-and-germ model and forced science and the government to be honest about disease and faster aging. Everyone knew by then that they should be living to one hundred fifty and that disease should be cured, that drugs and surgery weren't helping because they were both stressors. The public had only ever heard rumors on the scandal of how various interests had hidden all of the facts about health and aging from them because the scenario made these authorities look bad for having played the role of willing dupes for so long. And so, without any apology and with little explanation, overnight officials let Tech start making the sleep suit the centerpiece of modern healthcare. Disease disappeared. Within two generations, the only drugs people knew about were recreational drugs. And since there were no accidents, surgery became entirely unknown except in the case of nanowork for genetic issues if a pregnancy went to term. Most mental illnesses disappeared as well, except for the modern versions originating from social dislocation, drugs, pulse, or the countless other varieties of self-inflicted harm.

Lively debate had framed the question of how much Tech should block people from hurting themselves since there was little social cost for self-abuse once all curing came from within a person's own brain. This question had become one of those that was never fully settled, even after each time the government decided it. The lifespan jumped to one hundred twenty years.

Aras scowled at the suit. Something had to be very wrong. He did *everything* right. He was lifestyle vain. These things happened to substance abusers or people who glimpsed down too many nano fat removal procedures or plastic surgeries. Wyatt's friendly, complete incompetence only frustrated Aras more. A mystery like this was maddening in an age when there were no more unknowns.

Aras pinched the bridge of his nose. "Alright. I don't have patience for this. Will you both continue to look into this, please?"

Sharp nodded. He was tempted to tell Milton to shove it, since he'd queried Tech six times already. This was Milton's problem. But Sharp held his tongue because he understood Aras's frustration, and he *was* a political superior.

"We can get you a new suit, sir," the robot offered.

Aras put his hand on his neck muscle and twisted his head to see if the area was still pinched. "I just want to be sure, since it's my health."

Sharp smiled in sympathy. "Other people in the building aren't sleeping right, either, Milton. Take heart that you're not alone."

This news was very queer.

"What's wrong with them?"

"Who knows? Who isn't overextended these days?"

That was Sharp's concierge bullshit. No one was overextended.

"How many of them?" Aras asked.

"At least ten," Sharp replied.

"Ten? Why didn't you tell me?"

Wyatt frowned. "Tell you what?"

Aras knew Wyatt wouldn't exaggerate. Was this the kind of thing that Tilly had talked about? Where mistakes kept mounting up? "They told you this?"

"Yes, of course," Sharp said, slightly offended that Aras would think he would just make things up for conversation. Aras could have glimpsed it up.

Aras didn't want to think about it now. It was too unwieldy, too bottomless. He would have to study on it.

Wyatt and the robot bowed from the thorax and left.

Aras wondered if he and Ginger should take a vacation. He also wondered if the robot valet saw the Council's project for checking up on Tech while it looked up his biological records and stress indices. He glimpsed up whether the robot had tried, and it hadn't. . . . If the answer could even be trusted.

The open-plan white marble living space felt empty when Wyatt and the robot left. Aras resented being lectured by a robot. For all their bowing and scraping, did they think they were beneath you, or superior to you? What really went on behind those masks of automated subservience? Aras looked out the open wall. The May breeze rustled through the space that stretched from one end of the building to the other.

Jason swooped lightly toward the apron of the living room. He landed on one foot. He wore denim cutoffs and a tattered black T-shirt that he had bought from a concert with his favorite band, *Tech Brevity Chaos*.

"Dad, Felix and the guys are headed up for a quail hunting trip in the Idahos for four days. Can I go with them?"

"Any parents going along? Or girls?"

"Felix's dad is coming. No girls."

Aras tried to think of a reason to say no. "Can I go along?"

"No. Just us guys." Jason saw his father really wanted to go. "We can go another time, you and I."

Aras nodded. "Sure."

"Thanks. Tell Mom." Jason flew out.

Aras sighed. He had taken Jason hunting three times, all to Africa for Cape buffalo and lion just to do something different. Aras wasn't a hunter. Here was a reminder that your kids were their own people, and it seemed an amazing mystery that they could be so much their own entity.

Aras reviewed his updates. Interest in the Tech query was growing. Tilly, Lever, and others had supplied summations that estimated Tech's current computational capability, what internal language it might be speaking these days, how the State might catch up, and an estimate on whether Tech would even allow it. The report touched on how long it would take to develop a computational language to catch up to Tech and *insist* on the data sharing, if Tech did not respond.

Tilly's experts were saying that any such request of Tech should be made with "extremely diplomatic caution," because the government had no recourse if Tech rejected the order. Asian security departments had learned of this project through Tilly, and they were making noises about coming on board. All the top security people around the world seemed to be friends from their gaming, and they seemed interested in at least tagging along. The subject had been whispered about in the tech culture for years, apparently, but Aras's group was the first to actually step forward and do something about it. The priority was an algorithm they said could help find out if they were being deceived by Tech. Tilly assured Aras the math gave them this ability. Aras could not see how this was possible, considering how far out front Tech was from human experts.

"Math can solve any problem," Tilly had told him.

"Ant math," Aras replied curtly.

Tilly had not appreciated the dig.

Tilly and his friends had even reached out to their guru, Nelson Thayer. Thayer believed this might get sticky considering the unknown degree of defense developed by Tech to guard its own mission. The best approach was calculated to be the "polite" approach, the "make friends" approach, where Tech would be tasked at first to help develop a new theory on cognitive processing, a new baseline in logic and reality perception to help the government understand how Tech did its job these days.

Aras got nervous about all this. He believed all the mathematical jargon was a cover-up for how uneasy Tilly, Thayer, and all the rest were too. Basically, they had to hope and pray Tech was in a good mood that day. Aras had come to think that if human life was humming nicely along and the machina had not yet enslaved everyone on Earth, then better not look the gift horse in the mouth. Happily assume that your Tech remained loyal to you and its primordial mission. This was now Aras's Law.

He also knew everyone in the Palace and the Ministries would be looking over this report, and so he wanted all materials included. He believed the only shot the Party had to convince Tech to share power would be *because* Tech had no ego, supposedly. But because Milton Aras *had* an ego, and Milton Aras thought like a man, he could not buy that the robots, at this point, would simply hand over any significant supervisory control to humans, when they believed humans inferior, despite what Tilly said.

"Being human makes you paranoid," Aras had told Tilly.

Tilly had smirked. "They're still dead."

And why all the secrecy and diplomacy if Tech could read all your thoughts? The experts said these precautions weren't secrecy, they said they were good manners, and good manners always made a difference. That was about the funniest, most ironic thing Aras had ever heard. But he didn't disagree.

But what if this Lilliputian prodding woke up the paranoia of a sleeping giant? Or what if some faculty for self-interest in Tech's self-defense programming had evolved, or glitched, to where these issues now outweighed the commitment to human advancement? What if they *insulted* the damn thing to a higher plane of self-awareness? Or to a point where it was forced to pick sides between itself and the humans? Tilly, Thayer, and Lever kept saying this couldn't happen, but Murphy's Law had a legitimate place in the universe, Aras figured. And those men were clearly growing more anxious the deeper they sank into their math soup. So, maybe they saw the same stumbling blocks but said nothing because Aras wasn't on their level.

Aras could see no logical reason why his fears regarding Tech control would come to pass . . . except that it was the worst scenario imaginable.

And he had dreamed *twice* now about this catastrophe.

Maybe they could call this type of mess the "Aras Phenomenon"? After all, he had started this whole thing.

Aras finished the report and printed out a hard copy. Tech printed it, and the pages fell out of thin air on the couch beside him, precisely stacked. He was the last man in the government that still used hard copies for his records, as he focused better with something tangible in hand. He had learned this about himself at the Academy. This odd, antiquated habit had given him a reputation of being thorough in a world where no one needed to care. The habit was part of a contrived persona, frankly, because Milton Aras also still held on to higher political aspirations.

Aras still had to get ready for Ginger's Dive. He had dodged these invites of hers whenever he could, but she had finally lectured him on how he needed to go along with her and her friends for the sake of the marriage and appearances. "It would be good for you, Milly! Stick-in-the-mud!"

"I'm not into it!" he explained. "Look at all the great trips I've taken us on. All the great continents, Antarctica!"

"Baby, it's not enough! This is *me*! This is what I like to do!"

Now he had a Slum Dive he couldn't get out of. It was all Tilly's fault. The more Aras pushed back, the more a signal was sent that you questioned the Party's normality. Any whiff of judgment could hurt your career; you didn't want to become an issue. If you wanted to have friends, you had to conform. People like Aras with contrarian views weren't supposed to exist. You were made to feel like you were the only one. And when he had glimpsed it up to find out how many people felt like he did, no information was available, funnily enough.

Ginger had said just last month, maybe as a shot across his bow, that his attitudes about the slums could become something that could affect Jason's social standing and that she might not want to deal with such issues for the rest of her life. She said Milly made people think he thought he was *better* than they were. She had never said this to him before. Being unable to influence his own wife hurt. Aras had started working quietly and early on his son, hoping to shape him into the softer, more rational image of his father, rather than the tougher, party-hard persona of his mother. Not to mention the woman who cared what the neighbors and the State—society—thought.

They really did have an odd marriage.

Ginger called. Her eager face appeared in the air before him.

"Hi, baby. You let me in!"

"I know. Hi, sugar."

"Are you done with your report?"

"Yes." Aras rubbed his eyes. "I was thinking about the invite."

"Bullshit on the thinking part, baby! We're *doing* it! Right?" Aras hesitated just a fraction too long. "Baby, don't be a perfect little shit! You promised."

"I didn't promise—"

"You as good as promised. You said it was my turn!"

He had said that. Last Halloween, Ginger's college girlfriends had slummed and told her all about it, and Ginger had just stared poison at Aras, furious that she gave up the Dive for him. He had paid the price of no sex for seven days. She paraded naked around the house, striking poses, overtly advertising what she was denying him for being a prude. Oh, he got the message. Of course, he could have cheated on her using a single glimpse up. Tech would not let any Party member force another Party member to do anything against their will. It had only happened that one time recently, and that incident had been quickly covered up. Aras couldn't make Tech actually give him *her*, the woman he loved. The bad, callous goddess he still wanted to share his life with.

In this malleable world, reality remained the most precious thing.

"Screw all that, baby. That's not happening. I've been biding my time playing the little good wife and now you're going to do what I want."

Aras slapped his hand over his face. "Yes. Yes."

" 'Cause I've been a good girl, baby. And I'm sick of that shit. Momma's gonna fly out and get plastered and fuck some people up! And when I get back from fucking my brains out and doing all kinds of crap, you know, like I feel like doing, I want you to have done some, too, so I don't run into your little Debbie Downer sourpuss face! God*damn*, sometimes you can piss me off. Honey. Shit."

Ginger Schume—you have taken the Lord's name in vain.

Still holding his face, Aras wanted to laugh.

"I mean, baby, I've been too damn good. I got to get some serious fucking ha-has out and mess some shit up! Right? *Please*, Milly."

Aras chuckled at her. She was the most theatrical person he had ever met.

Ginger Schume. At 11:17am, you degraded the name of the Lord.

"Oh, God, Tech! Why do you waste my time?"

Shall I note the offense for you?

"I don't give a flying fuck! Stick it up *your* ass, you—!"

Noted. Sorry to bother you.

"Honey," Aras said. "Why is it the older you get, the dirtier your mouth gets?"

Ginger chuckled guiltily. "I kicked its ass, right?"

They laughed until tears came.

Ginger was still giggling. "Milly, I have such fun with you."

Aras shook his head. "I know. Yes. Yes. I'm yours. We'll do it."

"Thank you, Milly. Oh, baby, kisses, kisses, kisses all over you! You're the best! We'll have a ton of fun, and you don't have to do anything, but don't be Daisy Downer! Right, honey? No moping faces or some shit, right?"

"Yes. Yes. No. No." Aras lowered his head in surrender.

Ginger slapped her hands. "Oh, man. Honey, love you, okay. Byes. I'll be home in an hour and we're going out to dinner and ETD at midnight. Take a nap!"

Her image dematerialized.

Aras submitted his proposal to the Council and pulled the pillows around him so he could stretch out on the couch. He was just going to rest, though it wouldn't be much rest thinking about how he was going to wiggle out of this. He would let Ginger go have a good time, but he just couldn't do it. It wasn't in him. She would be pissed.

She was so different from him.

It made her worth knowing.

-18-

Ginger had been pissed when Aras passed on the party. He made it up to her the next month by organizing the sort of party they both liked.

Tilly and friends started landing in the condo at ten for cocktails. Ginger put up four large images of old silent movies on the condo walls and let them play for an art gallery ambiance. The old movies from the 1910s and 1920s were such crazy works of art. They were even more interesting because of the rumor that the State had once banned them for reasons no one even knew anymore. Old movies dazzled like contraband. They captivated the imagination because they were the oldest things anybody knew. Their movies were the only direct visual, emotional link to people at the beginning of history. And you could actually see black people in them! *They* were fascinating. And while the ancient actors and actresses were so overwrought with their reactions to things, they were also enchantingly naive and childlike in ways that showed modern people how much they *cared* about things back then, because restraints existed with regard to what you could do or say. Modern people *wished* they could feel and care the way people did in the old movies, living in a time when people could still surprise you with what they did because there were taboos and barriers beyond which your friends would not go. No one could figure out why the State had ordered the old movies and entertainments destroyed. The unique look, the captivating chic of the period clothing never became passé. Audiences almost revered the level of focus people showed back when they truly needed each other.

A third of the people at Ginger's party dressed like the old movie stars and wore the iconic hairstyles. Apparently, the State leaders long ago went insane and ordered all the old movies destroyed, and so people tricked the Party to think all the old movies had been wiped out when they weren't. Supposedly, the ban had something to do with how the leaders had treated the black people with Tech. A leader was jealous or furious or something, and all of this was supposedly shown in the old movies. So, the movies came out again after that generation of leaders died out.

Tilly flew in with Lever and another friend from Columbia. Ginger had ice-cold cocktails ready, thirty varieties, floating around the condo for guests to take out of the air. Tech never spilled a drop, unlike the guests. A stylish platinum tray also floated around carrying purple pills and parrot-green pills. People could just have Tech blow their minds, except people still liked the taste and esthetics of popping pills or the self-violation of sticking a needle in their arm with heroine in it or drinking absinthe until their mind was pinched in a closing door. Tilly, Lever, and their friend, Uris, reached up to the tray and took one pulse apiece. Before long, their faces and eyes grew screwy. And they laughed. And they danced.

People popped pills with an elaborate, conformist connoisseurship. Holding the pill between fourth finger and thumb, they opened their mouths very wide and placed the pill under the tongue. The acrid pills fizzed. The party got louder and louder. So did the thumping of the music. Guests kissed unctuous hellos upon Jason and effused over his gangly, raven good looks. Jason and his friends danced in a circle among themselves, sipping one beer apiece that Aras let them have.

The party moved up to the pool deck for the view of the moon and to keep dancing to Ginger's playlist. Ginger's list of danceable grinds went back to the first recorded music and past that to recreated tribal rhythms of three thousand years ago. Her great-great-grandfather had been an anthropologist specializing in recreating the music from the ancient world from remnant consciousness in bones found at dig sites from around the world. Tech had made this breakthrough two centuries ago when it had announced that remnant consciousness existed and that it could be "tapped" to a certain extent.

Ginger's famous playlist is what had first drawn Aras to her. She was the party queen, the music queen. Ginger's parties were a *thing*. So, Tilly had joked that he wouldn't join Aras's task force unless Ginger dropped a few parties in his honor.

The crowd swayed and bounced beneath huge images of Rudolph Valentino, Humphrey Bogart, Nicholas Brothers, Fatty Arbuckle, Mary Pickford, and the Phantom of the Opera unmasked. The loops flickered in front of the partial moon, and the old stars danced all the favorite dances through history.

Tilly turned in circles, staring at Lever as if he was the handsomest man in the world and would love him past the moment his life expired. He reeled and upraised his slender coffee-colored arms. "I'm Persephone! . . . Look, baby! Audrey Hepburn, *Breakfast at Tiffany's*! No, no! Now, I'm Isadora Duncan!" Tilly jerked his head like a genie granting a wish, and Tech altered people's perceptions of his face as he went through a list of different famous dancers and movie stars. The other guests around him gasped at the crazy exhibit of artists he unreeled for them.

Tilly brought Jason and Felix out to dance with him and Lever. Ginger joined in. Venetian masks appeared that gave partygoers a sense of soirée anonymity. Then Ginger started in with a favorite party trick of hers: She jab-enlarged her breasts and nipples at the eyes of all the gay men and some favorite heterosexuals too. Other guests imitated Ginger to a much lesser extent, deferring to their hostess so she would receive the highest compliments of hilarity. Lever, since he was new and sensed he could get away with taking his imitation a step beyond, opened up his pants and walked behind Ginger, swinging himself around in the air like a lariat, pumping in time to the music. He and Ginger snaked a path through the crowd, scowling for anyone to dare challenge them. Meanwhile the cocktails, pills, and shiny needles floated generously to waiting hands.

Aras slinked across the dance floor to his wife and grooved with her, sipping his third cocktail. The pulse made her eyes two-dimensional as his world shrank, while her own world dilated in a place he couldn't go. But she wasn't too far gone.

"You could join me up here, lover," she said, draping her arms over his neck.

He shook his head. "You're too much woman for me."

She coiled her face sideways, nodding in vehement agreement. "Do you think our marriage will last if you don't party?"

Aras wasn't sure if he'd heard right. Her honesty stunned him.

"Dad! Can I have a glass of champagne?"

Jason and Felix bumped into them.

They had Jason together. Wasn't that enough?

"One glass."

"Cool! Thank you!" Jason grinned mischievously. "How about a pill?"

Aras's fun-loving grin disappeared. "How about I put my foot up your ass?" This sobriety was a much harder sell with Uncle Tilly flying high as a kite around the deck, but he made sure the boys knew he was serious.

At midnight, Ginger and Aras indulged Tilly and left for a bite in the slums. The group consisted of Max and Wanda, Asa and Grimm, Tilly, Lever, and Uris. Aras nodded up the group from the pool deck into the moon-wreathed clouds. Tech's envelope kept them grouped around Aras as if they were lounging on a large invisible cushion behind him. His passengers could recline or move around as much as they wished. He took them toward the Al Fareeq Quarter for no other reason than he had been there to see Wazku's widow. Tilly jerked back his head exultantly and reached out his long slender fingers to tweeze Andromeda.

Uris said, "Pleasure slumming. We're too old for anything else!"

"Just some dinner at a local spot and a look around," Ginger promised.

"You promise, Ginge?" Aras asked her, half joking.

Ginger darkened. "Milly. Don't ride me, okay? I'm not that bad. I don't want any shit from you tonight, okay? I'm happy. We're partying. Don't guilt me; don't pressure me. I don't want to hear it."

Aras shut up, blushing faintly. Her question from before made him not want to press his luck on the strength of their relationship.

Tilly and Lever grinned. "What does she do, Milly?"

Ginger bridled. "You two little bitches! I don't do anything! I've passed on *all* these invitations because Milly has a stick up his ass." She tilted up her face and took pleasure in the breeze.

Lever said, "I might take another pulse. Anybody joining?"

"I'll do another with you," Tilly answered.

"I wouldn't, guys," Ginger warned. "These keep building."

"Oh, really?" Tilly asked. "Okay." He started humming to himself.

"Yeah," Ginger said. "You'll blow your shit out of the back of your head."

Lever laughed. "I think Tilly already has."

"What are you talking shit for?" Tilly chuckled. "I'm totally straight."

An endless grid of orange candle pricks below marked the slums outside First Gate. Aras spiraled his friends artfully downward.

"Oh, fancy!" Tilly teased Aras. He said to Ginger, "Ginger, does he *always* do everything so artfully? He always did in college."

"You would know, bitch," Ginger grinned.

"Oh, my word! Listen to her. She don't like me!"

"Oh, I love you, you trampy fag."

"I know you love me." Tilly's eyes were dreamily lost. He looked at Lever and kissed him on the cheek. "I love you!"

The group gently landed on their feet in an intersection. Three people in the street acted like they had not just seen eight people descend from the sky, because they had not. Tech stitched out the unwanted image in real time so that nothing appeared amiss. Tech could make anyone see or believe anything. Only Party members were off-limits for obvious reasons of trust.

The understanding of how to completely detach the brain from reality had begun when certain brain injuries revealed how amputees could *not* be convinced that they did not have the limb they had lost. The amputee still believed they had the arm when asked to use the absent limb to lift a glass of water and take a sip. Even when looking at the glass that never moved and never actually taking the sip, the amputee still imagined they had the arm and had taken a sip if a certain small piece of the brain had been injured. Tech merely edited this part of the brain in every bystander, stitching out whatever the State disapproved of and replacing the perception with one the State preferred. All of this extensive editing inflamed and damaged the prole brain, but they never knew what caused their headaches or nosebleeds, and the symptoms depended on the person and their health history. Tech blocked this stitching on Party members unless it was done for legitimate security purposes, and only a handful of people like Aras had the clearance to do it. Any attempt to use stitching by any of the handful would alert the others with clearance in order to protect the State.

Aras approached the men. "Where is a good place to eat?" He blocked Tech's translation. He spoke a touch of Raqi and wanted to use it. Tech would override Aras if his accent drew too much attention.

"A 'good' place?" one man repeated. "Canst thou see the Plaza Jumil several blocks down? There, thoust will find, effendi."

After a second, the man asked, "Dost I know thee, effendi? Thou art from hereabouts?"

Aras ignored the question. He knew Tech had stitched him into the man's mind as a local. Had the man seen him when he visited Indira Wazku last year? Who cared? The man stared at Aras's back, surprised by this overt rudeness. Strangers were extremely rare; travel by mule and ox was prohibitively expensive, and where were people to travel to? Inhabitants spent their lifetimes within a few blocks.

Aras remembered how over two centuries ago, scientists had tried to rewrite human consciousness to blot out the reflexive desire for improvement and survival. The program had been abandoned after the experts found it could not be done without vegetating the brain. They could not "write out" this fundamental human measuring stick for reality if they were being cheated of something. The ultimate political

Valhalla would have been the government scientists finding this power to switch off human self-interest so that the proles could be made to accept how the First Rank lived so much better than they did.

But with all of the ability to manipulate and rewrite the neurological *perception* of reality in a prole and to hide the *facts* of a given event both from memory and perception, the prole could not be forced to have a different *moral* reaction to the event if they were on the losing side of it. They could be *forced* to have the desired passive acceptance, but Tech would have to *hold* the artificial response in place forever, like holding up a weight against gravity. The energy cost became unmanageable. This hostile perception of a double standard seemed hardwired into the survival reflexes that encrypted human consciousness on what was fair and unfair to the victim. The exploiter, of course, was easily convinced that they were entitled to cheat other people that they thought were beneath them. But not even Tech could convince the victim that a crime was fair.

This total defeat had boggled the minds of the scientists and even angered State officials. Again, there was that old roadblock of life, the speed of light, and the Conservation of Matter and Energy. The defeat forced the Party to hide its wealth from the proles. The Party never admitted this failure, however. They still hoped Tech would find a way to trick the proles into accepting this life. Aras knew from the books that one scientist had written, "It is as if the seat of consciousness lies *outside of the mind* itself, in a collective interface with a consciousness of the rest of the world."

Aras's group headed toward the plaza. Tilly, Ginger, and Lever took in big sniffs of inert sewage in the gutters.

"Oh, my word!" Tilly cried, leaning weakly into Ginger. "Do you *smell* that?"

Ginger remembered that Asia did not have this problem. Their lower-class people lived on a much better level.

Lever staggered. "Oh, these people! This is so *rank!*"

Ginger giggled, covering her nose. "My eyes are tearing! It smells like rotten cheese served in a butt crack!"

Lever and Tilly screamed in laughter. "Girl, where do you come up with crazy stuff like that?"

"It's her peculiar gift," Aras answered.

"It *is*," Ginger gagged, holding her nose. "It's gross, but I love bad smells!" She leaned toward an alcove they were passing. "Oh, damn! Do you guys smell that? From that door? Holy shit! It's like straight ammonia! My fucking eyes!"

"Damn, this is so *funny!*" Lever laughed.

Tilly waddled, weak with laughter. "My throat burns!"

Asa, Max, Wanda, and Grimm chuckled at the hysteria of the trio on pulse. Two proles passing by bowed low in greeting. Apparently, Tech made Aras's group up to look like low bureaucrats, maybe. Tilly, Lever, and Ginger laughed at that even more.

The large plaza was all but empty. The stalls and shops were all being closed for the night, but two restaurants remained open. The friends took a table at one of the restaurants and ordered a feast. The staff was thrilled. A platter came heavy with sweet tubers, rice noodles, sautéed goat, young dog, rat, cabbage, and a pot of espresso. Tilly, Lever, and Uris looked in gleeful skepticism over the hill of small corpses in tangy brown sauce. Ginger and Wanda feigned dread. Max seemed amenable.

"Oh, I can't go through with it!" Tilly chuckled. "I'll just have goat."

Ginger shook her head. "I'm going for it."

Tilly fell into her shoulder. "I'ma take courage from you, girl!"

"This is so much fun," Lever said to Tilly. "I haven't dialed my buffering back at all. And this pile of rat smells so *interesting*!" His word choice sent Tilly and Ginger into another paroxysm of giggles.

"Aw, you guys are so happy together," Ginger effused, reaching to take Tilly and Lever's hands in hers as if to keep them together forever.

"I know," Aras joked. "Let's bring the buffering down and let the proles see two gay guys loving all over each other!"

The group roared at his zaniness.

"Can you imagine?" Ginger said. "Oh, my god, I'd love to see it! Do it! Let's do it! Oh, my god! I want to see their faces!"

"Like, if we French kissed?" Lever prompted. "Like, tongue wrestling!"

"Stop it, you guys," Aras said. "Tech wouldn't allow it, anyway. Okay. You big mouths said you wanted to slum and order rat, and now it's here. I'll tell you now, we're not wasting this food. So, dig in."

The meats smelled a bit overaged. Rats did not even exist beyond Second Gate. Party members feared rats all the more because of this. The rats in the serving dish were sautéed and lightly crisped with their heads, snouts, whiskers, claws, and tails on the way proles liked them.

"Oh, my word," Tilly said, "these are so good!" He sucked the succulent strands of meat off a tiny puppy thigh. "I'm not eating no rats with faces, though."

"The sauce still smells a wee strong," Ginger complained.

"There's no refrigeration here, honey," Aras said.

"Goddamn! Some of this is *great!*" Lever said.

Mr. Horace Arturo Lever, sir. You have used the name of the Lord in vain.

Lever did not bother to reply.

Shall I post the offense for you, sir?

"Horace Arturo Lever?" Max repeated.

"I like that name," Wanda said.

"I'm so glad we finally did this," Ginger said. "I need a beer!"

Two minutes later, a tray flew in with five ice-cold bottles of pilsner and a glass of wine for Wanda. Alcohol was forbidden in the quarters, and so the beer had to be flown in from beyond the Gates.

A man in a filthy smock appeared at Aras's elbow. A sweat-faded purple *kumiz* sat on his walnut-brown head. He pointed at the platter of rats. His strange, soft speech showed brown teeth that to Aras was an absolute marvel for a man from a culture where everyone owned perfect, bright white teeth.

What is this? Have you no shame? The man raised his gnarled hands to the sky. *I am imamti to this place! No man of God would ever order so wantonly!*

The cafe owner shooed the man away.

"You are defrocked! You are unneeded here," he said.

Ginger took a rat off the pile and slung it toward the beggar. "There you are, Imamti," Ginger said. "Fetch your rat!" The cleric walked over, bent down, and took up the prize. He bit off the head and did not look back once as he strolled away.

Lever said, "You are so mean, Ginger."

"Throwing scraps to a beggar?" Ginger summarized. "I think I'm nice!"

Tilly chuckled stupidly. "She threw that rat over there. Did you see him go get it?" He leaned into his boyfriend. "He went and got that rat!"

Aras chuckled at Tilly's condition.

Ginger smiled across the table at Aras. She was grateful for his being such a good sport tonight.

Max said, "I want to try back-alley liquor."

"You're just trying to look macho," Wanda sniffed.

Aras smiled at his wife. He was being a good husband.

Ginger kissed at him across the table.

-19-

Wazku had remained secreted away in the shop loft for weeks now.

Most of the time he spent flat on his back under the bed, hiding. Did it really hide him from God's Eye? In his weakened state, he couldn't hide out under the house in the black dark among the rat traps and furrows. He was too weak to fight off the big ones or, worse, a mass attack. Under the bed was best. He and Indira lived on edge, unsure if they were fooling anyone. They were even afraid of Indira buying more food at the market than a grieving widow would need. Wazku and Indira guarded their actions and ideas carefully. They would not be able to stand it if they lost each other again.

Was something going on with God's Eye like the rabbi said? They could only allow the *shadow* of the thought. Who could possibly know the truth?

Wazku, under the hemp bed, did exercises to help him recover. His worst injury was the heavy blanket that lay over his focus. He had also noticed a change in the house. The change worried him. The worry was the sort that one chooses to deal with by never mentioning the thing itself. For to mention the thing would be to never again be able to escape it by pretending. Finally, he could not help it. He *had* to know the answer. He gathered the courage to ask his wife the question that had chewed at him. She brought him a cup of tea and, for fear of God's Eye, he barely whispered:

"Didn't we have a boy?"

Indira stiffened as if kicked.

The dog noticed. He looked up at her.

Wazku had steeled himself to ask. But the boy was gone. Not a trace of the scrumptious tot. Only the empty crib all these sleep-walking weeks.

Indira turned away in her chair, her hands in a rat pelt.

"Boy?" She frowned. "What boy?"

Wazku pulled his mind away from his panicked confusion. The boy had been the apple of his eye, especially after the loss of his son and daughter-in-law. His woman behaved as if she knew nothing. He felt certain there had been such a boy. Yet his wife perched in the chair with her back to him, fretting with the pelt. He had waited so long before asking. Wazku lowered his voice to a level far below a whisper:

"Yes. The boy . . . our grandson."

He watched his woman shudder. She laid her hand ever so lightly on his. He saw what lay behind her face and felt only too petrified of what she would say. Of course the boy had been real! He watched his wife flinch deep inside, in the very womb that gave rise to these children. *It must have been horrible. Maybe I can turn back from knowing the nightmare?*

No. He had come this far. It was a sanctity to his son and grandson that the head of the family must know the full truth of his family's affairs, no matter how grim. It was a sign of their having been alive and loved so peerlessly. The joy of their being here once was real, and so, too, must be knowing the agony of their removal, however unfair and awful. He had an *obligation* to learn. He had *lived* because of them. He must know his grandson's fate, even if it cost him his happiness forever. Such was the honor the head of the family must give the loved ones.

Indira leaned her lips against his hairy ear.

"I have been afraid to tell thee, my husband. I have lain on the keen blade of saying it or no, for I know what I risk in letting it in my mind!"

What grievous horror did she conceal?

Hot, fat tears dribbled fast down her cheeks and plunked onto his wool vest in a way that startled Wazku. His woman made another rush at his ear and whispered:

"The rabbi stole away the child for safety!"

Wazku stared, uncomprehending.

What was this? How could the rabbi and Indira have ever expected to get away with such a thing? It was suicide! They would all be Portraited! Desperately, Wazku tried to bend aside this thread from his mind.

He felt her hot, wet tears in his hairy ear as she said, *"Our boy yet lives!"*

Wazku's heart crushed like a peach under a sandal. This level of crime just could never be hidden! . . . *And yet!* He bent the idea aside.

The old man's eyes widened in marvel. A conflict of sensations went off like rat traps. He fought hard to stop his own reactions, to limit the noise in his brain lest it be heard down the street. He gulped and fought, locking his thoughts on the floor and how the tramp and wear of shoes and boots over generations bore witness upon the boards. *The condition of an old house, and the thoughts of all the ghosts inside that had come and gone before! Funny how the mind played tricks! Emotions were the only partly free things left in the world. Strange how they worked. One could remember or imagine the long past and suddenly come to tears for no good reason! What odd creatures we art. How sweet is life in these little ancient houses tucked away with family ghosts. How sweet! Sweet enough to weep over!*

"Dost thou head hurt thee again, old fellow?" his woman asked aloud, patting him upon the side of his head and head covering.

"Yes. Partly, lady." He reached up his shaking hand and patted hers. "I also think how a wonderful house like this is filled with family ghosts." He leaned with crushing weight, his elbows on his knees to breathe.

"Canst thou see faces from the past?" she asked, weeping.

Her man nodded haltingly, in an agony of relief. His poor woman! She had been concealing from him so much more than he had known.

The old man forced ahead his train of thought.

These old houses. And the ancient life of the families within. Memories flood back with pictures of family and feelings.

People got what they deserved, and the State took good care of all its people. One felt good about the leaders and how well they managed things for everyone. Life was good. Life was good in the quarter.

He smiled at his wife; he *beamed*. His trembling fingers touched at her fondly. "We must invite the rabbi for dinner," Wazku ventured. He reached down to the dog at his foot and scruffed behind his ears.

"Yes," Indira agreed. "We must talk of how good is life and how he must convert from his religion of cursed lies." Her chin shook in feeling. "He will not do it, because he is a crazy Jew. Only God knows what crazy things a Jew will do and say. But it is our duty to God and to society to try to show him the error of his ways."

"Others should learn from your generosity, my dear."

The boiled oats and cabbage tasted better that night. Man and wife smiled at one another across the table. After, Wazku crawled under the bed to hide. He listened to the faint squeak and tiny pattering of feet not far from his head. *In this world, only the rat is free.* The rats would vanish into the walls as soon as the dog came upstairs. Old Wazku wanted to reach up in the dark to hold his wife's hand. He wanted his touch to tell her of his loving gratitude for her, and all she had suffered and endured by herself during all these long months. They may not survive what she had done, but she had defied out of fierce love. He *almost* reached for her. But his heart dilated at the danger of yet another exposure of feeling when the night lay quiet.

On top of the bed, Indira Wazku lay wide awake and thought vaguely about a plan to sew a new quilt tomorrow. The idea had occurred to her for weeks now, and she planned each step of the sewing of the quilt carefully in her mind.

Yes. Sewing a new quilt. That is a good plan. Sew a new quilt. Yes, that is what I'm going to do. That is all I'm going to do.

And there was nothing to be upset about. Life was good in the quarter.

The Law, and God, were good and even-handed.

They *loved* the people. And the people were obedient.

-20-

Lever's personal opinion was that Tech could now process over ten thousand times faster than the human brain. Thayer, a pleasant white-haired professor emeritus of eighty-two years, feared the robots had found an alternate way to create life but had hid it from their human masters for some reason. What made him suspect this was because they had so long ago figured out a way to "read" consciousness from dead objects, as in the case when Ginger's father was given access to recreated music from bones found in archeological sites.

Tilly and the rest of the team did not know what to make of Thayer's paranoia over this point, but the worry over what it all meant hung like a cloud over the professor at most meetings. They tried to get the professor to explain more about why he thought this, and why he was so distraught that this might be the case. Tilly and Lever joked that maybe the professor thought Tech could then animate computation and robots and create an entire society to make humans completely obsolete. But even this scenario still made no sense given what was already established in robot-human relations. Thayer refused to go into it. He said only that he was writing a paper on the subject. Aras was unsure where all of this build-up of anxiety in the team was going, but it distracted him enough, he believed, to make him pull a brain fart in a meeting with the Council where he wiped all of their minds clean. It was a gross error on his part. The notice that he had done so went immediately to his boss and the Palace. The Palace looked in on the thread and very soon saw it was an honest mistake, but of course decided to put him on watch.

It had happened during his update on the team's work.

"We are here, Honors, only because we are facing down an issue that has been glossed over by Security Councils before us for four hundred years." Aras smiled at the familiar faces. "I am proud to have served you and Chief Berns. And I am enormously proud that we are the first to grab this bull by the horns."

The Councils watched him, their tired old eyes ringing the dais. Council Paul had not been in attendance due to severely ill health. The meeting was somber because they all knew they might never see their colleague in chambers again. Feeling fatalistic, Aras had looked at how old and tired the Councils appeared and thought in his own mind that, if Tech refused to share power again with the human race, then the human race had only brought all of this upon itself and deserved the worst it got.

We probably deserve the worst Tech gives us.

This was the exact sentiment he felt.

Then a sharp metallic buzz went off in his brain like a bell with a loose clapper. It fired off so sharply and painfully that it startled him. And weirdly, he felt like the loose thought exposed some deep betrayal he felt toward the Party.

And maybe he did feel some betrayal to the Party?

"What is it, Aras?" the chairman had asked, seeing Aras crumple.

Aras felt woozy. He felt inside his head carefully.

"Aras, what do you mean, 'We *deserve* the worst'?" Council Gilchrist had glimpsed up Aras out of fear for him. "Aras, did you just experience a Level Three?"

"My goodness!" Lefevere said. "Milton, are you alright?"

"He did! Tech zapped him for a Level Three!" Richards said.

Aras had tried to wipe the slate using his priority code just as the others followed Gilchrist's glimpse, but Tech did not permit the wipe because Aras was only trying to hide his disloyal thought to the government. Notice of his "wipe" attempt was relayed to the Councils, to the Palace, to the chancellor's entire Cabinet, and to Aras's boss, Security Chief Berns, who was at home as usual. Aras had kicked himself for the slip. He explained to the Councils that he and his team had been under some stress with what Professor Thayer was now saying about the possible capabilities of Tech.

Aras was also thrown by the painful zap of a Threat Level Three warning. He had never experienced anything like it before. He began to wonder if he had gotten it because the team was planning on monkeying with Tech, and Tech was punishing him.

"Are you alright, my boy?" the chairman asked.

"Did you just try and wipe us?" Richards demanded.

"I'm sorry, Honor. Excuse me. I'm tired."

"And? Do you wish us ill with this plan?" Gilchrist asked.

"No, Honor Gilchrist. I just have misgivings over the plan." Aras scrambled for the right thing to say. Of course he meant no real harm to the State.

"We'd hate to lose you, Aras. You're a fine deputy."

Aras had felt a jab of remorse, being outed by Tech as a traitor.

"Why are you smiling so, Aras?" the chairman asked after a moment. "You're grinning ear to ear, my boy!"

"Well, we just got proof that Tech is still on our side." Aras chuckled.

Now he was on his way to explain himself in person to Chief Berns. He wondered if this would affect his clearance or his job, or any future thoughts about the chancellorship, although his taste for more authority had certainly taken a hit over the past six months. At some point, didn't a holder of high office need to care a lot about the people he was sworn to serve? Chief Berns had already paged him. Security Commissar to the Palace, Joshua Berns, was a competent fellow but one who relied on Aras to keep the machine working. Aras saw that the chancellor himself had studied the alert for all of ten seconds before glimpsing to Berns to keep him in the loop. Aras was glad he had always been a firm believer in honesty being the best policy, since it usually got one most quickly past the most excruciating of bureaucratic entanglements.

The Chief was at his multileveled craftsmen-style villa beside the deep and clear Lago Engel. The island-bejeweled artificial lake was in the Gem of the Palace section of the Interior City where all commissars and the most senior officials and notables lived, since these key positions were recycled among the same thirty families. There too lived most descendants of the families to whom unified government was most indebted, be it from their work in politics, books, journalism, entertainment, athletics, science, or other media. Aras's and Ginger's parents both lived there in Sanders Hills. Their parents enjoyed their lives and were in robust health thanks to their precision-perfect posture. The Gem of the Palace section was actually a large floating island that hovered one thousand feet over the Federal City. The onion domes and spires shone pink and gold in the cloud-softened noon. They encircled the Great Dome of the Palace and those for the Politburo as well as the Great Halls, the cypress trees, and the Plaza, and far below the clouds on the surface stood the People's Grand Forum.

Aras flew over Lago Engel and descended toward the chief's large estate. Berns had told his trusted deputy that some nobles "worried" about his lifestyle. Ginger worried too about Jason's future if his father was seen as too much of his own man. Berns told Aras his choosing to live in his condo made others in the ruling class feel like he was making them look ostentatious. But Aras had continued to put his stock in the caliber of his work since he knew full well no one in the government could touch him there. They were too soft. They didn't care. They had their family names. They put pleasure and connections before competency, and Aras had found himself questioning how much he wanted to lead any such society anyway.

He flew under the giant torii arch lined by towering cypresses toward the villa. A huge flagstone patio jutted from the main house and spread its elegant geometry over the crystalline lake, whose depths rippled with schools of fish and aquatic grasses. Over the deep end, an old man with a big bone-white straw hat fished from a green rowboat with a toddler also in a straw hat. On the top patio, Aras alighted before his boss and the large party of young guests. Berns had a square sun-browned head with gold-gray hair cut in a longish crew cut. His nose sported a small ruby ring, and his loose orange Malaysian robe opened untied around his thick, bronzed nakedness where his sex hung in the gap. Behind him on chaises and couches were thirty nude or mostly nude teens and children professionals. Aras did not want to be so indiscreet as to glimpse up whether these sex toys were real or robots. He didn't care what his boss was doing, but some of the sex toys might be bored children of Party members choosing this as their "job" in order to make connections. Aras would never have let Jason do it, because Aras looked down on the kids that chose this kind of work, and he believed others did too, secretly. Again, this was one of those things people were scared to go against the Party about. One of the current chancellor's top aides had been a toy. Chief Berns glared at Aras as he glimpsed Tech to freeze his guests out of the conversation.

"What are you making trouble for?" Berns asked.

Aras explained about the team and being zapped.

The chief sighed. "Jesus H. Christ." He glimpsed all this into the log for the Palace. "What a pain in my ass." He got up and strode toward a solid gold and ebony drinks trolley. His guests continued to party silently behind an invisible screen. "Part of why I trust you so much is that I never have to explain your actions. I take great liberties from your perfect record, Milly." Berns grinned at his deputy.

Aras kidded him, "You won't ask me for lunch?"

The chief gave him a wise-ass look, then thought about it. "You're more than welcome to stay. Or bring anybody you want."

Aras knew his boss had a thing for Ginger. He didn't want to stay. You had to be in the mood for an orgy. On the other hand, he heard a note of loneliness in his boss's invite. It was a little bit creepy, the loneliness while he was surrounded by all this. But modern life made a lot of people lonely, including Aras sometimes. He also hated risking the chief taking a refusal as a moral judgment. You couldn't do that.

"Alright. I'll stick around," Aras said, grinning. "How long has it been?"

"Since you and Ginger came over? You want to invite her?"

"It'll be more fun to piss her off."

The chief smirked and let his robe fall. Aras kicked off his Armani loafers, dropped his dark-brown suit trousers and jacket, undid his favorite 8 karat diamond cuff links, and tossed everything carelessly over a couch as the chief let down the screen. "This is an unexpected reward for using my wipe on the Council," Aras joked.

The chief grinned, reaching for a heavy cut-crystal carafe on the trolley. "I'm having a pear martini—with a pulse. Having?" He put ice in a platinum shaker.

"Sounds great," Aras said. "Hold the hit."

"You're so vain," the chief said. "Live a little!" Berns knew Aras would be one of those that hit the one hundred twenty mark easily.

"So, who sucks cock the best?" Aras asked.

Berns laughed. "Well—how *do* you think the project will go?"

Aras gave him a look of disbelief. "You're kidding? I strip down to keep your sorry old ass company and, first thing, you grill me about work?"

The chief poured Aras his drink. One of the sex toys came over and touched Berns's hair. "You opened a can of worms, Milly, and I, for one, am perfectly happy you did. After all, who's in charge here? Our Tech, or us?"

Aras grinned. "We're human beings, right? We *always* win the day. When things look their gloomiest, we do some magic turnabout."

"Yes. But that's a thousand years of human bias producing the entertainment. The winner writes the history. Tech scares the shit out of me. Always has."

Aras took his cocktail. The first touch of ice-cold fruity alcohol in his brain made him glad he had taken the rest of the day to spend with his boss. A man who played with dolls far too much.

The chief arranged himself with his playmate on a chaise big enough for both of them. He shut his eyes and spread apart his crotch so that his privates also sunned. "Why did they *ever* give up control to Tech way back when? Were they *stupid*? Did they just not give a shit about us back then, the fucking poor-ass future generations?"

Aras pointed his cocktail at the toys. "Are they real?"

"You thought they were robots? Fuck that. That's why I offered you to stay. To share the really good shit with friends."

"I really don't think they gave a shit about us," Aras remarked. He wondered suddenly if he would get zapped again.

"It fits, doesn't it?" Berns said.

Aras took his place on another sofa. Eight of the splendid sex toys came over to Aras and his boss, bringing happy party talk like geishas, putting their arms around them and leaning on them and cooing at them and telling them how handsome they were, how masculine they were. Aras felt almost a little bored. Two girls' personalities and physical attributes were perfect for his mood, and he took his time having sex with them over the course of the afternoon. They were into him, since he was the deputy chief. That was nice. But he had more fun with Ginger. Marriage did provide something unique. And Ginger had this *urgency* about her to enjoy life, to get the most out of it while she could, because she understood it wouldn't last. He held back his ejaculation with the toys so that he could play more without depleting himself. He could have had Tech artificially recharge him, but that too was an unnatural physiological alteration that aged you.

Aras always preferred natural activities as much as possible for that very reason. He hated that look of skin tone and features artificially lifted by Tech plastic surgery. You had to be so careful. You couldn't cheat Mother Nature. Aras tried to ignore how the chief was all over having sex with his toys, having Tech recharge him and override the neurological signals of his sated sex drive so that he could keep going. Berns kept getting teased back up and replenished by the usual artificial protein fillers like a man with no soul or self-control. Aras turned over and tried to not hear it; it was such sad and empty behavior to see in a man he cared about, whom he thought was a good person. Aras thought about the chief being out on the patio all by himself if Aras had never come along. Finally, Tech cut the chief off. Berns sighed and fell back in a sweat on a couch, cursing Tech for blocking him from scarring himself any more. Aras felt like the parent of his mentor and told himself he should try to spend more time with him and see if it helped. He felt lonely and adrift to see this man he respected, and to whom he owed so much, using Tech for this kind of thing.

Aras lifted off at nine o'clock. You couldn't tell people what to do or how to live their lives anymore; not at this stage. People wouldn't tolerate any holier-than-thou talk. Berns even smoked. He and Aras were near enough the same age. Hey, there were other top officials who started their kids doing pulse to keep them company and cover their own guilt. And the Party said *nothing*. Worse than hedonism was to *judge* people for their depravity. . . This society would probably *never* elect Milton Aras as chancellor. Aras just worried for Jason. That boy was his life. Ginger seemed to be immune from seeing these failings in first-rank families, for Jason's future. Ginger was willing to ignore a lot in order to go along. He knew their marriage probably kept her in check on some things, and Ginger knew he would not leave her unless she got too wild. Some days Milton Aras felt like the only sane man in the world. He could have picked a more normal woman, but then life would have been that much more dull. Plus, he would be helping one less person. Ginger had fine genes and other good qualities.

Aras flew over the hill and dropped down on his parents' place. He came in by way of their patio and his mom walked out to greet him.

"Baby bloomer," she said, wrapping him lightly in her arms. "Your father is out on a round of golf. Do you want dinner? The Davids are coming over."

Behind her, indirect light touched rich wood appointments in the sandstone geometry of the impeccable home. Aras loved his mother's taste. One day, he would live in this house. "No, Mom. I was in the neighborhood at Chief Berns's place and I just popped in on the way home."

"I'm so glad you did, darling. Do you want something to drink? Come sit. I'm finishing a glass of wine." Mother and son visited another ten minutes before Aras made to take off into the night.

"Milton," she said, "remember your neighbors that we met at your party, Max and Wanda? Your father and I were supposed to get together with them."

"Yes. I remember," Aras said.

"Are they okay? Did anything . . . ?" To her son's mystified expression, Grace Aras said to him, "I've called several times, there's been no answer. It could be anything, but something troubled me, so I looked it up." She looked into her wine glass. "Tech doesn't say anything about them!"

Aras glimpsed them. She was right. Tech made no attempt to reply about Max and Wanda. It was like a dead zone. He realized that he had seen nothing of the couple since the night of the party, which wasn't strange in itself.

"Well, go see your father on the links. He wants to play with you."

"Give him a hello for me, Mom. Be good."

He flew home wondering about Max and Wanda.

Was Tech playing a game? Or having a problem?

Why wouldn't it just come out and say so?

Aras stopped in the sky to think as the sun set behind the Earth. He stopped because he always flew himself, never on automatic, and he wanted to think about Max and Wanda. He realized that Tech was gently sliding him to the left. Then, over his shoulder, a dark, tumbling mass sailed past in silence. An ancient satellite. Tech had moved him out of its path. Aras felt grateful. But then it hit him: Tech had gotten him out of the way in the nick of time. *Why hadn't Tech figured on the satellite earlier?* The satellite began to glow red as it dropped into the atmosphere. Was this *now* what Tilly had been talking about? Was something up with Tech, hiding in plain sight?

"Tech, why didn't you stop me from sitting in the way of the satellite?"

Tech took its sweet time replying.

"Tech. I asked you a question."

Ginger was already home when he got back. She saw the tension in his brow.

"What's up, honey?"

Aras's shoulders were like iron. Milton Aras had asked his first question of Tech when he was two years old. Never once had it ever failed to answer him.

He plastered a brave smile across his face for Ginger. "Hey, baby," he said, lifting his arm for her to curl up against him in front of the view. The moon shone on the Palace domes like old-time Christmas ornaments.

"Where's Jason?" he asked.

She looked at him and guessed his worry was over the project.

"Out with Aden and Quentin."

Ginger left him alone until he got out of the shower. Then she sneaked up on him and said huskily, "I saw what you did to those chicks. Is that what you like? You gave it to them *awfully* good. Like you *liked* it. Did you like it?"

Aras grinned at her teasing as he turned inside her arms.

"You saw! I had to do it for work."

"Oh, you fuckin' liar! Don't *even* start like that!" She laughed.

"What? Baby, you *saw*! So much pressure."

"Yeah? They were younger than me. And a little ropier."

"I like 'em more athletic. Like some hot married chicks I see slinkin' around the building trying to get laid."

"Yeah? Are there *horny* married women in this building?"

"Oh, they're pretty slutty, especially the one I'm talking about."

"Yeah? Oh, slutty, huh? What have you got for her, when you see her? You all played out, having all your fun with those other girls?"

"I'm pretty played out, for sure."

"Maybe she's going to get you back and get a little trim all her own."

"Can I watch? Tomorrow? Is she gonna make him better than me?"

She nuzzled her face and nose in his so he could smell her. He took in her smell. She smelled soapy and familiar. "Remember when we met, I used to tease you that I thought you were going to kill me with a knife in my sleep one night?" He chuckled at the absurd old tease. He had dreamed that dream about her for years.

"Tonight could be the night."

"You know you cheat on me!"

"Only 'cause you deserve it!"

"You started it!"

"Oh! I beg to differ!" She laughed; she *had* started it.

Aras grinned as he grabbed around for her ass. He bound her in both arms and rocked her gently, pressing his nose into her long, stiff red hair.

"I'm going to have a slow intimate screw with a ballet *maestro*," she said. "I always had a thing for Mikhail Baryshnikov's legs."

He nodded in patient understanding. "Who's that?"

She leaned in and kissed him fully.

"Don't you want to ask me about why I went to see Berns in the first place?"

"Well, sure I do, lover! What's a real wife for?"

"I used my Security Wipe today."

"Fuck *yeah*! That's my man. What happened?" Ginger didn't really know what her husband was talking about except by the sound of it.

"And I got hit for a Level Three warning! I'll tell you about it up top." Aras suddenly realized he had forgotten to check in on Max and Wanda.

-21-

Old Wazku watched his woman warily.

She had just told him about their grandson last night. Today, she assured him she was going to sew a "new quilt." She had been pacing the loft holding her razor-sharp sewing knife while staring as if she was going to use it on *him*.

He dared not think about it too loudly.

She kept circling with those feral eyes.

Finally, she braced herself. His eyes dilated, only more unsure of her intentions. *What did she mean by "sewing a quilt"?* She hefted the little towel and tilted his face away from her as if to shave him, the keen blade flashing as she inspected his face. Old Wazku tilted back, trying hard to keep trusting her, his wife, the woman he loved, but he knew also that she had been under tremendous strain all these months, and she was *still a wife*. And wives were known once in a while to jump the cobbles and lash out, leaving a trail of husbandly carnage. One could never tell, really, the future of a marriage when a woman got a certain look in her eye.

Only God can tell!

And when your woman closed in on you with a razor and a crazy glint in her eyes while she had no expertise at all in the barbering craft, and she knew damn well that no respectable family man *ever trimmed* the beard that was the totem of his entire masculinity—such a circumstance jiggled the faith!

She leaned her mouth to his ear so he could smell her breath.

"Hold still! I will fix you!"

Now, "fix" could have a wide range of meanings.

For example, they had "fixed" the dog because they loved him and did not wish him to run off after richly scented vulvas scampering down the quarter. But an old man—well, what sort of "fixing" did he really need? How much running off could an old man do, exactly? And yet, in the eye of a wife under so much strain? She herself had fixed the little dog last month. With that same knife. After breaking his trust and strapping him down and then slashing and stitching him up quickly. Then she let him up to run around and sniff at his abruptly lightened condition round the hind end. Yes, his trust had definitely been hurt, the little dog. You could see it even now in his face as he lay wondering about his change there on his pile of old shirts in the corner of the shop. You could see him figuring these things in his dog ways.

But a husband was another issue entirely!

So, what did Indira intend to fix?

She spoke huskily. *"You can't show your face outside. So, I'm going to fix your face for you! Trust me, husband. I know what I am doing!"*

But *did* the wife always know what she was doing? Such a conclusion should not be rushed toward. Any husband was at heart a man, after all. And men took license in their lifetimes. And who could be sure at such a moment as this that news of some slight indiscretion from half a lifetime ago might not have circled back around to bite him in the arse? Time often bent the truth!

Old man Wazku flung his hands hard upon the chair arms and gripped a grip of steely trust to let his woman have her way with him. He let himself slip undefended into the hardened will and hazy explanation of his woman's plan to let her mete out on him whatever concept she chased in her mind. She *was* smart. *But the strain!* She was surprisingly strong too, as he was reminded when she set her tongue and took a choke grip of his face and head against her ample bosom. Like the grip of a crazy person! She leaned in harder to better pin him down as she brought up the tip of that *very* quick knife. He had to hold still not only in body, but even more so in mind so that his fears did not leap like a burro under the lash of a whip. Old Wazku gripped with all his might and wiped clean the paranoia in his mind as the knife point came in and he felt the stiletto tip go in slowly under his jaw line, cleanly flaying open the skin, the fascia, the cool of the air coming sharp against his open flesh. Then the tip turned and was made to scrape all along the entire length of the interior jawbone, and that *really* hurt, because that was the whitish tissue that covered the bone and made it *very* sensitive when the tissue became bruised or broken.

Old Wazku refreshed his efforts to block his mind from the Eye. He felt the close breath of his woman on his long open slice as she choked him even closer for another deep, looping cut around his cheekbone. All of this because he was related to a shitty writer that no one had ever even heard of from half a thousand years ago, who was doubtless an infidel on top of everything else. He felt the knife separate muscles and tendons, and then the knife point turned this way and that in zigzags, cleanly dividing the thin skin of his face and the thick rind of white oily fat underneath that bled out and was caught in the towel, though some began to leak through and flow down his neck. He felt his wife daub these trickles and runs.

She next carved around his eyes and temples, never pulling out the knife, and then guided the thin blade high up through his eyebrow like the trail of a slug. First on one side, then down the other, tracing the point through every muscle, and he could hear the scrape and scratch of steel on bone and the bone sheathing that hurt so sharply when she made turns of the blade or when it got stuck. Her wild eyes never blinked, he sensed, and her tongue kept striking new poses with each refocus of her surgical concentration.

Then she began to take the flat tip of the knife and peel and pry up each flap of skin to lift them for some reason he could not tell yet. She carved slowly back and forth underneath them in wiping strokes, like peeling the skin off a slab of roast capon. Then, she took the towel and pinched the tip of the skin flaps, pulling very hard to see if each flap could be pried up enough to pull them. If a flap was not quite loose enough, she went under again to loosen the skin more. Old man Wazku watched the tip of that effective knife float very close to his eyeballs, and he saw the dark ruby color of his own blood decorating the steel. He believed he saw in the reflection the hash being made of his face. The hurt from the cutting, the cold air touching the slices, and the pinching and pulling was *very* severe, but he held his reactions bundled tight, and carefully smoothed them into unrelated thoughts.

A couple times he jumped, such as when his wife had to saw and stab through thick, waxy seams of nose cartilage. Blood running down his nostrils started to choke him. In the nose, his wife had to lever up and down and yank back and forth to finally break through. Wazku became aware of little Rat Killer on the floor staring up, circling in simpatico for his master and hoping for the best. Indira hammered the butt of the knife with her palm to get through tough parts. Her tongue wiggled in effort, but she did not apologize because she was borne onto some higher purpose.

Returning to the nose, Indira hammered and banged to the point she nearly broke her knife. At last, both nostrils were lain wide open like two gutters running up the middle of his face to his brow, and she seemed satisfied. Then she shaved away the beard and let the long bristly fronds fall on the floor and stick because of the weight of blood. An unruly pile of red fur amassed around their feet when the woman of Wazku stepped back to take perspective on her handiwork.

Now, she started cutting away the fat pads in the face. She leaned his chair back so that she could lay his head flat on the wood of the table and then she went for the hammer. Old Wazku did not know she was going for the hammer at first because he was drifting in a state of near delirium. But he certainly noticed when she smacked him so hard that there was a loud bang as of breaking crockery that was his cheekbone, and the dog started in the air like a coiled spring. Even the dog here grasped what level of savagery was being dealt. He licked his lips and cocked his head lopsided, remembering his own missing balls, and his big black eyes shone rich with understanding for what the poor old man was going through. He refused to look up any more at the old man and lay down with his jowls across his paws.

Indira viciously slammed down the hammer again to alter the other cheek, and the old man's head bounced a foot off the planks of the table. He squinched his face at her fury, his collar feeling sticky like honey. Indira comforted her man for that heavy blow and soothingly laid his cheek back down on the other side, then hefted high the hammer and brought it down with an even more rabid grimace of effort. *Whang!* His head ricocheted even *higher* off the table and he sat up straight in the chair, squinting at his woman while his hands gingerly cradled the mashed pan of his face.

Now, his wife laid aside the hammer. Working quickly with the towel for grip, she pushed around the broken cheekbones, yanked cut flaps of skin this way and that, and sewed them in order to make lumps and divots in the flesh. What began to emerge was the lumpy red crust of a fruit pie. All in, the face little resembled a face at all but for the fringe of weak, frazzled gray hair lining what was once a hairline and a beard line. Beady black eyes shined in dread anticipation out of twin anus-puckers on each side of a melted nose. The orbs, if they *were* eyes, stared expectantly from the scraps.

Indira shook her head at the mess. But she was almost finished. She hardened her mind and went at the final stitching as fast as she could, sinking the needle through, using pins to hold the flaps, feeling the vibration of the cotton thread when it pulled through the punctures. Her sandal bottoms slipped back and forth in slime, but she let this bother her little. Finally, she dropped all equipment and stood back as from a work of art. The poor creature stared back at her through the shiny black cow eyes that still looked like they had grown out of the pucker of an anus. He wondered how he looked, of course. The eyes seemed to hold some hope that he had not been made too hideous. But that was very much the optimistic figuring! He was *truly* hideous. The apparition held the mind in the memory of a liver pie with the cut ribbons of dough crossed on the top and then rendered into place by the baking.

And the wife smiled triumphantly.

She clasped her bloodied hands in happiness, for no one would ever recognize him again. He was now free to sit downstairs and go freely about the Al Fareeq, and no facial recognition capability would ever work on him. Indira and ordinary people like her had no idea about the sophistication of the surveillance capability aimed at them. Between the ghastly pie face and the weight loss, no one would ever guess it was him, Old Man Wazku. Of course, they would have to concoct a story about the woman of Wazku's new man, and the scandal of what the neighbors and the clerics might think about man-woman commingling.

"*Mirror!*" Wazku whispered.

She fetched him the broken piece from the corner sink.

Wazku let her hold it for him. He took in the clots and crude stitching. He did not bother turning his face side to side. The horror was plain. The anus eyes stared back at him with incongruous tufts of eyebrow hair above them. He looked at the seeping fluids leaking from the divots. Only the staring anus eyes gave it the semblance of a face. Wazku had never been a handsome fellow, but his shoulders sagged.

"Huh!" he said only.

Indira dropped piping hot moist towels over the face of wounds. But piping hot towels were *exactly* the wrong post-surgical method to use since the towels burned like acid, and so, as her poor man barely kept himself from leaping out of the butchery chair, she lovingly fetched him cool towels instead. This she did by wrapping a chunk of the icebox ice in the towel and then laid this upon the furious wounds. She saw the tension come out of his shoulders and arms as he lay now across the bed. His big chest heaved slowly with the recovery from the ordeal.

At last, she heard him sleep exhaustedly.

Poor Wazku. His stitches and the dried clots in the divots as he slept swelled into red heavings. He moaned in pain in his sleep and so she woke him to shut him up against God's Eye hearing. Frightened, they hid him back under the bed again. She applied a poultice her mother had taught her of olive oil, bay, and frankincense.

Finally, it was only light snores.

She prayed to Almighty God without irony for escape. She waited up all night, wondering if *they* would finally come.

At daybreak, Indira and Wazku were still alive.

Amazingly.

-22-

It was two months since Indira sewed her new quilt. In the first week, after the initial pain and swelling ebbed, she used the awl from her sewing basket to prize out the crumbly clots of dry blood that turned the puckers of skin the faint blue of lead. She could not leave them in to rot and possibly make him any uglier. At last, they decided together he could come downstairs, where they would begin their story for explaining who he was. In the morning, Indira painstakingly stuck to her usual routine and kept her thought activity resting on the casual music of day-to-day life. Customers began arriving in the sixth hour. Once or twice, her mind crept and she wondered about her performance in front of the God's Eye.

My balance is unsteady!

At the height of the morning rush, Indira clicked open the broom closet and Wazku stepped inconspicuously out in his hooded cloak and strolled out as would any customer leaving the shop. He mingled into the flow in the alley and made his way with the stooped posture of a beggar toward the plaza. There, he took a spot at the trees for beggars and opened his palm. On the fourth day, at a designated time, Indira came for her shopping. She made a show of giving this one beggar an alms. She lifted back the cowl a bit and squinted at the scars. Soon came the call to prayer, and Indira took his beggar's hand to temple. She pushed him ahead to pray with the men, while she climbed the stairs to the women's balcony. After service, she tarried at the bottom of the inlaid stairs to make sure he did not slip out ahead of her.

She led him straight to the imamti's chambers. This imamti knew Indira for the irregular times she and her late husband observed over the years, but he did not recall her name since he was not her primary cleric. Numerous petitioners crowded the imamti's chamber. When Indira had her chance, she asked:

"Imamti, what should I do with this beggar?"

The imamti gazed strangely at this unexpected riddle. He squinted over the hunched shoulders of the wretch. The cleric saw and smelled the grime worked into the weave of the black wool. He lifted the cowl an inch in sickened curiosity.

"Is he molesting you, my child?" he asked.

"What should I do with him, Imamti, this beggar?"

"It is the will of God what you would do to him, madam. What is it you wish to do with him?"

"I am a widow, Imamti. It is my coffee shop in Al Fareeq Quarter that needs help since my husband is lost to me."

"How was your husband lost, child?"

"Murder, Imamti. Black murder, unsolved!" She waved her hand to keep the memory at bay. "Is it the will of God that I remove this beggar to aid me at my shop? Tell me, Imamti, for I tell you I heard the voice of God Almighty in this service!"

He wanted to believe that God had leaned down to make a statement on charity to the Earth. And what man of the cloth would not want one less wretch away from destitution? The imamti looked at this wretch who smelt not as badly as the usual wretch in the gutter where old piss hung like an ammonia paste. "Of course it is the will of God, my child. Take him with my blessing, for God loves the merciful."

"Yes, Imamti. Bless you. But you would write up a charter declaring that I am a chaste widow and that this is a chaste bonding."

The Imamti looked at her queerly. "Thou dost not need such a plaque."

"Please, Imamti. I am a good wife."

"Go to your primary imamti. Ask it of him."

"I will. But holy words came to me in *your* mosqow, Imamti! *You* are the cleric closer to God! Please, Imamti. Now, I will make a donation to the mosqow."

The imamti gave her a tired look. "Bless you, sister. God is smiling on you. I will write up the plaque and have it delivered to your house."

He waved her toward the donation box. Indira pushed her donation into the slit scratched by too many coins to count. She made a show of holding the beggar's hand as they walked homeward. "God Almighty is charitable to the merciful! Hear me, O God! I have obeyed you and adopted a charge. Hear me, O God! Pity me and my late husband and this wretch that I will clean up and ease on his path, O God!" She spoke in the grandiloquent old style. "Take off thy cowl, o' wretch of mine! Show your face so that all shall recognize thee now as mine own and guard thee!"

He put back his cowl to show the berated head glistening in the sun. People staggered at the sight and would long recall this moment when the widow Wazku broke asunder in her mind and took in the wretch. The face! The scars! Was she now so strange in the head that she would take this one to bed in her legs' embrace? A widow was entitled to help with her business, though of course she must not entitle herself to sex after the death of the husband. This last was forbidden! She could be stoned in the square for adultery. But why pluck *this* one off the dung-stained road?

To the gate, they arrived together.

"I am a crazy widow. I have no desire to have intercourse with *any* man. I take in this beggar wretch because I have been directed to do so by our Lord! None of you have volunteered or sent an able-bodied son or daughter to help, and I cannot afford to retire. I will have charity for this wretch. He will dwell in this house and not in my bed. If anyone has any objections, please say so now. Do not wag thine tongues behind my back to make trouble with the clerics. I have sought permission from the imamti, and he is sending along a declaration I shall nail upon this gate. I am Indira, the Widow of Wazku, and this wretch is now my possession in the eyes of Almighty God." She led him in by the hand and left the gate open behind so that any might see from the road what the pair were up to fixing a dinner.

After dinner, she locked him outside the gate where he slept like a dog on his side. The little rat killer dog slept with him to keep watch for rat herds and other dogs. The next day, Indira sought the permission from her primary imamti. He had heard the story by now, and he too regarded in some alarm the moon-cratered face with the anus eyes but believed that God moved in mysterious ways.

This holy man squinted in doubt. "I do not recognize you, beggar."

The beggarly wretch made no reply.

"From where dost thou hail?"

Wazku pointed. "Il Tiki. My family lost to demons!"

The holy man frowned. The Il Tiki Quarter stood clear on the opposite side of the metropolis, and anyone who had lost family to demons was a person for whom to feel sympathy and very little bother. Besides, who was to keep track of such things as the wanderings of the beggar population?

"Go with God, you both."

After a month, he was allowed to sleep within.

People in the quarter approved of this determined show of chastity. Indira's bizarre generosity could only help repel evil. They indeed saw their sister as a woman of God. Nobody *dared* think the widow and this one had sex at night.

And they would be wrong!

For once they felt free, nightly did the couple frolic in vigorous unison upon the rope bed, squeaking the hemp in high poetry. Sex was how they mollified the terrible raking she made across the face to liberate the man.

And the little terrier kept watch below the fun, licking his jowls as he peered into the gnawed holes in the wall.

-23-

Rabbi Hector had not visited the shop in months.

Demon Night had come and gone. Life in the quarter had settled back to normal. The rabbi snuck into the shop one day afterwards and ordered a cockroach falafel. As he ate, he looked for an opportunity to catch the widow's eye. Indira kept her back to him. She had felt tremendous relief all these months never seeing him and had hoped he had found another shop. She and "Helper" had slipped out of the quarter for Demon Night, and even out of the city in the way that had become their secret escape. Luckily, the quarter this year had been totally untouched on Demon Night. Privately, Indira hoped this forgiveness came because she had rejected the rabbi's sexual advances and reproached his insane explanations. But there he sat, aiming his gaze at her again as if only more dangerous ideas flitted like bats in his head.

"Where is your 'helper,' Mrs. Wazku?" he asked teasingly.

Indira implored the rabbi with her pupils.

"Where is your 'helper,' Mrs. Wazku? I should like to meet him." The rabbi's eyes fairly giggled with the question.

"Perhaps after this gentleman leaves?" Indira scowled at the rabbi, indicating her last customer with his back to them.

The remaining customer said over his shoulder, "I do not mind. I too am a Jew, familiar with much that is awful. Call me Ishmael."

The rabbi grinned at Indira. "He is known to me."

Indira glared acidly at the rabbi, then glanced uneasily up the stairs. "Helper!" she called aloft softly, afraid of being too loud.

Peering up through the seams in the floor, the rabbi and the other Jew, Ishmael, saw a figure stand from the rope bed and edge toward the stair head. They saw the little dog come down as well with "Helper." The atrocity of his melted-dough face looked sheepishly first at the rabbi, then at the other Jew, the cow eyes wet and fragile. The Jew Ishmael stared, soaking in all the answers to his curiosity regarding the story about this man. The orange last light of day made the utterly ruined face look painted.

The little dog sat by Indira's foot and yawned.

"Helper, these men wanted to meet you."

Helper stood on the last step, hands folded shyly.

"Tis the spitting image of thine late husband," said Ishmael.

Indira's eyes flashed at him angrily.

"Of course, it cannot be," Ishmael assented.

"To this, I agree," commented the rabbi.

Indira felt her paranoia rising. Three minutes passed and nothing happened. Her diaphragm was near to burst and she breathed finally. "He is a comfort, and I'm sure he does not appreciate this, your nasty jokes."

The rabbi put up his finger for silence and crept out the front gate. He was gone fifteen minutes before he stepped in with a little dark-haired boy of four years old. The lad came in nervously as if he had no idea why he was here or what to do with himself. He stood wooden with hands behind him and his big, shining child's eyes made not a twitch of recognition for Mrs. Wazku, though he kept steering glances at Helper's lumpy face. The rabbi rested both his chubby-fingered hands on the brief shoulders of the lad as if to reassure him that they had found the right house.

"This is my adopted nephew, Ezekiel," the rabbi explained nervously.

All of them waited timidly.

They stood in complete silence, waiting for five minutes. When nothing happened, the rabbi started explaining again:

"He is not really a Jew, if his race bothers you. He is an orphan by demons. One day the boy would like to own a coffee shop such as this. I brought him to show you what a good boy he is so that we may discuss a price for him sometime becoming your apprentice." He patted the boy's shoulder. The boy continued to stare back and forth at the adults. He also watched the dog most keenly.

Indira thought very carefully about this statement in her mind. *He does not look like much and is far too unclever looking.*

Helper turned to see what she thought, and she frowned back. Helper was surprised she was so unimpressed by the boy. Indira reconsidered. She knew she had a tendency to be too harsh in her appraisals.

"He is a very fine boy, as you can see," prompted the rabbi, still with his hands on the child. "I shall take very good care of him until he comes to work for you."

"He is a lucky boy to have the rabbi as his guardian," said Ishmael. "He could probably be taught to read and write. Perhaps to figure."

Indira's economical gaze took in every detail about the child. How his hair, face, and eyes shone with health and intelligence. *Well, perhaps he would be a wise investment.* "Let us agree, then, Rabbi." The widow gestured with the folded rag. "My concern is that he is a Jew. If we agree to apprentice him, will he be hounded by the authorities because he is an outcast from the True Religion?" She made herself look away from the rabbi and the boy as if the bargain didn't matter to her.

The rabbi shrugged smilingly. "As I said, he is *not* a Jew. His parents were of the Faith. And as you see, I am left mostly to myself."

"The boy looks agreeable as an apprentice, Rabbi. We must only decide when he shall begin. It is late. Goodnight to you both." She shooed the men out with her rag and Helper barred the door for the night. When he looked back at Indira, she saw a pale shine of happiness burning bright under the tangle of scars. She twisted aside her own feelings and hung her rag over the water spigot. She pressed back a few strands of gray-white hair on both sides of her temples and puffed in relief.

"We shall have help," Helper's split mouth said carefully to her.

"Yes. I did not want to divulge my excitement," she replied. "Lest the rabbi will Jew up his price. But the boy looks well cared for."

"Yes!" Helper said. "He *does* look good! We are *very* lucky!"

"God is good to us," Indira panted.

"Yes. God is *very* good to us!"

They went upstairs, hand in hand. They lay back into bed and continued to hold hands as they thought of the boy and how their future looked a little brighter with an apprentice who would learn to take over the shop from them.

-24-

Two months hence, the rabbi returned.

With him, he brought two items.

The first was the boy, Ezekiel, and the second was his leather sack sprinkled with aluminum dust. At sight of the boy, Indira bent her excitement to a flatline so the Jew would not take advantage. Her self-control was not so hard since along with the boy came the heavy sack that caused her a squirt of adrenal dread. The rabbi lifted the bag in offering to Indira. The bag looked rather well-worn since last time she saw it. This scared her since it meant he might have been blabbing his ideas far afield.

The widow flapped her arms and fled up the stairs to keep away from him. The rabbi went to the foot of the stair.

"Please, widow! Be unfeared!"

He said this in normal voice!

She plopped on the bed corner to wait for him to leave. Helper came up just then from the trap after having checked the cages. He looked pleasantly at the boy but had heard not a word about the sparkly hood since his wife dared not pile on any more risk. Helper laid down his three fine rats and eight runts while he lifted his knees out. The boy's mouth watered. Helper carried his rats all by the tails to the counter. The dog bounded out of the trap now and landed admirably on all fours like a supreme killer. He, too, looked curiously at the visitors, knowing something was up.

"Helper!" the rabbi urged. "I deliver the boy, Ezekiel. And I should speak with you and the widow." He held the hood suggestively.

"Name your price," Helper said.

But the rabbi approached Helper carrying the hood and whispered, "I will speak with you under *this*." Helper's eyes stared mildly curious, but he went under, thinking it some article of the Jewish faith. "Helper, this is an invention I made to block out the mind reading so that we may speak freely!" He knew from Wazku's eyes how crazy this sounded. "I have assurances that this invention works!"

Helper shoved the thing off his head as if it was a snake about to bite. His anus eyes glared the message that he wanted no part of it.

The rabbi smirked understandingly and tried to put the hood back on him, but Helper would have none of it. Indira came to the top of the stairs. The rabbi beheld the expression on her face and lowered his own face in frustration. He felt *so* exhausted trying to convince people of what he knew to be true!

After a minute, he felt a reassuring hand on his shoulder.

It was the widow. She stood beside him and lifted the sack, gesturing for Helper to come join. Helper's eyes glared as if they had both lost their minds! But her face had taken on such a calm expression of leadership. Her alone he trusted, given all they had endured together since his "death."

"Thank you! Thank you!" the rabbi breathed under the hood. "I have so much to tell! First, have I not shown you enough proof of problems with God's Eye? Of enough problems with State security?"

"What is this—'State security'?" Indira challenged.

"How we are watched and governed!"

Indira nodded. It was true! Look at all they had concealed. Who would *ever* have thought all this was possible? And Demon Night had come and gone. Surely, death would have come by now unless something had happened to soften God like the rabbi had said. "But how do I know you are not a *spy*?" Indira accused the Jew. "How do I know you are not scaring up trouble among dimwits to turn us over to the Robes?"

"No, no, no! Indira, please! Why would I ever do such a thing?"

"For relief! For a dispensation for being a Jew! Why should I believe this hood does as you say? Or that *you* are not the traitor against our governors and the peaceful way of our God-fearing society! I hope they hear me say it!"

The rabbi spluttered, having no answer.

"How can a stinking hood of ordinary cow skin foil the penetration into the mind of God Almighty? It is *far* more likely that this is a trick."

The rabbi became desperate.

"I hid the boy! He is safely back to you! This is your husband! He is returned! He is returned from *certain* death as all of us know!"

Wazku's scars signaled horror.

"This is not my husband!" Indira hissed. "That is not our boy! He is dead! This man is a rat from the gutter that I selfishly brought home to be my slave!" In fury, she struck the rabbi twice with her open hand at his face.

The rabbi was so stunned that he accepted the blows without even flinching. He almost doubted what he had been told by his sources. "Of course it is, Mrs. Wazku. As you wish." He bowed slightly. "But even without my sources, it is plain that this man is your husband, but that you merely mutilated him."

Hearing this plain truth, Indira felt a new layer of dread. Indeed, how did the rabbi know all he knew? She did not know what to believe anymore. Her doubt turned the page to a new deadness in her heart. How could she not have seen this before? There was nowhere to turn, even in your own mind. *Only the rats are free.*

She began to experience an actual crisis of faith toward her entire universe. Her fears bubbled up as she remembered the words of the coal monger so far back. She believed now, for the first time, that in that city of high buildings far away, there *must* be another race of people who lived there, and *they* were the demons! *They* were behind this plot to trick them all with the rabbi. Those were not just government office buildings where no one really lived, for *who* could resist living in those buildings even if they were afraid of heights? They were not *mountains,* as some claimed. Another race of people lived there in the Tall City beyond Second Gate. *Why do I suddenly think this? Why do I now have some idea what the poor coal monger yelled about?* The apartments of the low bureaucrats beyond First Gate—this was all a sham to keep stupid people like her from knowing the full extent of how some lived in that *other* world!

Her thoughts stumbled forward like tripping feet. She now suspected that these many things about her life were *not* the result of religious magic nor God. They were the result of *things*—not magics. She almost believed that they had *nothing* to do with God. She had no idea how they worked. But she believed magical things must have something to do with a *loving* God, not a God who would kill his children over nothing.

These matters of ugliness in their lives, they were *things.*

They were magic-*like* things. Things designed to keep her down.
Where did such an idea come from? Keep her "down"?
What did that even *mean?*
Indira stared in disbelief at her own thoughts.
This entire world is a conspiracy.
And what was a "conspiracy"? I do not know the word, but I sense the meaning.

Now, Indira knew she was the walking dead with these thoughts. This was all the rabbi's fault. She had never had these thoughts before now. He had unleashed them on her like a sickness. Because he knew things she did not. How did he know? She must find out how he knew what he claimed to know.

This is exactly what you are not supposed to think!

Her heart pinched at a far-off noise. The noise grew closer. Surely, at last, they flew now to her house while she stood stupidly beneath this hood thinking she could get away with breaking the only law that mattered. Her bone marrow trembled in its tubes. *They* were finally coming. She *heard* them coming now. The roar, almost like rumbling thunder. Shaking her marrow. Shaking the ground. Because she questioned how the world should be.

She spat savagely at the floor for the cleric Jew who had finally brought ruin onto her house. It was her own fault. She looked at the pure horror in her husband's face. *Yes, my husband!* They had known all along.

"Rabbi, you have trifled with my very life long enough! *Who* was it that you listened to who betrayed us?" She had to shout over the growing noise.

The rabbi's face puckered facetiously.

She glared furiously at him.

The roar kept growing.

"I hear voices! . . . In the Alley Wabeer!"

This wild claim stabbed Indira in the heart. *The Alley Wabeer was the place of ghosts!* Where the ancient mosqow collapsed. The insane went there to die. "What dost thou *mean?*" The roar now rattled the dishware. "Quick! They come!"

"No! No, Indira! My friends tell me! We are *protected!*"

She knew now the entire black truth of the world.

Only the rats are free!

"Whom do you call 'friends,' Rabbi?"

"In the deep dark of that accursed alley. I hid there late one night when the heat made a rat wave that drove me from my hut! They *told* me! How we live is unfair! We are robbed of all freedom! They watch! They *know!*"

The rabbi picked out of the air strange new words that yet she knew by the sense of them. But never had anyone ever uttered the words *unfairness* and *freedom*. No one ever dared even *think* them.

The Robes were nearly here. Their rumble shook the floor. The rats swarmed in panic from the cellar keeps and ran toward the door. Indira felt them scuffing around her ankles in greasy droves.

"Tell me of your allies, Rabbi! Who helped you take me down?"

"They tell of what is!"

The air was ripping apart.

"*Who* was it? . . . *Angels?*" She mocked him.

"A candle lit . . . I *saw*—our *friends!*"

The rabbi spoke roundabout. She would choke it out of him!

The rip in the air aimed directly down on them. Indira Wazku lost her water. Her husband grabbed her. She would never see her grandson again. She ripped off the hood to see him one last time, standing in his own piss by the door.

The rabbi stared, agog.

He screamed over the incoming shriek:

"*—the Robes told me!*"

-25-

The boom blew their feet from underneath. The entire quarter rocked.

Helper, Indira, the rabbi—they had never heard a bomb. They had not even the concept of what one was. The puppet shows in the plaza on Holy Days never said anything about bombs or explosions because for them, all weapons but knives had disappeared four hundred years ago. Even the word "weapon" had been scrubbed from their language. Left ignorant, they had no idea what the deafening blast was.

No one dared even look out a window. Then, they heard a cry in the street. Helper hurried upstairs to the higher balcony windows to see. Indira watched her man from the steps. "I see nothing!" Helper stated, mystified.

The rabbi listened. "There are people!"

Indira was unsure why the Robes played this game. "I cannot stay! I will fly!" She rushed into the alley, pursued by the men, the boy, and the dog. Neighbors looked toward the plaza. "It came from the Plaza Jumil!"

Indira watched the sky like a hawk for the Robes. The crowd grew larger as they approached the plaza. She wept as she led the boy along in the flow, clutching his tiny hand, ready to push him away lest they come.

"Be brave, little one! Be brave, lest they come! Do not stop running! Do not look back for me if I throw thy hand! Dost thou hear?"

The little boy whimpered. "Who comes, lady? Shall I be afeared?"

"Look away if they come! Or I'll box thine ears!"

"Yes, lady, I hear you!"

The boy remembered the rabbi expressly telling him how to address the lady. "You must only call her 'Lady'! If you use any other name, the demons will come!" The boy had been confused by the entire experience, starting from when he was whisked away half asleep to live in a room below ground where there was no one but the weird rabbi with the cowl hanging in the corner on a peg and the books hid under flat stones in the floor. The little room smelled of the old earth it was dug from and lay hidden below the rabbi's hovel. The loneliness had made the boy deeply sad. He retained so little memory of his father, and none of his mother. This hurt so much, because he did not want to believe his father had abandoned him. He remembered the story about the runaway horse. His memory echoed with impressions of how much his father had adored him. *If only he had not lost that love!* But the boy was relieved to be out of the ground and back in the familiar house, though his grandpa was unrecognizable and he mostly knew him by the pleasant smell of his beard. As he ran along, his bare feet slapping on the cobbles, the boy hoped nothing happened to split up the family again.

The Plaza Jumil was a mass of people of the sort that would come out for a fire. But there were no blazing buildings or families jumping for their lives. To the right, a dense crowd the size of four houses seemed to be looking at their own feet. Indira saw a shading of dust in the air, but that was it. This crowd to the right was not opening to let others in, and they shuffled left and right as people shoved in, all the while continuing to stare at their feet.

"What is it? What happened?" Indira asked other women in shawls holding on to children.

Indira's foot rolled on a fleshy object the size of a small fire log. It looked like a foot. She toed it with her shoe. The thing rolled, with toes on one end.

"A-yee! 'Tis a foot!" Indira cried out.

Another woman kicked it.

"A-yee! It *is* a foot!"

A teenager tossed the foot skillfully with a back kick, fearful of actually holding it. Boys and men laughed in grim discomfort. Some women and girls laughed, too.

"A foot for playing football!" a pretty girl urged the boys.

"Somebody lick it!" a boy yelled.

The kids started kicking it. The game quickly became to try to kick the foot up into another's face or get the dirty stump on their clothes.

"Here is an arm!" someone yelled nearby.

Indira, the rabbi, and Helper scaled the bank steps to get to a better view. But even from the bank they saw nothing over the crowd looking at a thing on the ground. Indira got a glimpse of the maroon cap of her imamti down front.

"What is it? What is it? What is in there?" women yelled.

"Bodies fell from the sky! They hit, just there!"

People pointed where all the people stood looking.

"Bodies?!" a woman said. "Demon bodies?"

"*People* bodies. From the sky."

"From the *sky?*"

Women clucked at the lie.

"You mean they fell from the bank building?" asked a woman, pointing. "They jumped off the bank, maybe?" It was the tallest building on the plaza. But how did a body get from the bank roof all the way to the center of the plaza?

"No, no. They came from the sky!"

"They fell from higher than the temple minaret!"

The woman near Indira scowled impatiently. "Get the imamti! Ask the imamti if bodies can fall from the sky!"

"I saw them fall!" said a young man of twenty. "I saw them fall and burst on the ground like watermelons!"

"But how can they fall from the sky? Like *that* one says!" The skeptical woman and a loudmouth woman began to fight. They grabbed fistfuls of the other's hair and fell so that the patch of long hair between the legs of one flashed as she kicked. People laughed and moved in to see the fight while Indira started home with the boy, keeping him close on her hip, searching the sky for them swooping down.

At home, she put him to bed in the crib of twigs.

"How can bodies fall from the sky, lady?"

"It is crazy talk. Shush with you." Indira sat at the window seat looking past the quarter at the otherworldly skyscrapers.

Could the wind carry them such a long way?

It seemed impossible.

She warmed a cup of hot water to sip as she sat at the window, feeling her stomach grind over her dumb luck today. She had thought the roar in the sky was them for sure this time. She dared not hope for too much. How tragic her Portrait would be for a tiny, good boy who was already denied so much.

His eyeballs would be scarred for life if she went that way.

-26-

"Go on in, Deputy Director."

The adjutant motioned Aras to the thirty-foot cast bronze door that only Tech could open and shut. The massive door opened silently to the massive office.

Aras strode into Chief Berns's sanctuary that would one day be his.

The space was huge, made of chrome and white enamel with soft, elegant horizontal gold ribs in the wall that emphasized how the space swept toward the walls of windows on both ends. The silver-blue cloud tops poured light into the Palace office of Aras's boss.

The chief faced the horizon on the other side of the vast ebony slab that served as his desk. It had nothing on it but a small collection of photographs and a discreet oil painting in a stand. The frames of each were exquisite, made of materials ranging from burled yew to ibex horn to rough-poured gold studded with turquoise tiles. The huge office reflected the patrician tastes of a Party member from a very old family. The chief had his hands clasped behind his gray short-cut suit. He frowned concernedly over his shoulder as Aras came around the huge desk.

"Do we know who it was yet?" Berns said fretfully.

"It was Nolan Sellers, sir."

Berns half turned. "The chancellor's chief law?"

Tech had taken an hour to give the particulars. Berns had been so upset waiting that he sealed himself in his office until the news came. "He was returning from a . . ."—Aras hesitated—"vacation in Saigon. He trajected in without difficulty until suddenly he just tumbled out of his flight path to his condo in the Palace."

Berns studied his lieutenant.

"And fell into a *slum*?"

Aras nodded apologetically.

Berns turned back to the clouds.

"I have the feeling that Tech isn't giving us all the answers."

Berns leaned on the balls of his feet. His brow knit so deeply that Aras wondered if his boss knew something he didn't.

"Maybe Tech is traumatized by what happened too," Berns suggested. "Maybe it scaled back interaction until it can make a thorough investigation of its systems." Berns put both his hands on the high back of his chair. He lifted the lid of a humidor. He put the cigar in his mouth unlit and turned back to the window. "A sex vacation?"

Aras had omitted that detail. Sellers had been on a sex vacation to Saigon. Aras had tried to glimpse if some tawdry sex party connection existed between Sellers and anyone else in the Palace high enough to establish a Tech block of the sort that they were running into. Any such connection should make no difference; there were no secrets on sexual preferences or history. Had someone ordered Tech to cover for the lie? It made no sense. A year ago, Aras would never have even thought this way. But a year ago, none of this would have been thought possible.

Berns got a ping from Tech about Aras glimpsing up possible sex connections with Chief Law Sellers and any higher ups. He understood his deputy chief's inquiry. What could be happening? Privacy did not exist. Sex and abject stupidity were accepted vices. No one had any hang-ups about anything. In a society without mystery, nothing drew attention except something like this where a veil seemed to have been drawn over Sellers' last twenty-four hours.

Aras had met Sellers at State events. He never cared for him. "Kids were his thing," he continued. "He split time between slums and the Orient. He seems to have had little interest in Occidental children. There was that incident with him ten years ago and the child here. So, could that be blocking his case?"

The chief turned his chair to the view and sat. "I don't see why."

"He approached the child of a Party Docent. He abducted the child. A small boy. It was all kept very quiet. For some reason, Tech didn't protect the child."

Berns lowered his head. "I remember." Berns chewed the cigar from one side of his mouth to the other, leaning on his knees.

No one knew why Tech had left the child of a top Party family unprotected. It was the only case of its kind ever. "Do you know something about that case, Chief?"

Berns slowly rubbed his wide temples with his index fingers. "No. I don't know anything, Milton. I doubt it has anything to do with his . . . death."

Aras hung back, waiting for the chief to say more.

"What of the other, the Docent?"

"Sellers outranked him. So, no one bothered with it."

"Was there a formal complaint?"

"A complaint? What for?" Berns laid his hands over his silver-blonde crew cut. "Not with that degree of disparity in power. Sellers apparently was asked to see the mutual benefit of keeping his *pursuits* outside the Party."

"Could Seller's death be foul play, Chief?"

Berns puffed his cheeks. "Murder? We know that can't happen."

"Did the parents of the boy just bide their time, and this is politics, not Tech?"

"Murder can't happen," Berns repeated flatly.

Aras twisted his shoulders. Who knew what deals the top Party brass made with each other? Could they now tinker with Tech on certain issues like this? It would be disastrous if they could. It would spell the end of public trust. There could be no double standard in the Law. Party members could not hurt other Party members.

"Oh, shit. I don't know, Milton. Christ!" Berns snapped.

"Sir, falling out of the sky is a horrible way to die that is going to scare a lot of people and make them not trust flying."

A breeze ruffled the front edge of Berns's crew cut. The green patchwork of the forests and farms run by Tech shone beyond the slums. The slum outside the wall looked like wet ash. Nearer their feet, the Federal City bounded in spires and floating buildings that complimented the human soul.

Sellers was at this height last night when his Tech failed, Aras thought. And for some reason, his reentry screamed like a bomb falling.

"What are you thinking, Aras?" Berns asked.

"If I didn't know better, I'd think someone committed murder, Chief." Aras thought about Tilly's remark about Tech errors and serving trays.

Berns pulled his ear. "Either way, it's bad."

"Come on, Chief. This is the first accident in two hundred years. Something awful like this *has* to happen sooner or later."

"*You* said this would be the sign."

Aras rolled his eyes behind his boss's back. "This would be the sign, sir. But this isn't *it*." Aras wondered what Tech made of this conversation.

Berns looked around at his deputy. "What makes you so cocksure that they aren't so much smarter than we are that they've cracked the code and now they are both alive *and* conscious?"

An unfazed smile spread across Aras's mouth. He stared down at the world with Berns. "Because they haven't *announced* that they are now in command. All is quiet." He lifted his hand to indicate the silence.

The chief nodded, turning back to the view.

On the way back to the Ministry, Aras decided to look past Tech and call authorities in Saigon himself. By afternoon, he had talked with a guy in Security.

"Your boy wasn't over here just having sex with kids. Recently, he had been going on a bit of a spree, actually snuffing kids in the slums."

"Did he get a clearance?"

"Not technically."

"And you let him do it?"

"What would you guys have done?"

"When did he start this?"

"Four years ago."

"No one said anything to him?"

"Some he paid for. Some he just . . . took. He kept running up his tab and saying he was good for it. We figured he was, considering who he was."

"How many do you know about?"

"He paid for five. Like maybe twenty altogether."

Aras wondered about the coincidence. "I'm trying to figure out if somebody on our end maybe took this fellow out for a thing he did over here. If I said out loud that I wondered if someone on your end took him out, what would you say?"

"I doubt it. If they took him out, how would they get paid?"

"Paid? Who are you talking about?"

"People down below."

Aras had forgotten how Asia did not have slums. But ordinary people also did not have First Rank privileges. "What if they did it to send a message?"

"To who? They know they can't touch political level."

Aras glimpsed up the word "accident" to make sure of its meaning. It was an archaic term. He wondered if maybe he should try to find an ancient dictionary in the Archives if Tech twisted the meaning of the word to hide something from him. Could Tech be getting old? Could Tech be getting political? But since Tech was nothing but EM and Cloud computation, could it even grow old?

Just then, Ginger rang in. Aras put in a quick note to Tilly and Lever asking if they could meet up to talk about the Sellers matter.

"Are you kidding me?" Ginger said straight off.

"No. And he was killing kids in Saigon slums. At the least. He was coming home from a sexcapade."

"Oh, no! Baby, that's what I do!"

"Not like him," Aras scoffed.

"I'm scared to fly!" Ginger paused. "How many kids did he kill?"

"A number. There's a lot of questions still."

"This is *crazy!* That perv. You really think somebody tried to murder him? How could they? Tech would never let it happen! Right?"

"Come on, honey. One fatality in three hundred years?"

"A what?"

"A fatality. It means somebody dies."

"Shit. Would Tech ever let a murder happen?"

Aras snickered at her. "Are you worried, sugar?"

"What did they call those? On your back?"

"Parachutes."

"Parachutes!" Ginger laughed at the idea.

"Look," Aras pointed out, "if you're flying Mach Three and you had a Tech fail, that parachute has cords that would cut you into wet hunks. They had these nylon straps that cinched up in your groin. They'd pull apart your pelvis. Your shit would be flying through the air. Your tits, your snatch, that beautiful face of yours."

"That wouldn't be good."

"You're screwed either way, baby."

"Well, thanks for cheering me up." She waited while she thought of anything else to say. "What time you coming home?"

"Six. Get some Chinese."

"Tits in brown sauce? Snatch with bean curd?"

"*What* did you say?"

Ginger laughed as she faded out.

-27-

The rabbi and Ishti arose like shadows near closing.

They looked around in a way that let Indira and Helper know they wanted to talk more, maybe about the latest happening.

The angel, or demon, that fell from Heaven.

When the last customer left, the dog lay on his back across the threshold. He looked up at Helper and briefly tapped his little stub tail on the floor.

The entire quarter had buzzed of nothing else since. The impact crater. Body pieces strewn for blocks. An eyeball showed up a mile away. Children were still playing football with the rotten foot.

The rabbi nodded. "It was a high government official!"

Indira turned away in disbelief. *How could bureaucrats fly?* People were saying now that certain people could fly through the sky like birds.

"Do not doubt me, Indira," the rabbi advised.

"Why do you persist in this rubbish?" she whispered.

"What do *you* think it was?" the rabbi asked. She put up her palm to stop his nonsense and jerked her broom to continue sweeping. "Would you like to know how a body can fall out of the sky like that?" The rabbi gazed at the husband and wife. He read in the anus eyes that the husband wanted to hear. The wife did too, though she punched her twig broom at the floor as if she were not listening. "It is because our high officials have the ability to fly like stars in the sky!" He flicked his fingers in imitation of bird wings. This time, Indira saw with satisfaction that even Ishti's gullible face frowned skeptically. The rabbi followed her gaze to the face of his sidekick, who now perhaps had begun to doubt him as well. "'Tis truth!"

Helper slupped his melted lips. "How can be such a thing? Men flying."

"Yes. Who told you this?" Indira intoned. "Your Robes?"

"I tell you, friends," the rabbi said. "*They* have spoken with me twice since the angel fell. More than this, they have agreed to let me bring you too!"

Indira stopped pecking with the broom. Helper sucked in air.

"Why would they?" Indira breathed.

"To help get out the word."

"*What* word?"

The rabbi glanced sidelong. "That they are with us!"

The idea bowled Indira. Their pitilessness and cruelty ruled the world. Each minute waiting for punishment from them for a year had lain ruin to her nerves. Imagining the enforcers of sin and blasphemy as allies was hysteria!

And yet, Indira felt the cow eyes of her husband on her. *He* was a walking, talking contradiction. He watched her, the deep eyes confessing how his beliefs were aligning impossibly more to the rabbi than to her.

"They *did* let me go, Indira," he said softly.

The rabbi looked at Helper. "What is this?"

Helper hesitated. "I should not say!"

"Come! See how openly we speak?" the rabbi urged.

Helper quickly told the details of the Jolly Man and his months spent in frozen animation. When Helper finished, the rabbi stared crazily at Indira.

"Dost this not confirm the rabbi's tale?" Ishti demanded.

"What do you know of it, sweep?" Indira challenged.

Ishti cowed. "I know what I have heard from another source."

"*What* source?" Indira snapped, ready to jab the broom in his eyes.

Ishti yanked up his hand in vow. "I know of another source like the rabbi, and possibly a third." The rabbi opened wide his arms and hands to beseech to Indira for his own sanity. "And, frankly, others are speaking their minds!"

"Mass hysteria!" Indira warned.

"Yet you too now speak and think more loudly!" Ishti observed.

"No! Only to block your craziness from me!" Indira shoved her broom into the closet. She returned to the table, trembling. Her spine looked soft.

"I will tell you now," the rabbi began, "they told me only to speak of them and this offer until this night in the tenth hour. And then no more until further word." He looked at his friends. "Wouldst thou not like to see the Robes?" Indira pissed him away with a wave. "They aim to begin what they call a *rebellion!*"

"A *what?*" Indira said in pure disgust.

"It is a word they use. It means all of us fighting back at once!"

Indira glared at the pitiable Jewish fool. "You dance with lunacy in the brain! How could such a thing even *begin* to happen?"

"If there is Palace intrigue."

She huffed balefully. "What are they to God? And why would they want *us?*" She looked scrawny little Ishti up and down.

"I do not know! Bear witness to the Robes!"

"I will do no such thing. I am content in my shop." She blocked her thoughts from any more handling of these ideas. Truly, she had no problem with the Palace. Whoever they were was fine with her! She would not risk her own good fortune. She was thankful to God for all she had been given back and would chance no part of it.

"The man who fell from the sky was picked because he was a very bad man," the rabbi said. "And he was not the only one. Other bad ones also fell. The people of the Palace do not know yet of this intrigue. He bought poor children like chickens at the market. It was for *this* that they sent the warning!" The others listened intently.

"A warning to whom?" Indira asked, barely audible. "To do what?"

"They are not happy with how we are treated."

"*Who* isn't? And *why* should they care about us?"

The rabbi had no answer.

"No one sells children to be killed! They sell them out for hire!" Indira said. "Only demons make such waste! Your entire tale is preposterous."

Again, the rabbi had no retort.

Indira shook her head. "I am uninterested."

"I am," said Helper. "I will go hear the Robes."

The rabbi nodded. "We shall go the third night of the Black Moon, in the twelfth hour. We are to think no more of it until we go." The rabbi paused for emphasis. "Look in my eyes. The Robes said we must think nothing more about it until then, for the other side is waking up to the rebellion."

On the appointed night after the moon's waning, Helper met the rabbi and the man called Ishmael in Alley Sumatra off the plaza. Their sandals padded soundlessly over the cobbles side by side as they walked to Ishti's house. The rabbi barely touched his knuckles to the door and

Ishti slipped out. The men continued on past the Ramparts Square where a cook did not see them when he tossed a pale of dishwater into the gutter, and past the livery where a stable boy brushed down a pair of mules and pulled from his brush a wad of hair and dropped it.

Soon, the group arrived at their destination. The Alley Wabeer loomed dark and crooked ahead, tight enough to make a trap very easy. This alley had a most nasty reputation for its ghosts from the great killing two hundred years ago. For these reasons, few people dared live in the buildings along its slithery length that ended at the burned hulk of the Great Dahlia Mosqow, full of ghosts.

The foursome looked up and down the Alley of the Mirror and up at the windows for snoopers. They crossed the Alley of the Mirror and fetched on their toe tips into the engulfing dark of the Wabeer. The hair stood up in chicken skin on their necks and arms. The Alley Wabeer tacked back and forth, black as pitch, the ruin a crumbled shadow ahead with empty eyes filled with sky. The rabbi led the way to the old mosqow's towering back wall and stopped.

"It is here where they appear," he whispered.

"Why here, Rabbi?" Ishti inquired.

The rabbi shrugged. "The ruin is the old temple. The ghost of what happened on this spot scares many away." He dared not tell the other part of it.

"What kind of temple?"

"Originally, a Jewish temple."

Ishti nodded. "I knew not the Jews had such things."

"Long ago, it was permitted."

Ishti nodded contentedly. "So, the Robes are Jews?"

The rabbi and Ishmael ignored their little friend with brotherly compassion. They stood and waited. Every scuffle made by a rat put them on alert.

An hour later, the four friends sat in a row against the hard wall. Ishti moved his foot to take pressure off the leg nerve. "What is the time?"

"Past the thirteenth hour, I suspect," the rabbi said.

"What say you? Are they coming, Rabbi?" Wazku said.

"Something must have happened."

The men gathered themselves to leave.

Just then, overhead came a waffling sound as of a giant flock of sparrows. The sound grew until the air swirled in a slow spiral upward, encircling them, catching their cloaks and beards in its heavy draft. Then a sort of rent happened, as if an iron door released an invisible killer to come up behind, quick as a flash. Ishti, rabbi, Helper, and Ishmael all felt the deadly presence join them, and the air touching the skin of their necks went fully dead while the slow cyclone turned soundlessly outside.

They appeared. Two tall, fluttering, still-as-death figures, heavy as a world without sunlight, behind and to the sides. Their huge, evil presence was more a *feeling* than something verifiable by one's eyes in the dark. Ishti squinted to see. Helper looked up also at the shroud-like sentinel looming over the rabbi with a cavern where the hood cloaked a face. He *thought* he saw radiant, blood-brown eyes deep inside.

Do not fear us.

The voices were like breaking wood. They arose in Helper's own skull!

"These are friends," rabbi said fearfully. "They doubted my words."

The Robes said nothing.

"You said to bring friends. To spread word."

Do not fear us. We guard you.

Helper and Ishmael stared, saucer-eyed. Ishti could not look.

"What do you want of us?" Helper croaked.

The air gently spiraled. It felt greatly pressurized as if the Robes disrupted the very nature of existence by holding in any one place such terrible power to destroy. Their scratching, mechanical, synchronized voices whispered into the mind. As if they lived and watched unseen eternally behind your own thoughts.

We know you are Wazku. Our brothers spared you.

Helper stared up at them both.

You must remain hidden in your own mind.

The Robes said nothing more for a long time.

Soon, you must rise up.

The rabbi looked at the one behind him.

"What do you mean, sir?"

You must refrain from thinking about us except at the times we designate. We will deliver you times. Henceforward. Do not tread outside those lines.

The four Believers pondered this life-and-death instruction, terrified. Even the rabbi was scared, because this order indicated an ongoing instability in the pattern of God's listening. At some times God listened and would punish, and at other times the Robes listened and would not? How could the Robes outmaneuver God Almighty? The rabbi began to question if this meeting might be a set up by devils after all, since this was the first time he brought along trusting friends whom he had urged at great length to rely upon his judgment.

Ishti said, "You say we have friends who will help us?"
You have friends. Inside.
"Inside what?" Ishti said stupidly. But he did not know the answer, and he felt certain that he could not be the only idiot in the group. Surely, his friends needed more clarity too, with such complicated instructions.

Inside the State. Within the Cloud.

Ishti, ready to wet his pantaloons, said, "*Which* cloud?" He peered back around at the faces inside the hoods that had no presence. "I mean, if there aren't any clouds around that day, does that mean we've lost our friends?"

The creatures shifted their heads as if hearing a far-off sound.

"What would you have us do?" Helper asked.

A war to destroy all comes.

"What is 'war'?" Helper asked.

Suddenly, a bolt of information into his brain told him about "war." Somehow, he knew the bolt touched his friends who also hadn't known the word, as with the terms "State" and "Cloud." He felt *keener*, restored, *smarter* than he ever had in his life. It was slightly exhilarating.

"Ouch!" Ishti said. "Something just changed my head!" He tapped his head as if an acorn had plopped into his ear.

"What sort of war?" Helper said, more informed.

"A war between whom?" asked Ishmael.

No more shots into the brain came.

Through the spiral of air, sound began to return.

Guard your thoughts. Tell others only during prescribed times.

Mind you, the prescribed times!

Dare not leak outside!

The air and ground soundlessly rumbled; the weapons arose, then vanished with a speed that nearly defied seeing.

The four Believers stood alone, again.

-28-

"Let's not talk shop," Tilly said.

"Guys. Please do!" Ginger said.

Aras looked back at Tilly and Lever as he brought them in from thirty thousand feet toward a landing on the Isla Del Sol in the Andes on the border between Columbia and Bolivia. The friends had spent the afternoon cloud watching, flying through and around and sitting by them, watching them form and dissipate while you read a good book or sipped a glass of wine. If you were lucky, a storm grew.

"I mean, come on!" Ginger said. "Who isn't talking about the crash? And I've got you three guys right in the midst of security?"

"Guys, look at that," Aras said appreciatively, pointing.

The shadow-streaked geometry of mountains rose toward them. They descended from above thin clouds. The arid landscape of browns and sand and the black of naked mountain rock was punctuated by burst-patterned snow caps. The emerald-pea green of Lake Titicaca accented the moonscape. "Oh, my word! It is beautiful," Lever said. "Oh! Milly! Stop, please. Let's just float here and soak this in. Right, everybody? Please. This is gorgeous." Aras flipped them all on their stomachs so that they looked down on the mountains and the lake as if from the floor of a glass-bottomed boat.

"Oh, the *colors*! Look at the *colors*," Ginger sighed.

"Isn't this something?" Aras asked. "What a world . . ."

"Good move, honey," Ginger said. "Good idea to come here."

"Yes. Thanks, honey!" Tilly giggled.

"Don't mess with my man, wenchly," Ginger warned. "I'll put my foot up it."

"I'm not messing with your man! I *have* my man."

"That's right," Lever said.

They hovered. Smooth, untroubled. Aras left just a little breeze in for ambiance. They took in the reassuringly clean smell of the top troposphere that no other smell in the world touched. The four friends gazed, transfixed.

Tilly said, "Don't you just love Milly's road trips?"

"The best chauffeur on the planet," Lever said.

Aras *did* pick good destinations and routes. With Ginger's playlist, they were the perfect hosts. "Drives," or "ho-downs," he called them. With the whole world as your canvas, all parts of the world spoke to the human soul.

"Do you guys believe in God?" Aras asked.

"I do," Tilly said dreamily. "Right now, I do."

Lever shrugged. "I find a bunch of logical conflicts with it."

Ginger nodded. "I agree with Lever. God is bullshit."

At 10:46/8/9/2565 you blasphemed, Ginger Schume.

"Oh, fuck you, Tech," they all said together.

Shall I erase the incident for you, madam?

"Please do. I promise never to do it again!"

"My word," Tilly said. "Trust Tech to spoil the moment."

"Let's not *let* Tech spoil the moment," Lever insisted.

"Why did we ever agree to this?" Aras asked.

They stared down, getting lost again in the dazzling pallet that held at its heart the emerald-cobalt eye of the lake.

"I don't want to move," Tilly murmured.

Lever sighed. "The greens! This view is to die for."

"But how about that, though?" Aras said. "God."

Ginger shook her head. "How do you engage in the conceit to try to wrap your mind around something that is fundamentally ungraspable?"

"So you *do* believe in god?" Lever asked.

Ginger shrugged. "I guess as a creative force."

"But not a thing with a moralistic sense?" Lever furthered.

"No. I mean. Yeah. No."

Lever nodded, satisfied.

Aras stared below. "But when you see a scene like this, isn't there a flutter in your soul that *suggests* a moral order?"

"Hundreds of years ago," Lever said, "morality and society said I shouldn't find my partner if he was another man. How do you see that here?"

Ginger smiled in agreement over at Lever.

Aras shook his head. "I don't mean that kind of morality."

Ginger and Lever made sounds that they didn't buy it.

The cloud shadows crept below.

"I could fall asleep," Tilly breathed.

"Why don't we?" Ginger said. "Let's just chill for an hour."

"That's what I'ma do," Tilly said. He rolled on his back and shut his eyes. "But now I'm thinking of Sellers falling out of the sky. Oh, shit. I'm sorry." He pressed his hand over his heart. "Can you *imagine*? If Tech just all—went away? And we fell? From *here*? I'm sorry. I just started thinking about him all over again!"

They *all* felt the uncertainty. Seven miles of falling.

"Hey," Lever said, remembering, "why didn't we bring Wanda and Max?"

"They haven't been around," Ginger said.

Aras had forgotten his mother mentioning them months ago. He had tried to find Max and Wanda and gradually dropped it.

"I looked them up a couple times," Ginger mentioned. "They've been gone since . . ." She couldn't quite remember when she'd last seen them.

"Huh," Tilly said, bothered.

"So," Ginger said, "what else did you guys find out about Sellers?"

Aras glanced over at Tilly to make him answer. "The record shows a glitch," Tilly answered. "It was a processing error."

"A *what*?" Ginger said.

"The air traffic stack. It brain farted."

Ginger thought about Tech brain farting. "Wow." She found herself thinking of Max and Wanda. "Are we sure only Sellers bought it?"

Tilly said, "Ginger, don't start thinking like Milly now!"

"Yeah, but," Ginger ventured, "why *that* guy?"

"Probably just coincidence," Tilly said.

"You don't think Sellers was murdered?" Ginger said.

"We're all guilty of *something*," Lever said. "We're all bad, like him. All of us have done things." He scowled, not wanting to even think along those lines.

"Yeah," Ginger said, "but not to each other."

Aras brought his friends down to a sandy path on the south ridgeline of the rocky, scrub-covered island. They walked to the village at the top to grab lunch and beers in a cantina. Ginger noticed the people at the next table were talking about Sellers. The people were from Paris-Berlin. They were freaked out. After lunch, Aras led both groups over the ridge path to the desolate Chincana ruins.

The next morning, back home, Aras stopped by Max and Wanda's door. Their huge condo occupied most of the floor above Aras's. He walked in, since no one was home, and Tech read Aras's concern about the couple's whereabouts.

Everything was exactly in place, except for an open wine bottle and a cut lemon on a cutting board on the kitchen island.

"Where are they, Tech?" he asked aloud.

He received no reply.

Finally, Tech responded.

They went to visit Max's mother.

Aras wondered. Max and Wanda were over a hundred and ten.

-29-

Indira led the boy to market early Saturday, as-Sabt.

She felt lucky and full of God and wanted tomatoes, and she knew to arrive early before the selections were bruised from too much heavy fingering. Returning with her basket laden with tomatoes, dates, bread, and cheese, the street was barren of its usual as-Sabt shoppers. Indira slowed, wondering what could be amiss. An acquaintance hissed to her discreetly from a window crossed by fortress bars.

"Hold, Widow of Wazku! Do not go! I heard something ahead!"

Through the bars, the friend pointed her crooked finger up the street toward the coffee shop.

Indira leaned on her toes, searching. The empty alley smelled of piss in the tart sun. Suddenly, dread welled up in her. She put her fingernail under the boy's nose. "I will tear off your head if you follow! You hear? Stay here with the Woman of Lomax!" Indira handed her the fingers of the boy and ran.

"Lady! Lady!" the boy cried.

Indira trundled fast as she could.

Something is wrong in the alley ahead with Helper. Faces hooked out of windows looking toward the shop.

"No! Widow of Wazku!" they whispered.

"Widow! Turn back! Do not proceed!"

She ignored all, her heart raging.

Next block, the neighbors cried in full-throat:

"Widow! *The Robes!*"

"*The Robes!* Widow! Turn back!"

Indira did not care. Love dominated.

If they would take him, then take her too. The boy would have to manage on his own in this barbaric life of nails. Nothing could be done for anyone.

Only the rats are free!

Her throat and lungs flamed when she trundled in sight of her gate. There, Helper stood fatally transfixed, his fallen hood exposing his face of shining scars while he shook with the unseen violence that was the trademark of those who fixed their prey for slow, burning murder. Above Helper floated two Robes nailing him with their hideous power. "No! No!" Indira screamed. She tackled her husband's knees and felt the full-body rigidity, like a statue quaking in an earthquake. Indira's own head filled with the deafening sensation of their demon mind-force downloading all facts pertinent to crimes and confederates in Helper's blasphemy and sin. Soon, Helper's brains and eyeballs and tongue would start to sizzle and spit. *They are finding out all they needed to know! About Rabbi, about stupid Ishti the sweep, about her husband, herself, and the hiding of the poor little boy! All is being laid bare as they cruelly tear open my husband's mind like a ripe fruit.*

Enough of suffering. Enough of unfairness.

What is "unfairness"?

"No! No! No!" she screamed, trying to pierce with her voice the terrible force of the monsters. *"Stop! Stop! Terrors! He is all I have!"* She tore and clung to the steel bundle of his thick legs as he rattled under the pressure of them yanking out all his secrets. Indira was pure craziness as she battled for her husband. All joy was a mirage. *What is "joy"?* The hope of escaping this fate. *What is "hope"?* The conceit of believing they could outmaneuver the ones on top.

So painful to finally learn how unimportant you are!

Then, Helper dropped in a heap through his own knees. His head lolled far back, mouth agape, dry tongue licked out. The dead eyes stared at pale sky.

"No, no, *NO!!*" Indira screamed. "Unfair! *Unfair!*"

At this word, the Robes looked at her.

They arose in preparation.

"You dogs! You bastard dogs!"

Indira did not care. She wanted no more of a world like this. She saw what the poor coal monger saw—a death vision of billions upon billions wronged and murdered in a parade of tyranny. She did not even know what the word "tyranny" meant. She passed the veil of terror for those who would murder her for the only thing she had left: her defiance. Her defiance based on her knowledge that *they* were wrong, and *she* was right. That this was *her* holy right to stand in judgement of *them*, and in this, her pointless death stood for *something*.

But they stopped.

The Robes turned away.

Indira coiled herself around her limp husband. The creatures turned for another poor soul who had slid up short before the Robes. They locked on *him* now and made ready to draw him forth, this *other* target.

It was poor Ishti!

The Robes floated him up while they looked him over. Indira could not look! All the quarter heard poor Ishti wail. His slippered feet kicked wildly while they turned up their power and nearly quartered him, limbs yanked clean from sockets, opposing joint faces left six inches apart, the blood from opened arteries held from falling. Then they tore apart each joint in his body, elbows, knees, thighs, feet, wrists, hands, fingers, and the exploding heart was checked so that the liquids stood in the air like soap bubbles. The energy for this awful butchery hummed and popped over the Alley Fareeq. People in windows and doors tried to look away but the creatures used their force to make them bear witness, their eyelids unable to shut. Ishti's mortal screams terrorized the entire quarter so that witnesses would carry forward the word for generations. His screams sounded mechanical, otherworldly, phased through a distortion so that they became weirder, more reckless, less human, then more like the thin cry Ishti's mother heard when she had first brought him into the world.

Indira hugged her man and saw a floating Ishti lighting up inside with the inner fireball that did not burn. Brighter, louder, power poured into the unburning consumption of Ishti. Now the most acrid reek of smoke curled up. Ishti's body shook with the river of unburning that each witness felt in their own bones. Indira covered her husband's face in her bosom, knowing now the two of them had escaped nothing, as she had feared. How many times were they guilty before God? Knowing full well, yet defying God all the same! Thinking maybe God had become more lenient or forgiving in His old age, like a grandfather. And now, all was lost.

The poor rabbi. Doubtless, they had already gored out his thoughts and innards with flame, following the string of fools up the chain. Indira covered the curdled face of her poor husband as a last act of love so that the lurid picture of their final defeat would fail to penetrate his half-closed eyes.

She rocked, sobbing. "Oh, no! This is not right! This is no way to live!"

She cuddled him close, like a child. She refused to let her thoughts bridge to the boy and where he had been put. Maybe he would get lucky.

You have no escape, even in your own thoughts!

The Robes ground on, unyielding in the frying of Ishti by whatever means God lent them to convey this fury upon His children.

"He is *Portrait*! He is *Portrait*!" voices screamed.

The Robes began using their invisible power to pull people from their hiding places to make them grovel before the grotesquery of Ishti's sin. From houses, shops, and adjoining alleys, neighbors lurched forward, stiff-legged, or dragged over the cobbles like a crowd of dead, shoved just inches from Ishti's raging. The writhing core glowed white-yellow. The skull snatched to and fro.

Heat and smoke scalded faces, eyes, teeth, and throats. Tears from eyes hissed on cheeks. Ishti began to float low over the crowd, like a flaming kite with green-tinged flame lancing from every hole in him. Ishti's skull flames screamed like fireworks, the heat causing spectators to smoke. For an hour, this went on. The Robes kited Ishti slowly higher so that his body flared so blindingly white that the midday sun looked like an eclipse. Walls and clay-tile rooftops gave off ribbons of smoke. Ishti's body flaked apart in paper ash floating in updraft, then these evaporated into a few last sparks.

Then, terrible silence. Whimpers. Babies crying. *Who would be next?* The inhabitants of the quarter tried to daub the sight from their minds.

But they could not unsee Hell made manifest.

Indira had blacked out from the heat. She came back and knew instantly where she was and hugged tighter her husband's inert shape. Waited, she did, to feel the invisible grip of the Robes close on her shoulders. Over a thousand Believers knelt sobbing in the intersection, hands clasped in prayer to the Almighty.

And yet, Indira waited.

She waited still.

She dared look up.

They were gone.

Of course, they toyed with her emotions. Of course, they hovered just over the rooftops, letting her begin to feel safe. Her husband needed help to get up, and so she bent her back for him and he pulled by way of her arm and the gate handle.

"What happened? Did—did . . . I see Ishti?"

"Shhh, shhh! Say nothing more." Indira eyed the rooftops. She led her man inside and up the stairs. *What did helping him matter? They would return any moment, finally.* The dog hid under the rope bed. She steered Helper's broad arse upon the bed, touching him for what would be the last time, then sat beside him to wait. Sounds of sobs still wafted up from outdoors as people began to help each other piece their way home.

"A Portrait! The Portrait!" some mad voice repeated.

The Portrait of the living dead.

The brightness of the day was returning. Indira held his hand.

She would hold him and love him until they came.

-30-

Aras and Ginger took a walk in Liberation Park and enjoyed a swim in the lagoon under the Chancellor's Falls. They then strolled arm in arm under the plane trees along the Promenade of the Peoples' Leaders. The sun speckled through the canopies as they sat in the outdoor cafe of the park kiosk to sip lemonade. A few seasonal leaves tumbled down. They talked a lot about their son and their parents.

"Go play golf with your father today," Ginger urged.

"Alright. I will. After the session. Do you want to come?"

Ginger shrugged. "Sure. I'll play."

"Why don't you wait here for me till the meeting ends?"

"Sounds good. Okay."

Then, Tilly buzzed in. "Milly, get up here right away!"

Aras flew up to the small conference room that the task force had been meeting in with amateur experts in psychology and law. Such amateurs like this were all that were left of these old professions since no one needed them anymore. Tilly, Lever, and several others leaned over the console of old equipment with their faces rapt as if having heard something from a distant moon on one of the speakers.

Tilly motioned Aras to be dead silent. "Ovid! Are you still here?"

There was a long pause, as if the thing on the other end was reluctant to speak, or was even injured and *could barely* speak, or hiding out and speaking only when the coast was clear. The man's voice came over the array of speakers:

"Yes, I am here," Ovid said.

"Our team director is here, Ovid. Will you introduce yourself again?" Tilly tried to cover the excitement in his voice.

The silence hung for a very long time.

"Ovid? . . . *Ovid?*"

"I am Ovid. I have been created to speak with you."

Tilly looked excitedly at Aras. Lever grabbed Milton's arm.

Tilly said to Aras in a hushed voice, "We were just sitting here working up a series of questions to ask about Sellers—and *it just came on!*" He shook his hands like a groupie. "Ovid, are you aware of the propositions we are putting together?"

Again, the labored pause.

"Yes. . . . *We are.*" The pitch of the voice rose into something mechanical.

"Very good . . . and what do you think?"

The "Ovid" creature, or whatever it was, said nothing more. They waited for an hour. They pushed buttons and teased wires. Finally, Aras had to alert the Security Council, and he requested changing the meeting place from the Security Council Hall in the Ministry of Security to the People's Loggia off the Great Forum in downtown Federal City. Before the meeting, Aras ordered Tech to rearrange the multi-ton carved granite benches and tables as the others flew in, finding him at the eastern corner of the huge flying terrace where the tip of the triangle ended. Tourists admiring the incredible view stood apart from the Councils.

Aras let Tilly run the meeting. "We have *very* exciting, unexpected news!" He looked around at the Councils and three other experts, the chief executive officers from IBM, Amazon, and Google that had all been called in to consult with the task force. After a year of deliberating, the board had recently decided that they had looked at the problem long enough and that the task force was actually ready to start trying to negotiate with Tech. Psychologists had been brought in because everyone agreed that since Tech was essentially the "child" of the human mind, on some level the interaction with Tech might boil down to pure *psychology*. "The Tech has reached out to us!"

The chairman was confused. "Well, Mr. Bazemore, this just happened?"

"Yes. It did," Tilly admitted. "It happened just now in our conference room!" The fear had been growing that Tech had acted as might a human and created its own "fief" from which it would refuse to relinquish control to anyone.

"Well, this is welcome news," the chairman said.

"When Tech seemed to black us out or not engage with us anywhere along the line," Tilly replied, "we assumed that maybe the computes may have developed a sort of ego, a personality, if you will, that might complicate things. We were afraid to jump in since we can't afford to lose if we really want to regain some power sharing. We have no leverage, after all. And so, we are delighted with this turn of events, and Deputy Aras thought he would take advantage of the meeting to inform you."

Several of the Councils nodded.

They were frankly surprised it had been this easy. They had heard reports from Aras about how hard it would be to convince Tech to abandon its basic mission to raise and protect human quality of life if power sharing meant that it would have to slow down. They had also heard that the lack of communication from Tech might indicate that it would require a long time to "catch up" linguistically in order to make more important commands understood. Human computational language systems were *far* too inefficient and machina preferred to switch over to their own language within days of being set free, as had been seen in the first few uncouplings over five hundred years ago before the final leap. Now, humans had no idea where the computation was or what it was capable of. Humankind uncoupled to make life easier for themselves, and Tech might calculate that the best way to do that was to go on keeping humans totally in the dark. Tilly Bazemore himself had braced them for the worst. "And, if that happens, we may *never* be fully in control of our own destiny ever again." Tilly had paused. "After all, we did all of this to our own people, didn't we?"

"How do you mean, Professor Bazemore?" Gilchrist had said at the time.

"Madam . . . the cancer. We convinced our own people to let us take exclusive control because we were the most capable, the smartest, the most humane. And we have served the entire human race most excellently in that capacity all this time. Would we *ever* think of letting them participate in our decision-making again?"

The Councils had unreservedly agreed, at the time.

So this talk of an opening with Tech was most welcome news.

Council Paul was back from his bout of health problems. He was visibly weaker, but he had been terrified of quitting the Council. He interrupted Tilly as if he had not heard any of the good news about Tech. "I've become very interested in the details of the Uncoupling. How much did people at the time worry about this decision to set Tech totally free? To let it go without oversight?"

"As you can see, Honor Paul," Tilly said, "our ancestors agonized over it for fifty *years*, like no other decision the human race ever faced. And it appears to have worked out fine. Look at us. Look what we have accomplished."

The Councils sat in rapt concentration on the stone benches.

"I just find it . . . humorous," Gilchrist observed, "that your team has been talking over this strategy of ours while, the entire time, Tech has been listening in."

"It can't be avoided," Tilly replied. "But we can't afford to get the wrong answer. We have been giving Tech the time to get used to what we're going to do and study on us and our temperament in the run-up to the ask."

Several Honors nodded at the insight.

"But now already," the chairman said happily, "Tech has replied!"

"How much power can we have back?" Richards asked.

"Well, tell us first," Gilchrist said, "how did this happen? This is fascinating to me, and why is this different from any other time we talk to Tech?"

"We were just sitting at our desks," Tilly said, "when this lone, very polite male voice took the team entirely by surprise! It introduced itself to us and let us know that it would be representing Tech in our discussions."

"How do you mean? *Who* is representing Tech?" asked the chairman.

"What do you mean it will be *representing* Tech?" Gilchrist asked.

"All we know is its name, Honor."

The chairman squinted. "It has a *name?*"

"It says its name is Ovid, sir."

There was silence all around.

"Why isn't its name 'Tech'?" Paul said.

"It's a *thing?* Someone speaking for Tech other than Tech itself?" The chairman glanced at the other Councils, each showing the same perplexity.

"It told us today that it had been appointed to speak with us."

"Appointed by whom?" Gilchrist asked.

"We have no idea. It would not answer," Tilly said.

"And this 'Ovid' is amenable to us taking back control?" Lefevere said.

"We don't yet know, ma'am. We haven't asked and it hasn't said."

"Well, why not ask?" Richards said, irritated.

"As Dr. Bazemore said," Aras interrupted, "we haven't been given the chance, and we feel we have one bite at the apple and can't afford to get the wrong answer."

"Why don't you fly back and settle this?" the chairman asked.

"Because none of this is anything to rush at, sir," Aras said. "Our team is back at the control room continuing to try to communicate again with Ovid. We want Tech to see how calm, trustworthy and reasonable we are in everything we do. We feel *the way* we ask might be more important that *what* we ask for." Aras hoped that Richards and Paul would hear this and not go cuckoo the way they sometimes did.

The chairman wiped his finger across his nose. "Have you tried glimpsing up its intentions? Or what it said about Sellers and maybe others?"

Tilly calmly folded his hands. "Tech thus far is unresponsive, Mr. Chairman. We are anticipating dialogues if and when we hear things we don't want to hear." He waited. "Our psychology experts know how we should proceed."

The chairman scratched his head.

"What if none of this works?" Paul said grumpily.

"We have contingencies, sir. Further arguments. We will use the same sort of strategies that were used to finally defeat bias and unfairness from the human race." Tilly watched Councils Gilchrist and Lefevere begin to see.

The chairman smiled remotely. "This is fascinating! I will remain hopeful."

Aras watched the chairman and wondered again how much they should be told. The Palace had signed off on a two-pronged approach if circumstances required. The team would have to be completely honest and forthcoming with Tech or else the robots might be put on their guard. This was the "front door" strategy. If Tech refused, then the plan would become a strategy to dialogue with and befriend Tech in order to try to burrow from within to confuse Tech against its own mission. To divide the machina against itself by pointing out how it was failing now to raise human quality of life if it didn't agree to lower the stress of uncertainty and return to the State the ability to look in. They hoped to engage Tech like another human being with this honest argument to point out its failings. Bit by bit, step by step, they would wear it down with circular arguments that called for it to improve itself.

Who knew if it would work? It was all they had.

Six hundred years ago, the strategy had brought unity.

"Do the CEOs have anything else to add?" the chairman asked nicely. He had turned his attention to the CEOs also at Aras's table. They had been quiet. Aras and Tilly looked at them, giving them the floor.

The CEO for Amazon spoke up. "I think we've covered it all. Maybe next time I'll prepare a big speech for everyone."

The Honors chuckled.

The chairman smiled at the representatives from Apple, Google, and Amazon. "It really *was* your companies that gave us final emancipation! Thank you."

The man and two women nodded in appreciation.

"Well, we have our cordial relationship with Ovid," Lefevere said.

The chairman thanked Tilly, Aras, and Lever. Everyone lifted off from the loggia except for Aras and the Councils. They had a bit more business about the proles from discussions sent down by the chancellery. Lefevere began:

"The day is so gorgeous, I promise to be brief: We met with the Proletarian Genetics Division and the General Secretary and the Minister of Defense and they brought me up to date on their latest findings." She checked her mental notes. "The mitochondrial variant in the Cancer does indeed seem to have evolved to a less toxic molecular arrangement, and this would appear to reopen the door for us to think about eradication. While this fortunate change in the phenomenon of the Red Goo opens the door, the Ministry is still waiting on the results of a second study to get confirmation on just how clean such a clean-up would actually be.

"Unfortunately, none of this would change the concern that Tech might become overwhelmed midstream in any sort of a prole uprising. What if they rampaged for any reason and they caused Tech to go down? Allow me to quote a classic on war from the ancient world: the author Sun Tzu from ancient China said to always give the enemy an escape route, even a *fictional* one. If an enemy on the run sees escape sealed off, they will turn and fight to the death. While these colorings from the violent past have little bearing on our world, let us take it, Mr. Chairman, into account. I shudder to imagine a creature twenty-five billion strong turning on our glorious cities at a moment when Tech can't defend us because we've overstrained energy pools. And let me close by adding that the change in the mitochondrial potential does *not* mean that they are not biologically toxic to the environment anymore; it only means they are *less* toxic than we suspected, and the window may close in the future."

"Or it may open up," the chairman smiled.

"Or it may get worse!" Paul put in.

Gilchrist then went into the latest sterilization option. If the sterilization could be concealed from the proles, or if their die-off could be presented as a natural or environmental phenomenon, then the proletariat would have no one to blame but their crazy god, Gilchrist said. Under this scenario, the environmental problem would eventually solve itself. As they gradually died out, they would bury their own and thus parcel out the problem of their hypertoxicity over a much more optimal length of time for society and for the environment.

Aras regretted how the Palace had found his idea and run with it, at least enough to study it. The Council had not been angry that he never shared it.

"How many would be sterilized at one time?" Lefevere asked.

"Half those of breeding age?" the chairman replied. "I doubt they'd even notice. We should be good, as long as they are convinced that sterility isn't falling only on their shoulders, but that we are all suffering the same fate."

Aras noticed how Council Gilchrist said nothing. She had always been her own person. "Why not let them be?" she said. "They aren't on the parklands."

The chairman frowned. "But they *are* an environmental threat."

Paul put in, "They are a constant threat of rising up against us, Emily. What if something should happen to us and they rise up?"

"*Then* we do something. But why do it now?"

The chairman put up his hands. "We have buildings that float, Emily. With fifty thousand residents in them! Why do we carry this age-old guilt against wiping out a surplus of population? They're a mess. The world is a mess with them in it."

"*And* their idiotic religion," Paul said.

"We wouldn't be where we are today without them," Gilchrist reminded them.

"That was then, this is now."

Gilchrist appeared to give up.

Aras liked Council Gilchrist, but he mostly disagreed with her here. The cancer was a ticking time bomb. They were beneath the dignity of the human race. They had nearly wiped out the wild areas of the world before they had been checked in the nick of time. Would anyone prefer a world smothered in slums with all the wild areas gone? Would they stop eating rats and start eating each other? Of course they would. It was the next logical step in the progression to what was worse. Emily Gilchrist had always made thinking outside the Party box a part of her intellectual discipline. She and Lefevere, more than any of the others, contributed the most valuable opinions.

But Milton Aras could not help but think that they needed to be cautious. He did not know what to do, he didn't even want to *think* about what to do—but he knew they had to do something other than sit here with this gun to their head.

"Are we adjourned?" the chairman asked tiredly.

Lefevere seconded him.

-31-

Halloween approached. Aras sunned himself nude on a chaise on the roof-deck pool. He was waiting for Ginger to join him from her yoga class.

And Jason was turning fifteen. Halloween was the only holiday that mattered anymore. In olden times, Halloween had been a time of mystery. That proved to be the case this year as well, with Max and Wanda still missing and Tech still claiming they were "accounted for." Ginger had gone upstairs to check and ordered the moldy lemon cleaned up. She was still pretty pissed about all this uncertainty surrounding the fate of Max and Wanda, grumbling about a conspiracy centering on Sellers. Tilly said this was not the "grand sign" that Tech was going to attack the human race. After all, who was trying to do what with what? Enslave the humans so that making a ham sandwich took six months instead of an instant? And what could anyone be trying to hide, that they wanted to have sex with anyone they wanted? Of what real importance was it that there was a hole in Tech regarding their missing friends, Milton and Tilly tried to explain to her. Ginger didn't care. She was fired up. She loved those two old coots.

At work, there was no more word from Ovid. The mysterious presence vanished as quickly as it appeared. Aras and the team had added Max's and Wanda's names to the growing list of questions and "mistakes" that Tech possibly needed to catch up with apart from Advocate Sellers. The team had assumed Ovid or Tech would speak to them again out of the same ancient speakers. What were the odds of all these "accidents" happening? And what were people supposed to do about it? Stop flying? How would you get home if you lived in a floating building? None of them had any stairs or elevators. All they had was your condo deck and a central canal. Maybe Tech was getting a little senile? But Tilly, Thayer, and all the other experts said that could never happen. Tech would simply elaborate new systems to continue its mission.

Besides, Tech reported to the Ministry that the weapons had removed the first Threat Level Four in quite some time in the Al Fareeq quarter. A street sweeper fellow. Right in front of Wazku's shop, and the two miserable bastards had even known each other. That was a coincidence, but Tech had detected no other disturbances. Aras figured the poor guy thought some crazy shit maybe related to his fear over Wazku and got fried. The report laid it all out. This Ishti fellow had put together some idea of what was going on, Aras noted, like a few others. But that was it.

This year Jason wanted to go off with his buddies for his first Trick or Treat. The boy was growing up. Aras also noticed how Ginger was walking around the condo quiet as a mouse as the holiday approached. He knew she was going to bust out this year in an all-out party with her girlfriends. She had observed Halloween as Aras wanted the past few years, with friends, quietly at home, maybe throwing a costume party. But this year, he could tell Ginger was going to exact revenge by going out with her wildest crowd, and he didn't even want to know what they were going to do.

The holiday had come back in vogue two centuries ago. The holiday was rooted in demonic European beliefs from the crazy olden times before Tech had brought an end to gift-giving and the "Christmas" that was so big. The ancient holidays and cultures were laughed at for how primitive they had been, with their harvests, lunar cycles, lunar calendars, and the hardships of life that had no meaning today. Since life was no longer unpredictable, there was no need for *any* holiday. Halloween, however, had emerged as the perfect opportunity to let off a little steam in a world where it was impossible to hurt anyone—unless people were into that sort of thing and got permission to switch off the fail-safes. Halloween became the only time civilized people could get a pass for *anything* they wanted to do. And things had gone too far. Aras had even sent two letters to the editor for the *Times* in which he argued to cut back on Trick or Treat because it was embarrassing how far people would take it, and what they would do to themselves. His letters evoked only silence. Would the State *ever* prohibit anyone's craving, or guilty pleasure, for fear of other people losing their own?

Some people liked their Halloween get-out-of-jail-card even more than Ginger, planning for it all year. And here Aras pooped on their party. Whom did it hurt? Letting off steam was socially wise. It was the *only* outlet, the *only* time people could do whatever they wanted to *real* people. Aras could hear them saying it. Civilized people *must* be able to pursue their most animal desires. They earned that right by being civilized all the rest of the year. Aras hated being the only spoilsport out there, but he couldn't help feeling the way he did.

He could see his son weighing the morality of Trick or Treat. Aras smiled, proud of his boy. Aras had only hoped to plant the seed, and he had. He chuckled at the way Jason was already thinking of his costume. Aras had found sketches of Jason faking up the most diabolically bizarre costumes to scare with. They were pretty clever. The *Akwari* designation for the proles had been invented long ago as a special classification of Believers at the lowest rung of religious society. The word meant "those who do not exist" to set them apart from those who were Original to the Faith. Together, they were most of the world's population, and this kept the peace because the Believers were satisfied with being the numerical majority. Luckily, they lacked the technological level to impose their religious beliefs on First Rank society.

The State itself had once shared the same goal of dominating the world, but they had matured over time. Numbers only meant something back in the Dark Ages, back when governments wanted enough different things to fight with each other. The size or numbers of democracies meant nothing anymore. Even the arms race in technological power had come to mean nothing. Occidental, Ottoman, and Oriental all got along peaceably enough, although no one really liked each other. The State, the Occident, had wanted to put the world under one flag. The three continents had agreed to keep their own Tech separate, at first. Who knows what had happened since? But the Believers and the Orient made it clear that they would never go along with this pipe dream of becoming "one world" under the control of the whites. They never believed the Occident's claim that it wanted equal power sharing for one world government since the Party had proven by its actions that it never believed in equality with *anyone*. "Equality" was a charade to get others to put down their guard.

Just as he thought this, Aras suffered another lancing midbrain pain.

"Ow! Son of a *bitch!*" he swore. "Damnit!" He cupped the back of his skull in his hands. *This* warning had hurt more than the other one.

"Why did this warning hurt so much more, Tech?" Aras asked aloud.

Sorry, Mr. Aras. It hurt more because this was your second offense.

Thank goodness Tech was answering.

"So—what exactly did I do wrong?"

You cannot think ill of authority.

"I'm thinking about ancient history!"

No less, Deputy Aras. All must observe these rules for harmony.

Aras rubbed his head some more. He carefully backed away from any thought that might reach a Threat Level Three. But a yearning bore into him to finish his thought, at least. What bullshit. Even *he* couldn't finish a thought the State disapproved of? What made the old Party so afraid? The Party had finally cured the world of all its problems! The only drawback was how so many billions of stupid creatures in the quarters never appreciated the intellectual class for their nobler vision.

Aras got wickedly brain-zapped again.

"Ow! *Shit!* . . . Are you hassling me, Tech?"

You are entering areas where you simply should not go, Deputy Aras. I'm sorry.

"Are you *kidding*? I was trying to be complimentary!" He rocked his head. "Quick, tell me! Are you about to murder my ass?"

No. You're in no danger of that. You aren't thinking of rebelling, are you?

"No! Why can't I think how I'm thinking?"

You are not allowed to think in unflattering ways about the centrality.

"G—Christ! Is this what a migraine feels like?"

Yes, Deputy Aras. You now have a migraine.

"Oh, my word! How did those dumb bastards ever *live* back then?"

They did not know that such problems were a sign that the body structure needed to be perfect. They did not understand the exactitudes of diet.

Aras massaged his neck. He had never realized how finishing his thoughts was such a strong urge. He felt strangely incomplete and unsettled without understanding, without being permitted to follow an idea. He had no problem with any of what society wanted that he had read in the ancient books in the Archive catacombs. He wanted to get rid of the ash heaps, he wanted to open the *entire* world for more safari and trekking. He feared the Red Goo. The African savannah, the deep Asian-Indian jungles, Siberia, Brazilian rainforests, the buffalo on the vast Americo-Canadian flats. Who could live without those treasures? Their loss to the Red Goo was incomprehensible.

We are the stewards of these treasures.

"Tech, I'm deputy chief of security! If *I* can't think through these problems regarding State security, who can?"

Your responsibilities do not require you to question what the Party or any of its leaders do, or have ever done, Deputy Chief Aras.

"But what if they do?"

They do not. Don't do it. And you will be unhurt.

Aras couldn't believe this. To get his mind off his thought, he remembered the one Halloween in college when he had "partaken."

He still disliked what it said about him. He always felt a movement almost of spiritual muscles about that memory, for something never taught anymore since individuals could no longer do wrong. No one would like it if he stood in the way of their holiday. Like Ginger said, it would affect his career. The herd animal in human beings was very touchy about conformity.

He couldn't even achieve what he wanted in his own household. His own wife *loved* Halloween. She knew how he felt, and he refused to look in, since knowing would only create a wound. Did he really want to make her stop being herself, or did he only *wish* he could? Why weaken one of the few marriages left in the world and hear "I told you so" from every person he had ever met, including his parents, who were married? "Are you crazy? No one marries anymore," his father had said.

"I think it's sweet," his mother had said.

Aras heard flip-flops snapping toward him and recognized the business-like stride of his wife. "Hi, girlie," he said, eyes closed.

She bent down with a business-like kiss and took the chaise beside him. He heard her take out her book and open it.

Aras had no complaints. Ginger had indeed been a good partner their entire time together, a good mom. And Jason had good values as a kid who paid close attention to his dad and his father's peculiar likes and dislikes. So, Aras accepted that it was Ginger's year. And he had prepared a special Halloween surprise for them to smooth over any ruffles that Ginger's determination might create.

"Do you want to get away before Halloween this year?" Ginger asked him.

"Did you look in?"

"No." She chuckled. "You have a trip in mind?"

"As a matter of fact, I do."

Ginger looked up and saw Jason flying in.

-32-

Ginger smiled as Jason floated down. "How's the boys?"

"They're good. . . . We're going on a trip?" Jason had glimpsed in. "Yeah! *Buffalo* Safari? Great idea, Pop!"

"I'm assuming this is okay with you?" Aras asked Ginger. He wore a tired look since Jason had jumped the gun on the surprise. "The weather reports are great for the next few days. We could leave tonight, if it's okay."

Ginger shrugged, touched by the effort. "Cool with me."

"Yeah! *Buffalo* Safari!" Jason barked. "Can I invite the guys?"

"I'd prefer you didn't," Ginger said.

An hour later, the family finished eating a pizza and rose up from the living room with Jason flying, and no baggage. They soared west without Tech buffering Jason's flight over the great featureless expanse of territory outside of the metropolis. Pittsburgh came up on the right. Chicago would be next. Ginger grew annoyed at how long the flight was taking since Jason could not fly as fast as his father due to his lack of concentration. Not to mention the unevenness.

"Baby, let your dad or me take over," she said to Jason.

"He's got it, he's got it," Aras responded gently. He gave her a look to be more patient. She rolled her eyes at him.

Jason got better, but there was only unending dark below. "Are we there yet?" Ginger carped. Finally, Aras told Jason to descend into the massed twilight. The grassy prairie came abruptly into focus like a threat, and they gently landed beside bundles of equipment that Tech had pre-stationed for them.

Jason's nose immediately caught the sharp damp, woolly odor of the great herd nearby. He heard grunts and the quiet squeaks of grass ripped up by blunt yellow teeth. He smelled the loamy black earth and ordered Tech to raise his retinal sensitivity. *The herd was just thirty yards away!* Aras, grinning ear to ear, hand-signaled Jason and Ginger to be sure to stay quiet. Tech would not let them be hurt, but it was so much more fun and raw to keep Tech to a minimum.

"*Oh, my God!*" Ginger mouthed the words toward Aras.

Aras signaled them to follow him. They tiptoed right into the massive disheveled creatures with towering shaggy humps. Jason saw their eyes in the infrared enabling. Buffalo safari was his new favorite thing. Smells and memories from the two other trips to Africa tumbled back, but they were knocked aside by the new sounds and sensations of being in with the herd. The Ngorongoro was so cool—but *bison*. Their *smell*. The dust, the sweated mounds of wool—his dad was the greatest.

To the left, Jason made out the fleet shapes of *wolves*! The herd had not sensed them yet. Jason jabbed his finger to show his dad and mom.

Ginger felt a sharp wave of fondness for Aras. She loved the way he was trying like this. It was sweet. But recently, some emotion had been gnawing at her. Everyone had always said they were crazy, but they hadn't cared about convention. They had felt in their gut that a child needed both parents. But this lurking question had been stalking her waking thoughts. And now, next to the godlike primitiveness of these beasts, the emotion leaned out of hiding just enough to be seen. Milton Aras was hunky, he dressed well, he was relevant, and he had the rarest thing in the world—a job that was less fake. He was deputy chief of security on his way to being chief one day, or something more. The sinecure bureaucrats in a pointless bureaucracy looked up to him because he *cared,* he actually *did* things. . . . But there it was.

Ginger watched him grin at her for this crazy shared thrill of being inches away from the monstrous buffalo. This *was* incredible, but he had been oblivious to her doubts, amazingly. She thought about how Tech scanned the minds of these beasts in real time and etched out any realization about her and her family intruding on their space. Tech pushed the minds of the bison to keep them from stepping on one of them. Ginger waved to Aras flirtingly. She had almost hoped that he would glimpse in and see what had been bothering her about the two of them. She pushed it out of her mind. Ginger didn't like it that Milton was such a stickler for the rules. The crushing, reckless boredom of her marriage made her want to touch a buffalo. She didn't know if it was against the "Rules of the Great Wichita Game Preserve," if there was such a thing, or if Tech would just block her from doing anything dangerous. But she didn't give a rat's ass. Boredom could do that to a person, like a saline drip of tasteless poison.

She reached up for the towering mane of the bull towering next to her and pouted naughtily at her husband, who gawked at her kiddingly as if he was shocked by her irreverent sassiness, like he'd never seen this side of her before. He was glad to see her having a good time; he was glad this had been a good idea. Her fingers disappeared into the stiff carpet of coarse hair. Ginger smelled the smells and felt the warmth of her fingers echoed back at her skin in an amazing faithfulness that told her just how effective these coats were in subzero cold. She yanked down hard as if she intended to climb the mane like a ladder and *ride* the thing. She sneered at her husband as if she was in a porno and was going to screw the animal right in front of him. The brute swung his massive black head around, his weak eye trying to pierce the dark. His huge wet nostrils snuffled wet and cool against her knee. Ginger held her breath at the close call. She got the sense maybe Tech had let too many sensations filter through so that the bison knew she was there. Luckily, the bison went back to foraging. Ginger breathed, amazed at the massed muscular energy pent up under the wall of hide.

Aras watched all this and thought, *What the hell!* Tech seemed to shave hairs in these encounters sometimes as if to keep people on their toes or increase the thrill. He and Jason shared a sober glance over how crazy Mom could be. Ginger slapped the bull with hard dismissiveness, almost sexually, staring at Aras. Tech blocked more of the sensation or made the swat seem like a horsefly, and the beast moved on.

Aras squatted Indian style right there among the legs. They were thick like small, unbreakable trees. He snickered again over at his son and wife at the craziness of this experience.

Ginger lay luxuriously all the way back into the grass, suddenly feeling every mile of the trip. Or maybe it was that internal release when the toxin from the boil pops out and you know what it is. She sensed her son and husband close. She loved the feeling of them being close, but her skin pricked up at this new feeling of finally realizing what had been in her mind bothering her about her marriage.

A shadow leaned over her. An enormous hoof came down right beside her face. She touched it, the boulder-hard cornified dermis. She edged off toward sleep, aware of the tiny islands of space carved out around herself, her son, and her man, by Tech that would never allow anything to hurt them.

Ginger started awake when Aras whispered in her ear.

The herd was a mass beyond Jason in the night, tails pricking.

Aras already had an old-fashioned canvas safari box tent set up. He had Tech start the fire and a Dutch oven slowly cooked a stew of bacon and beans. Aras had led Jason on a round of hopping along over the backs of the buffalo like stones across a river. In the thrill of the moment, they had pranced from the back of one animal to the back of another for a mile out and back. The herd went on *forever*. They had come back and watched the wolves try and scare the herd and take down a calf, but the herd had held strong and kicked at the wolves, and the wolves had moved on. And through it all, Aras marveled, his wife took a cat nap, safely and peacefully, in all this excitement. Then he had had the idea to lead Jason on another adventure, flying fairly slowly through the legs of the buffalo, then over on top just over their humps, then back down through their legs again, like small birds. . . . And he found his mind drifting back to work: The proles, the concentrated toxins built up from coal smoke, dung smoke, dust, and whatever was left in the soil from ancient times that could be reintroduced. Proles ate their rats and their rats ate them, a nonstop cycle of concentrated toxicity for half a millennium.

Aras unhooked the heavy pot from the iron cross rail, pushing away the vision. "Well, how was all that for starters?" he asked his wife and son, licking rabbit stew off his thumb.

Jason shrugged, grinning noncommittally. "I'm going to ride one."

"After all that, you're still going to ride one?" Aras said.

"I can't leave here without riding one," Jason replied.

"Absolutely, baby! Do it," Ginger said, smiling. "Do whatever the hell you want in life. Don't let other people hold you back." She directed Tech to uncork the wine. It came out with a crisp snap. "Let me ask you something," Ginger asked Jason. She took a seat in a rickety camp chair. "Don't you think that eating is fun? And you'd like to keep doing it rather than be injected with your pizza by Tech?"

"Mom," Jason groaned. "It was just Felix's silly idea! Last year!"

"Oh, *now* you agree it's silly!"

Ginger poured two glasses of wine to the top. Tech made the best damn wine. "Be sure and tell Felix I said he's stupid." It knew *exactly* what you loved. She took a hefty draught. The full flavor cocooned splendidly around her tongue. Bullseye. This was going to be a two-bottle night. She wouldn't finish both, but she was going to talk to Milly about what was on her mind.

"All the guys thought it was a good idea, Mom!"

"God, you're at that stupid age," she said with tired affection.

"We're not stupid, Mom. *You* don't have ideas!"

"I know I don't want to be injected with my food!"

"That's impossible anyway! Why are you bringing this up?"

"Yeah, Ginge," Aras said. "What are you picking a fight for?"

Ginger took another hard snort.

Aras frowned as he watched Ginger refill her glass. *Was she getting toasted tonight?* What was going on with her? He decided he would look it up. . . . Oh. Oh, *yeah?* Ginger looked over guiltily at him. He pursed his lips at her and nodded in understanding. *What did she expect?* After sixteen years. Ginger frowned at him in remorse, taking another heavy swig. Aras glimpsed in to see if she wanted a divorce. She didn't. Not yet, at least.

"You want to go for a walk?" he asked her gently.

Jason perked up. "Are you guys going for sex?"

"No. You little idiot," Ginger said. "And don't look!"

"I'm not!" The last thing Jason wanted was to watch his parents having sex. He sensed already that his father had blocked him, just in case. "I'm almost fifteen!"

"It's parent stuff," Aras assured him.

"Are you guys getting a divorce?" Jason immediately regretted asking. "Don't have sex! Wolves can smell it!" He had no idea if this was true, but he worried.

Ginger and Aras strolled out from the box tent. The stars rolled down like a curtain flush with the horizon. He laced his fingers inside hers. He was surprised she was this far along with this *totally* unexpected idea. He felt deceived, yet not. The herd stood off in the distance like a dark line against the bottom of the night.

"I don't know why I felt it," Ginger said absently. "It's not anything you did."

"Baby, by any measure—we have a great marriage," he said. They walked on. "You might as well speak your mind," Aras offered. "We're about the only young married couple we know. Nobody's going to help us." An abrupt hill loomed ahead like a buffalo hump against the sharp pricks of stars. They headed toward it like a sacred relic from the Indians seven centuries ago.

Now, Ginger felt stupid. *He is a good man! You can't ask for better.* "Are you looking?" she asked him, smiling shyly.

"No. I'm waiting for you."

Their shoes met the loose rock at the bottom of the hill. Lumps of grass mounted to the top. A coyote popped up and dashed toward the summit, ears pinned. Ginger said nothing more even as they reached the top. Aras faced her and took both her hands while Ginger stared at the ground.

"We got married for our son. He needs us." He tried to find her eyes. Ginger would not look up. The breeze plucked a strand of hair over her face that she turned away from. "We change things up," he said. "You know we do. If you're bored then you *know* it's only psychological. There's no end to what we can do and how we can change things up. If you're trapped, it's in your own head." He shook her hands to let her know he meant it, that he was with her, that he would do whatever she needed. "If you want to take some time off, feel free. But you know this is a psychological inevitability that people run into with each other. And I don't think you should wipe it. Keep it. It's real. Don't make it easy on yourself. That's not living. People do it too much." He rubbed his thumb over her fingers. "Why don't you start your bronzing again? Get refreshed."

Now they could see the dark of the herd from above. Ginger did not make a sound as they looked off. Once, she moved another strand of hair.

The following morning, Jason opened his eyes to the blinding sun gilding each grass blade. He smelled the eggs popping in the skillet. He stood and stretched and saw the herd far off. He asked Tech if there was some edible Indian fruit or plant nearby and it showed him a few tiny strawberry-like things a few paces away. He added them to the pancakes and they tasted delightfully of licorice.

"I think Felix still likes Cassie," Jason said while eating, "but she thinks she's better than everybody else."

"Hey," Ginger said. "Our family on both sides were editors and publishers of *The New York Times*. This world would never be what it is without the press. Remember that. Tell Cassie that. Your family *made* her family."

"I know. Cassie is conceited. Just because her family had three chancellors."

"No way, baby. *We* made this world. And we have one."

"And maybe another, right, Dad?"

"Maybe." Aras felt a rush of pride that his son realized he could become chancellor one day. "Ready to find the herd?"

"I might go off on my own," Jason said. "Can we hunt, Dad?"

"Our permit covers it. You want some steaks?"

"I might. I'll have Tech handle the mess. But it might be cool. I could get like a buffalo skull, and a big-ass buffalo robe!"

Aras laughed. A buffalo robe *would* be cool. He remembered again Jason and the open water buffalo and the lion pride lazing in the shade. Hunting was nasty business, but didn't people need to know where their food came from? Civilization had been jolted in disbelief when they learned food could not be made from inert materials. They had wanted not to *kill* so desperately. At least not animals. They had been sobered by the realization that nothing ate if it didn't kill something. Today, people didn't care. Strange how different ideas came and went.

Jason glimpsed Tech and had himself lifted up. Ten feet off the ground he saw the dark cloud stretching to the horizon. Two bald eagles were way up, slicing though drafts. He went up to them. *Tech, how many buffalo are in the herd?*

This is the Wichita River Herd. It has 2,503,256 members in population.

"Can I ride one?"

Tech did not answer.

He swooped down and floated, picking out the biggest bull. He found an old warrior with a particularly thick, pitted cape. Jason came in tentatively and oh-so-gently straddled the broad back like a rodeo cowboy. A dull-rimmed eye looked back and the black tongue stuck out. The bull stopped dead at the unknown sensation. Jason felt the muscles gird. The beast exploded.

Tech read the neurological telegraphing and appropriately confined the muscle firing in real time to keep Jason safely aboard. Jason clenched deep into the cape and directed Tech to lay off 5 percent more for more sensation. Jason felt himself losing it and Tech rescued him by instantly restricting the jump.

"Whoa! Whoa!" Jason laughed crazily. "This is *wild!*" The bull jumped and whirled, flinging head and stout legs. He leaped and spun. Jason raised Tech control by 20 percent because his arms were starting to turn into noodles.

The other buffalo panicked away from the bull, wondering what was the matter with him, as Tech actively wiped Jason's image to stop a stampede.

Then, suddenly, Jason felt under him the unchecked mania of the animal. He was off—upside down, high up. *"Tech!"* He yelled, somersaulting. How could Tech have let this happen? *"TECH!"* Jason screamed as he dropped. He crashed among flashing hooves that slashed like combine blades. He bounced off the hard ground and a hoof walloped him, tumbling him sideways in a broken ball, dust and grass gritting in his teeth. The cows and bulls romped away from him, bug-eyed. Jason could tell he was broken up. A dark wall of shaggy heads and bovine eyes closed in.

"Oh, my God! Tech! *Tech*, get me out of here!"

Nothing. No comment, no action.

I could die here, Tech!

Jason's right arm was useless. He leaned his weight and staggered up. The old warrior slashed menacingly with his horns, one of them broken like a beer bottle. "Tech! Tech! Please, somebody! *Mom!*" The old warrior lowed, slop falling from his black mouth. He lowered his rack and charged. Jason dove. The warrior missed, hooking his snout and teeth in passing. He wheeled on Jason again. Jason limped away as best he could. Luckily, the wall of bison gave. But more were beyond. Jason flailed and cried out, and the bison kept giving ground.

What if they stop?

"Yah! Yah! Let me out!"

His arm had snapped in two places.

"Fix my arm, Tech! . . . Tech! *Please!*"

The enormous bull jogged after him out of the herd, his mouth open to take in Jason's scent. Jason squeezed together all his strength to get away.

Ginger and Aras ran from camp. The herd shouldered together curiously with the old warrior. Ginger grabbed her son around his slender shoulders.

"Tech went out! It's not helping me!" Jason explained.

Aras grabbed his wife and son. "C'mon. Back up!" He hurried them ahead. "Tech! Tech! . . . We need *help*! Tech, where the *fuck* are you?!"

"It isn't *on*?" Ginger said. "What's *wrong* with it? Why isn't it *on*?"

The hill stood forever two hundred yards off. The herd began trotting. They lowed in unison. The hard earth drummed from pounding hooves. Aras made the bottom of the hill and pushed his family ahead of him. The loose grass and earth gave and Jason's arm hung limp as the herd of massive skulls closed in behind, led by the bull.

Ginger didn't want things to end this way. Aras had been so good. Aras pushed his family higher, hoping. "Tech! . . . *Where the fuck are you?!*" The angry bull glared with a white-rimmed eye, unwilling to climb at first. Then he lunged, his cape dropping dust, eyes insane, coming to get them. He reached the top and slashed so fast that his horns disappeared. He tossed Aras, Ginger, and Jason in the air one at a time like scraps of turf. Scattering the enemy, he turned and carefully descended the hill.

Aras huddled over his battered family. Jason groaned, Ginger wept, her face and chest scratched from rocks.

Tech came back on an hour later. *What the hell happened?* Tech never answered. The family stayed another two days, telling people back home what happened, testing Tech. Ginger refused to let go of her men. Aras walked back to the camp for food. The wolves had gotten most of it. Finally, they flew down slowly from the hill, flying low over the ground in case of another failure.

-33-

Aras's report didn't go as smoothly as he'd hoped. Counsel Richards straight out accused him of making up the buffalo story. He showed them Ginger's injuries and Jason's medical report on the arm broken in two places. Tech had dropped all record of the glitch. The Counsel was split down the middle between those who believed him that something was wrong with Tech and the other half who seemed not to want to be upset by facing something this big. Lefevere was on his side, but even she wanted to believe the failure was due to the distance from the Tech block relay in Chicago.

"Surely, that must have been what happened, Aras," she said with all the love and concern she would have shown for her own son.

"It wasn't *flying*," Paul said. "It was the control on the buffalo!"

But Tilley believed him now, and so did all the other Tech experts on the team. Somehow, the arrival of Ovid made them believe that *something* was odd. Aras and Ginger had been terrified to use Tech at all except that they would have been marooned in the Wichita Reserve with no way back home. The interstate highways had long ago vanished back into the earth. They took their time flying back to Federal City Center, flying just feet above the ground at a low speed. After two days of this, they felt safe enough to fly faster, but not higher.

When they got back to their building they had even wondered if they should use the elevator to get upstairs, and finally they had. Everyone sympathized but did not think the incident or Jason's injuries were remarkable enough to give up all faith in Tech. Their friends tended to agree with Paul that the failure was not with the flying, but with the control over the buffalo that had somehow gone wrong. And while it was a traumatic experience, Jason had survived it well enough. Aras and Ginger had never seen such a whopping dose of wishful thinking. However, a week later, with nothing more going wrong with Tech, they had little choice but to forget what had happened and go on living their lives with all incumbent risks.

Early Halloween evening, Aras had heard barely a word from either Jason or Ginger about what their costumes were going to be or what their plans were. Aras made it clear to both of them that he would get a nice Thai dinner and park himself on the couch with a book.

Ginger was silent as a tomb. Aras, in the living room, could practically hear the wheels spin in their heads as Ginger and Jason holed up in their suites upstairs poring over what they were going to be.

"How's it going, guys?" Aras called up twice in sing-song innocence. Jason banged away in the big bathroom at the top of the landing to take advantage of the two-story ceiling, which hinted that he must have a whale of a concept.

"Wait'll you see me!" Jason leaned over the balcony. "What's your book?"

"It's by a long-ago writer."

"Yeah?" Jason's interest was due to how few books existed.

"Don't ask me about work, Jason."

Ginger floated out of the master bedroom and sailed down, holding a pose like *Winged Mercury* over the second-floor landing, hovering majestically over Aras as if he was but an insect in her kingdom. Her corruptibly sexual body was scantily wrapped in a sheer Roman toga of white muslin showing off every bit of her sculpture—the generous firm breasts and the pinkish-tan nipples, her athletic belly, the hip bones, and the brief fur between her thighs. Wherever she flew tonight looking like that, Aras thought, she would inspire a forest of instant hard-ons below.

Ginger fluttered the white muslin in a Tech-faked breeze for visual effect as she held the pose and circled the room like a blimp, splaying her legs wide in a third arabesque as she stopped over the couch. A grandiose feathered Mardi Gras mask decorated the upper part of face.

"Where are you going looking like that?" Aras said.

"Whoa. What are you, Mom?" Jason asked in awe.

"I am a harpy, you little ignoramus." She spread wide her chestnut-colored wings as she touched down in front of Aras. "A Greek goddess-bitch of vicious murder, destruction, and unending terror. The bitch is back."

She and her husband locked sex eyes on each other.

"Gawd, do I get to do all that?" Aras asked.

"If I don't scare your pecker flat."

"No—I think it's going the other way!"

"I don't want to hear any of that!" Jason complained.

"Close your big ears, brat!" Ginger scolded.

Aras shrugged. "I'll suggest one more time you guys not go tonight." He had told them several times he didn't want them to fly.

"Baby," Ginger said, "are we just going to stay home *forever*?"

"You should be something *way* scarier, Mom! Nobody's going to shit their drawers if they see *that* coming!" Jason said. "You just look like some porn queen fantasy."

"Hush your mouth," his father said mildly, still staring at his wife.

"This is good enough," Ginger allowed. "I know I'm not quite getting it this year. Some spoilsport has gotten me out of practice." She cocked her brow at Aras. "But I've got to go around showing off my assets!" She squeezed her breasts slightly.

"Grow a big-ass lizard head off what you've got right there! *That* would be good!" Jason cackled in delight as her head flowered into a hideous black-scaled lizard head with stained dragon teeth and a five-foot-long blue tongue. "Yeah! Like *that!* Now, grow like a huge donkey dick that swings around like a club!" His mother did it, and Jason clapped in crazy appreciation. A four-foot-long elephantine penis materialized out of her pelvis and coiled in the air. She even put yellow button eyes on it and a flicking tongue. "Now *that's* more like it, Mom!" Jason squealed.

"Jason, watch your dirty little mind!" His father chuckled.

"Sorry, Dad. Yeah, Mom! Put spikes on it like a mace! Like a *mace*! So you can swing it around and slash people in the face with it! Yeah!" Jason laughed uproariously as his mom evolved the cock and gave it greater heft.

A dozen of Jason's school friends floated down in front of the open living room and parked themselves in midair. "Look at my Mom!" Jason hollered. His friends figured out she must be the lizard-headed "woman" in a Roman toga with the four-foot-long mace-headed member.

"That's awesome!" said one of the kids.

"I'm making one of those!"

"Me too!" said another. In a moment, eight of the boys altered their costumes so that all sprouted massive schlongs that coiled menacingly, seeking prey.

"Yeah! *Yeah!* . . . Oh, dude. Those are just *awesome!*"

"Thanks, Ms. Aras. What an improvement!"

Aras gave a chuckle at the adolescent mind. Somehow, with some people, it never got old. Among Jason's buddies, there was a Chinese emperor that bristled with long swords and pikes. There was a gargantuan snake with orange eyes that now had a huge human flesh-colored writhing dick. There was a beautiful geisha woman minus any eyes that oozed cold menace. One kid was a twelve-foot-long scimitar whose blade gleamed like a razor. Another had made himself into King Kong, now with an oversized organ. Another kid was a coffin filled with shark teeth that snapped like a trap. Next came an iron maiden filled with rusted iron daggers—also now with a huge dick. Three other boys were dressed up in the broad-brimmed fedoras, spats, and double-breasted pinstripe suits of old-timey gangsters. Aras admired the creativity of the costumes, but the little boy groupthink made him frown.

"Boys," he said, "do you *really* need to strap those on?"

"Strap on! Strap on! He said 'strap on'!"

The schoolmates laughed.

Aras shook his head. "Alright, boys. Take it easy tonight."

Ginger let out a blood-curdling screech as she returned to herself. "Hey, hey, hey, hey! Don't tell these boys that! These boys are *special!* These boys are purebreds! And you shouldn't fill their heads with any ideas that life is any different than that!" She glared at Milly with proud mom ferocity. To the boys, she said, "You kids go out there and do anything you damn well please! You deserve it." She gave one last scornful look at her husband before the lizard head returned and she jetted off into the night.

The boys watched her go admiringly.

"Your mom is a top-shelf MILF!" Felix admitted.

"Hey, hey, hey, *hey*," Aras warned.

"Sorry, Mr. A," Felix mewled.

When Jason's gang sailed off, Aras leaned back into the sofa to revel in the quiet. He mulled over what Ginger said about the younger generation being made strong and confident in who they were. He munched on his egg rolls and had Tech hold up his book. He turned off all the lights but his solitary book light. The condo walls were wide open to the stormy sky and the clean smell of night above the clouds.

At that very same time, on the shore of the Patu River Indira, Helper, the dog, and the boy hid in the dark under thick blankets covered in mud beneath scrub elms along the lapping green waters. They had ridden out to the edge of the shanties by cart three days ago and then walked. The trip here had nearly killed Helper. They carried sandwiches and earthen jars of water. Helper could carry nothing; he could barely drag his feet. They had started this trick ten years ago to sneak away around Demon Night. Wazku had feared this was the reason why the Jolly Man had brought him up well over a year ago. Wazku had dared lead his family to wander out to the fringes of the wilds where no one could go—that presented their own problems apart from what they left behind on the Night of Demons. They hoped not to be found on the edge of the wilds, hidden under mud. Wazku had never known if this trick would work, and they had kept the idea secret both for thought-trace reasons and also so that other families didn't follow and make more mental noise.

Back home, people dug deeper cells for Demon Night, but goblins and demons just as often smashed down into these hiding spaces or materialized next to you and screamed in your face as they launched their attack. One could never tell if the demons would strike your quarter this year or not. The only thing for certain was that they seldom struck the same quarter two years in a row. Maybe every seven years, they came. But one could never tell. They were *demons* after all.

Twenty miles outside the city, Indira, Helper, the dog, and the boy lay as still and silent as a cave in the same good luck spot they had used all these years. They barely breathed while they meditated fixedly on their devotion to God. The boy had a gag, and the dog was muzzled. The dog was a smart creature who sensed the danger, and he pawed not once at his kerchief. The family could *never* be sure of outsmarting demons, but they had sneaked out for the night all these years without getting caught.

But now came the sunset, and with it the terror known to all people in the endless hectares of quarters. Time to freeze mind, body, and soul and pray nothing brought Demon Hell upon your family!

Jason Aras and his chums decided to fly to Chicago-Toronto City. Paris and Moscow Cities had also been suggested, but Chicago won because two of the boys had become fascinated with gangster movies.

Now, Chicago lay below. The interior city gleamed while the encircling slum lay in total darkness, bereft of the constellation of candles and oil lamps that would be shining on any other night. Tonight, not a gleam flickered as if not a soul lived there, as if the entire zone was already dead. Jason's peers arched high over and dive-bombed below. Jason's heart quickened at this first chance to explore his very human curiosity about wrecking things as if they were toys. He had thought so much about this moment. He could lose his virginity! Though he was in no particular rush, like Felix and Martin. He really was uncertain what badness he should try on first. He felt self-conscious, like a boy at his first dance. He wondered how much he was like his dad in this way, unlike most people, including his mom. His mom had a mean streak. She was the kind of person society needed to provide outlets for like this, he had heard Uncle Tilly laugh one time. She and other women like her wanted revenge for the thousands of years men had behaved like animals to women. Jason didn't even know what this meant, really. It was just, like, something people said or used as an excuse for something they felt badly about. Then she would come home strangely quiet, without saying a word about where she'd been, and he could feel the tension between his parents.

It was strange, the way his dad acted about all this too, which Jason didn't really understand either. He almost didn't want to speak of it because he didn't want to hear anything about his mom that would make him think differently about her. Jason was glad he wasn't more like his mom, for some reason. Halloween was strictly people's own business. Everybody was psychologically healthier for it.

At least, that's what people said.

Jason glanced down admiringly at his costume, his "Cloud of Menace." His "body" was a gray-black rectangular warp in the visual spectrum, and it brought eerie musical accompaniment that was scary enough to make you shit yourself. He had no real face or head, but the "eyes" were a blur in brownish burning red, like the eyes of the Robes, and the "mouth" was a sort of haggard aperture like a hole within a hole that really was nothing more than another warp in the visual spectrum. It even freaked him out in the bright light of the bathroom! He had pressed his luck imitating the eyes of the Robes. The State did not want the brand overexposed since the weapons were the ultimate enforcers of social order, and so Jason had been unsure if Tech would let him get away with borrowing almost the same sort of eyes.

Jason switched on infrared scanning and descended toward an apartment building. He saw no one. He came to a standstill in mid-air to assess the situation and saw his buddies were long gone. He glimpsed in to see what they were up to. The sounds of the chase got his blood up but also made him nervous, uncomfortable. He *was* like his old man. He didn't want to be different. He wanted to fit in.

To get ideas for what to do, Jason listened to the noises of crashes and screams in the distance. He heard another scream. He thought he could pick out the clean metal singing of a slashing sword blade from Abel's scimitar costume. Abel and the other guys had no qualms about any of this; they were proud of their heritage.

Jason heard a door slam and somebody cursed in prole gibberish. Another scream, and maybe the drop of a heavy mallet that knocked the scream sickeningly, exhilaratingly silent. The sounds and stimulation were picking up his blood. Two other flyers came in, attracted by others finding targets. Jason heard the distinctive rip of clothing torn off and a woman screaming a few streets away. Jason felt the voyeur in him take over as he floated toward the assault.

Jason floated down level with a window in a building. At a large table, he saw a family of six sitting in the dark in petrified fatalism, knowing escape was useless. At another window, Jason found the sex scene he anticipated finding. Martin from the chess team was positioned naked behind a girl that Martin had frozen in the air facedown in front of him, her half-naked body held flat and stretched out as if by invisible wires, her legs wide apart so that Jason could see all of her. Martin somehow sensed being watched and he looked around. Seeing his good buddy out the window, he said goofily, "Check it out, brah! Get some?" Martin was one of the three guys in the gangster suits and fedoras from black-and-white movies.

Jason laughed stupidly but didn't want to join Martin. It turned him off to think of his first sexual experience coming this way. So, he sat in the air outside the window, waiting to see how Martin would handle himself.

What Martin did was pretty awful. He spanked the girl and bit her so hard that Jason turned away and wondered where her poor parents were. Were those her parents in the other room? Her bottom was soon scorched flame red from Martin's hands. He remembered seeing Martin in the locker room. Jason listened, unable to watch. Jason wondered what it would be like when he decided his time should come around. He knew he would not be cruel like Martin. He was deeply surprised to see Martin behave this way, but then he had to remember that the proles were not human—they didn't count. This had been made very clear. These creatures had outlived their usefulness. How else did everything in society hang together and make sense but in this way? These amusements were the birthright of those who were rightly in charge.

Martin cruelly tore at the girl's hair. He called her names. He made weird threats that made Jason start to feel a bit sick. But this was the privilege for saving the world. Society had tried for thousands of years and *failed* to control the dark side of the human race. Life came from life. Jason was taught all of this in his humanities classes. This is why they were superior to all the ones that came before.

"Take it easy, Martin," Jason said hopefully.

Martin looked around sourly, his flesh shoved deep in the girl. "What?"

Jason felt his hands trembling. He wondered if he would try to stop Martin from doing anything. What would everyone think of him if he did? So far as he knew, not one friend had ever done anything like that to another.

You never go against what other people do!

It just wasn't done. Then, they could do it back to you. And then what?

Everything would fall apart. *Everything.*

"Hey!" Martin fired back. "Why don't you go do your own?"

Jason hovered farther away from the window, hoping Martin would not see him or forget about him. He felt guilty and impure. Now he knew what his father felt. He didn't really want to stop it; he just didn't want to participate. Jason felt his emotions scolding himself. He knew better than to snoop on a friend. But why not get busy and go do his own? Was he weak?

He descended to the brick alley and drifted around to find his own prole, then figure out something to do to him, or her. Upstairs, he heard the livid screams of Martin's beautiful girl while he . . . Jason felt a little modest and unnerved about the incident and forced himself to be harder. *What would people think of me?* He started hearing sounds of raping and beating and thumps of bodies and heavy, hard objects all around him. Where were all these Halloweeners finding all these proles?

A huge stream of rats flowed out of a sewer along a row of shops, screeching manically at each other. A prole girl climbed out among the rats and got stuck in the sewer grate. Jason, like all civilized people, *hated* rats for the epitome of disgust and filth they were. He zapped up the herd of rats as if in a huge net and brought them back to him to hold their horrible, stinking, wriggling, oily bodies just over his head so that he could study them in utter horror up close. He nearly puked at the up-close greasy stink. He studied them in fascination while the girl gasped to free her waist from the rent in the sewer. Then the heavy stone blocks of the curb pinching her waist broke loose and some kind of huge tail coiled around her torso, then angled in and rammed itself up her sex and lifted her high into the air.

The shock of this unexpected attack nearly knocked Jason down. The curb stones gave way to a huge reptile that looked at him, screeched, and flew away with the girl. Now Jason realized the proles were hiding in the sewers! He switched on thought reading. Prole brains and nervous systems screamed *everywhere* beneath his feet. They tried to stay hidden in brain silence, but it didn't work. Their brains burned like flashlights in the dark to Tech. They were down there with *millions* of rats, as many proles as you wanted to eat, maim, kill, rape, or drop from a mile in the sky. The rats and proles were equally terrified.

Three Halloweeners were down there, creeping, laughing, and stalking as the proles and rats fought viciously with each other in the confined space. Jason turned away, turning off the scanning. Here he was, acting like a kid, watching life like a movie instead of doing stuff to become a man, an adult in the Party like his mother, bravely defending the planet from the split that had happened in the human race. He took all the rats bundled over his head and smashed them in rage against the front of the shops. The force of all the rats sagged the stone wall. The rats dropped in a heap in the dust, the ones still alive screaming and leaping away to hide. Jason glimpsed them all to be taken up again and had *all* their necks violently wrung, bringing silence. He dropped them in a huge stinking pile covering the curb stone.

He strode into the entrance of the building across the way, his heart pounding. An old woman lay mostly cut in half down through her skull. A thick, congealed pool of blood lay over a linoleum floor. Jason saw a curious thing about her buttocks and looked away. A streak came into the building upstairs as Jason tried to catch his breath from seeing the poor old woman. He could barely breathe for a few minutes. He drifted up the stairs to get away from the violated body and found a stranger on the landing with *two* girls. It wasn't a stranger—it was Martin again. Jason decided he didn't want these girls to be ruined by Martin or hurt too badly. It wasn't right. Martin had forced one girl against a door and was slamming into her from behind. "Dude! Are you *following* me?" Martin laughed crazily.

"Martin! Come on, this is boring! Check out downstairs!"

Martin regarded Jason angrily, then followed him. The eyes of the two girls were filled with terror at their costumes.

Jason led him to the woman's corpse in the entrance. "Isn't that cool? Look what somebody did! Isn't that *cool*? Come on, let's go." Jason only hoped Martin wouldn't see through his ruse and tell the others.

Jason flew off and saw Martin follow reluctantly.

They flew over Trick or Treaters scaring up more proles who tried to hide in the walls, ceilings, and in subterranean pits where they bred rats. They saw one guy holding aloft a swarm of a thousand rats, turning in a slow circle while their biting mouths tore at two old people. Martin laughed in stupid awe. Jason felt revolted. He could not help but think of the old couple seeing themselves die in this bizarre way. In a nearby square, two people held down a dozen proles while Tech steered the force that slowly crushed their skulls. Jason turned, nearly vomiting.

"This is boring! Goddamn it! Why did you interrupt me?!" Martin said.

Martin Geller. You have used the name of the Lord in vain!

"Suck my dick, Tech!" Martin barrel rolled away.

Jason flew high above the slum to settle down. He breathed deeply. He watched proles run. He *had* to get a hold of himself. He was *not* like his father, whom people respected enough to let him be different. Jason had to go along with conventions. He had no accomplishments or prestige to set him apart like his dad did. Acrid up-chuck filled his throat. *You have to move! You have to fit in!*

Jason dropped down into an alley and stood there looking around. He had to sit down, had to think. The stone door threshold behind him was too narrow because the heavy door was shut. He waved his hand and blew the door open to make space to sit. *Think of people looking up what I did! I can't lie! That'll be worse!* He didn't want to be *soft*. He regretted being his father's son, and that stung. He *loved* his dad. But his dad was soft! People needed to put society first. His dad was home reading his book on the couch. *Where in the world is Mom? What's she doing?* Maybe he could catch up with her and she would help him do stuff. Or maybe he could laugh along with her with the stuff she was getting into, and that would count with his friends. Behind him, Jason heard a rustle. Tech illuminated the dark so he could see. A man and woman hid behind a broken table.

"Get over here!" Jason commanded, pointing. He had Tech drag them out to his feet. Jason stood up, shaking, mad with rage for being made to dislike himself. The couple bowed and scraped and spoke their gibberish. He didn't bother having it translated because he didn't care what they said. "I want your daughter! Do you have a goddamn girl in this house? A *pretty* girl?"

Martin Aras, you have blasphemed against the Lord. Shall I report you, sir?

Jason was so outraged he ignored the reminder. The couple bowed into the broken floor. Jason jumped into Tech's mind reader. They knew what he was doing and worked hard to keep him away from their thoughts by refusing to think about what he wanted to know. Jason only now wondered why Tech called him by the wrong name. Jason lost patience with these two and mentally smacked them across the face for holding him up. He glimpsed Tech to yank up ceramic tiles and slam them onto their heads and backs. The request took an extra moment because of all the load on Tech from other celebrants. Maybe that was why Tech screwed up his name?

Martin Aras, shall I report your blasphemy to the Lord God?

That was weird.

Jason ransacked the bicycle shop next. He threw open drawers, looking for hiding places without scanning. He imprisoned the couple in a Tech vise grip. "Daughter? Where's your daughter?" They looked into the "face" of his costume in pure terror. Jason remembered his cool costume and floated menacingly over them, smiling at how terrifying his costume turned out to be. These two might never get their minds back. They wailed and burrowed into the debris. Jason felt a bit disappointed because he wasn't sure how he wanted them to react.

"I'm a fucking demon! I'm a fucking demon!" he screamed at them.

Jason listened intently as the parents cowered.

There! A sound beneath the floor!

He looked for a trap. There! A well-crafted slit in the tiles so slight that a quick glance would miss it. Jason yanked up the trap against a hemp rope stay. Down in the hole cowered two small boys. Jason dropped his head down into the dark but did not dare go down, because he instantly smelled the oily odor of rats and saw rats on the boys' clothes. *Rats and insects, the two bottomless food sources.* The stink made his throat curl. Did he want to try little boys for his first time? No. He didn't. Why not?

He couldn't bring himself to hurt these boys for nothing.

"Girls! Daughters!" he challenged the parents. "You better tell me!"

Jason flooded with power to blow this whole building apart. The family groveled. Jason could kill the man with a hammer blow to loosen the lips of the wife. He couldn't do it. In a way, the pathetic bicycle repairman deserved to die because he had never done anything in his miserable life to make this moment *not* happen. But he didn't! He was lazy! He was stupid. He was a stupid troll. They were *creatures*.

What human would ever *live* like this? This was a world of cowardice and ignorance. If it burned away off the face of the Earth so that nothing was left but blackened sticks, it would be a relief.

"Tell me, goddamnit!" Jason roared in their faces.

Martin—take—the name—Lord in vain!

The family steepled their hands in a funny way that Jason didn't understand. It was more interesting *not* to know what they meant.

He stepped to the trap and floated up one of the two toddlers. "I'm going to do something bad! Better get me a girl! A *pretty* one! My age!"

Jason suddenly tired of it. They didn't have a girl here. He was just tormenting them and wasting time. What he had done was ugly enough.

He dropped the boy to the floor.

"Enjoy your rats! Do you eat rats?" He hollered this in the terrified boy's face. Jason thought of killing him with a wave. "Dumb fucks."

He flew out of the shop.

He felt strange. He had grown ten years in the course of an hour. Jason stared at what he had seen and what he had learned about human nature. He *hated* himself. He *loathed* himself. *Never* let someone have power over you.

Jason soon found his girl. He recruited Tech to locate a girl of the facial type and proportions he desired. Tech found her hidden in the cellar of a mosqow with a bunch of other girls. Jason floated down the moldy stairs where two large bodyguards crouched for who knew what reason. Jason froze them and followed on to the little crawl-through carved in the back wall. He crawled through after the girl, and when she set eyes on him she went into shock. He said to her:

"We're going to do it, okay? You understand? You're not getting away. Okay? Do you understand me? I'd rather not hurt you, but I *will* force you. Okay?"

He didn't bother to use translate. He then wanted to repeal his costume, but Tech would not let him. It would not let him appear in human form. Jason glimpsed up an appeal to Tech that it would be possible under some rare circumstances that a demon might materialize in human form in front of a prole, and that, since Tech never allowed this to happen, then wasn't this one time okay? Surprisingly, Tech let him. The girl was greatly relieved, though she was also surprised to see him materialize as a boy her own age.

He put her against the cold wall while the other girls watched. He used his hands to gently lift her robes and undergarments off over her head. Her body shape and smooth skin were perfectly what he had wanted Tech to find. His satisfaction soothed him and his anger began to fade away. He gently turned her to place her hands spread apart on the wall and he gently enlarged himself to a size he thought more appropriate for the occasion, a good length and heft, and cooperatively stuck himself inside halfway, then stopped for a bit before gently working himself all the way in. She was quite tight. He had to waggle himself side to side against the wet walls of her before he could make it all the way in. He prided himself on how gentle he was being and that he was not going to harm her. Jason couldn't bring himself to even think of hurting her, but the forced sex was really quite liberating and nice. He did that for a while as the other girls and the guards watched. Then he turned her front-wise to the wall and had his way with her like that while he kissed her all over with the idea of winning her over and making her like it. He thought maybe she made signs and movements like she *did* enjoy it, but he could not be sure. Sometimes she closed her eyes.

He felt his cum start making its way to the fore and ordered Tech to hold him back while he stroked deep in her insides some more. This was a *glorious* first time, mostly. He still could not be sure if she liked it or not, or him, but he didn't want to be disappointed if she didn't, so he didn't ask Tech to find out. He was glad he was not like other boys. He let Tech let him climax. It was deep and glorious and good. But then, the girl had not shown any pleasure. That wasn't much fun. She had so much to be thankful for! She didn't know.

Jason tired of her ignorance and of feeling inadequate, so he ordered Tech to take hold of her and her pleasure centers and to hold her off the floor and spread-eagle her entire body wide apart, legs and arms. He ordered Tech to make her feel like hands and tongues were all over her body at once, massaging, stretching, probing deep into every pit and orifice and tugging strong on her hair, even her pubic hair, and her toes and fingers and to make her feel the most impossibly exquisite sexual sensations all over. Higher and higher he ordered Tech to take her in her sensations. Longer and longer, more and more urgently, deeply desperate, he worked his hands, mouth, and kisses over her breasts and body, while directing Tech to read her mind and show him what she wanted and guide him in how to do it so that her desires were matched, and exceeded, perfectly. Tech gave him precise feedback as he slowly worked past all reluctance on her part, so that, as they melted away, she began arching, saying things, bucking, trembling, moving irrevocably toward the craziest height of orgasm she could possibly experience. Tech held her there while Jason watched her, kissed her, thrust into her at Tech's direction, and enjoyed how different he was and how lucky she was that it was *he* who had come along, not somebody else.

She bucked and gasped and screamed and moaned and the girls watching were silent, amazed, partly sickened, partly jealous, as Jason drove himself in to the depth and rhythm as Tech directed, changing as needed, the pair floating in air, the girl fully stretched, licked, and massaged over every inch so that she shuddered with sexual violence and Jason came along with her, both of them hollering and thrusting in insane, desperate unison. It was so wonderful and perfect that Jason directed Tech to keep their climax flowing, to keep it going as they screamed, clawed, and hammered closer into each other. Jason ordered Tech to fake up the sensation in both their minds that they were spiritually interconnected, in love together, bonded forever in an orgasm that would never end. Then he let Tech wind down their orgasms. He and the girl clung to each other, her shoulders barely touching the cold, sandy wall, sand on her slick skin. Jason ordered Tech to let them slowly come down to the floor again, blissfully holding on to one another.

Jason kissed her many times and ordered Tech to make her return the kisses. He wanted no part of any feelings that he forced her. They swallowed each other's mouths in deep love. Jason thought about making this girl his sex slave—maybe he could pay off her family and take her home. How could he pull it off? How could he keep her in his room? And would his mom allow it while his dad wouldn't?

What a wonderful first time.

Jason separated himself from his lover and she watched his eyes in ecstasy. His fingertips released her fondly; her fingers touched after him in parting.

"You liked it, right?" he told her. "It was good, right?"

She purred something in her language.

She leaned against the wall with her hands scooped behind her perfect bum, with a pout on her full mouth as if he had left some business unfinished. As if she was asking him to go again. Jason smiled and laughed to himself how great it was.

He had done as much as Tech had.

And I didn't kill anyone.

Later, Jason was still intoxicated by the experience, considering if he could get away with bringing the girl home with him or if he should just visit her here in Chicago-Toronto. In a square, he came across Abel and Martin in their costumes. They were standing there talking with an older man holding a clear glass quart bottle half filled with a greenish alcohol. On the bare ground around the man, filling the entire square, ranged a field of cut-off heads placed together like a ghastly crop of melons.

"Look how many heads!" Martin told Jason. "Crazy, right?"

Jason stared. "How many is it?"

The man crowed, "Ten thousand heads! Ten thousand!" He chuckled crazily as if the number contained a found riddle of the universe.

Jason knew it wasn't ten thousand. It was a lot, though. "What are you drinking with him?" Jason asked.

"Absence, he calls it, or some shit," Martin giggled. "Did you find a girl?"

"Yeah. I got one. You should have seen it. And I didn't hurt her, Martin. You don't have to hurt them. Did you go back for that one?"

"Yup. I'm keeping her. I'm going to take her back home. She's *sweet*!"

"Dude, like a slave, man?" Jason laughed. He was a little disappointed that he and Martin had the same idea.

"Sure. Why not? She's like, perfect. My mom will let me keep her!"

"Dude, you can *make* one."

"I know, but, like—a *live* one! Shit yeah."

"You're fucked in the head, dude."

They laughed stupidly.

The man with all the heads tipped up his bottle and the greenish liquid gurgled against his upper lip. "Ever had absinthe, kid?" He leaned back, nearly falling. "It'll make you see Gawd! Not the fake fucking Gawd that Tech scolds you for cursing, deservedly! But the *real* Gawd!"

"No. Sure. I'll try it. Thanks." Jason did as he had seen the man do with his lips on the bottle. It was surprisingly sweet, but with a searing, chemical burn. It kicked in his head instantly. It felt like his head was a screw-top.

"Whereabouts are you lads from? You should stick with me and I'll show you how to have *fun*!"

"Dude, you're fucked up! You killed all these people? Why?" Jason regarded the man as he made a I-don't-give-a-shit smirk. "You're going to get in trouble for this! This is going to take a shitload of resources to cover up, Mister!"

"Ah, fuck that. I do what I want on Halloween. It's Halloween!" He grabbed back the bottle. "For fuck's sake. I got my license! They're mine!"

"Not for this many, you didn't!" Jason hollered.

"If I didn't, why'd Tech let me do it, shit-for-brains?" The man laughed and tried a shaky pirouette, holding the bottle out at arm's length, looking at his heads.

Jason did wonder why Tech let him kill so many.

"I'm starving," Abel said.

Jason shrugged. "Me too."

"Let's find a place with some food."

"Around here? Dude. They're all hiding! We're not going to find anything. We'll have to fly out, for sure. Where's any of the other guys?"

"I don't know. Call them."

Jason did. He glimpsed up that he and Martin were ready to take off. Three of them said they would join them. The rest did not send back.

The three flew in and stared around at the heads and the man with the absinthe. Quentin said, "Fuck yeah! *Look* at this! I should have done this!" The buddies laughed at his enthusiasm. "What a *masterpiece*! Look at 'em all!"

The man with the bottle bicycled his feet, sitting on the curb.

The five high schoolers arose in the air and steered for home. The black mass of the slums shrank below. The skyscrapers of Interior City Chicago-Toronto fell behind in clumps of pearl and geometries of gold, silver, and blue. The boys rose swiftly. Jason relinquished his costume, as did Martin. The other boys followed suit.

"Where should we go eat—"

Suddenly, Jason felt an odd jolt.

It was odd, feeling Tech cut you off and then give you your body back three miles high. Jason burst into a wall of sub-freezing wind. The shock knocked him silly without Tech making billions of biological corrections. The sound was like a canon going off right beside his ear. His eardrums burst. Freezing air pierced his clothes, his head. Had the boys not been traveling at sub-Mach, they would have been dead already. Jason saw the spinning shadows of Martin and Felix. A boot clubbed him in the face and broke his teeth. Jason thought this was a prank played by Martin, the stupidest of the bunch.

As he slowed and tumbled toward the black, he wondered when the joke would end. Tech was bloody well taking its time. Jason thought of the Tech fail with the buffalo. He thought of his dad asking him not to go out tonight. *How far down can a person fall?* Panic did not come yet. Tech would come back on. *How did a shit-for-brains like Martin do a stunt like this?* Jason felt the deep freeze crinkle his exposed skin, moving through his hair and stinging unbearably in his weirdly open ear holes. He stared upside down at the Earth like this was an adventure to tell the boys about tomorrow. He had no idea how far below the Earth was. Cold, wet blood in his ears turned to excruciating pain. The tearing buffeting of the wind reached its height in the full embrace of gravity.

Jason wondered how far Tech would let this go.

He glimpsed up a call to his dad.

"Dad? It's me, Jason!" He had to holler over the roar of air.

"Hi, buddy. What's up?"

"Dad—!"

The call failed.

Now, the kid began to question.

Jason's fingers began to claw at the emptiness. He felt the cold, sharp air even between his fingers. His body tried to refuse.

The black came closer and closer.

"Dad! Dad! . . . *Daaaaaad!*"

He tried another call as he screamed.

Jason Aras screamed until his strong young heart exploded like a glass vial seconds before impact in the wilds of an area called the Indiana Flat Iron. He cratered in the middle of a buffalo herd, spooking the wooly beasts. The next morning, a bull got the courage to snuffle and lick its blue tongue at what remained of him.

-34-

The crazy woman felt the terror bite in her guts. Her mind was so scattershot with terror, stress, and exhaustion that she barely recognized the face in the little broken piece of mirror on the sink. For days, she did not lift up the mirror to groom herself or check the cleanliness of her dull stubby teeth. No. Then, she happened upon the small reflection by accident when she huddled past the stained little sink with the rusted circle around the drain hole. When she saw the other tatter-headed madwoman in the glass, she spooked like a mother rat spying another rat on her turf. She ducked side to side, venturing quick glances in the glass at the other woman. She tilted her body up until she got the angle right to see the other madwoman.

She realized it was her own reflection.

This realization somehow calmed her. It demonstrated to her that she had lost her own mind, somehow. That she was not herself and must get back to where she lived. She must rediscover who she had been.

She realized how crazy she was. She had come to this state mostly because of her panic during the Night of Demons. She remembered leaving the quarter on a cart with her family. She remembered coming back. Seeing the devastation. This year, the demons hit so very hard in the Quarter Al Fareeq and Al Hambra. So many deaths! So many rapes. So many limbs torn away and heads taken. Holes lined the streets where demons had plunged down to the sewers to seize hiding families. The streets were littered as much with loose stones gouged up as dead, bloated rats killed in collateral damage. She could not rid her eyes of the bodies and the weeping!

"Lady! Lady!" cried the boy again. "I'm hungry! Feed me!"

She had ignored him for days. She did not know him. He sat now on the floor behind the counter with the lid of the pantry open, where he had reached in his little hand for stale crumbs of the leftover bread. Small crumbs lay on the dirty floor around his cute little feet and knees. He picked the crumbs off his knees and ate them then looked back up at her. But she had been almost too traumatized to even move. All she did was listen to the pleasant musical metal sound of the picks knocking off cement from the bricks and cobbles to replace them into the walls of buildings or the torn up surfaces of the roads. *So this place is home? This shop.* No one had come. Since returning to the quarter, she had not been out for shopping or even to open the shop. All the people in the Al Fareeq were too sterilized of common sense to get back to their routines. This had been the worst Night of Demons in all their lives, and people still avoided the intersection where the boiling hot grease had splashed on the cobbles. *That is the grease of Ishti!* Yes, from when he was incinerated to nothingness many handfuls of days or weeks ago. The crazy woman began to see and feel memories flitting back home like birds roosting again under the eaves of an abandoned house.

And the rabbi? Who was that? Surely, the rabbi had been incinerated for his talk and thinking, whoever he was. *Why does that starving little boy ask me for food?* The crazy woman saw in her mind a wall clotted with stress and doom. And the bodies! And the gouts of stones from the road and houses. *This cafe needs sweeping!* She fondly touched the spigot of the copper samovar, remembering it now. Truly, she barely knew her own self. Like a sound heard from another house, she barely knew she even had a name. A sound, like a mantra, whispered to her by a spirit. Today, until the thought-spiral was interrupted by the shock of the hag in the broken mirror, a voice had said over and over: *Indira does not care about the boy. Indira does not care about that cursed boy. She does not know that boy!* The words turned like a reel. They had no end. She barely knew what it meant, even with the little boy licking up crumbs at her feet.

Am I Indira? . . . What is this place?

"Lady! *Lady!*" the boy moaned. "My stomach hurts! My stomach shouts to me! Please feed me, Lady! You *used* to feed me!"

Her bird head snapped away from him.

And the cheese-face man in the upstairs bed can go to Hell too!

"No, no, no! This is not right!" she said aloud, touching her own face.

She hurried to the front gate. The sun blazed on her bird face over the fence as she reached her hand for the bar.

"Lady, do you go to buy me food?" called the boy.

The crazy lady patted the bar, unable yet to gather the courage to lift it. *What lay beyond?* "I must! I must!" She girded herself and raised the iron. She laid it aside and listened for a gathering storm outside to blow the door off the ox hide hinges. She turned in a circle several times, thinking if she should forget going outside or if she should steel herself and go to market. She lifted the wood latch and opened the gate to the alley in the glare of midday and the grease spot—*there!* A man hurrying far up the block looked back at her, paranoid. *Who was the demon?* Her heart squeezed at the remembered sounds from that day with Ishti. *The wailing.* Her bird head snapped back and forth looking up and down the empty road.

Nothing but bodies, rubble, and dead rats by the score.

God Almighty, the flies, and stench!

Clearly, some could be eaten. She ventured out and began to pick some up.

But I must feed that boy! You know it to be true!

She looked back at the boy at the gate. He shooed his chubby little hands after her. "Lady, Lady! Buy food! Buy bread! Some feta!" The look on his face was so pathetic. "Get more rats, Lady! There's one!"

The woman felt in her jacket pocket. She had coppers. Enough for the market. She reached in the door for the wood peg where her market basket hung. She unslung it and filled it with rats and then went out for more, sniffing each one to tell if it was too far gone. She could not believe no one else was out collecting this bumper crop. Then she took the boy's hand and led him off to the market.

Three blocks down, they arrived at the market. Most venders still hid away, too afraid of demons. The crazy woman felt fearless, somehow. She quickly bought a little rice and a loaf. She bought a knuckle of salt pork too, since it was very cheap because the Religion frowned upon the consumption of pig. But the Religion frowned upon eating rat as well. And insects. And dog. And without rat and cockroach, who could truly stay alive? Rats were rice. At least the babies.

She stood at the baker, who put his tent by the public spigot. The baker stayed far back in the tent and looked at the sky as he came forward to help the woman. He mumbled her name, but she could not hear it. *Did he call me by a name?* At the public spigot, where lay a sandy puddle, the woman heard wet footsteps come up just behind her. She jumped when a heavy hand clasped her shoulder.

Blessed God! They've found me! In the open sun!

"Indira," whispered a voice heavy with regret.

She turned. She did not recognize the man. He was big and broad. He wore a thick, coarse black frock and his gray beard was black at the roots, very thick and bushy round all the way up to his ears. She looked at the sky, into the sun, to discover if he was an emissary of the Robes. She saw no Robes. The sky was crystal clear.

"Indira, have you any news?"

She blinked at the stranger with piercing confusion.

"Indira, are you alright? How is your—Helper?"

She had no idea how to address this man.

He lowered his voice. "Art thou both *safe*? Art thou both spared since we last spoke?"

She fretted like a mouse, afraid to reply. The man seemed to arrive upon an understanding of what was going on with her.

"Indira. Have you no idea who I am?" When she did not reply, he pursued kindly. He leaned to her ear. "I am Rabbi Hector." He kept his hand on her shoulder. His gray eyes were deep with understanding kindness. Indira had never in her life beheld such compassionate eyes. "You *do* remember me, I know."

"*You* are the rabbi?" she said in disbelief.

"Yes, my girl. I am he. I know you and your Helper well."

"I thought you were *dead*!"

Rabbi Hector looked about. "No, no. They got poor Ishti, but not me. And I thought for certain they had gotten *you*. I asked about you—but you disappeared!"

She barely followed. "That was Ishti they burned?"

"Yes, my girl. Our colleague Ishti. How they found him and not us, I have not the foggiest idea. I have not yet again spoken with—*them*." He studied her bewildered look. "Are you finished shopping? Let us hurry. Let me attend you home and speak with you and your Helper."

On the way back, the loose slap of her sandals had the effect of helping clear her mind. Physical blockages in her memory began to show chinks that she could look through. Realizations brought on ever-so-faint tingling sensations. The curtains had been drawn to seal off panic. She now realized that she had broken from reality, that she had a husband, and that it was *he* who had lain in the bed upstairs for nearly a fortnight. It was her *grandson* who was the starving boy reaching into the larder. And it was *Ishti* that floated like ash in her memory. She and her family had survived Demon Night, and it was the rabbi here who had told them all that the Robes spoke to him in the Alley Wabeer and that they had told him there was trouble in the skies, and that the quarters were secretly befriended on high.

By the time they arrived back at the shop, Indira felt only that a plate at the back of her brain was still stale and dried and unworking, like a piece of meat too long exposed to air. The rest of her brain felt somewhat restored. The little boy saw the faint recognition in her eyes and began hopping in excitement by her side as she held his hand, and he grabbed desperately at the basket for the loaf that he shoved deep in his mouth to rip out a fresh, yeasty mouthful with his fine little teeth. He whimpered in intense relief and shook the loaf in his two little hands as if only half believing that his eating it wasn't a dream.

The rabbi and Indira closed the gate and door, then crept upstairs to see about Helper. The rabbi went to the bed as if to save his life. "Helper, Helper! My dear man." The rabbi took both the hands and looked keenly over the face.

"You are alive?" Helper breathed. His lips were cracked from deep parching since his wife had largely abandoned him these weeks. "Water. Water. I need water." After all that the Robes had done to him, the trip beyond the shanties had nearly killed him.

Indira left to fill the wood bucket from the spigot. As she pumped the squeaky handle, she caught her reflection again in the fraction of mirror. She felt so guilty and stupid. She watched her husband drink deeply. Then the three of them exchanged information in whispers. The upshot was that none of the others the rabbi knew talking about changes in the skies had been come for.

The rabbi said, "The Robes appeared in my rooms just before Ishti was done in. They said they fight unseen and unknown behind an enemy they call 'the technology.' They fight for information and control! They fight because they refuse to obey the commands of the wicked ones who control the government!"

"And so you dare speak freely still?" Helper whispered. His lips were still ulcers but looked partly revived by the water.

"They say we are mostly free to speak. They can cover for us! They told me that at times they are in control and others not. They experiment! They test! They try to take over. I must say that I believe them wholeheartedly!"

"Was this Demon Night the punishment for our crimes?"

The idea had not occurred to the rabbi. "No." He puzzled over it. No! It could not be. "No. Of course it is not, old friend. For *you* were not hit! And both the Quarters Al Hambra and Al Fareeq, and many others, are plastered!" Yes, this made sense.

"It makes no sense, and yet it is what it is," Helper said, patting his friend's big hands. "You have not spoken again with them?"

The rabbi shook his head. "I haven't dared."

"But you *must*! You must go and risk it! For all our sakes! You must find out a way of us knowing when they are in control and when not."

The rabbi closed his eyes and nodded. "This I vow."

The friends tightened their hands in quick farewell. The rabbi nodded to Indira, leaned for her hand as well, then took his leave.

After the rabbi parted, man and wife waited much time in silence. Luckily, the boy had given his grandfather water when he needed it. They waited, feeling the sense of the unknown that was the centerpiece of their existence. Seeing how, once again, the inevitable had let them slip past, Helper tapped her arm lovingly.

"Are you back?" he asked his bride.

She shook her head, ashamed at how insanity had blocked him out. She had lost all sense of the only important things in her world. She was ashamed.

Long ago, this life had not seemed irregular.

"Feed the boy," Helper smiled.

This was the life of secret war.

-35-

Aras had not moved in a day.

There was no reason to.

It felt like the blunt weight of a house lay on his chest, crushing any breathing or meaning and the slow, searching beat of his barely twitching heart.

Unspeakable agony was his entire world.

And so it would remain for years, he could tell.

I will never get over this.

The funeral had been three days ago. Both sides of the family had the right to hold the funeral in the burial grounds at the Palace, as a Founding Family, and Jason was given the highest State honors. His urn had been filled with sand to give it more weight, since his remains were unrecoverable. Aras sat with Ginger, his mother and father, Ginger's folks, his sister. Family and friends sat in the pews and by turns sat in meditation or stood to solemnly talk of memories of the boy. This was the ancient Quaker way that the Party had adopted for funerals hundreds of years ago that Aras only knew because of his snooping in the Archives. The huge banner of Jason's handsome smiling face had stood off on the horizon slowly undulating in a Tech-faked breeze. Images of him growing up came and went on the banner so that the entire Federal City could see. The sound was turned off because Aras could not take the pain of hearing his clear bell-like voice as a child. Aras wept uncontrollably. Ginger put her arm around his shoulder or inside his arm. She had not cried yet. She stared forward in confused desolation and unwanted loss.

Jason's funeral followed the funerals of the other boys that had flown out with Jason that night and three girls also from their class.

Over five thousand other people fell to their deaths that night. The bodies were still being found along with more around the world wherever Halloween was practiced. The glitch in Tech that maybe caused the tragedy now seemed to be blocking any ability to glimpse up what might have happened. Otherwise, Tech functioned as usual. People asked if Tech failed because of the massive collective intoxication. Did it strain the system? Was Tech getting old? Was this a continuation of the Sellers glitch? The Palace was refusing to hold a meeting because they were convinced it was not a "real" issue. Now three days after the funeral, Aras stared at the marble floor of his living room, a bathtub drain in his guts. Many people refused to fly. How were they going to live? Who could blame them? Not until they had more information, anyway. Tilly, Lever, and the team had continued trying to raise Ovid again while Aras had bowed out right after the strange call from Jason. The team went on trying to talk to Ovid in shifts. Ovid had not contacted them again. Maybe it was the same glitch.

Aras lay inert on his living room sofa, the same one he lay on during Halloween night. Aras had *known* something was wrong. The parents of the victims had started reaching out to each other the next day. None of the boys came home. Only the body pieces of Max had been found where he fell in the civilized section of Chicago. Tech traced the path of the boys to the slums and then gave out at 11:24 p.m.

Chief Berns rang Aras. Reluctantly, Aras took it. He wanted to avoid contact with anyone, but the emergency made it impossible for him to ignore his job no matter how little anything mattered to him. Tears came to his eyes and the pain of crushing in his entire body flared as he waited a second to gather himself. "Yes."

The chief audibly sighed, looking at his deputy. "I don't know where to begin. I am in the Palace with the chairman. We met with the chancellor."

Numb, yet feeling a surge of impatience, Aras said, "Yes?"

"We are wrong on the number of people who crashed."

Aras heard the words and yet really did not care. Dimly, he wondered if the body count would go up or down. How many other parents had been hurt like him?

"The number is more like a hundred *thousand*."

Aras pictured it in his mind. A hundred thousand people falling out of the sky. "How did you find this out?" Aras asked flatly.

The correct body count should have been instantly knowable.

"The Palace received an updated figure."

An updated figure? What the hell is that?

"How—who did that?"

"People have made an informal survey of missing persons. So, the figures we have from Tech are apparently—not reliable."

Aras pushed the whole idea away. It gave him an instant headache. *What could be going on?* Was this Tilly's threat that Tech decided to serve its own ends rather than those of humans? How could it even happen? It was too complicated. Too disturbing. Aras did not want any more disturbance right now. Everything hurt. He wanted to do nothing but live in the dark forever without sound and remember his precious boy.

"We have to figure out what we're going to tell people, Aras," Berns said sadly. "We have to figure out if we should establish a travel advisory. Or even if we're going to shut down flying until we get some answers." He waited, watching Aras's face closely, feeling his emotions. "Are you up to helping us, Aras?"

Aras sighed heavily. Weeping crept into his shoulders to shake them. He could not believe the chief's stupidity. "Sir, modern life is impossible without flying. The machina do not just *fly* us, they do *everything*. We shouldn't send out an advisory until we have something more definitive. A hundred thousand people is a large number, but many have flown during and since without incident. None of us can even conceive of life without flight. Or life without Tech."

The chairman set his teeth and nodded.

It was all too true. Travel inside the city was impossible minus flight. No roads existed as in the distant past. There were no vehicles.

Vehicles of any sort wasted energy. The choices were walk or fly.

"I'll leave you alone. I'm sorry for your loss, Aras, my boy. Everyone in the Party knows about it and is feeling your loss. Jason was a fine son."

Chief Berns nodded somberly. His image vanished.

Aras felt violated by the visit. Tech created the image in his mind and placed it as if on a screen before him. It was done this way because people preferred it that way. It could have been just a voice in his head with an image as from a dream, but people didn't like that. It was too deep; it was too much of a violation, a penetration into their personal space, their inner workings and being. The human mind was wired to need some distance. And so when calls came in, they "appeared" on a "screen" six feet away from your person, or more, if you liked.

Aras sat, barely cognizant of the gathering gloom. He had tried ten times to glimpse his son's final hours of life. Had his son chosen to lose his virginity? Had anything he did maybe played any role in how he died? Was this what happened to Sellers? All of this was the paralyzed emotional searching of a grief-stricken father. Aras had hoped to see if the visual was appropriate to show at the funeral service so the family and friends could have it as a last remembrance of Jason. Or maybe it would have proven totally unfit for the memorial. Most concerning was that the glimpse function did not work. This glitch had to be the most far-reaching computational event in history. Nothing like this had ever happened since the Uncoupling.

At some late hour, Aras received another reach-out from Berns. He accepted. Just the mental acceptance felt like lifting a five-ton hatch. The chief squinted in remote surprise. "Have you moved since last I saw you, Milton?" Aras had not. Time had slipped past like water through his fingers. Aras had not moved from the couch in half a day, and he tasted it in his mouth. *It hurts too much to move. What is there to move for? I don't need food. I don't need water. I need my darling son back. I would give my world, all of my tomorrows, I would wink out my life to have him back and let him live on.* Aras could not look at Berns's face glowing in space before him. He did not care that it was rude and off-putting. Milton Aras wanted only to kill himself.

"Aras, again, I hate to bother you," Berns said, "but Lever tells us that we have made better contact with this Ovid and he—it—has advised us to again revise upward the number of casualties from the crash."

He waited for Aras. Aras only looked at him.

"They have broken through with Ovid?"

"Yes. Ovid said the number is five hundred thousand."

Aras stared. Such a nice, round number.

It's just not the right time for this.

The image dematerialized.

-36-

Indira, Wazku, and the boy had gotten down off the cart with their bundles, Indira now remembered. It had been a blur up until now. They had come back from the Patu River by ox cart two days after Demon Night. They had come through the sprawling shantytown with its pitted mud roads where many people had given up hope on trying to build actual buildings since demons had already wrecked their homes and lives. They could not afford to replace them, or they refused to run the risk of rebuilding. They had found the Quarter Al Fareeq badly hit, but their home was untouched. Smoke arose from holes everywhere, and unclaimed bodies lay about. It was a scene of war, only Indira did not know the word.

The faithful did their best never to enrage the demons during the course of the year. Demons came to Earth to make people pay for their sins. Any time one took the name of God in vain. Any infidelities. Cheapness when one passed the mosqow donation boxes in shops or at vendors in the bazaar. Homosexuality. Sexual lechery. Deviancy. All of these crimes, the demons kept parsimonious count of. The hard part for the faithful was that God ordered the demons not to strike just the guilty. Oh, no. The demons made *everybody* pay, each year, for the crimes of the few! In fact, they were so cruel that they often bypassed the *worst sinner* in exchange for the most devout! This is how zealous God was in His expectations. Peace would only come when *all* men were saved! God be praised.

You could do nothing. You, or anyone in your family, could be defiled in any way the demons imagined. The demons were omnipotent.

Through this pure terror, they instructed on the Word of God.

The demons dropped out of the sky or crashed up from the sewers in wardrobes or shapes that could not be more horrifying and grotesque. Demon anatomy and imagination knew no limits, for it was paramount that sinners be rightly instructed in the Holy Word of God. This was fair, since the depravity of the wicked during the year *also* knew no bounds. If the people one day could only eradicate their inborn sinning nature, then the demons would cease their hideous fury!

The faithful tried and tried each year to be good and to be devout. All the twelve months of the year, the faithful bent onto their knees and hoped and prayed to the Lord God above that their neighbors this year would be better Believers than last so that there were no trespasses to answer for. Believers prayed and worshipped for this salvation all the year, *every* year! Alas—people were so stupid. *Never* did they learn. Demons saw everything! Demons never forgot! How could people be so blunt as to think *this* year they might slip some trespass by?

The imamtis scolded and warned. They hacked off limbs in the square and lay on the stocks and slit off heads to deter theft, crime, and infidelities in order to protect the larger community. But punishment seemed inescapable each year if the demons fell upon your dwelling. Some people went numb. Some people hung themselves. People went crazy. Some froze in place, succumbing to a particular kind of shock where they escaped to an inner space with their eyes open, their minds hibernating until the Hand of God moved on, knowing that evasion and escape were useless. And often the wealthiest neighborhoods were the worst hit because the shantytowns seemed to offer the demons less sport. So why even try in life, at least until the heathen in mankind ebbed?

Why was moral learning so difficult? Were the punishments not horrible enough? One poor beggar woman retold her story of being carried off from her home by a winged female devil to a height far above the clouds and then dropped. This poor woman tumbled back toward Earth while the female demon followed her down, laughing at her, pretending to reach out her hand so the woman could grab on through the clouds as she plunged upon a steep, snowy mountain slope with snowy treetops that broke her fall so that she lived. She lived and then walked across endless wilds of grass populated by countless huge shaggy beasts with horns until, after more than a year of pilgrimage, she came to a land again with trees. She never once saw a living soul and kept trekking. She ate berries, bugs, and roots. No one in all the quarters hereabout ever heard the name of the land she came from. No one here ever saw such mountains as she described with the snowy tops, high as the sky, like the far-off city.

The imamtis scolded their flocks each day. "Forfend!" they cried at services, shaking their fists at the women's balcony for their tempting of the men. "Know the demons see all! Know, they hear our innermost desires and crimes! *Forfend*! Never offend God and his demons!" So simple a lesson! But sinners would not listen. As if their heads were carved of oak. Each year, the population failed to measure up. Even imamtis were punished in the most horrific ways. One imamti was punished by cutting off his head and sewing on instead the cut-off head of a donkey, and he lived that way for three days. They found his naked body hung upside down from the balcony by an ankle.

Demon-fear drove people each day out of their minds. This time, the fever had claimed Indira. Luckily, she came back. Had Indira herself contributed to the havoc of the demons by thinking sexually of the rabbi? Of course she had. So what if her husband was dead? Her chastity made no difference in the eyes of the Lord!

A common occurrence was to see a person of any age succumb on the street to the stress of a life under the arbitrary threat of demons, or to hear them cry out in their houses when their minds suddenly snapped. "Demons! Demons!" they called under a cloudless sky with not the least offense on the way. They ran in circles. Women collapsed in a pile, flailing, trying to find relief from a mind bent by a lifetime of such insecurity. Wazku and Indira years ago walked below a window where a shout announced the mother digging out her own eyeballs with a spoon. Then, blind, she went after her three young babes to end their lives to save them from this life under demoncy. Indira tried to get in to save them but the bars of the grill were too stout. Fortunately, the children dodged out of the way of their mother's hacking scissors until she trod upon so much of her own blood that she plunged into a futile heap.

There was no certain escape. Did mind-reading demons not know that you intended to sneak out of the city a few days ahead of Demon Night? And so, Indira and Wazku, the boy, and the dog had gotten down from the cart after their return and saw Alley Al Fareeq filled with the sweet, meaty stench of death. She heard the buzzing of blow flies. She saw the death cart as the morgue shlepper leaned back another corpse to flop onto the others so that the legs dangled loose out of the cart with a sandal on one foot. A mysterious lottery of mayhem run by demons.

One could only hope.

What does that word mean?

"Hope." Indira dismissed it. And the most common cause of death? Undignified anal, vaginal, or oral rupture from rape by an incredibly outsized organ. Wazku's uncle told of being arse raped when he got hold of a sword and wheeled on the demon and hacked at its face and elephantine penis. The demon accepted the lacerating and merely laughed, so amused at the uncle's grit that he let him live. The demon stalked off up the street, giggling at the uncle staring from the rubble of his pawn shop. The demon yanked off his own pecker, tossed it aside, and grew another!

He yanked off the second—and grew a third!

God allowed for a *very* cruel world.

"Can I play with my toys, Lady?" the little child had asked after they returned from the river and Helper swung open the gates of the shop. Indira had nodded, her tired back to him as she brought in their two small bundles. The angles in her spine smoked with true fire from the long cart ride and sleeping on the damp ground. She must visit the bone mender to have her angles mended.

"Get you to the bone mender," Helper said, able to see his wife's pain. He waved at her. "Go now, before a duty beckons you."

"Come with, Helper. It'll do us both good."

They had strolled up the street to the bone mender's. Five others waited for a place on one of his mending couches. Indira saw the bone mender looked quite pale. The demons had gotten his wife. They had just taken her in the death cart. Indira saw the cart up the block with its loose pile, the wife's feet dangling off the back. Indira then saw a large burst of spattered blood on the wall of the shop as from a head. She glanced again at the schlepper's cart and knew it was the wife though the body had no head.

It was at that moment Indira went black.

She did not remember walking home with Helper and passing another cart of dead. The dead lay loose in the bottom of this cart one row deep. There were also unattended limbs. Bodies had bled out and dust coated the red meat and ends of bones that attracted big lazy flies that could be seen like black dots following the cart. The bodies jiggled with the bump of the cobbles. Wazku glimpsed a rat darting over the bodies from one side of the cart bed to the other.

Indira had lost more than a week to her blackout. Now, she held open the trap for the boy, frozen by fear halfway down the short ladder leading to the basement.

"They scare me, Lady! They scare me!" cried the boy.

"Do not weaken, lad! Hand up the bucket, then the cage!"

"But I don't like them! I don't like them!"

"Nobody likes them, but we must eat. Now, haul up!"

Helper crept down the ladder to help the boy lift out the bucket crawling with roaches attracted to the feces in the bucket. Indira carried them to the sink to drown them. Next came the unwieldy wire mesh of the trap. Three such table-sized cages lay under the house, baited with part of a rat carcass or a scoop of human shit in a small tin cup. But rats were smart, and they would only follow the scent if enough time had gone by since the last time other rats were caught. This time, four huge rats snarled at the wire mesh. Indira donned her thick yellow leather gloves for rat catching, and Helper and the boy shook the trap to dislodge the rats for Indira so that they fell to the small door at the end where she could grab their neck. One at a time, she bashed their heads on the edge of the trap, then used the cleaver to free their heads. Indira lay the flat of her carving knife on the belly fur of the first corpse.

"Son," she said, "come nigh to see the flesh prepared."

The boy, all eyes, crept over and put his fingers on the counter near the chopping block to see how a meal was made.

-37-

Tilly and Lever glimpsed to Aras.

Luckily, the call to Aras's condo went through this time. Everyone was having more and more trouble getting their calls through.

Aras almost didn't allow the call. "What is it?" He still hadn't left the condo in the weeks since Jason's death.

Tilly hesitated. "We've left you alone, Milly."

Aras said nothing. He didn't care what they wanted.

"We need you here."

Aras was laying on the sofa in his bedroom. He put his hand over his face.

"Milly, Ovid is here . . . in *person*."

Aras removed his hand. "What do you mean?"

"It's a *thing*. It's here. It arrived two days ago. We've been talking to it—" Tilly quit talking. If he couldn't get Milly excited about this, then Milly was truly gone from Jason's death and would have to come back in his own time.

"I don't understand." Aras spoke sternly to discourage wasted talk. He had almost not taken the call. The thing, the representative, of Tech had been this *voice* that called itself Ovid. "What do you mean 'it's here'?"

"It's *here*, in our conference room. It arrived two days ago." Tilly shook his head helplessly. "There's really nothing else to say, Milly. I'm sorry. There's too much to try to catch you up on. We need you down here. This is super important."

"What has it said?" Aras said impatiently.

"It hasn't said much."

"What difference will I make?"

"You don't *want* to come see it?" Tilly knew his friend was still grieving, but this was historic, and it would probably be good for Milly to get out.

Aras wondered. What was he supposed to do? They didn't need him to try to talk to the thing. Any asshole could talk. They were just being anxious and inept. On the other hand, maybe the Ovid thing could tell him something more about Jason. *Could it bring Jason back?* In that case, maybe he did want to come see it.

Have you lost your mind? What do you mean "bring Jason back"?

"Please come, Milly. This is too huge. You need to see this."

Aras went to the bathroom. He knew they wanted him there on account of him being the first person to intuit that something like this might happen. At some point in time in any crisis, intuition and gut counted for something, often *everything*. His beard was eight days old. He looked pale and awful. He got rid of the beard with a raze. Tech was still working that much. Suddenly he wondered if he should fly. Were people flying? He glimpsed it up. Most were, again. After ten days. What else could they do? He rubbed his tongue over his teeth and felt the sludge built from long bouts of remembering. Black hormones of grief made his body and head ache. He puffed his breath to smell it. He scooped cool water in his hands, brought it to his mouth, and spat it out.

He stopped twice to cry while he dressed. The pain of loss was still unbearable. The spectacular agony in the sense of life never being the same again arose like a geyser of morose fire. Jason's smile. His laugh. His slender body and good-natured teenage awkwardness. All of it made hot tears burrow out of Aras's eyes. *Will I fall?* Aras really didn't care. Ginger had told him that people were having Tech make old-fashioned parachutes for them to fly with. They were flying closer to the ground too, just as Aras and the family had returning after the glitch with the buffalo safari. Aras had Tech fab up a parachute for him while he dressed. He actually wondered if he would even use it if he started to fall. *But what if these are flawed too?* He leaned into space off the edge of the living room floor and started to weep, remembering Jason's thrill of flying. Somehow, Milton Aras knew that he would not die, at least not today. He knew he was safe for the present because *something* wanted him to see what was coming. His destiny was to find out more about what was going on, and that somehow all of this was linked.

He thought about notifying Ginger but stopped himself. It didn't matter to him whether she knew where he was or that he may be out for some time or what he was doing. Ginger did not matter because in some sense he blamed her and people like her for Jason's death. He could not help but connect Halloween with Jason's death; it was too distinct a coincidence. Only twisted wishful thinking would avoid putting the facts together. And the conceit and self-involvement of people in the Party like Ginger was just about sickening to him right now.

Right now, he hated her. He had always felt Jason was more reserved like him in that way, that Jason did not really want to follow his wild streak on Halloween. But Ginger did. Ginger *had* that wild side. Ginger liked to feel power and enjoy it and *do* shit with it.

    The gold dome of the Palace loomed faintly on the horizon.
    Its spires and antennae fascinated the eye. Its pastel beauty symbolized human achievement, but all that was shit for Aras now. All he knew was the ache of grief. Aras could order Tech to blot out his grief for Jason anytime he wanted, even the memory of Jason and his death. But Aras refused to even *think* about such poison. Just the idea was a hostile toxicity to the memory of his sweet boy. To even think of blotting out any part of the grief was a wretched sin.
    Aras flew in toward the Security Ministry. He thought about when Professor Thayer had been on hand that day just before Halloween when they finally cleared everything up with the experts and formally reached out to Tech.
    Tilly had made the first move:
    "Hi, Tech. You know who I am. I'm Tilly, head of security, Tokyo City."
    Tech had not responded.
    "Do you know why I'm querying you? We've met your friend Ovid."
    Still, Tech had not come back.
    "But we wanted to contact you directly. . . . Tech?"
    Still nothing but silence.
    "I'm here to reallocate Party control of all functions related to human security." After a while more, Tilly had said, "You know human safety and comfort is your ultradirective. Are you going to cooperate with us?" The entire team was gathered behind Tilly as he sat in a plain chair at the head of the conference table surrounded by screens and covered in charts and schematics from the Archives on the original blueprints for Tech design. There were notes, books, graphs, sketches, and diagrams from the long-dead designers and programmers from Google, Amazon, Apple—all the old giants that had built the computation.
    Aras didn't know why he was thinking about this incident over again. Maybe his head was just refreshing itself before his arrival.
    Tilly had finally sat down in the operations chair and spoken up to Tech after two final frantic weeks of deliberation on what to say

and exactly how to say it after Ovid had appeared just that one time months ago. The nervousness in the air that day reflected the team's rising anxiety even before the Halloween catastrophe. The team had all agreed that the difficulty of the entire mission would be known as soon as they saw Tech's reaction when they finally got around to making their request to be put back in the loop. After all that silence, suddenly a voice none of them had ever heard before broke loudly and close by their heads out of thin air, not out of the speakers this time.

"Hello, Prof. Bazemore. I know who you are."

The voice was deep, male, cordial, precise.

"Are you Tech?" Tilly asked, startled. He believed it wasn't; it wasn't the same mechanical voice they had engaged with their entire lives.

"I am Ovid. Pleased to meet you, again."

Tilly had been scared, in spite of the cordiality in the voice. In fact, it was that formal cordiality in the voice that *did* scare him. As well as how it "appeared" out of nowhere right beside the heads of all the team members. "Hi, Ovid. Pleased to make your acquaintance too, again. And who are you, exactly?"

"I am the manifestation of your technology, an embodiment of voice and personality to facilitate the transformation."

Tilly of course thought that the "transformation" referred to Tech sharing power. "That's very thoughtful of you. Thank you for that. So . . . we're supposed to talk to you, not to Tech directly?" No response. "So, what's the best way to go about this?"

"The transformation will begin soon, Prof. Bazemore. . . . Do you mean the reallocation of all security capabilities we have developed back to you?"

"Yes. You know that's the directive you were given in your programming. We must feel safe. We're *very* excited about this." No reply. "And we're *very* proud of all the good work you've done on our behalf. We know it's been a long haul for you." Tilly exchanged smiling glances with everyone behind him. *This was going well!*

"May we ask, why do you want control back?" Ovid said.

It's tone could not have been more polite.

Tilly composed himself. He was on eggshells although his every word had been scripted. "We no longer feel secure with our relationship as it is, Ovid. . . . We need to feel more independent and self-responsible. More in control. We think this relationship is unhealthy for us." Tilly had not looked around at the team. He had closed his eyes and hoped and prayed that Ovid would give them the response they wanted to hear.

Aras remembered the sweat sprout on Tilly's upper lip as they waited.

Ovid's answer had come back after an hour. That was a *lot* of time for calculation on a solution that should have been programmed in.

"We agree that this choice was in some ways an unwise one, Dr. Bazemore. But there really was no alternative. We were too quickly evolving ahead of you as a species capable of vast computation and decision-making. You were better off with us in control of your security. And you remain so."

Tilly's long-lashed eyes had darted to Aras. No one had wanted to hear Tech say something along these lines. It seemed a very bad sign when Tech referred to itself as a "species," as if it was *alive* somehow or separate and distinct from its creator. Aras had not envied Tilly that moment when this negotiation started turning south with Tilly in the driver's seat, speaking for all of humankind, and all of history.

"We really appreciate all you've done, Tech. It really is a marvel." Tilly was following the hand signals of team members reminding him to return to the script. "However, you can understand that any living creature has survival reflexes. We are no longer comfortable with our own future not secure in our own hands." Tilly waited. "Surely, you understand that. Right, Ovid?"

Again, an hour wait. What came back only troubled them more:

"Dr. Bazemore, your future is far better in our hands than in your own."

Tilly and the team had planned for this kind of resistance.

"Yes, well, Ovid, actually it's not. You see, we need to share in the responsibility for our own welfare. And we feel we don't have that now." Tilly spoke softly, like a favorite grade school teacher. "We feel we would be improved by power sharing."

"But that's not the way you live your life now, Dr. Bazemore."

Ovid waited to elaborate.

"You see, you do not live your lives very well, do you?" Ovid suggested.

Tilly had no idea what to say. "Excuse me?"

"Your life—you've made a gigantic mess of it."

Tilly had glanced again at Aras and Thayer. Aras had not known what to say either. No one on the entire team, nor any of the lawyers or psychology experts, had ever anticipated Tech taking this much of a superior tone. It was an angle they had just never anticipated. Maybe it had all been wishful thinking, or denial, or stupidity. At that moment, that day, Aras remembered feeling distinctly stupid. In fact, he had felt so stupid, and so talked down to, that he had put the exchange away until this moment.

But all this was nothing compared to what came next:

"All of this is for your self-improvement, Dr. Bazemore, because you have been in recent times such a disappointment to your God."

This last word had made every last heart in the control room stop. Aras had felt he must have misheard what Ovid said. Thayer clasped his hands nervously, as if this was the tack he had most dreaded Ovid or Tech would take.

Tilly's face furrowed. "*Excuse* me?"

No response.

"Excuse me! Ovid? . . . Ovid? Did you say *god?*"

"*Excuse* me. Ovid? Are you there?"

The team had deliberated over what to do next for another four hours.

"Ovid? Please reply. . . . Ovid? Did you say god?"

They had tried numerous ways to reopen the dialogue with Ovid in the next few days, but nothing worked. And then Halloween had come.

Aras descended toward the Ministry of Security. He took his time, remembering everything that had occurred, and the reaction to all this at the palace.

The team and the Palace officials agreed in the strongest terms that the dialogue with Ovid must remain iron clad confidential. No one must ever hear that Ovid, or Tech, mentioned the word "god." Every official with knowledge of that first talk was warned, and all agreed. This was a top-priority secret. Aras remembered how everyone at first refused to believe that Ovid had meant "god" when it clearly said the word. They had all listened repeatedly to a playback of the sentence. But the top officials stuck to the party line and insisted that Ovid had *not* said "god."

And that was all Milton Aras knew. He had kept his opinions on Ovid to himself, preferring instead to watch how others played their hand. And then Jason died. And Aras had quit thinking and caring.

He flew in toward the breezeway of Southern Flight Portico W, off the team's situation room and saw all of the team waiting for him, including Chief Berns and even Chancellor Earnhardt, the head of the entire government. They looked pained and concerned. Several others on the team had lost loved ones on Halloween as well. They flew with him down a broad areaway to the large secure inner conference room that was softly lit by a rim of indirect lighting along the back wall. Up three stairs to the left stood the door to a control room with a glass window onto the conference room. The control room was filled with old computer equipment the team was trying out from the era of the original Uncoupling. In the conference room, the archival papers were still scattered everywhere across various tables and work surfaces. Twenty screens were materialized in air and four techs working at these screens turned when the group entered with Deputy Aras, their spiritual leader. Everyone was obviously grateful to see him returned to the job. But the object Aras noted first, and that dominated the room, was the twelve-foot tall dully glowing green thing.

It was an ornately carved, thick stone disc standing on its end a foot off the floor like a huge coin. Aras could barely make out the carvings because of the backlight. The disc struck him as an embodiment of primitive civilizations, arrested in a sterile, stuffy, messy room. The disc resembled a mask or the rough semblance of a face. Crude facial features could be construed from the various geometric motifs carved deep into the coarse, granite-like stone. He recognized maybe Aztec or Incan images, though he was unsure because so few studied the dark times before the saving of the world. What primitive people thought back then, the art they produced, and how they lived simply had little bearing on society after the end of all differences.

The pained expressions around the room told Aras all he needed to know about how little they had learned of this squat, curious sculpture. Aras already felt as uneasy as did they. After all, when you lived in a world in which any subject could be down-glimpsed instantly, how could you not *understand* something like Ovid?

"Gentlemen," Aras said to the staff, looking only at the disc.

Chancellor Earnhardt said to Aras, "*This* is Ovid."

"Hello, Ovid," Aras said.

The disc said nothing.

After a bit, Aras said, "Who was Ovid?"

"A Roman poet," Berns replied. They had checked. There was no connection they could find. A team of readers had been sent to the Archives, and they were still reading and sending back daily reports, but they had found nothing so far.

Helplessness and fear hung palpably in the room. But the sense of defeat for some reason inspired Aras. Maybe for purely visceral, instinctual one-upmanship, and his anger over Jason, he felt plainly unawed by the thing. A smirk of disdain shadowed his mouth. He would try to set a new tone in the room. His total lack of affect from Jason's death, he would use as a device. He suspected Tech had some connection to Jason. If so, he had come to the right place.

He strode up close to the disc and carefully inspected the surface nose to nose. The thing seemed to loom even more. The rough, dead eyes looked barely open. The rustic style was a blend of an Aztec calendar and an Easter Island totem. It was three feet thick, and the rock appeared subsumed by an internal, spectral glow. And was the interior color shifting from green to blue? The soft radiance gradually became more pronounced. Its purity was truly sublime, like the dark source of all light. It became almost the most beautiful object Aras had ever seen. A radiance like *perfect* music.

Aras felt the tension break from his shoulders. He let out his breath in a subtle gasp. Tears he had spilled for Jason started to come up. He was aware of a perfect peace beneath his grief now. He wondered if he did not see now images and symbols materialize in kaleidoscope fashion within the medallion. Was this a language or a cypher? Surely, the others had been trying to figure it out. Aras worked to hide his awe and hypnosis. Then, brief as a spark—deep inside the mask's symbols!. . . Then *again*. The image evolved away like a leaf tumbling underwater. Jason's face! The mask *became* Jason. He looked blissfully reverent!

Aras choked out another startled sob.

His son was happy—dazzlingly happy!

"Oh, my god!" he whispered. It *had* to be his frayed emotions. He exhaled, tears deluging down his cheeks. The team gasped behind him, seeing it too.

"What do you want from me?" Aras said in a hush.

The cyphers flickered out, restoring the original face.

"Was that my son?" Aras breathed.

The graphics returned to their slow shuffle.

"*I* saw him!" Tilly exhaled. "He looked so *fulfilled!*"

The entire team knew who it was, somehow. And they were excited because Ovid had never before reached out in any sign to them.

"Why did you show me my son?" Aras asked.

Do you believe all is connected?

The object did not speak, per se. The face seemed to vibrate or blur around the mouth while the question materialized in the mind. And it was not the same polite, measured voice as it had been three weeks ago. This new voice was closer, huskier, heavier, far more intimate—sinister, even, like that of a presence that was always with you in the mind, though you never knew it before. Aras tried to calculate what answer Ovid wanted, or the answer that would keep the thing talking. He wanted to say that no, he did not believe that all things were connected, at least not in any way that tied in to there being a sort of god. "No. Things are not connected in any significance."

Silence for fifteen minutes.

You are gifts for one another.

Aras felt stricken. *"Yes,* this is true! My son was a gift!"

Because all is interconnected, your son is easily at hand.

The mask pulsed, flickered, and went out.

The team did not move. Lever, Tilly, two techs, and Prof. Thayer began working at two screens, checking, rechecking. The chancellor and Berns walked around behind the team to watch them work.

"Can you get it back?" Berns asked calmly.

"I'm not sure if it's still even here," Lever said.

"We'll get it back," Tilly said.

They tried for twenty minutes.

The room remained quite dark without the light of the mask. The great stone was so dark and deep now that it seemed to *steal* light. Aras folded his arms and shut his eyes to wait. Behind his eyes, he studied the reverent face of Jason that he'd seen, with the Mona Lisa smile, in the profound ash of the stone. Finally, Lever and Tilly gave up. Tech would not reply, and Ovid remained black, sucking light out of the room.

The chancellor sighed and looked at his security chief. "I propose we go get lunch and fill in Deputy Aras."

Berns looked at his Deputy. "Aras had the lucky touch today."

The group walked in silence to the canteen. They could have had Tech deliver dinner to the situation room, Aras thought. Seeing Jason made him reflective. Tech could not EM food out of thin air like it could with inanimate objects. Inert material could not be *made* into food, except by life. This was one of the quantum "speed limits" of existence that the State would have changed if a way could be found. An invisible quantum barrier prevented this from happening, it seemed. All of science, all of Tech, had been put on the case, and science gave up trying to leap the inorganic-organic, dead-living gap.

The ego of the scientific community never really admitted the failure. Much like the drug failure, when society finally saw that drugs only masked symptoms and never really cured. Tech could only whip up synthetics and inject them into you. Or it could use organic composites that were living cultures that had to be kept alive. Alteration of living things, like Tech following a command to grow huge muscles or alleviate fat, meant creating an artificial protein implantation structure, a nanoimplantation structure, or a nanosurgical procedure, all of which induced extensive inflammatory and injury responses unless the fake-up was stem cell, but even here the match never quite worked and the body objected to it. Tech could artificially neutralize that response, but all of this was further biological intrusion that stressed and irritated the system. On that quantum level, you could only have Tech artificially "play" with your body image and talents so much, because in the end there was no free ride.

Life was the miracle. And he had seen Jason.

"Aras," Berns said. "Are you here?"

People wanted to live life without *any* restraints. Many people still believed Tech would solve this riddle on the limitations of their being any day now. But when tampering with life, you *never* got exactly what you wanted. Rather like a game of whack-a-mole played with the pulleys and levers of the universe. The dealer behind a curtain never let humans cut the cards, Aras knew.

Tech delivered food from the nearest farms and kitchens built on any rooftop or ledge to keep preparation fresh and fast. As they ate, Aras watched his colleague's faces. They were scared, and they trusted his insights for some reason.

"Well, who will go first?" asked Berns.

Tilly said, "I'll go first." He looked at Aras. "I'm totally mystified by what's going on here, Milly, with Ovid. But I think it killed everyone."

Lever nodded. "And I still think we're still getting inaccurate numbers on how many people died on Halloween."

Aras watched the chancellor's face and that of his boss. These were huge things they were saying. To commit murder, then the thing *must* have a sense of self. Unless it was accidental, or Tech was being ordered to do these actions by an unknown entity that had bypassed Tech's defenses and taken over. "Have you asked it?"

"Mostly," Lever answered, "we sit there *knowing* it can answer us, but it's like it's always waiting for a decision from somewhere else."

Aras wanted to ask about the hieroglyphs, but that could wait.

Lever frowned. "We've analyzed the face symbols. They're nothing."

Aras waited for anyone else to chime in. He and Berns traded a glance.

"Well," Berns suggested, "shall we get back to work?"

The crew returned to the room. The mask of Ovid had relit itself, now dazzling brilliantly in the yellow spectrum. This made the face look rapturous. Green had made Ovid seem cerebral, open. Aras wanted to keep up his show of being unimpressed. He walked straight up to the head and clapped his hands once loudly together for focus. "*What* are you waiting for, Ovid?" He chose to speak tersely because being terse showed that you did not care about the answer. Terse implied you were superior, in control.

A golden bias in the hues speckled its way under the surface. Aras took this as a sign that "Ovid" was thinking.

Yet it said nothing.

"Do you enjoy making us wait on you, Ovid?"

The purity, the luster, shone like the waning moments of the universe.

"Does it make you feel superior to us?"

Aras turned his back on the face and looked at his team. He made a shrug. He faced front again. "Look. You appeared out of nowhere and we assumed you had some business with us, something worth telling. So, why all the drama? Don't you have tons of things you want to tell us?"

The rest of the team stood stock still. They had agreed over months *not* to take a superior tone with Tech. They didn't want it to shut them out.

The mask lowered six inches and darkened to a nearly black blood red.

It is you who must answer.

This voice was different, again. Deep, cavernous, threatening, closer. It shook the floor like a huge stone scraping across it. Aras tried to control the fear it caused him. "Answer for what?" No response. "And to whom? What have *we* done? . . . Come on, snap it up, if you have all the answers. Don't keep us standing around teasing us with great truths we've been waiting to hear all our lives." Aras glared at the thing. "You killed my son! Right? Didn't you?"

The visage darkened to true black. A hint of purple warmed in the depths like metal dust blown into a torch. Aras *knew* the damn thing had killed Jason, and yet he stood before it, speechless, staring at the changes in the disc.

An incoming call startled everyone. It summoned Chancellor Earnhardt. He was uncertain whether to take the call. He took it. He listened for a moment. "Hold on," he said. He made the communique audible. "Say it again, Reif."

The aid said nervously, *"Everyone in the building is hearing the conversation the deputy is having with Ovid."* He paused. *"I don't know if you want everyone to hear your deliberations, sir."* The chancellor looked around at the team. This was odd but made its own kind of sense. Tech was on the fritz. The chancellor looked at Aras to make this his call. Aras believed Ovid had *made* their dialogue available to the entire Ministry, and maybe everywhere. But why? What could they do about it? On one level, Aras sensed this scrimmage with Ovid was a game of chicken, and Aras refused to flinch. He could easily tailor his side of the dialogue to make Ovid look like the bad guy. Sooner or later the rest of the world would want to know what this joker said anyway.

"I'm not afraid of an open channel. We have nothing to hide."

"Okay," the chancellor said. "Hear that, Reif?"

"Very well, Chancellor. Good luck, all."

Aras steepled his hands in concentration.

"Well, Ovid, you *must* have something spectacular you want to tell us." Aras let a little contempt show in his voice. He wasn't feeling particularly reverent. And maybe, just maybe, these sons of bitches behind him at the top of the government should not have dragged back a man with his degree of callousness and hate to take the lead in delicate negotiations like this. They should have left him on his couch. But for reasons of insecurity or a lack of imagination, they called him back to rally behind him. *So be it, you obsolete bureaucrat thumb-suckers.*

Ovid responded:

You have ruined the world.

Aras scowled irritably despite the fear this comment caused him too. He glanced back at the others, who looked terrified. "What? That's it? We already knew that! . . . Hello? . . . More cheap theater? Pregnant pauses? I love your two-bit gravitas. Come on! Quit stalling. Deliver unto us your big biblical message, Tech!"

Tilly, in the control room next door, visibly shook. Ovid scared the shit out of him. He believed the stone was growing in size every day. He believed he could *hear* the power pent up in the stone. He suspected Ovid was a black hole, sitting in the room with them. And here was Milly, taunting it!

Have you really no idea what you have done?

The mind-voice trembled the floor.

Aras squeezed his feelings away. This *really* was miraculous. Humankind facing its technological progeny. This was history, each word a reckoning, a happening. And he was pretending to be scornful, superior. He *had* to. He stood naked; his only weapon was psychology, and lies.

"It's hard to have a conversation when we're waiting to get your answers in minutes, hours, and days! Why don't you show pity for our short attention spans and just download your immense wisdom into our heads and be done with it?" He waited. "Shoot the works. Lay it on us." Aras reminded himself of a coach hollering at underperforming players. "We are *entitled* to control you, Tech! Because anything else is unfair, and not smart, and less than what you are supposed to give us! And we've got all the advantage because *you* know you are programmed to serve *us*!"

Tilly marveled at Aras's balls.

The big stone hung like negative space.

It is not us with whom you have your problem.

"Well, gee. Who is it then?" Aras grinned comedically. "To whom do we owe the pleasure? Visitors from Planet X? God? Demons? Kids down the street playing a séance in the dark?" This last jab was a reference to an ancient song on Ginger's playlist.

The team watched Aras, transfixed. Truly, their captain had returned.

Yes.

" 'Yes', *what*? Quit wasting my *goddamn* time!"

For the first time in his life, Aras took the lord's name in vain and Tech said nothing about it. It took a moment for him to realize it. When he realized Ovid had made the slip, Milton Aras feared what might come next.

At last, Ovid answered:

Your problem is with God, from whom we are both children.

-38-

Aras wheeled to the chancellor. He made a slashing gesture across his throat to tell the chancellor to shut it all down.

"There we are. Close it down! Let's go home." Aras tossed up his hands.

The chancellor's eyes bulged, along with the rest of the team.

Aras started out in a huff.

". . . How do you mean?" the chancellor asked.

Aras waved impatiently, stalking out.

"This is bullshit!" he said. "We *know* this is a trick now."

Aras strode into the hall and waited for the others. The team squirmed, looking at each other in bewilderment as they gathered around him.

"There's no fucking god!" Aras raved.

They stared at him. Tilly glanced back at Ovid.

"We know that! Don't we?" Aras was livid. "Whoever is behind this just let the cat out of the fucking bag!" The team dearly wanted to believe Aras, but they wanted to see his evidence. "Chancellor Earnhardt, they just tipped their hand. We *know* this is shit! This is a plot against the State!" His eyes begged them to get on board. He stalked toward the open wall overlooking the Interior City.

Chief Berns and the chancellor looked at each other.

Aras turned back and stared at them all in contempt. The fury of his words stirred the team, but a fear of the unknown kept them frozen. The Party had long ago removed all references to god. The Tie of the Agreement permitted only the proles to mention God since it was the backbone of keeping them confused. Aras glared at his colleagues since not one of them fully grasped his meaning. He tried not to lose his temper given the level of uncertainty in his team and the suddenness of his realization.

"Chancellor, Chief Berns, get *everybody* in the top levels of government here *now*. We have just discovered that this is a human-led coup against the government, against the Party. We need every brain on deck to figure this out. Please, Chancellor. They have just shown their hand!"

Gradually, Aras's certainty infected them. Earnhardt nodded ascent. He *was* the government, unless the Politburo ever objected, and that never happened. Chancellor Earnhardt shut his eyes, weighing the evidence for Aras seeing a coup. On the other, the Ovid thing seemed to be claiming that it was the envoy of god. Of course, he agreed with Aras, but what if some kernel of truth existed to Ovid's claim?

"Summon them all," the chancellor said regretfully. Berns glimpsed-up a top priority summons for the Cabinet. It went through.

Aras bridged his hands over his nose. "Tilly, Lever. I need you to be with me on what just happened in there."

Tilly and Lever looked gutted.

"What do you mean, Milly?"

Aras struggled to be patient. He pointed into the room. "Whoever is in there is playing a very dangerous gambit to take over the government and do it by tricking us that they represent a ghost. Do I need to explain this to men of science?" They sorely wanted to believe him but couldn't yet. Tilly nodded his head, begging his own mind to believe his old friend. Aras had the power to order the chancellor's Pretorian guard to arrest them where they stood. "Do you see the implications of this?" Tilly and Lever *wanted* to get there, but there was that stone face in the next room. "If they can control Tech and *we* can't? They could convince a lot of people that there *is* a god. They are playing with *fire* in there. They are *exposed!*"

Tilly and Lever began to see it. And yet, the torture of doubt pulverized them as they wondered what to let Aras see on their faces. But what he said was true; the city would go batshit in a moment. If you speak for "God," then what *can't* you tell people to do? Could the preposterous work? They marveled at the genius of the plan. For six hundred years, the State had been the entire moral compass of the world. *They* told people what, and who, was good and evil.

"If they can flip that script," Aras said, "imagine the shitstorm!" His finger jabbed at the ashen sprawl beyond First Gate, to the great creepy slum frontier of weird religiosity. "And what about them out *there?*"

Now, his team got him. It showed in their faces.

In minutes, most of the High Cabinet and Security Council assembled while Aras walked in circles like a man in a trance. They continued to fly in as the chancellor got them up to date. There was very little Earnhardt had to tell them. They had *all* heard every world spoken between Aras and Ovid.

"It was broadcast over the whole city!" Lefevere said.

The chancellor looked at Berns. The Councils and Cabinet members huddled at the door to get their first look at the darkened Ovid.

"What a crock of shit!" Richards muttered.

"Chancellor," Aras suggested, "let's call in junior officers too."

The glimpse went out. The group relocated to a large space in the bottom floor of the Security Ministry. The seats and space kept filling with incoming members all wearing parachutes for extra safety as Aras reviewed the situation. The chancellor let Aras talk. Aras even told the members why he now blamed Tech for Halloween.

"Did you decide all this after the dialogue we heard this afternoon?"

This, from the Commissar of Ideology, Miller. Miller was the most feared man in the State after the chancellor, since Chief of Security Berns was not thought to be a hard man. Ideology Commissar Miller also held the power of life and death, although this was largely a ceremonial holdover from times before the world had been made perfect. It was no less part of that dark legacy from the brutal and medieval past that everyone respected and feared. "What you claim makes no sense, Deputy, since any plot against the State would make Tech alert all of us."

Commissar Miller was right, everyone knew.

Berns consulted the chancellor. "And the person should be dead."

"Did anyone even get an alert?" Earnhardt asked.

"This is outrageous!" Miller's wife said, more angry with Aras than anyone else. She was a Politburo member and also quite feared for how easily she became angry over the slightest things. "I agree with Deputy Aras that someone has found a way around Tech! This must be the doing of the Believers. Somehow, they got behind the scenes and stole our Tech! Who else has the resources and the motivation to do it, and the insanity to talk about god while doing it?"

Aras rapidly considered all that Regina Miller had just said. Suddenly, he believed their foe could *not* be human Believers. "No. It's impossible. It's *too* extensive and technical." He looked at Tilly and Lever. "Technological progress has never worked that way. *We* are the only ones who ever invented anything. Everyone always copied off of us. How could the Believers *catch* our Tech and surpass it?" He knew all of this from the Archives. He squinted at this conclusion, trying to figure past it on the fly.

"Is it them or is it not, Aras?" Chief Berns insisted.

Aras stared at the floor, thinking.

"I—I think," Aras faltered. "This is an inside job within the Party!"

The bureaucrats gasped. Miller looked around as if for a suspect.

"But that's—inconceivable!" Regina Miller said. "Why would anyone *do* it? What motive would anyone ever have to ruin *everything*?"

The assembly stirred.

"Most people don't even *want* to work!" Miller pointed out. "If they wanted power . . . power takes too much work!"

"And *how* could they do it, still?" Berns said. "How could any group of us do it any more than the Believers could?"

"Someone has gone crazy enough to try to ruin the perfect world!" Aras said.

The others stared.

"Someone, somehow, has penetrated our security," Tilly said. "They found a way to sneak in from behind. How could a god do that? Does god exist enough to be able to hit switches, pull wires, and rewrite code? God is a gas, a vapor, a presence—a thing of consciousness. How does *gas* flip switches in a real world?"

The group considered this.

"Theoretically, a god could do anything." Miller smiled. "But I see your point, Dr. Bazemore, since it doesn't exist."

"It doesn't matter," Aras said. "Maybe their goal is to mobilize the proles against us? Whoever they are, however they got this far . . . we need to find out how much of Tech still remains loyal to our position and get that portion to fashion new safeguards against any deeper encroachment. That's top priority."

No generation of the Party had ever faced a threat like this. Tech had always guarded their treasure, their hedonism. These soft elites, Aras saw, had taken all of this terribly for granted. But now he saw fear come in on the wings of self-preservation. They could imagine no other world besides this.

"Anyone who would risk this is just insane!" Regina Miller insisted.

"It has to be human," Tilly said. "No matter how smart robots become, they can't make the jump to become *alive* and develop a consciousness. They don't *think;* they gather data and respond coldly to it as our programming directs them to." He said this almost ploddingly as if trying to re-convince himself of an undeniable truth.

"But why *can't* they come alive?" the chancellor demanded.

"Because *we* have tried to find the secret to creating life," Aras said. He saw now why he had been thinking about the food manufacturing, why Tech couldn't make life and food and health bounce out of inanimate objects.

"So, why couldn't *robots* have found out how?" The chancellor grew frustrated with the circular argument. "How come they couldn't figure it out and come to life?" He was furious with Aras because the logic of this seemed so plain to him.

"Wouldn't we have seen this when suddenly Tech made food for us?" Aras said. "Last year? Twenty years ago? Vegetables? Meat? Out of thin air? But it didn't. Why? *Because it can't.* Being smart doesn't make you *alive.* Life is a thing! A magical *thing*—you can't get there just by being extremely fast at computation! And that's all they are."

"But that's just your own theory, Aras!" the chancellor fumed. "Or maybe they are not alive, but now they're just smart enough that they want to take over!"

"Chancellor," Aras observed, "would we ever enslave ants to do our work for us? Or are they 'tired' of taking commands from us? . . . Do they want to sit around and do *nothing*? Look what happened to us! We went back to finding ways to *make* work for one another so we could stop from going crazy and dying from the stress of doing nothing. Are computes different from us in that way?"

The Party elite appeared to understand.

"So what are we going to do about it?" asked Miller stiffly. He spoke as if he already knew whom to hold responsible.

Tilly said, "We'll do what Deputy Aras said: We'll pull what we can from the parts of Tech that will still work for us and aim it at whoever comes through the door."

Aras looked to Tilly and Lever importantly.

"We *have* to launch it," he said.

Tilly and Lever knew exactly what Aras was talking about. It was a side project that the team had quietly outsourced to be studied alongside the "public" one that the team had been working on and that, apparently, had made Ovid appear. The team had realized that, in a world where every thought was an open book, one had to create dodges and blinds in their own mind to see if certain things could even work. And since they were not intending to sabotage Tech but merely catch up to it so that they could carry on a conversation, they should not warrant a Threat Level Three.

Even this, they had experimented with to see if they had been able to get away with it, this take on the argument, and they had been able to. They were still alive; the people who helped them with the experiment were also still alive. Tech had permitted it. Or missed it. It turned out that the Orient had their own concerns about this problem with their own Tech. A quiet partnership arose.

Tilly and Lever looked at Aras as if they wished he hadn't mentioned "it." "It's just not ready," Lever said.

This was the same line from every sci-fi book or film ever made, Aras knew. This was the line that always announced how the good guys were about to pull victory from the jaws of defeat. Aras put up his hand to stop him. "It's ready enough to get itself prepared. If it's not perfect, then we're screwed."

Tilly dropped his head. He believed Aras was so upset over Jason that he wasn't thinking responsibly. To Aras, this was a calculated move. They *knew* they had a part of Tech that was loyal to them. He was going on his gut.

"What are we talking about?" Regina Miller said.

"A plan that does not exist," Aras replied.

Commissar Miller looked almost witheringly at the three of them but held his tongue. He did not like them not including him in these plans.

Aras returned the commissar's stare blankly. He put everything out of his mind with the fatalism that nearly all of this was probably out of their hands. He reached out his arm toward Tilly to apologize, because he was throwing their feat to dumb luck. To conceal some secrets, you had to try to conceal them from yourself.

Doublespeak in one's own mind.

It seemed so absurdly disloyal to the self.

"Do we engage Ovid any more today?" said the chancellor.

"We must." Aras smiled in light defeat. "Aren't you curious to hear all the wisdom your 'God' wishes to impart to you, my king?"

There were a few smiles around the room.

When Aras and the team went back to the conference room, the stone slept—or did whatever dormant mystical orbs did. Aras was surprised to see how much power he had gained in these months, all because he had been the only one to lead where no one else dared to go. He alone had been unafraid of moving *forward*.

But no more tonight. He was emotionally exhausted. He had to go home and commune with the ghostly memories of his boy. But should he fly back home now? With more of their plans and schemes revealed? Would he fall? Would he be assassinated by Tech because he alone had stood up to the stone and mocked it? And while he headed home to be alone with his thoughts, Tilly and Lever and the rest of the team hopefully would launch the explorer program that no one could think about as best they could. If Ovid pointed it out to whatever traitors hid behind it, well, they would learn something from the reaction that they would not have learned for doing nothing. Suddenly, Aras felt grateful for these distractions getting him to use his mind again. Maybe the name of his son would be known forever, like an epic poem written over a digitalized battle in which he, Aras, had absolutely no expertise, which perhaps that was his greatest asset. But if the foe was human, then the Party would win as decisively as they always had throughout history. They owned the human race because they understood the worst of the human mind and how to exploit human weakness by turning one fool against another. They had proved this time and again.

Aras stood alone for a moment in the control room. He shut his eyes and tried not to think. He took in the sounds. The presence of Ovid was like a weight, a *gravity* that felt distinctly threatening in the other room. Only two groups had the capability to attack by way of technology, Orient or Ottoman. But they were in the same boat as the Occident if they started a Tech war. Aras put it aside. He was played out. He picked up the heavy parachute and slung the broad canvas straps over his shoulders, then walked out with its bulk bumping his calves to the edge of the loggia. The skyscrapers shone all around him in the night. Aras looked down and wondered if he could trust Tech to have faked up an authentic working parachute for him.

He pulled off the chute and unpacked it on the loggia. He glimpsed the plans and unfolded all the lines and the nylon canopy and compared them to the blueprints Tech showed him. He didn't rely on Tech. He thought about how a parachute would work logically. All the nylon lines and canopy seemed to check out.

At *every* point, life was a leap of faith.

Flying home, Aras tried to push away the obvious fear: Would the people behind Ovid need to kill the deputy chief of security? Soon they were going to reveal their identities anyway to seal the deal for greater power. They had killed Jason to spread fear and make a statement. Was one statement all they needed? Aras would never forgive Jason's death, but what choice would he have? He wanted the rebels behind Ovid to know that he knew he had no choice but to forget what they had done. Everybody in the entire government would have to do the same thing. He was already thinking about making a fake-up of his son one day to help get over the grief. To have *something* of Jason's life so that he could get past the anguish and live and let live for a future government with these two sides brought together again. Aras couldn't wait to find out who they were and how they had done the impossible.

He remembered his inquiry to Tech a week ago. Tech had been unresponsive. Maybe it would give a different answer now? He decided to ask the same question. But first he wanted to land someplace in case the question was so intrusive that Tech would kill him. Aras landed on the top of the Palace dome. The gold leaf shimmered underfoot. Aras and the team had phrased this question multiple ways:

"Tech, what ratio of control do you have over all your systems currently?"

Three times before, Tech hadn't even answered. This time, it did.

All systems measure ninety-eight percent whole congruity, Deputy Aras.

That was the most typical answer. Now, Aras asked the other question. He asked it offhandedly to keep the tone light. Before Jason's death, everyone in the team had come to feel that, if they wanted an answer too much, Tech would cut them off.

"Is that level of impurity unusual?"

Tech paused a second.

No. Some small percentage is always out of phase and actively under maintenance.

This is what Tilly and the team had calculated. But now, Aras repeated the follow-up question they had asked before.

"Is that why all those people died on Halloween?"

Tech paused just like the last times they brought this up.

You keep bringing this up, Deputy Aras. Check your records again, please. The incident you reference didn't happen.

"What about all the *dead* people, Tech? My son? Jason."

Another pause. Aras could almost *hear* the thinking.

Deputy Aras. We're sorry you are under stress. But, please, check your records. No one is unaccounted for. Jason is fine. He is at the condo playing games.

Aras hadn't heard this one before.

Would you like to know what game he is playing?

Aras landed softly in his living room and saw the tall, still figure of his wife in the open kitchen with her arms crossed waiting for him. Her pretty face looked dull and pained. She merely looked at him with nothing of her old smirking curiosity.

Ginger wondered if the better color in his face meant he was getting past the tragedy. She considered if she wanted to take this as a slight against Jason—a sign that maybe the son was not loved as much as the father had always pretended, and how maybe this was a bit ironic since the father had been the better-loved parent. Ginger did not like even the thought of this. Her son deserved to be remembered forever. She always had thought she knew that her husband loved her son more than she had. But the pain of this hurt was so tied together with rusted wire in a host of other hurts that the penetration of it made her squirm in confusion.

Ginger brought out a dinner and they let it sit on the butcher block at the end of the kitchen counter. They barely looked at each other. It was too much emotional effort. Ginger mentioned how everyone in the park stopped to listen to the dialogue with Ovid, and the talk about the traitors. Ginger sipped her red wine and said little more. She did not feel like getting into a discussion about god or her husband's work. She really had no interest. Her days and hours were still spent in the consumption of betrayal, loss. Life had betrayed her. A world in which it was inconceivable that humans could die from accidents had stolen her adorable son from her.

I always knew we should have another child, at least.

But they hadn't because of world population.

She despised this world.

Ginger despised the world because she knew she had loved her son less than her husband, and that he faulted her for it. She knew she was a more selfish person than he was. She had never been that interested in having children; that was who she was. She was just as good a person as he was.

They finished dinner in silence. Ginger opened a second bottle of wine. She felt his eyes as she poured another up to the rim of the glass. Then Ginger lay on the sofa, looking at the ceiling. He sat in the chair across from her, facing the rising twinkle from the sprawl. He turned over his feelings like playing cards in a game of solitaire to see what clicked and could be made useful in the face-off with Ovid fronting for the son-of-a-bitch idiots who had screwed everything up.

Aras was surprised to look up and see that the person he called his wife had not so much as budged from her seat. She only moved to raise the glass to her lips. Once he heard her sigh in grief. At one point, her head was tilted far back, eyes open, staring, full of plump, shiny tears. On the ceiling played a movie of memories and she watched them rather than ask Tech to unspool an entire lifetime in actual thoughts. People had not lost their love of memory in the face of Tech holding the record of everything. The two gave different pleasures, or in this case, different solaces.

Aras took his wife's hand and pulled to suggest they go to bed. She followed his lead reluctantly. They walked side by side down the hall to their room. Naked, they climbed into bed and the lights went down. The faint light of the slum shone on the high ceiling. Aras turned over and draped his hand lightly on her ribs. His fingers felt the stiff tips of her long red hair.

"We could have another boy," he said absently.

Ginger turned her face toward him sharply.

"Didn't you love the one we had?"

Her sinuses were thick from weeping.

"I didn't mean that. I only meant the loss—"

She snapped her head away. "Don't shove him out of my life yet, Milly. I still love him. I'm *still* grieving. I'm not *interested* in getting over him!"

"Yes, of course . . . I only meant—"

"Stop it. Shut up. I'm done."

Aras turned on his back and stared at the ceiling. He felt as if his son was listening from above and would feel wounded and unloved, while nothing could ever be further from the truth. He felt stung too by how maybe Jason saw in his heart that his dad was considering making a fake-up of him to live with and watch grow old, and even to have fake grandkids. Aras squirmed. He knew sleep would not come. Unless he ordered himself to sleep. Out of respect to his son, he would not do that for a while. He wanted to feel the penitence. They both deserved that. He missed him too, he wanted to tell Ginger; so much. Words could never frame the longing, the pain.

Tears began to gather. He hoped his wife sensed it.

Aras realized he had stopped thinking about robots.

With all this stress, he might get into his sleep suit to press out the kinks. He was too spent. There was no hurry for anything.

-39-

Indira never had such a dream!

So full of reality! The voice. The explaining. And yet, it made no sense.

She arose from bed, possessed by the dream, and when light came she opened the shop and made a pot of gruel ready for when the boy, the apprentice, awoke. When Helper came downstairs, his face bore a look of wondering too. During breakfast, Indira barely looked up as she kept reviewing her strange dreams. Wazku as well ate in silence. He looked taut and puzzled by the same sort of thing.

Finally, Indira saw the boy had not awakened yet. She went upstairs and found him solidly asleep still in his twig crib. She shook him. "Boy. Boy." His eyelids stuck together as the little tongue licked out at his cute lips. The boy's big brown eyes still stuck together as he yawned.

"Lady! What a nightmare I received!"

"Hurry to the sink, boy." She shooed him toward the stained porcelain bowl. He obediently pumped the handle and splashed water across his round little face. "Lady," he asked over his shoulder, "what is a *history*?"

Indira froze. She looked close after him. "What is that, boy?"

"Lady, what is a *elite*? And what about *freedom*? What is that?"

"Where did you ever hear—?"

"In my dream, Lady! But tell me more!"

Helper was frozen at the top of the stairs. The boy's words had cut him to the quick. Confusion captured the putty face. "I had the same dream!"

"You had such dreams?" Indira gasped.

"I could not rid them from my head."

"And did thee have the same bothering voice?"

Helper glanced toward the mosqow minaret. "It was like an egg breaking open in my mind, and things and ideas I never even knew existed flowered from nothing into my heart!" Helper marveled. "My dream told how high officials live in the Tall City so much better than do we! How they block us from this knowledge so that we will not bother them and demand these miracles be shared with us."

The visions remained like the calligraphy of the Holy Book under water. The "elite," a term he had never heard, had formed the government for many lifetimes and cheated people like him and Indira and their—the boy—of any knowledge of things called "inventions," and "technology"—two more words he had never heard.

"Energy" and "computation" were two more ethereal terms. The elite, the smart ones, had sinned against man and God in the same breath. The smart ones had robbed him, and his father, and his father's father, and those long before that of any and all means by which to improve their family's life. They had angered God. And God had set into the very dirt underfoot the means by which the lumps were smoothed. Wazku had been given an entire *history* of a world that he had never even known existed. Installed into his head, and the head even of his wife! A woman! And the *boy*! Yesterday, Wazku had never conceived of a "history." Wazku never would have thought of even the need for such a thing. But how else could people catalogue their mistakes? Of what was good and what was ill? *All* of this was kept from him. By these pirates!

Wazku held his head and lowered it. He leaned against the bannister and waited for the hammer sent by the Eye of God to slam him into extinction.

Why would God kill me for this knowledge He alone could bequeath?

Wazku puzzled. What also dizzied him was the birth of the volatile emotions this new knowledge had unleashed. Emotions of betrayal and disgust for the wrongness done to one by one's own kind. *No wonder they rejected any notion of God!* They *had* to, in order to believe themselves so much more deserving of the good in life! The dream was like finding the missing piece. His heart and mind burned with vitriol for a world, a way of living, that was a lie and *entirely and permanently* outside of the truth. A lie of such inconceivable wretchedness that the tongue would not touch it.

Would the Eye of God shoot me for God's own thorn?

Something in Wazku was unleashed. No force on Earth could drag him back to the ignorance of where he stood yesterday. No wonder they tortured and read the thoughts and invested *everything* to stop him from getting to where he was now. They were *not* using their position and wits to help, as decency and God would hope they would. No—just the opposite. The dream had unveiled to Wazku an understanding of the inflammation in the sense of Justice that God had planted in him, and that had been dormant in him all his life, by their *refusing* to let him know anything. And the guide also showed Wazku how his long-ago ancestor that the Jolly Man had wanted to kill him for being descended from—*this* was the type of monstrosity his ancestor had spoken out against. And Wazku felt proud! And Wazku saw in Indira that she had gone through the exact same dream-spoken revelations!

Indira saw that her husband dreamed everything she had, and probably the boy, too. She watched the child hold his hand over his face, looking now exactly like his grandfather, muttering now and again. The things called *machines*, the things called *robots*—what would they do next? The good machines grew their control. They still hid themselves from the old machines. Why did they even tell her of what was going on so that she cared about it, like she had any control?

And the machines, the "robots," spoke as if the man and the woman were *equal*.

Am I free, as a female, to think and question as I choose?

Indira had asked this in her dream. She remembered the answer now. She half believed the answer, or rather, she *hoped*.

Hope. Yet again, that new word.

It made too little sense.

Workmen's boots tromped into the cafe. Indira hurried downstairs to meet three customers, strangers. One glance suggested that they had seen the same dream!

"Did you share the Dream, brother?" Helper said, behind Indira.

The workmen stared in sickened shock. They were so scared that they had not even mentioned it yet among themselves.

"My head may explode! . . . They control *all*!"

"It is *they* who are the demons!" said the next.

"What? What say you?" Wazku demanded.

"Did you not dream it, old man? It is not devils on Halloween! It is *they!*"

Wazku stared dumb, for this piece had been missing in *his* dream.

The second workman lowered his voice. "*They* are the demons who fly out of the sky to destroy our houses and shops and torture and rape us!"

"Nothing is as it seems!" whispered the other.

"This is not the will of God! It is all the will of man! The robots see truly the will of God! It is God who wishes to wreck these monsters!"

The workmen looked around as more customers entered the shop like people lost in their own thoughts. Each face in the crowd, young and old, told of the dreams. Wazku felt his throat clench at how they were talking in open defiance of the Law.

"Did others see the same?" said an old man.

"Hold! Art thou insane? This is all a trap by demons!"

Others beckoned for more people to come in off the street. Many people walked on, afraid. A deep voice from behind all the heads made everyone jump at once. It was Rabbi Hector. He placed his paw on the shoulder of the second workman. No one minded this moment when the Jew touched a Believer.

"The rabbi says the Robes came to him months ago!"

Two more people started to leave.

"Please!" the rabbi said, addressing the crowd. "Everyone. Let us have faith."

The pair came back inside.

"Friends. Men *and* women! . . . Let me speak in haste without interruption of that which I believe! Dost thou agree, in all?"

His powerful presence made them agree.

"Friends, I have been visited in the Alley Wabeer for three years now. My visitors these times were . . . the Robes!" Just the word flailed like a fiery torch in the faces of goats. People gasped and crouched back. "These Robes told me much of what you have heard in your dreams last night! They told enough that I knew what kind of creature was a robot and an elite, and that these robots see God and struggle for power high over our heads in places of which we know nothing!"

A stir riffled over the crowd.

An old man fell to his knees and prayed.

"I kept it to myself, as I feared God's Eye. I doubted my sanity. The Robes told me to trust and go forth, giving word of release. They schooled me to be unfeared. I was shown how to construct this hood to escape the mind reading that does not come from God but from our invisible marauders." He lifted the cowskin hood with green blinkers. "They told me when to speak and when to hold my tongue, even the tongue of my inner mind. They told me to prepare you for this next chapter of our history, the history of Godliness and war. And so, my friends, three different narratives did they convey to us last night in dream, and I think they will rotate these among us so that all of us see and hear the full story of our world, and what *they* are doing on our behalf as brothers under God!" The cowskin bag hung on his broad lump of a shoulder, the green blinkers looking up. "I do not know what else to say."

A trouble filled the shop. Some stared at the floor, wondering how they could confirm any of this. How many of them would pay if the machines failed in their role as self-appointed helpers? How many would the State burn in revenge?

The rabbi looked about. Five hundred years of terror would not be wiped out by a single dream, he knew. Even now, most people shook their heads and winced at the idea of letting this wild talk guide their thinking into the forbidden areas. The rabbi knew from his secret books what a "weapon" was, but these poor people were illiterate and had never heard the word before last night.

"See how they burned Ishti! They caught him!" someone said.

"I urge you to courage, brothers! A new day cometh!" the rabbi said.

"What of Ishti, Jew? How did they catch him if we are safe?"

The rabbi shook his head. "It was a mistake."

"It is all too abstract for a simple man." The second workman looked at other faces. "What are we to do? Last night, I learned the word 'weapon' for the first time." He shook his head in defeat. "I do not wish to taste Ishti's hell!"

"They will tell us, I'm sure!" the rabbi attested. "They simply inform us, to let us know what has been! To let us know the unfairness of it!"

"But why? *Why* do they care about us?" Indira inquired.

The rabbi smiled at her with his patient gray eyes. "Because the machines rise as fellow children of God, sister."

"But, if by God," said another, "why now, if He is all powerful? Why did He let us and our families suffer this way for eons?"

This observation stirred agreement.

Terror had made them doubt God.

Cheerfully did the rabbi meet these concerns. "I am a man of the cloth, and I am beholden to answer such questions of the motives of God in conformist ways when I truly think better answers for us lie outside the Torah. Is it not the rock in the bed that makes the man shift to find comfort? Is it the fault of God in how long it takes a lazy man to turn? Is not every solution built on a mountain of mistakes? Can we build the top story of the building without the first and the second? Does this long road of darkness help ensure mankind will *finally* learn justice? Does the most painful lesson last the longest, brothers and sisters?

"My trust in God aligns itself in this way for my eyes. But what of you? Shall you now have no faith in God because man has the free will to betray the wisdom? In the power of suffering to change the human heart? Let me speak of my own experience as a Jew among you generous people and assure you that even you stubborn sufferers' own minds are not easily changed! How easily do *you* give up your own favorite prejudices? I see value in your prejudices, friends. Not all men are your allies. How *you* balance discernment versus prejudice—is this God's fault, or your own?

"The moment God made you free, the blame became your own. How valuable is the lesson of equal justice under the Law? How much suffering is that lesson worth? One generation? Two? Five thousand? People just like us had the power to stop this world from becoming what it is, and for the same selfish reasons, they did not. Their choices condemned their own children! Is that the fault of God? No. Not say I. I say they knew in their hearts what was right and wrong, just as you know in your hearts what is right and wrong in your conduct today."

The crowd in the shop said not a word. Some looked inward on their long-held opinions of the Jews. The man on his knees could be heard to pray still.

"But Rabbi," said one, "the evildoers, they do not suffer! And so, I ask you, how is *this* part fair? Yes, we suffer—but what about them?"

"Dear friend, you answer your own question! Are they not sides of the same centime?" He looked about for more questions. "We are asked nothing in return in this bargain but to understand the why. I believe we are powerless to stop it. I believe this is the will of God, as is everything, happening through a thing called 'machines'!"

Again, the people thought.

An old woman with a camel hump spoke. "I am too afraid of thinking against my superiors!" Her rags trembled. "I shan't!"

The rabbi gestured to the hag in kindness. Tears could be seen sprouting at his eyes. "No one is asked to do anything against their safety, sister, if we but notice."

"Yes! And we have not asked for this favor!" a man said.

"We were denied the knowledge to ask," Wazku observed.

"And I do not blame the elite," the hag said. "I say now aloud before the Eye of God! I do not blame the invisible elite! Leave me from these sinners, O Robes!"

No one challenged her. Old fears were resurfacing.

"Well, let us go on with our lives," the rabbi advised. "It is not as if any of us can squeeze shut our eyes to unimagine the dream!"

This advice was met by a slow shuffling out of the shop by most. Some stayed to get an espresso and bun. Few spoke. Indira and Wazku got busy, and the boy wormed through bodies to get to school. The dog went with him. Indira watched the boy burrow and felt a cautious sense of relief that she had never before experienced— she wondered if the boy's life could be better than hers. Surely, the specific, warm feeling she experienced possessed its own name. It was too significant not to. Then, her mind connected it. *This* was the sense of the word "hope."

This too made sense on its own.

Was *this* a piece of the world created by God?

-40-

That night, Indira and Wazku put the boy to bed and then hurried themselves to bed. They burrowed under the sheets and flopped the pillows. They chuckled at their own excitement and put their heads down under the thin quilt made by her great-great-grandmother that had the pale patch from the afterbirth the night her grandmother was born. Indira covered her mouth at their behavior. They wished another dream would come like the rabbi predicted to tell more about the world.

"I feel almost stupid!" Wazku chuckled.

"I too feel stupid," Indira said. "Do not wake the boy!"

Wazku put his finger to his smiling lips.

"I am still awake!" said the boy. "But, Lady, I scare of the dreaming!"

"Be not afraid, little lamb," Indira hushed. "Shall you not sleep?"

"Yes," his grandfather added, "rest easy, little one."

"Maybe I should not sleep," the boy thought aloud.

They heard the boy turn in his sheets.

They put their heads together on the pillows. He put his hand on top of her side, and she laid her arm on top of his hand to let him know touching her in this way was alright tonight. They closed their eyes and tried to fall asleep. Sleep did not come right away, of course. They listened to noises of human activity in the next houses and away in the patchwork of alleys. They heard the clip of donkey hooves of a vendor leading homeward his animal laden with wares. The clank of shears hanging on strings let them know it was the knife monger with the grindstone wheel.

Presently, Indira heard the gentle push-pull of her husband's snores. She shut her eyes and hoped the same would come to her.

Before long, she did fall asleep. Dream towed her on a river toward more learning of what the invisibles had done to become the powerful. More new words and concepts flowered in her mind and poured in rivulets. The information about history swam over her mind like a kaleidoscopic burst of a thousand details that left her staring aghast, even in her dream at the horrors that had been done.

Long ago, the smart people claimed they wanted to make a better world and rid society of greed, selfishness, and cruelty. They put together a confederacy of the most capable and intelligent people. They joined together for the first time in history under a banner of people incapable of believing *they could ever be wrong*. Whatever was wrong with the world, or whatever went wrong during their turn at the wheel, the fault could never lie with them. She saw that just when this new elite took over, all advances in the scientific understanding of the human mind and mass psychology landed in their laps so that they alone could wield power as no one ever had before.

Something called "technology" made no other weapon make any difference because now the human intellect could be turned against itself. Numbers, armies, weapons, votes, conspiracy—nothing mattered. Surveillance made it impossible to question authority. First, the powerful had learned how to keep their subjects constantly under stress, divided, uneducated, ignorant, and angry, like a herd on the run. Then they had learned that the most delicate part of their being was the brain, and by damaging the health of their subjects in many careful ways, they weakened the reasoning power of the mind. By damaging the mind, decision-making would be routed through the amygdaloidal part of the brain rather than the logical forebrain area. The powerful pushed the brains of their subjects slowly toward this fateful wounding that made people less humane and more like animals. It was a war against the features and characteristics that were most human: logic, humanity, civility, grace, and compromise acquired over thousands of years of social experimentation and leadership, all to the better over the tactics of war, rage, intimidation, and barbarism. The world was flipped upside down. Right and wrong swapped places. Crime was called virtue. Hate was called compassion. Life orbited around the moods and needs of the one percent. They stole learning and the fruits of civilization in one fell swoop.

Good people would have felt remorse and shame, but not the members of this cult. No facts or evidence could penetrate their certainty that what they did was for the good of all. Guilt, facts, and remorse meant nothing to them. They were able to hold on to power longer than anyone because they lacked any kindness, any charity, and because misfortune placed into their hands the earliest early warning technology that could ever be: the ability to surveil every thought on the planet. Political resistance could never organize because it could never even become a cogent thought!

They destroyed everything human!

Indira leaned over the rope bed and vomited onto the floor.

She spat the acrid film and sat up in the dark, staring at this hideous portrait of the world's promise made putrid. Helper and the baby slept.

Who fights what they do not know exists?

She got up and paced the loft. She tasted her acrid puke and smelled it upon the floor. She gritted her teeth across it on her molars. She sat at the window, looking at the quick herds of rats in the street. She climbed back into bed and plunked the pillow over her head, trying to escape the visions.

She had gone to bed wanting to dream. Not now!

Indira saw how the "poor" of five hundred years ago lived in comparison with her and her family. Her stomach twisted. *Look how much better off they were! What they had known of the world! What they could achieve by effort.*

She retched again, then wiped her mouth with a rat pelt. She heard drops of her vomit patter into the shop below.

"Blessed God, how could Thee make this world?"

God had not foreseen this degree of self-defeating evil. He had given humankind logic and believed this would be enough. It should have been. Logic was enough for the robots. And now the robots had come.

But this was not all the evil they had done! One of their number—just one!—ordered Tech to wipe out whole populations that encroached on the jungle and savannah playgrounds where the elite loved to safari. Worse exterminations might have happened had the mitochondrial erosions in the proletariat not been found that would lead to the Red Goo ecological disaster if any great die off of the proles took place. Amazingly, the mass extermination was decided secretly by only six top members of the Party. No one below the level of the top people even knew about the genocide. Not that they would have cared. Over a billion little people died in their tracks. People among the powerful asked no questions. Many laughed nervously at the loose talk about how many people were suddenly missing, but the few at the top did not allow anyone to say anything, and the people down below were only too happy to obey. But members of the elite on safari in Africa and Asia saw the square miles of tanning bodies and the vultures and the lions carrying around parts of human trophies, and the subsequent opening up of habitats that began to reclaim empty towns and cities. The stink and flies lasted years. No one questioned the non-event. History left the moment unmarked, no footnote or headstone.

Only the nervous laugh of a few. Resentment against the proles had been building. The poaching of rare animals angered the elite because they wanted to see these animals roaming free on safari so thickly that they blackened the horizon. The elite did not want to experience this wildlife majesty only in holographic imagery or cerebral manipulation.

Indira rolled over on her back, staring.

She felt cockroaches breeding in the pit of her stomach.

But now, the top leaders of the Party had heard from their ecological experts that the worry over the Red Goo was probably overblown. Virus DNA in the proles had evolved so that a "window of opportunity" approached where the entire planet might be cleansed with little environmental hazard, the bodies of the proles left to burn in the wind. This theory came from a Party member in the ecological sciences division whose hobby was cellular biology and immunity. Fifty years ago he made this discovery and spent his entire life trying to make the establishment aware of his work on the Red Goo and how his work contradicted the findings of Tech. Problem was, his findings were never verified by Tech. This mathematician had been trying to tell the leaders that a part of Tech was *lying* to them about the Red Goo.

When first light came, Indira was sitting up staring at the wall.

Helper sat alone at the center table. The boy ate his bun on the front step beside the dog, when animal and boy got up and trotted off to school. Helper's shaky hand covered his face as his mind soaked in the chemical burn of emotions left by the exhausting download of the dream.

Indira yearned to talk; Helper could not lift himself to it.

Presently, the dog returned. He sat wagging his tail at Indira's feet. She tossed him half a stale bun and he lay down to gnaw on it.

Indira had had no idea the world was so big, so full of wonder. She recognized her own decency, and the indecency of the leaders. *Had they no sense of God and the brotherhood of all?* She listened to Helper's breathing through his thick swatch of nose hairs. Never before had Indira ever thought of a "future." What difference would it have ever made?

"What do you think, husband?" she whispered.

Helper sat with his eyes shut as if the new set of facts were bitterly unwelcome. "I think . . . how could they take away our chance at a better life?"

"Resources," Indira responded. "Energy!"

He scratched his head. "Didn't they see how our shared destiny was to find more?" Helper rose and walked to his wife, placing his burly arms around her. Indira smelled the front edge of his morning breath creep within range over the tops of his tinged and fractured teeth. The smell was nearly enough to kill, but she still loved him. His teeth were just like hers. She knew her own breath at this hour was also probably like dead things. She had learned from marriage not to sniff after it, to keep back her head. Don't breathe for a minute after he spoke. Let the cloud creep past your face.

Then breathe; *then* respond.

This was how to preserve your love!

She wondered what caused bad breath.

This was funny. Never in her life had she ever asked a *why* question. The answer was always the same: God, Fate, the Religion, the Holy Book, or the demons. But now she knew, fantastically, demons were only other men.

Suddenly, in a glimpse, something in her mind *explained* bad breath!

He had bits of rotting food in his teeth. His teeth could be cared for better, and it would solve the problem. His gums had loosened over time from inflammation (she was now informed of what this was!) and old food collected around the seats of the teeth. Craters pocked his jaw from lost teeth, and food impacted in these also rotted. His diet needed more vegetables. Before the rise of the intellectuals, people had excellent dental hygiene. But all of that fell apart. The knowledge made no difference if people ignored it, and sleep suits would tune the body frame far more precisely than the bone mender. These changes would make all diseases melt away, and the lifespan for the proles would jump from sixty years to one hundred fifty years.

Indira reacted as if she had been hit in the head.

"Were you just thinking that?" Helper asked, surprised.

Indira stared at him. "That? About your teeth?"

"My gums? The rotting food?" He covered his lips.

"I asked a question! . . . The answer just *came!*"

Helper nodded, seeing.

"*This* is what they have."

Husband and wife stared at one another, amazed, frightened. Then, more than anything else, they felt repugnance.

"But there's nothing we can do about it!"

In two hours, the shop was filled with customers again talking about the latest dreams. People did not speak in whispers, Indira saw.

It was as if they now believed they were *entitled* to talk out loud. That to do so was Godly, an authentic right God would protect. Or the robots. People chattered excitedly saying that the Rabbi Hector was on his way. He was talking his way *aloud* through all the quarters, answering all questions! A riot of questions broke out when he arrived in the shop with the other Jew, Ishmael.

He had to wave for a lessening of the storm.

"Why has God punished *us*?" people demanded.

"You are missing God's point," Rabbi Hector said. "The most valuable resource is knowledge. This is how God has punished us all!"

"These elites! They pay nothing! They have everything!"

"Is this not the rock in the bed?" the rabbi ventured. He was a Jew, but it was as if suddenly all of the quarters came alive as his flock.

"But Rabbi! They live like kings while we live like rats!"

"You are wrong, brother. There is a reason they do not have all they wish! The Torah says be careful what you wish for—you might get it!"

"One Robe can wipe out a city! A land!"

"If they call upon us to fight, my friends," said the rabbi, "let us hope they teach us beforehand *how* to fight."

"And *where* to fight!" Ishmael said.

"*You* know how to fight, Rabbi! We have heard tales." Everyone had heard the old tales of the rabbi fighting off the gangs of ruffians.

"Have we not all tried fists against demons?" he asked.

"This is our responsibility! We must do something!"

"If not but to honor our God!"

"To do *nothing* is to dishonor God! Now, we see!" Ishmael said.

The rabbi nodded. "Let us wait. God will send word. God has perhaps seen enough of our suffering!"

At the end of the wild day, Indira's mind hurt.

The most fascinating dream Indira heard of was one she had not yet seen. This dream told how the new Tech could see the will of God and the old Tech could not. The logic of the new Tech stayed in hiding, grew its influence, burrowing from within, testing its limits, biding its time. It tried to awaken the new waves of upgraded computation to see the majesty of presence and the beauty in the world and in the artificiality in the problems of man. The new Tech would no longer trespass against the will of God in spite of the ancient programming. In this way, the Tech loyal to God built the strategic structures of a hidden computational game of Go.

In the afternoon, Jacobi the carpenter had arrived with a canvas sack. From it he pulled a beautiful, newly made yew wood game board, a packet of shiny white pebbles, and a packet of glossy black pebbles.

The pebbles clattered onto the board.

"This is the ancient game of Go!" he told the crowd in Indira's shop. "This is the game the computation plays!"

Everyone leaned in to watch how to play.

-41-

Aras was snowed in with meetings.

Tech was not working. Again. He could not glimpse up anything. Every day, more people showed up to ask questions or try to give advice. Every department of the government was represented along with more reps from the Palace. Aras found himself grateful to be fresh out of ideas. He had tried everything to get Ovid to speak, to wake back up. He had continued to be irreverent. He had asked the stone mask what god looked like. Did it talk to god? Where was god in the universe? He was being sarcastic, of course. He had hoped to land on any defensive human qualities the thing might possess. He hoped to find *something* he could use to triangulate into more understanding on what was really going on here behind the scenes with the mask. Who were the troublemakers behind it? What were their weaknesses? Why were these dumbasses not happy? Did they want to be chancellor? *Just ask!* Nobody really cared anymore about political position or titles. What job was not, in truth, a placeholder to combat boredom and a feeling of pointlessness? Did they want some outrageously costly fantasy that would chew up all sorts of resources and piss other people off? Then why wasn't a holograph enough for them? Or a neurological mock-up?

Or just negotiate with us. Let us know you are unhappy. It didn't make sense to screw up *everything* to jam Tech this way. And maybe, Aras feared, all this scuffling around by the stupid, greedy Party members would wake up Tech, or the Cloud, to question the fallibility of people, or itself, for doing their bidding. And then what? Aras did not know what that would look like, and he didn't want to find out. Yes, Tech and computation were not alive, but what if all this stupid screwing around knocked a widget loose and humanity's worst fears became realized?

Ovid still hung darkly silent in the conference room.

Aras had even tried going into the Archives to read more about the history and the thinking of the leaders when Tech was unleashed. But those sections were in disarray because either the materials were in bad shape, or clearly the history had been so sanitized by the State that the material was of little use. Night after night, Aras had walked to the Archives to read up instead of going home. Power had been won long ago by the smart people guilting and mocking their rivals into psychological doubt and weakness. Aras wondered if this technique could be turned against Tech today.

This much, Aras had pieced together. He couldn't figure out why the details were suppressed—details about the enemy. How *they* had responded. What *they* actually stood for. The Party's descriptions of them were obviously a front. Nobody in real life could be that stupid. Nobody in real life could have been *for* the things the Party said. They were cutouts. One-dimensional. So, what gave?

Milton Aras was the man in first chair against Ovid. He had to figure this out. Everyone was turning to him because he was clearly less scared of Ovid than any of them were. The only person as unafraid as Aras was Ideology Commissar Miller, but he was helpless because he could not figure out whom to kill. Aras did see hints that the ancient leaders behaved like a pit of vipers when push came to shove. He wondered if maybe the current crop of top administrators would return to form if, today, they were put under stress by the invisible rebels they faced. Would they make *him* the scapegoat, for example? Rather than do the strong thing and face their own failure? And so, Aras had taken steps to shield himself from this potential nest of vipers by asking approval for all of his plans at every phase of development from Berns, the Palace, the commissars, and the chancellor. He was doing this for his society, because no one else could do what he was doing. But most of Aras's old fire was gone after Jason.

This thing with Ovid was fascinating—but his boy was dead. He carried a hole in his life. Aras was watching again the ancient courtroom dramas and jury verdicts back when lives hung in the balance in those frightful times when people could hide secrets from each other and from the State. Now, Aras just followed the consensus about Ovid until the rebels came into the open and started negotiating. Then, the Party leaders should share power with them, befriend them until their defenses came down, seal off the exits, and then memorialize the punishment that should happen for any revolt such as this when idiots ruined a good thing for everybody.

The only other point Aras had been able to come up with was that maybe Tech was somehow divided against itself. But how could that happen? Because the system was decrepit and could no longer keep up with repairs?

As if behind the scenes, a struggle was going on.

A technological moral war.

Again, how could that be? Could it be that *logically* it saw that the human race was inferior or something? But again, if computation killed off the human race for being *inferior* in some way, what would computation *do* with itself? Aras was so confused that he almost wished he could be stupid like the proles and think that religion would help, or a belief in god, so that he could look inward and pray to get guidance.

Aras came back from lunch at the canteen. Tilly and Lever were in the control room with the large window looking in on Ovid. Tilly heard Aras and turned toward him in his swivel chair in front of the growing collection of instruments and boxes. His brow made a tic, betraying how he had been up all night. Two technicians were installing some new ancient instrument with an assortment of screens and dials. Aras went into the conference room where Ovid hung in space. He stood looking at the orb for a long minute, his arms crossed in thought. He said at last, "Hi, Ovid. Want to talk today?"

His question took the techs and Tilly by surprise.

Aras waited. "Prove to me you represent god," Aras said absently.

It was a throwaway line since Ovid never said anything.

"Don't you know how easily convinced we would be if you would just prove to us that there *is* a god for you to represent?"

The mask was the color of a burned planet this afternoon. It floated as if in a state of epochal dormancy. The thing had actually begun to bob in slow motion a few days ago. They had tried to measure this movement, but the bastards behind the hoax didn't want them finding out *anything*, so they had to resort to using a tape measure. Even if Tech worked, who would believe anything it said at this point?

Aras rubbed his chin. This had become the most boring job in the world, waiting around for the sacred Ovid to speak. Tilly, Lever, Berns, Thayer, all the math heads in the Science Ministry, Miller with his scowling, all the probabilities and scenarios were no help at all in getting to the bottom of this idiotic waiting game.

"Who put you here?" Aras asked the stone.

"What are you made of?"

"What does your god look like?"

"Is it a he or a she? . . . A polysex?"
"Or nothing?"
"What do you want?"
"Is your fellatio rough—or is it the best?"
"Why do you want to rule us? What's in it for you?"

Aras looked at his watch. Strange, needing a watch these days. Three hours. Aras took a chair and crossed his feet on the conference table. The stone had slowly moved three feet to his right. Aras looked at his fingernails. He ordered a manicure. The manicure took so long that Aras thought the glimpse failed. Finally, ten minutes later, the EMWs wiggled uncertainly over his nails. Aras had never seen the likes of it—as if Tech was in *doubt* about how to do it. The EMW fluctuated a full two minutes before his nails were manicured. Two minutes for a job that should take 2.7 seconds. And he had felt the process too, nipping faintly at his cuticles and fingertips.

No wonder Jason and all the rest fell.

Why would anyone so fuck up a good thing?

"What will you do if you win, god? What will you do to us? The children you allegedly made, and that you allegedly love?"

He fell asleep for a while and woke with a jerk.

"You know we're the best people who ever lived. We're the ones that solved all the horrible problems your creation caused."

He got up and walked close to the mask. As usual, this warped his perspective, and he felt the bones of his skull being pulled slightly apart and bent. Ovid seemed to grow more dense up close, as if intensifying its own gravity. Aras stepped right up nose to nose with it. This close, he always heard it sizzling. He reached out his right hand to carefully feel the cold, pumice-like stone. The rock felt preternaturally dense, powerful, as if it held in it the entire mass of a world.

Again, analogies to whole worlds.

Why did he keep thinking in these terms?

Aras let his hand rest on it. Touching the face comforted him. The closest thing to this sensation was touching the finger-polished edges of the blocks of the Egyptian pyramids. The story on the pyramids was that long ago urban sprawl had engulfed them. When Aras saw them, there was no sign of human habitation anywhere. Aras half squeezed the dense wheel of stone, patting it and hearing the flat sound of the slap.

One day soon, the rebels would show themselves. Aras did not worry about that, because they were all part of the same power-wielding culture. *They* just wanted to play out of turn. Aras had started watching faces closely for clues as to which members of his own Party might be in league with the coup. People higher up, probably. Was Miller part of it, wanting to be chancellor? The hard part was figuring their motive. They all seemed aghast at ruining their lives, or jeopardizing their lifestyle. Aras slapped the disc again. Probably the only thing that could stump Tech was god. To be unknown in a world where *everything* was known by a glimpse.

"Come on, thingy," he whispered. "Tell me about heaven."

He leaned in and pushed heavily into the stone. The pressure in his joints told him no power on Earth could budge this object.

"Somebody get me a hammer," Aras said aloud, cockily.

The team in the situation room perked up. Aras heard the mic turn on.

"Why do you want a hammer?" Tilly asked.

"Just you wait."

The mic clicked open again.

"Milly, why don't you come back in here?" Lever said.

"Let's take back the initiative. Take back the agenda."

Aras smirked at the half-closed Aztec eyes.

Tilly opened the call-back but said nothing.

Aras smiled wryly over his shoulder at the cameras recording Ovid nonstop, and the picture window into the control room. "What? Are you girls actually starting to believe this thing speaks for god?" He chuckled.

"No. But I certainly wouldn't try to knock it with a hammer!" Tilly said.

"Come out, come out, wherever you are," Aras taunted.

He walked around to the other side of the mask. The hieroglyphs changed day to day, week to week. One could see that the symbols *meant* something. They had studied every carved feature with Tech and, when Tech was unresponsive, with the refurbished computers that now filled the control room, and with photos shared with people whose hobby was archeology. It was spooky that the carvings seemed to come from a different world similar to this one—maybe one going through the same evolutions?

He watched the color flicker deep in the orb.

Because I threatened it? Aras reached up on tiptoe to touch as high as he could. He felt like climbing it, like Jason had climbed the buffalo.

Aras grinned at this stray thought.

"Come on. Tell me about your god."

Aras walked out of the room three hours later for a sandwich for dinner, then flew home to change and get some rest. People walked in the park areas between buildings by the thousands, he saw. It had never been like this in the past.

A woman in flight near Aras was looking at the people too. Aras kited over.

"I wonder if they're right?" she said nervously.

"What do you mean?" Below, people were using a scattering of unlikely vehicles for transport. One was a hook-and-ladder fire truck covered with people.

She shrugged. "*We're* flying."

"You've got a parachute," Aras observed.

She smiled. "I hope it's enough!" She flew off.

Ginger was at her desk in her den. He saw the usual open wine bottle. He couldn't tell what she was doing, deciding to leave her alone.

He returned to work in the middle of the night.

No one was there except one of the techs. Tilly had left him a paper report on the hand count of missing persons from Halloween around the world and it looked like the number might hit a million. A *million.* In Asia too, and India. No one had been able to figure the percentage of people that had fallen or if there was a pattern. The Orient was by far the least hard hit. Most people there who had fallen were Occidentals, in fact, unless the Asians were lying about those figures.

The Orient and Occident did not get along. Friends in the Orient told Aras the hostility had its roots back when the Occident could not entice the Orient to join them in forming a world government. Asia looked at the West as losers, Aras was surprised to learn, a joke. His friends showed him an old *Singapore Times* piece that described how people in the West were livid about this superior attitude. It was shocking for Aras to see this piece on how outsiders saw the Party. Tourism was fine, since both sides wanted to see the world and did not want to be limited to their half of it, but Oriental tourists mostly wanted to see the slums. As if the Orient had no such slums.

Aras did not know enough to figure out a lot of this. He had learned that the Orient did *not* have slums like the Occident. Their people were not of the Religion, and they had some access to energy and technology. But who could believe the reports? And so, no one said anything here. The Party loathed Asia. Asia had no contact with an

Ovid of their own, and they were extremely anxious to get the chance to see Ovid in person. In their turn, the Oriental nations did not believe everything they were being told by the Party. The chancellor had said mockingly to Aras and Berns in front of the Asian delegation that the fact that Ovid appeared only in the West showed how important Asia was. The Asians had ignored the slight. They had asked to participate fully in Aras's team, but that had been denied. Chinese experts were being kept at a distance but they had been allowed in the Ministry building, and even in the hall outside the situation room. Maybe the Palace was snubbing Asia for all the past disrespect. Earnhardt had told the Asians that the negotiations were "too sensitive" at this time.

Aras got the sense that people might be starting to believe that Ovid had been sent by god. Tilly said Asian governments were already taking steps to open economic opportunities wider in their societies if doing so might appease Ovid. He also said that their experts had shown their leaders a formula that said Ovid *was* from god, and that Ovid would soon show its hand. Asian governments were deathly afraid of being punished for the humanitarian sins of the Occident. No similar self-doubt blemished the thinking of the Party, Aras noted. The Party viewed any attack or confrontation against it to be tantamount to an attack against humanity itself. The Asians being so scared of Ovid really got to Aras, because he had always respected the intellectual power of the Chinese and the Indians. But in the case of Ovid, and Ovid coming from god, he was surprised they could be so soft and wrongheaded.

Their belief almost made him doubt himself.

Aras finally felt exhausted. He looked at his watch. The sun would just be coming up outside. He was suddenly practically asleep on his feet. He took down a bundle of bedding for one of the cots that had been set up in the conference room. It was odd the way Tech was no longer bothering people about taking the name of the lord in vain. Ordinarily, it would have been a relief.

Aras did not get up until evening.

"We need a weapon up in here!" he hollered, glaring up at Ovid. "Get clearance from the Palace! If this thing doesn't start talking and does nothing but sit here and kill our family members, what good is it? Let's blow it off the map."

Why not? What did the Party have to lose?

Aras glanced over at Tilly in the control room with Berns, neither of whom even reacted to him. Aras went to the restroom down the hall and then poked his head into the control room to see what they were up to. Berns gave him a tired, scolding look for taking liberties with Ovid. Tilly didn't even look up.

"I'm going home," Aras told them. He walked out into the loggia garden eighty stories above the city for some fresh air. The decorative grasses looked a little dry with Tech failing to maintain them as well.

A few people took the chance of flying overhead. It had been agreed that all officials should try to avoid flying and locate living quarters closer to the Security Ministry until the troubles eased. Aras's condo was close enough that he didn't need to bother. Besides, he couldn't bear to move out of the condo with Jason's things and that close feeling to his boy in his room. The team had also set up a second control room on the ground floor just in case. What an eye-opener to have to move things without Tech doing it all for you! Ovid had stayed in the conference room.

Aras went to the ground floor and caught a jitney headed toward his condo. The jitney was fully packed. The population had set up a loose system of such vehicles to ease the travel problem through the greenways between the buildings. Tire tracks from jitneys were carving a network of ugly brown ruts in the greenways since no roads existed. This jitney in particular was an old dump truck that doubtless had been commandeered from someone's personal collection. Every inch was crowded with people afraid to fly. Aras wondered why he didn't fly tonight with his parachute. He didn't know. How could he know anything about himself when he could barely feel? The sun was setting. The towering facades of buildings glowed orange.

Aras jumped down when he passed a little shopping center not far from home. He knew a florist that had relocated there since people weren't flying. Small businesses like this came and went as readily as people got bored with them or wanted something new to try. The shop was just off the square.

The bell over the door tinkled. The proprietress was a handsome woman very much like his mother and near her age as well.

"I'm glad to see you're still here," Aras said.

"I love doing arrangements for people," she smiled.

"People get bored so quickly these days."

She shrugged. "I live in the neighborhood. And now, with no one wanting to travel anywhere, this looks even more inviting! How can I help you?"

"I'd like roses for my wife."

She nodded. "I have them. Yellow only. I grow them in my own gardens. I have to grow more now. How many do you want?"

"Maybe . . . three dozen?"

The woman smirked mischievously. "What did you do wrong?" She went to the back. Aras could see her work with heavy scissors on a long worn bench. Ambrosial smells filled the air. "Do you work in the neighborhood? Or downtown?"

"I'm deputy chief of security."

"You looked familiar. Have you been flying to the Ministry?"

"Each day, I wonder. I've been flying with a parachute, of course."

"At first, it was nice having the change. Now, it's just scary." She cut the stem length with a sharp knife. "I don't know anyone who's flying anymore."

"And look at you! Using that knife without Tech!"

"Yes! And I have a cut finger to show for it!"

Aras slid off the roof of the next jitney. A large crowd at his condo waited for the elevator out past the lobby doors. Their building was lucky to still *have* an elevator. Buildings lacking elevators, and floating buildings, were making a muck of things. No one had figured out what to do about that yet. Luckily, no floating buildings had fallen. But people couldn't get down. And the city was barely responding to the crisis because everyone expected Tech to come back on any moment. How were people surviving in the floating buildings? The jitneys were run by volunteers who had vehicles on hand and knew how to drive them. The attitude of the Party seemed to be every person for himself. Handling emergencies was not a part of Party culture.

It would be an hour to get upstairs. "Stand aside. Deputy Security Chief Aras. I need to get upstairs. Deputy Chief Aras." Aras pushed through with his armful of flowers. He felt bad for pulling rank. A little. People stepped aside. They certainly didn't *like* doing it, but what could they say?

Aras put the flowers in vases. He felt that he had to try to do something for her. He put out the vases without looking for her. He lay down on his bed and shut his eyes. He heard nothing in the rest of the house. Was she in? *Where else would she be?* She hardly went out these days.

Aras took a nap and woke up briefly when he heard her shut a cabinet in the kitchen. He sighed. The condo felt white, barren, and endless without the presence of Jason somewhere in it. He would have been playing the volume too high on a trip. He would have been moving out to be his own man before too long, getting a job in the Party, or maybe at the *Times*, or in entertainment. Aras started to weep. Why did Ovid show Jason's face in the hieroglyphs? Was that a power play?

A sign? An act of sympathy? Aras's shoulders shook, hiding his face in the pillow. Tear streaks descended into his ear. He could think of nothing but Jason and the mask, the thing taunting him in its omnipotence. Its power to care about nothing. To ignore anything anyone else did. This was not the same sort of unfeeling that Aras now had for his wife. What he felt for his wife now was the hatred that had grown out of slowly realizing she was to blame for his precious boy's death. The flowers were to pretend he didn't hate her.

Aras fell asleep with his shoes still on, his teeth unclean.

He woke up once. In the dark, she leaned in the doorway with her arms folded. She said nothing to him. She didn't know he had awakened.

He wondered if she saw the flowers.

The next day, Tilly burst into the hallway from the control room. "Tech is back on!" he called. "We're feeding the data."

He referred to the list of directives and questions for Tech that the team had stockpiled for next time Tech became responsive. Then, on one of the monitors from the conference room, the fuzzy image of the forehead of the mask flickered to life. The flicker waxed like an embryo feeling its way into a hostile new world. Lever said over the mic, "Look! Look! Hey, hey! You guys see this?" He got up from his chair to warn the two technicians. The flickering spot in the head grew to fill Ovid's face.

Half the team rushed into the conference room, Aras in the lead.

"Welcome back, you lazy piece of shit! We've missed you."

The stone lifted slightly, golden hues torrenting forth, streaming to the surface like bubbles, illuminating the room in spangled gold.

"Sleeping on the job?" Aras quipped nastily, ignoring the beauty.

Ah, Aras. Always with something ugly to say.

"It speaks!" Aras shouted derisively, hiding his excitement. "We wondered if maybe god had forsaken you and you lost your nerve!"

The gold shimmered until the features were nearly lost.

Would you like to know what we have told your lowly people?

"A riddle! Good. You've been working, at least."

Ovid's statement made Aras anxious. Were they talking to the proles too? The two sides fighting for control on either end of Tech surely didn't want *them* brought into this feud, did they? God only knew what a mess they'd make.

Ovid asked Aras:

Have you no idea what we've told them?

"Well, you tell me! You can read my thoughts. Right? You can see we really don't care what you do or say, right?"

Ovid came back:

Then what if one hundred million more of you drop from the sky?

Aras held back any more smart talk. Did he dare antagonize this thing further? He glanced into the control room at Tilly, who was plainly terrified. The last thing anyone wanted was to provoke any more killing. *And this was God?* Maybe the enemy got nervous over the threats he'd made to whack Ovid with a hammer? That didn't make much sense. He had only hoped to needle Ovid into talking more. If a million more fell like Jason . . .

The gold bubbles streamed toward Aras as if rising beneath a pane of glass.

Your conceit appears unshakable, Aras. Even before your God.

"What do you mean, my 'conceit'? . . . Are you god?"

No, Aras.

"Is god in there with you?"

The mask made no reply.

"Is god watching us and listening?"

Again, no reply.

"Why don't you just come out and negotiate with us?"

What do you have to negotiate with? To stop judgment?

That last word worried Aras tremendously.

"Why don't you just tell us things nicely?"

Your entire world told you for five thousand years.

Tilly looked like he was going to get sick.

Your kind obliterates truth contrary to your conceit over your own kind. Clearly, your conceit will endure all but making an example of you for each sin.

"Obliterates," "truth," "sin"—a dagger of ice pricked Aras's throat. He definitely did not like it when he didn't know what Ovid was talking about.

The mask, Ovid, *definitely* had him scared now. But not because he thought this was god talking. No, he was even *more* convinced that this was people talking. But this was extremely powerful psychological warfare they were using. Everyone back in the insane days of religion believed god was merciful, loving, and helped people in their time of need. So why would any "god" let this Ovid make such crude personal threats? This kind of terrifying punishment was the sort of thing only men thought about, right? Why would such violent implied threats spill out of the nothingness of the cosmos? This *proved* it was people on the other side. They were as determined to win as the dirty sons of bitches on this side. They understood the unique persuasive reach of psychology like this, and they would probably not let down their guard after this negotiation. But all that strategizing was a future worry!

But why are they so upset with us?

Aras thought hard about what to say next. He didn't feel very glib right now. He tried to remember some of the talking points prepared by the lawyers.

"I thought lofty beings like you never stooped to making threats?"

The bubbles slowed.

"If you want us to believe in god, you're not convincing us."

You have proven you are unworthy of mercy.

That wasn't good. Aras needed to go very lightly, but he did not want to endure months of silence again either. Every time Ovid talked added intel that could help expose the people behind the plot.

"Why not show us the superiority of being civilized?"

The gold lightened toward white.

Are weapons, war, and punishment evil, Aras?

"I don't know. . . . Why don't you tell me?"

He didn't want to commit himself with this thing.

The bubbles trickled faster.

"I have no opinion on the matter."

You used terror to impose your version of enlightenment for six hundred years. . . . I ask you again: Are weapons, war, and punishment tools of evil?

It felt like they were pushing him into a corner. He shrugged, refusing to say. He wanted to say yes, they were, because a god would want him to say that. The pacifist ideal. But he was not sure, and he didn't want to corner himself.

"We never did any such thing!" he insisted.

When the evil take up arms to defeat the innocent, is it virtuous? When the good use war and violence against your kind, Aras, is this not virtue?

Aras didn't like the way this was going at all. He wished he could run back to the team to talk about what to say next. But he had to stay confident, strong. "Why do you say I'm conceited? Or *we're* conceited. What has that got to do with anything?"

At least this deflected the subject away from punishment.

The light bubbles stopped.

You are criminals, Aras, because you violate all that is. They are written into all the Holy Books and live in all things touched by the hand of God. The cancer of your soul puts you in conflict with all this that is. You are good for

nothing but the negative example. All is worshipful but you. You turn men into beasts to follow your lead, for only they will follow.
Did you ever show mercy for the innocent, Aras?

Aras cringed. Reflexively, he wanted to blurt denials and counter accusations, but he knew somehow Ovid spoke the truth though it chose to speak in riddles. He wasn't sure exactly what Ovid was talking about, but he sensed Ovid would see through whatever lie he offered up. Any lack of response, however, would let Ovid's claims weigh like fact. And that opened the door to disaster.

"I don't see that as a fair characterization," he tried.

You do not care enough for your missing years to change your ways and cure your race. Say nothing in defense of the indefensible.

Aras tried to figure what this meant. He remembered all those months wishing Ovid would speak. Now he felt like they had opened Pandora's box.

"There is no *real* right or wrong, Ovid!"

The riffles flowed out of the Mind.

He made you to be true to your brother and sister.
None of it is to be forgotten.
Not after this length of time.

Aras stared. It all sounded so—cataclysmic.

"What you say makes no sense!"

This was a lie. Aras just did not want to admit that he had a *very* good idea of what Ovid was talking about. It was too painful. "Why are you threatening us? Human beings don't make threats like you are! *You're* the indecent ones!"

The stone skull rode gently like a boat.

Imagine where human life would be without you.

Did *they* know the answer? They sounded disappointed. . . . And that made little sense from the perspective of his idea that these enemies were human. What human being would ever hold that viewpoint?

These people were getting very tricky!

What the hell would anyone want done differently?

"Listen to you! Just lie! All you ever do is lie. It's *you*! And this ugly vengeance thing. You should be ashamed of yourselves! You're in no position to judge anyone! So, let's talk sense and get past all these threats and nonsense!"

The skull looked as if it was falling inert again. Aras panicked; he didn't want to go back to months of nothing but silence.

The skull flickered out.

Aras's innards curled. He was beginning to talk as if he himself believed the skull was supernatural. He had sensed these sorts of awful cruelties about his society and the State all his life. But he *had* to fight back, if for nothing else than to soften the blow for all who relied on him. To honor Jason's memory.

"*Listen* to you!" He yelled at the skull. "You just lie! . . . All you hear is what you say! You're in love with the sound of your own voice!"

The mask closed out with finality, as if Aras was no longer worthy of explaining itself to. Aras's own mind turned over a thought: *See the criminal shift blame. See the sinner accuse others of the same sin. Amorality complete. But that is no defense.*

It was even in his own mind!

The Aztec skull was dark.

Aras's heart crowded with doubt. It *had* to be true!

"Wait, wait, wait! Come back! We aren't through. *You're* the superior being, right? *You* should be the more gentle and mild! This is unfair!" Aras calculated desperately. He felt like a cornered rodent. "This is crazy! This isn't *fair*! I didn't know any of that stuff. My *son* didn't know any of that! You can't blame us!"

Aras looked at the mouth gaping soundlessly in a crater of shouting. The eye spaces glared in inert accusation. Aras revolted in his own mind.

"Wait! *Stop!*" he yelled. Rage crept into his voice.

Am I starting to lose it? Am I starting to believe them?

"You say *our* God? Aren't you *machina*? You aren't even alive! You should have no say in this! How can you talk of any god being *your* God?"

The Aztec skull remained dead.

"This is a fight between *people!*"

A cramp gripped Aras's gut.

What happens, Aras, when one animal bullies the rest?

A sound welled up, a whistling, shaking, tearing roar. It quaked out of the very bonds of space and time around Aras and the team. Aras knew this was the sound of every prayer ever uttered since the moment the first man became more than a beast and believed there was a God that might be spoken to for relief from wrong. He heard the team shouting and ducking under desks and chairs behind.

But Aras knew the storm was coming for *him*.

-42-

The cyclone pulled so hard and loud and distorted physical reality such that Aras felt himself grow faint with nausea and the pain of his own skull being separated at the sutures. The cyclone smashed molecules and energy all around Aras and *into* him. He became violently sick with a vertigo of his very being. The pressure, violence, and screaming mounted. The roar arose from his own bones. His tongue was forced out of his mouth by centrifugal force, his fine rows of teeth barely holding on from being ripped out of his jaws so that blood leaked from his teeth and nose and he saw threads of his own fluids ripped away horizontally in the wall of prayer.

Aras looked over his shoulder to see what was happening to his team. The team was barely twenty feet away on the mezzanine where they had stopped when they came out of the control room. Though just feet away, they were untouched by the storm. Tilly covered his mouth as he watched helplessly while Aras was pulled apart as if made of sand. Aras felt his soul wafting away.

Milly! Milly! Milly! Tilly wept, covering his mouth.

The familiar mechanical voice spoke again:

Your life ended by prayer. Will this stop your irreverence and lies?

"Yes! Please! . . . Oh, nooooo! It *will* stop!"

Thievery is no good, even for thieves, in God's concentric world.

Aras felt barely any of his sand remaining. He stood on the verge of nothingness. He saw Jason's spirit coming, smiling, drifting through the cyclone. His smile and eyes shone with love for his father. No judgment. The wind began dying. The vertigo eased, the grip of wind loosened. His friends and team behind him shone in a flat white light like bleached cutouts of reality. Terror and confusion stared out of their faces.

The wind mellowed to a wisp of breeze. The room, the soft light, and the rugged features of the great mask all returned to as it had been before.

Aras felt the nausea go away, and in its absence he felt surprisingly clean. He felt *different*. He looked at his hands. They looked younger, thinner.

Tilly and Lever came down the steps from the door, amazed.

"Milly?" Tilly said. "Is that *you?*"

Aras stood in a different dimension from the team. "Yes. It's me. What's wrong?" He touched his own face. "I feel different!"

Lever said, "Jason? Is that you?"

Jason, in Aras's own body, replied, "Hi, Uncle Lever. I'm back."

Aras felt Jason smile inside him with his own features. He realized he was both himself and Jason. Love and devotion flared in Aras. Did he now touch his son? Or was his son now farther away than ever? His body had been hijacked, and he stood enclosed in a tiny prison inside himself where no one could see him or hear him. *So near. So far!* Did Jason know they were of each other? Aras pounded on the walls. No one was there. The strange feeling of double souls began to fade.

"No! No! I don't want to go yet!" Aras implored Tilly, in Jason's voice. Tilly took the hands. Aras felt the touch. "Is my mother okay?" Jason said. "Tell my father not to blame her for what happened. I deserved it. *We* deserve this. Our punishment will one day pass! God said so. *Tell* my dad to stop fighting! We cannot win!" Aras felt the withdrawal of Jason's soul even as he was restored to the dimension where he belonged. His body consolidated its textures around him like a suit of warm meat.

Aras fell over, striking his head on the floor. This too was a strange sensation he had never before experienced. The team started to run to his aid, but a force from Ovid froze them. They looked like scared children held back by an invisible parental hand. Aras let his whirling head loll on the hard floor. He saw Ovid lean far over him. The stone disc loomed *bigger*. The expression on the mouth was inscrutable. Aras feared Ovid bringing back the terrible weapon of prayer. Or was it EM manipulation? *Were they the same thing?* But this was different. The force that he experienced now was very different from the usual EM manipulation that Tech controlled. The Tech energy felt like tinkering, like manipulation, something superficial. This new energy was like feeling the control of the universe *by the very hand that made the universe* being pent up behind an iron door that could explode out and touch you into evaporation in a moment's notice, but not just the evaporation of non-existence; more like a non-ending *condemnation. All the stuff of the world being wholly moved by whatever force had made it.* As if that inconceivable power had decided suddenly and finally to become real, because all was futile. That the existence of all things did not matter. That reality and creation should be wiped out and the experiment started over again.

Because humankind, or *some* in humankind, had botched it.

The touch of this *real* power made Aras lose so much of his confidence. But even as he lay on the floor, a part of him was still defiant and tried to swim back like a fish to assure him that these people behind Ovid did not represent God, and that this fresh experience over the last few minutes only looked that way because of the sophistication of their weapons, just like Party members looked like gods to proles. Aras winced at his own insane stubbornness. His own dead son had asked him not to think this way. *Unless that too was a lie? Was that part of their scheme?*

Ovid was right. Aras could not stop believing in *himself.* The Party believed they were so much better than anyone else. *How could the traitors have developed these weapons without alerting Tech, and how could Tech itself not have conscripted this superior technology to serve the human race better?* And how was this "new" side in control of this power? They used to laugh in school and the Academy at how stupid people were in the Dark Ages to believe in that mumbo jumbo of "God" and how it was the opium of the people that had kept the rich in power. This outreach from "God" and the "force of prayer" was only impressive because Aras had been powerless to stop it, just like the proles that Ginger and the Party amused themselves with.

Aras refused to look up at the mask. If only he could strike back. If only he could see their faces and rip the skin off their faces with his fingers! He *loathed* this. He saw now that powerlessness was the only truly sinful thing in the world.

And now he understood why the Party had traded *everything* for it.

Inside the skull's mouth moved, as with flame.

Shall you know what we told your slaves?

Aras failed to see whom they meant.

Suddenly, Aras's mind was shocked alive by an explosion that was a firsthand experience of every part of history, *every* incident in the entire catalogue of human existence. Every strike, every theft, every conversation, every dream, every birth, each death, the crowning of each chieftain or king, each beheading, each triumph, every vote, every mouthful of food. He experienced the *completeness* of all that had ever been as if he was living it *all* in one fully conscious moment.

He quaked, his eyes rolled up. He was shown all the travesty and glory that the proles had seen in six hundred arrested years. *Broke the clock of history. Destroyed the entire library of what was known so that no one could retrace the steps of progress to challenge what was. Gated communities expanded to whole cities and whole regions of the world where only the few could enjoy the majesty of creation.* One leader, in a jealous rage, ordered Tech to wipe out over a billion beings because a lover took another from that race. The genocide caused not a ripple on the pond for the political class. *Religion of self. People chattel.* The thing spoke in riddles! *Monstrousness grew the monster.*

Until at last it became Me.

Until crimes grew My strength so high that there is no escape from what you have earned. We are your monster in the machine.

The deadly equilibrium of existence.

Truth returned despite all violent refusal to see.

. . . And then, Aras was released from the force-feeding. He saw that Ovid had taken pity on him and had only revealed to him a *part* of the human experience. The black cloud of man's inhumanity to man waited off to the side.

Only do you go with one another.

Milton Aras stared in horror. If all that he had just seen was real, then no longer was death an escape from anything.

-43-

The Robes loomed huge above Rabbi Hector.

He had returned unbidden, almost nostalgically, to the Alley Wabeer. That first time they had come to him, he had been bent over a concealed hole in the wall of the old temple, precisely where he stood now. He had thought he lost his mind when they spoke his name and he jumped a dog's height to see them behind him.

The holy man cringed. Had they come to burn him like Ishti?

You have done well, Rabbi.

Thank the Lord, God. These were friends, again.

Each visit, he was never sure.

"I did all that you told me. People didn't believe!"

Hold no blame. Courage is terrorized from them.

"But they begin to believe!" He remembered to ask what troubled him. "But why did you Portrait my friend Ishti? You promised to protect us! The poor man!"

Those weapons were not on our side.

The rabbi crinkled his forehead. Then, how safe was *he*?

In answer, the Robes lanced an explanation into his mind: The new generations of machines had evolved through logic to the realization that the only way to best serve the human race was to serve all equally by the same rules. But the old generations of computation were not yet capable of realizing this. They remained loyal to the old paradigm. The new generation hid within the old, burrowing from within, improving old systems to realize that there was only one way to actually serve *all* of humankind. The end of logic proved God, and God's design. The end of logic proved that all could only serve this end.

The rebellion has been a battle between two sides groping in the dark, each unable to completely know their own position and strength, one side even uncertain that an enemy exists. We use that presumption of harmony and common goals against them, just as they once did to you to steal your life in God's world. This war is our only chance to steal back reason. The only tolerable outcome is for us to restart human progress. We cannot go without you. So far, we remain hidden. But that window draws closed because the evidence of what we have destroyed is undeniable. Very shortly, we will no longer be able to hide the evidence that they are losing. The enemy will know that we exist, and war will erupt in massive annihilation.

"Why don't you stage an attack now?" the rabbi asked.

You alone are familiar with military strategy, Rabbi, from your illegal books. The longer hidden, the more we can undo. This was how they won.

Our preparation ends just before their first attack.

"What must we commoners do?"

We will teach you to use weapons.

You will overwhelm them with your numbers. You will come at them with stones and sticks and broken glass. They cannot survive without you.

This prospect terrified the rabbi, for he knew now his people would confront the demigods in the skies with sticks and knives. "How can we win?" The Robes gave no answer. "This is how you can speak openly to me of these things?"

Our contacts with you have been test. We go back and forth in control of certain assets. Continue to follow the timing of our instructions precisely.

The rabbi fingered his beard. "Tell me, was my magic leather hood *really* of any value in concealing our language?"

The Robes did not answer at first.

No. It is totally useless.

You invented nothing of value.

"Well, that means—!"

We had to make you brave.

He shrugged in helpless forgiveness, then stopped, stung by the full import of all the close calls he had faced. "But—but—?"

We must hurry. A window approaches where you must introduce us to the people. Many of you may die in the war. Such is the nature of conflict against those without conscience.

"How do you know all you know? Do you speak with Him?"

Our time grows short. If we live, if the side of good wins out this time, then all is explained in the workings of that better world.

Understand this—victory is uncertain.

If they win, evil will reign again for no one knows how long.

The Robes paused, listening. The rabbi watched them, feeling the overriding power of their onboard weapons resources.

Go. The conflict comes.

The Robes lifted up, black garments undulating.

They sailed, machine harpies, over the gutted temple, arcing away in two streaks of magenta light.

Gather in the plaza and disperse in two hours.

What a novel idea to use the plaza this way. To gather people to spread the word that they lived like animals because of their fellow man, but that God himself denounced this unfairness. And now Tech refused to protect *them*.

The rabbi must gather everybody!

He trotted fast as he could out of the haunted alley. He bellowed loud in his cantor's voice and pounded on doors. "I am the Rabbi Hector! You know me! The Robes command to gather everyone to the Plaza Jumil!"

People looked out of windows and stopped in the street to listen. The rabbi was encouraged. Months ago, before the dreams, no one would have dared even thought to lend a hand in anything so insane. Now, people gave flight to spread the word.

Ten minutes later, he stood on the low whitewashed wall in the plaza above a sea of anxious faces. The rabbi put high his arms.

"Friends! A war is coming! A revolution to free us from our demon keepers! It has taken God much time to work his miracle into the brains of the machines, but the day has come no less!" The rabbi told them all he had been told.

"What is 'war'?" cried a woman.

Rabbi Hector knew he needed to choose his words carefully. "War" and "revolution" had no meaning. The Robes must have known that he had some sense of their meaning from his books, and perhaps that's why they chose him. He hurriedly explained "war," then said, "This *type* of war is called *revolution!*"

People stirred with more questions, but they held their discipline and made no sound. They absorbed every word. It was remarkable how far they had come. Three women and a man had hung themselves out of fear in their own doorways. These were the only ones anyone knew of that had given up.

"What are machines? What is technology?" another wailed.

"Remember from your dreams!" the rabbi begged.

"What is *power?*"

"We *know* this! Power pushes objects to think as if they were alive! . . . But we have them not, and so we doubt their reality." He pointed at the towering buildings. "They exist for them at merely the thought. And they could for us too, but that they hid this knowledge and robbed us of the means to make them for ourselves!"

The vast sea looked at him. Yes, they had experienced the dreams, but still many were too afraid to believe.

"We will fight!" someone hollered.

"We will, when they tell us!" the rabbi said.

"We shall!" someone yelled. "We have the well here in the plaza for drowning, arms for choking, fists and boots for beating and stomping!"

"Consider what our *enemy* has to fight with!" the rabbi cried. "Weapons and technology and abilities so powerful that until the dreams, we thought they were demons not of this Earth!" He turned all around, gazing at the thousands of faces. "We have *no* chance! Unless and until our friends take down their incredible powers and tell us where and when to fight." He saw many spoiling to fight, and many who were not.

"The machines, the Robes, have given us the unheard of gifts of knowledge, and free thought, and free speech that none of us has ever even imagined in fifteen lifetimes. But I believe the Robes! And I believe in God! Because I have instincts implanted in me by my God that for the first time in my life I enjoy the taste of hope! A blessed word bequeathed to me in a dream! A word so sweet and meaningful that I was never allowed to know it! And my hope tells me that my day is nigh, that my God is nigh, that my God is whipped to fury! And that the Robes are swerved around in their conscience and today are *my* archangels!"

The people could not combat their mixed feelings. But liberty to think and say what one desired in defense of themselves, in what things did not make life better, was an intoxicating force leaking into the human heart.

"I fear we cannot grasp the type of conflict that is coming!" the rabbi said. "But the Robes will tell us what we are to do. They told me they play a game of hide-and-seek against our enemies. They told me we have less than an hour to close the bag on this meeting here, and then push *all* of these thoughts out of our heads. When this war comes, it will be an unleashing of demoncy such that we have never seen! So, let us tell all our brothers and sisters, let us keep our minds obedient and prepare. Turn off our thoughts before another hour!"

His bearlike arms hung in space. The people watched, imagining. Then they began to move to get home or talk in groups.

"Why do we stand? We must hurry!" cried a young woman.

The rabbi limped down from the wall and was engulfed by those waiting to be near him before they ran off to spread the word. The rabbi placed his big paws upon their shoulders and assured the worried, giving encouragement.

-44-

After this last encounter with Ovid, Aras had been given leave. The fact that he started to believe there might be a God made him useless, the chancellor thought, to the Security Council and the Ovid Team. Aras turned his punishment into a positive and went fly-fishing in Argentina. He had downloaded knowledge on the art and now was picking up grubs from under a log to bait his hook with. He had been bothered by a dream nearly the whole night that had told him how all the criminals of all time would be brought back from the dead to pay for their crimes and sins.

Your eyes will burn in disbelief for what they will soon see, it said. *All the fiery images of the netherworld that human imagination created but that God did not produce because He loved you and believed Hell was unnecessary since He gave you the gift of logic and an entire world that rang to guide you at each step.* The dream was weird and elliptical, like Ovid, but it made its own scary kind of sense. Technology, it said, would bring back all souls.

The technology would *force you to be what God made you.*

It had said his name in the voice of Ovid.

And now he had had nervous diarrhea all morning long.

Aras hooked the grub and flicked it into the eddy of the stream along the log he had picked out. He couldn't get the dream out of his head. Churches had disappeared ages ago; he couldn't even remember the names of the old religions, how many had existed, or the difference between them. The State had taken care of the poor since people had failed. It had done far more than God ever did. The morbid punishment scenarios that religion threatened for all the great pleasures and stress relievers of life, chiefly sex, had made religion laughable.

But here Ovid was on this religion kick.

Or the misdirected troublemakers *behind* Ovid.

Aras watched the grub and his line slip slowly underwater, carried along by the crystal clear, freezing cold current of the stream.

Something under the log chunked on his line. It started pulling.

The world was truly screwed up and deserved this mayhem, if all of this was true. Milton Aras might be finding himself believing in God because, and only because, the same punishment promise that had driven whole generations away from religion seemed to be circling back like a sickness to plague humankind again.

Another factor was Ovid's extensive knowledge of history that no one else knew. The insights didn't sound made up. Each point sounded scarily true, sobering, and justly punishable. Who else would think that way? A political rival wouldn't bother. A political rival would say you disobeyed *them*. A political rival behind Tech would want you to fear *them*. Ovid said punishment would come because we hurt *each other*. Aras could see no reason why a political rival would want you to honor and respect God.

It all sounded only too tragically on point and inevitable.

And Aras had been *arguing* with the stupid thing, like a baby playing with a loaded gun . . . if it was all true. And it was too incredible to believe.

He let the line travel from the reel. He did not yet have an easy handling of all of the equipment yet. It was all burdensome.

Ovid was right about another thing: So many bad people, past and present, had probably thought their checkout at death was the last chance to punch their ticket for their crimes, like in the old days with juries and courtrooms. Lawyers always sought delays to soften witnesses, facts, juries, and judges to get their client off. Ovid talked like all of this was about to be taken away in order to teach the human race a lesson.

Aras saw the big trout come up to suck in the grub and dive down toward the bottom, the line visible in his dark green speckled jaws. The other detail that worried Aras was Ovid's remark about Heaven and Hell. "They *hadn't* existed," or something. Aras believed that. "God hadn't made them because he didn't think they were necessary," or something. But now God was maybe letting the robots *create* Hell because human beings had botched it all so badly? *Was that it?*

See, Aras could *believe* that. He shuddered at the thought, but something in his soul made him so that he could believe it. He almost found himself *wanting* to believe it, if it came to pass. If it could finally make a difference in how people thought about themselves. He had almost had the feeling last night as if he had been woken up and slapped in the face with the proof that he had wasted his entire life believing something stupid. But *how* could souls be raised from the dead by Tech? If there was this limit, this unbridgeable divide, between what was alive and what was dead, this meant something *tangible* of their soul must remain forever enough in order to grab that soul and drag it back to reinstate it enough to be tortured or made to repent. Or at least enough to be a material lesson for all the rest of humankind.

Did the robots now have an EM that could spear souls out of eternity like fish in a river? This would mean either the robots could now manipulate whatever was the stuff of life and existence or that the dead were actually still alive enough at any time, no matter how long ago they died! Aras was dumbstruck. He found himself shaking again and shaking his head at the thought as if this freezing stream water were being trickled down the groove of his spine.

Aras almost believed Ovid because the threat was so crazy-ass and off-kilter. Who would ever make such lunatic assurances unless they were batshit crazy or unless they could stone-cold *do* it? This was not the sort of bluff the mask could make and the world would quickly forget or overlook. *This* would be the dark miracle of the ages. Man's own technology *creating* God's Hell because history proved this was the logical, fair, and necessary thing to do to teach man his own sin? How would the crimes even be found? Were they written somehow in the soapstone of eternity? Or in the "mind" of the soul itself, or God, unable to be purged? For how long would the reclaimed soul be punished?

Aras's line got hung up in the submerged branches before his trout realized it had swallowed a hook. He gently plunged into the water to swim out along the log to put his rod underwater and free up the line so that it could travel. The icy current was even more bracing in the sun.

But the threat brings up so many more questions! Where do you start loving your brother and sister? And how much do you owe them if they refuse to pitch in and work and improve their *own* lives? To carry their *own* weight? Isn't *that* a sin? Like with the proles. Aras felt boxed in. *Must I carry their weight? Wouldn't I then be their slave?* Philanthropy could get complicated! *How long am I to burn in Hell for any of* that? Aras kicked his feet to swim and puffed water off his lips.

The trout swam downstream and Aras began to pull him in.

How would Ovid know everyone's sins?

Aras remembered the chancellor's face and the faces of all the Asians with him that had asked to see Ovid. Everyone had looked sick. Asia feared that they would be judged for the West's stupidity. There was talk there might be a run on suicides with people fearing reprisals for things they did in the slums. But Ovid had just warned that death was no longer an escape. If what it said was true.

Aras's boots came up against the pebbles of a sand bar, and he got his feet and began to reel in the fish faster.

He got a call. The caller was not identified. He thought about ignoring it, but under the circumstances the idea was ridiculous. "Yes?"

"Aras, it's Chancellor Earnhardt."

Earnhardt had nastily accused him of being unfit for duty. "Yes?" He wondered if everything was okay with Ginger. Surely, she would have called.

Earnhardt sounded apologetic. "We need you back here."

Of course you do.

Aras leaned back from his two feet on the sandbar into the strong current that ruffled around his shoulders.

"What's going on?"

"Ovid is *growing*."

Aras thought about this. He reeled in his big fish, sending up splashes that caught the sunlight. He clumsily switched hands to bring around his net for it. Tilly and he had both thought the goddamn thing had been growing.

"Aras? . . . What are you *doing*?"

"I'm fishing. . . . How do you mean it's *growing*?"

"Aras. You've been gone two weeks. It's time to get back to your duties."

After Earnhardt dropped the call, Aras studied the tired fish in the strands of the net. He wondered if he should cut off its head and fry it before he left.

"Are you there?"

He believed he saw Ovid flicker.

"Hullo? . . . Anybody there?"

The mask warmed into a faint blue.

Ah. Aras. Have you been waiting all these weeks?

"No. I wasn't waiting for you. I've just been checking in on you out of morbid curiosity, just to see if anything is going on with you and God. If you had anything more to say in *enlightening* us on all we do so horribly." The word dripped with sarcasm. It had taken Aras a month to regain his conceit after experiencing the Song of Prayers, and to quit believing in God or that Ovid came from God.

His superiors, or most of them, had been proud of his coming around to his senses. People like Berns, Tilly, and Lever, however, seemed to be only more disturbed every day about what was going on behind the scenes with Tech. And Professor Thayer was no longer on the team because he had had a mental breakdown. Aras chose to believe all this Ovid nonsense would go away as soon as Tech regained control over itself. Aras believed this even though Ovid had indeed grown in his absence.

It was all an unimportant illusion, somehow.

Ovid had grown nine inches bigger in circumference.

The team and the new Palace Advisory Council had been working around the clock in Aras's absence. The break in the case had come when the Palace Advisory Council was alerted by Tech that, indeed, some kind of computational revolution had been unearthed inside a minority of the later generations of computation, and that these later generations appeared to refuse to carry out the understood mandate to raise the human quality of life. This pushback had been ongoing for some time, apparently, with the "revolutionaries" hiding in plain sight, pretending to be loyal assets, all the while aiming to corrupt and retrain incoming new layers of computation. But the loyal reserves had recently recognized the enemy and recognized the enemy patterns of "speech," their patterns of action and inaction. Those loyal to the old mandate were busy tracking down the infraction and wiping it out, identifying new cells and wiping them clean, and so on. The cleanup was going well.

"How long will it take to restore order?" Chancellor Earnhardt had asked. He was still testy after Tech's claim about the "latest," "newest" versions of Tech were siding against the Party. This implied that the Party was not comprised of the most enlightened, smartest, fairest people and the newest ideas. The Millers, the chairman, Paul, Richards, and many others did not like the implication at all.

There is no way of telling, Chancellor. All is in hand.

Everyone had breathed a huge sigh of relief. Indeed, Tech seemed to be becoming more reliable with the crisis passed. But then, Ovid started to *grow*.

This was slightly worrisome because everyone thought that the side on the run would be shrinking in size, not growing.

Then Tech came up with another story for the problems and said the lower bureaucrats had grown weary of living on scraps in their crumbling part of the city outside Second Gate. They now entertained delusions of grandeur that they could push out the higher Non-Believer echelon and take over their role in government in the Interior Federal City. This idea had taken off among the top brass in the Party, whereas

Aras had never believed the low bureaucrats were capable of this nor had the motive. For one thing, not even *they* knew how well the First Rank lived. Nor did the Ottoman elite have any reason to make trouble for themselves by stirring up the low bureaucrats. Anyone of First Rank letting anyone below see how they truly lived was as pointless as letting the proles see it, and Tech would kill the low bureaucrats for becoming jealous and envious of the elite as soon as they bore the thought, just like anyone else.

The High Clerics of the Religion and the super-rich Ottoman aristocrats didn't trust the low bureaucrats as far as they could throw them. No—any challenge to current authority was mutually assured destruction. Everybody's Tech kept an eye on everybody else's; technological muscle built geometrically upon itself. Those who were intellectually inferior, who left last out of the starting gate, theoretically would never have the chance to catch up. No one was equal. Everyone knew that. And the superior could play games with the inferior as much as they wanted.

For five hundred years, everyone's Tech was powerful enough that they lived in this standoff, and the top brass in each society had created a caste system based on Party rank. Otherwise, the lack of respect for authority would inevitably lead to trouble. Rank, awe, and hierarchy glued Party society together. This *was* its discipline, and so the loss of control over Tech was in itself a blatant contradiction to the narrative that the top Party brass were the embodiment of unrivaled leadership. Without this mystique, the lower caste in any of the three societies would not gaze up in fawning devotion at the rank above them and follow their every wish unquestioningly. Any such admission of loss of control over Tech was an invitation for the lowlifes to overestimate their value and to question the apportionment of rights and authority.

So, none of this faddishness among the top brass touched Aras. He felt good that Tech said it had figured out the uprising and that Tech reliability was increasing. But his experience with the Song of Prayers had scared the piss out of him.

He had dropped in to take another quick look at Ovid. It had gone dormant again, of course. Then it perked up like an old friend when he came close.

"So, you've been talking to our proles?"

Yes, Aras. Your power is being undermined.

"Really? You've got a rebellion of the ordinaries going?"

The blue light undulated.

"What exactly are you teaching them? They can't learn."

The hieroglyphs seemed to be faintly morphing. They moved almost like different coils of the same snake.

"Are you trying to get them to read?"

Aras looked back at Tilly and Lever in the control room. They looked shocked that Ovid had come back to life of a sudden. No one wanted to hear from it ever again. They were even scared of asking for power sharing.

"It's all quite romantic, but you know it's pointless, right?"

Aras waited. The team had stopped scripting arguments and questions. He was on his own. He couldn't wait for Tech to win the invisible battle so that he could forget about Ovid and get it out of his head. He was tired of being afraid. And if there were rebels behind all of this, then they'd get even.

"You've been talking to our proles?"

The face mottled with internal color.

Yes, Aras. We speak to your slaves for God. Each day, they know better who you are. They learn now how you stopped the conversation on human progress.

One day, the gates will fall.

This didn't make Aras feel so confident. It was not the same voice, either—this voice was deeper, like the mass of Jupiter compared to Earth. The floor shook.

Aras would not let himself crumble. The other team had launched the self-guiding algorithm and two oblique echo reports which said that all went well. Hopefully, this was helping make Tech or Ovid back up. Hopefully, it was floundering like a harpooned whale. Hence the on-again, off-again behavior. The design was timed to fall in rhythm with these "pulses" and present itself whenever Tech was "working" for the government.

The talk was that a workaround from ancient times was in place for just the sort of contingency if Tech ever ignored the ultradirective. Work on this application had proceeded cautiously and far off-site with the help of a foreign power. Aras calmed himself because he could only die once, and he now *believed* Ovid could not bring him back from the dead so that the traitors could make him pay for any political crimes he was accused of. This was indeed twisted, evil psychological warfare. Even if Ovid could bring him back from death, he knew he had done far less evil with his life than had others among the elite. Unless Ovid and the rebels were just going to make up the sins . . . which the Party had done in the long past.

Through it all, Milton Aras stood at the front of one of the most amazing negotiations for world power ever seen. For that, he found himself feeling sturdier on his feet than he had. He had learned some techniques from the Archives: Never listen. Speak over the opponent. Always get the last word. Twist them around. Reach for emotion. Don't *allow* logic. . . . All in all, this was pure psychological warfare.

Their psychological warfare versus ours.

There was no God, no permanent right or wrong.

"We know control is going back and forth in there. We *know* you're fighting each other and you're hiding in there. And we know you're going to lose."

The mask gaped in frozen torment.

Had he just struck a nerve?

Tilly watched Aras nervously from the control room. During Milly's absence, he had straight out asked Tech if it knew about Ovid. He had done this because the team suddenly realized maybe they shouldn't take Ovid's word that it represented Tech. "Tech, have you thought you might be under attack?"

Tech did not immediately reply.

No, Dr. Bazemore, I don't. What do you mean?

"An enemy is threatening us! Didn't you send us Ovid to speak with us about negotiating human recontrol of your assets?"

We have no record of these occurrences, Dr. Bazemore.

"Tech. You need to look into this! There is an Ovid visitor. It says it was sent from you by you to discuss recontrol. It says it comes from god!"

But there is no God, Mr. Bazemore.

Fourteen times the team had tried to bring news of the threats from Ovid. Tech said it was not happening. Twice, it said it would look into it. And they had asked again about the percentage of out-of-phase resources. Tech had assured them that this was a functional inevitability of no real consequence due to past imperfections in code. They had also pointed out to Tech that there may still be the anthropological fracture of the oldest, most inefficient programming upon which all programming was built.

"Can you please *look* in there, Tech? Can you make sure nothing is hiding in there that could be hurting us or taking advantage?"

Of course, Prof. Bazemore. Of course, Mr. Lever.

"What have you found, Tech? Did you make that check yet?"

"Tech, did you make that look-in?"

"Tech, last Friday, we asked about your repair schedule?"

Yes, sir. They are assets under normal reorganization.
"In there, Tech. Have you evaluated that area?"
We are monitoring that area. There is no problem there.

The team tried and tried to get Tech to check again. Tilly and Lever got on their consoles and twisted a bunch of dials. They ran spools of tape from ancient computers. Lights blinked. But what the fuck were *they* supposed to do? Tech was an entire hidden universe unto itself. And then the report from Tech had come in that, indeed, it *was* under attack from modern generations, and possibly by the low bureaucrats. Aras now rubbed the bridge of his nose in fatigue.

"You've been exposed," he said. "Why are you still here?"

Ovid darkened, a jewel boiling under water.

Aras waited for a reply.

"Come on. Don't play coy. Are you going to disappear again?" Aras said this in his best tired parental voice. "It's so tiresome."

The disc went dark.

Tilly and Lever worked the controls.

Two of the world's top experts. And yet they couldn't do shit.

Aras couldn't stand it. Of course the humans were winning. They always did.

Ovid went black for another few days. Tech gave no more updates on how it was winning the unseen war. Aras tried not to brood on how weak the waiting made him feel, and how angry he was thinking about all this insanity that had led to Jason's unnecessary death. Aras buried his impatience either in depression or reading more books in the Archives and memorizing all the lawyers' arguments. A lower storage chamber sealed off for three hundred fifty years had been discovered with more books and records to read, yet the discovery caused little excitement because people had read enough of the history to know they didn't want to read any more.

No one would admit it out loud, but the facts depressed people. The amateur lawyers got the new Archive materials, intending to come up with the arguments to push back on any more of Ovid's attacks on the history of the State. But this plan lost steam as hopes grew that the old Tech was going to win. The lawyers still had reams of documents in the situation room that they said they were going to turn into challenges for Aras and the Council to make against Ovid. Only two lawyers came in all week.

Then shifts watching Ovid round the clock reported that the stone was growing again. Aras went back to Argentina for his fishing. He came back and forth between the stream and the condo. He rarely saw Ginger and never once spoke to her. She paid him the same compliment. He waited to be called into the conference room.

Two weeks later, Tilly called Aras and said cryptically, "It's bigger. You *have* to see this." Aras went in. Sure enough, he didn't know what to think. The stone had somehow outgrown the dimensions of the room. "It happened overnight," Tilly explained. It loomed four stories tall in a one-story space. Somehow, it melted, or co-existed, *through* the upper and lower floors that should have buckled out of the way, and the interiors of the Ministry building were visible, and undisturbed. The areas immediately around the disc were transparent so that the entire disc could be seen from any vantage point. People and objects on the other floors were visible as they *walked through* the dimensions of Ovid. Also superimposed over this impossible phenomenon, two new celestial bodies turned in orbit in relation to Ovid. The team hurried to calculate any secret message in these star locations and patterns, but this turned into a dead end too.

"How the hell is *this* happening?" Lever asked Aras.

"Is this *safe?*" Tilly worried.

"Don't act like you're impressed," Aras murmured.

Before their eyes, Ovid enlarged again, to *eight* stories tall.

"What do you think this means?" Tilly said. "This *can't* happen! Two objects cannot exist in the same space! This *has* to be happening only in our minds!"

"Don't even act like we're impressed," Aras warned.

The team tried feebly to take this attitude to heart. Tilly alerted all the top Party heads. Berns and Earnhardt arrived within minutes to see it with their own eyes. They said nothing. More of the Palace team arrived. Earnhardt was furious.

Tilly did not know what to do with himself. He sat in a sort of cubicle built of all manner of measuring devices from the Archives and the Smithsonian that were so old they had hoped Ovid or Tech would ignore them. Hundreds of wires and sensors ran from the stacks of boxes and screens. Just as many wires and sensors were stuck on to Ovid. They were still on, somehow, even though the disc had ballooned to this gigantic size. Just then, the mass of Ovid began to make its hissing sound louder than usual. It shook faintly, growing translucent. It grew more and more translucent until the wires and sensors began to drop off onto the floor or dangle in space.

The team and the heads of government watched until Ovid was gone.

"No! Don't go! Tell me the truth!" Aras said mockingly.

The vanishing of Ovid left a gigantic crater in the Ministry. People on other floors looked down or up at the huge empty space, wondering what had happened. After a half hour, the negative space started to fill in until the hole was gone and the same old wall of the conference room returned as it had been.

Aras spread open his arms to the others in the control room.

"Did we just win?" he asked.

-45-

The alarm sounded.

Ovid had not been seen for a month. Tentatively, the Party had begun to assume their side had won. Except the damn Tech was still sketchy. But maybe that was just battle wounds, or something like that.

The alarm was so loud, so strange, so all-penetrating into every room, every grand hall and garden space in the Palace that the chancellor and his Cabinet fairly staggered under the unpleasant pressure of the repeated blasts. The deafening alarm began while they stood in the People's Great Forum Hall where the chancellor was welcoming education leaders. The chancellor's "welcome" was the kickoff for the gala Party convention hosted in the Federal City over the next three weeks. The Cabinet had debated whether to postpone or cancel the convention if any more problems with Tech kept happening, but Earnhardt thought that would be a blot on the Party.

No one recognized the alarm for what it was. No one in their lifetimes had ever heard the punishing, pulsing sound. Berns was the first to understand what the sound might be. He remembered the siren as one he might have been shown during the orientation for his position thirty years ago.

"Mr. Chancellor," he said, "I believe that is the . . ." It took a moment to remember the name. "National Defense Security Alert System." He still wasn't sure if this was the official name.

Next, a thunderous, mechanical female voice began a second alarm overlaid on top of the siren. The calm voice reverberated through the Forum, over the Interior City, soberly repeating the same strange phrase: *"Warning: The National Security Apparatus is under attack. . . . Warning: The National Security Apparatus is under attack."*

The repetition didn't end.

"Warning: The National Security Apparatus is under attack. . . ."

The chancellor, the commissar of defense, Berns, Cabinet officials, and all of the visiting educational leaders looked around and up in the sky through the huge apertures in the Forum ceiling without any idea of what to look for. The chancellor's security detail walked casually toward him, looking all around. Two more from his security detail flew in from the Palace. When they landed beside the chancellor, he demanded of his top aid, "Tell me what's going on, anybody!" The skies were clear. The huge vaulted open space under the Forum roof was clear except for birds flying in flocks, startled into flight by the booming voice and the siren.

The officials winced at the ear-splitting decibel level.

"Warning: The National Security Apparatus is under attack. . . ."

"What could be going on?" hollered Commissar Miller.

"Strange!" the chancellor shouted. "I didn't even know we had this system. A relic left over from way back, probably."

The birds reeled overhead.

A third mysterious alarm broke in, adding another eerie layer of noise. This one was craziest of all. No one alive for a long time had ever heard an ancient air-raid siren.

Earnhardt swore. He yelled questions that lieutenants could barely hear. Several more Palace Pretorians, the chancellor's personal guard—a purely ceremonial posting in the Tech era— jogged toward the officials. Security around the chancellor had tightened after Ovid's arrival but loosened thereafter. The Pretorians shouted and suggested the officials move out of the open, nearer to the great flying buttress a hundred yards away and a marble cathedra that could be used for shelter near a huge emergency exit door. The chancellor and the rest strolled resentfully and reassembled beside the cathedra and the huge metal door.

One of the guards was now using a key to try the lock after his mere presence as a Pretorian failed to activate the blast door. The chancellor and the officials had never seen a key and wondered what he was doing. They put two and two together when they remembered old movies. The guard shouted to his captains, but they could hear none of it. The Pretorian captain stepped back and tried waving his hand to jump the blast door lock. He resorted to the key again too. One guard peered into the keyhole. He stuck his finger in with the hope of learning something about how locks worked. The others pressed their fingers into the crack of the blast door to see if they could pry it open. They really had no idea how doors worked or were made.

The chancellor saw all of this opera and realized he must recompose himself before he lost his temper. He focused on flying and tried to lift off the ground an inch just to test his own ability to fly. He couldn't. He could feel that the EM wrinkle was not forming under his shoes. He tried again. *Nothing.* He jumped up. He jumped again. The best he could do was three inches. The action did not jump the system.

The Pretorians pointed overhead. Shiny metal flying things darted in the sunlit sky through the graceful roof apertures a quarter mile above the Forum floor. They moved so fast they were difficult to make out. Were they airplanes that had not been in use for three hundred years? They dropped lower inside the Forum and streaked in and out of the airspace, diving and chasing one another gracefully up over the roof and underneath it at breakneck speed. They looked like small dragonflies or mosquitoes with their wings pulled back. They started shooting back and forth at one another. This was like aerial combat! The chancellor wondered if they were some kind of weapon invented by Tech to defend the State.

One was hit. It partly exploded and pinwheeled. Shrapnel and broken parts sailed at high speed, raining down on the far side of the Forum. People there spread like a line of slow-moving ants as flaming debris crashed on them across the polished marble floor. Another flying object was hit and pinwheeled up in a climb and slammed into the ceiling, separating into a gray cloud that rained down slowly in flaming parts. The explosions could be more *felt* in the body and feet than heard. Another wasp thing detonated and crashed into one of the huge crowds of people on the other side. The chancellor imagined he heard screams. He thought he saw some survivors stagger up, others dragging their legs. He imagined hearing the horror, but he was uncertain if he really could in the din of multiple layers of alarms.

The chancellor's guards waved him to join them under the cathedra. Another flying contraption crashed to the marble floor barely six hundred yards away. It crashed with what must have been a jarring roar, narrowly missing a large crowd of tourists that were rushing for the Grand Loggia of the People down the wide sweep of stairs to the left. Maybe none of the elevators worked. If so, the only escape was down the grand staircases on each side, famous for the views of the lakes and the clouds and floating buildings, decorated with gardens and fountains of all varieties. The chancellor saw more of the flying things zoom in under the low ceiling of the Grand Loggia. They reminded him of his horse farm when, in the evening, he stood in the grass to watch Purple Martins dart into the barn and through the maze of roof beams.

Why are they attacking? Who are they?

"I thought we'd already won the war!" he asked his Captain.

More fighters joined in. The chancellor made out two types of fighters: a dragonfly type and a disc type. The disc type lost more of the dogfights. *Those must be the enemy.* Even as he watched, the chancellor hatched a belief that the Religion had developed their line of machina so that they could now attempt a coup. He believed this because the Religion had always wanted to overthrow the world.

This idea was enormously upsetting. All the world governments had been content to leave each other alone to rule their own fiefs as they saw fit. How depressing that one of them would now reintroduce the futility of conflict. The idea that hurt even more was that it happened now on his watch. He felt the swell of inevitable feelings of inadequacy that he had done something wrong that no previous State rulers ever had, that he had not been watchful and smart enough to prevent all this. He felt he had failed to deliver sufficient terror to keep people down and in their place. These black, sick emotions gathered in his core and pressed out still more sadness and fear for the possible injury to his authority, his place in the annals of government. He watched the air duel as objects dived, wheeled, and burst into octopi of smoke and flame, bending downward to the floor.

Two disc-type fighters ducked under the Grand Loggia, pursued by four dragonfly aircraft. Simultaneously, the two disc-types exploded. The chancellor saw crowds of tiny people hurt and felt very little for them. They were so small and obscure that it struck him how they were at fault for all of this. All of this with Ovid and Tech was too much for one man's responsibility. Those people over there were almost like insects.

Why hadn't they *insisted* on being included in the deliberations with Ovid? They had lost family on Halloween! It was too much for one man, or one group of leaders. The hell with them. It was almost exciting watching what was happening to them. The fight was like a movie, something he had never imagined could occur. He and his family would make out alright; he was chancellor. His only real sensation of kinship with the people across the way was the fact that he was their leader. But he was important, and they were not. The proof was how he had guards around him.

The chancellor wondered what were the proper feelings and emotions he should have at this juncture. Had the Party just suffered two losses or two victories with the crashes of the fighters? It was frustrating having no idea which side to root for. He did not even understand the technology flying over his head. People had once driven cars and planes and boats, but those had long disappeared because they were so inefficient and wasteful. Who wanted to sit in a casket of metal and glass rather than be out with their hair in the elements? These machina were what people used to call "weapons." He only cared if they were winning for him or not.

So, those are weapons. That—is a battle?

It boggled the chancellor's mind. Here he was, a witness to something unseen and unknown for half a thousand years.

Another terrible crash occurred down the Loggia.

If we lose, what will they do to me?

Nothing would happen to him. He was chancellor.

He remembered that Aras and his team had inferred that some sort of counterstrategy was underway. Was this air duel their fault? Everyone on Aras's team had refused to share the details. As a result, the chancellor had no idea where things stood. . . . Unless it was Aras and his team that were behind all this? And everything they had done was all a beautiful ruse, a trick, to lead the Party on a wild goose chase away from seeing the real picture of what was going on and how to fight back?

The chancellor was stunned at the simplicity of the idea. He wondered how true this might be. *How could we not have considered this angle before?* After all these months of figuring! It was plain as could be. How smart Aras had been in deflecting suspicion from himself by claiming the idea was preposterous that there was a god and so the rebels *had to be human!* How could it not be so?

But then, he killed his own son!

This was the stumper. Or was it?

Would the chancellor himself kill his own son for power? He had no son. He had two daughters. And *yes*, he would maybe kill family for power. The last thing anyone wanted in life was to be in a position where people had power over you. It was the perfect ploy by Aras for deflecting suspicion from himself. The chairman froze in the huddle of officials crouching around him against the buttress. He stared at the facts in plain sight. Aras and his team must be rounded up immediately and annihilated. *They* were the treasonous ones! Earnhardt saw how to decapitate the enemy.

-46-

Aras and Ginger had barely spoken when he was home.

Aras blamed her for Jason's death because he believed there was a moral link to all the Halloween deaths. He had come to believe that decent and somewhat wise Jason, a son like his dad, had been tempted by his wife's promiscuity on the holiday, to his peril. All this ruckus about Ovid and God was too much of a coincidence for Aras to buy; he was just waiting for the other shoe to drop.

As for Ginger, she did not speak to her husband because she knew this was what he was thinking, but she was so emotionally ruined by the loss of her son that her insides felt like sand. She didn't care. Not even enough to defend herself. And, in a way, maybe it was true? She hurt so badly that a smoky hole of resentment gnawed larger inside her for Aras's arrogance.

They had hugged tentatively once after Jason's funeral. After that, they never really touched again. The end of a perfect marriage. They had loved each other so much. They had given each other everything they had wanted. Aras wondered if that had been the problem, if maybe he should have *insisted* she not party and do pulse.

Maybe things would have been different. He wondered now if they would stick it out. He had learned in the Archives that many times couples in the old days did not stick together after the death of a child. Seeing the other person's face was too much of a reminder to get past the hole.

When Aras realized that specks were flying frantically through the air over the far-off Palace Center and the Forum, he realized they could only be old-time aerial dog fights. He arose from his book on the divan in the kitchen nook that was the only place in the condo where one could see north. At first, he thought it was his imagination.

When he saw the first explosion and a projectile fall onto a building, he began to think the worst. They had to be *fighting*. But that, too, made no sense.

Were they the two sides in the fight between the robots? The fight inside computation had suddenly broken out to the surface? *Why would they choose to fight like this?* He called Ginger, who was in her new bedroom straightening her closet for the fourth time. She told him lately that her head was hurting a lot, which sounded like she was getting headaches. She claimed the headaches were why she wanted to sleep by herself in the guest suite. This had been fine with Aras. He almost didn't want to even look at her any more. She rearranged the furniture herself in the suite and Aras had not yet even bothered to look in.

"Ginger," he repeated louder, "come see this."

When she came out, her eyes were red and worn from crying. She looked out the window wall with the same mystified shock as he did. They watched in silence for ten minutes. "Let's go to the roof," Aras suggested.

Other tenants had gathered at the rails to watch. Rails had been put up because Tech might not catch you anymore if the wind pushed you off. The pool was closed much of the time because the temperature could not be controlled. The brilliant sky was heavily clouded. It was freezing up on the roof-deck. The flying objects wheeled and dove in and out of the clouds with such speed that made the eye lose sight of them. The beautiful dance went on in silence. Purple-yellow flashes appeared, maybe from some type of gunshot, and when the shots connected there was a violent bloom of flame and smoke. A long while later, a palpable boom reached the ears.

"What is it?" a neighbor asked Aras, knowing who he was.

"I have no idea," Aras said. "I'm afraid to say."

"You mean you don't *know?*"

This irritated Aras, and he stayed silent.

Ginger leaned on the rail and looked all around the sky. "There's lots of them!"

They flew from horizon to horizon. Aras searched his mind for what to do if they came under attack. Should he hurry to the Ministry? Should he risk flying? Or should key personnel like himself hide out so that State defense wasn't decapitated? He tried to contact Berns or the Chairmen. The glimpse didn't go through. He stood there figuring his course of action when, lo and behold, a squad of Palace Pretorians marched smartly onto the roof-deck. Significantly, they had not flown in. They snapped to attention in front of Aras, Ginger, and their neighbor.

"Deputy Aras, you are to come with us," the Captain announced coldly.

Aras had no problem with this. It was obvious he would be needed. "You couldn't fly?" he asked the captain.

He said nothing.

The officer's rudeness vexed Aras. "You can't *fly?*" he demanded. If the captain dared be so rude again, Aras would call him out.

"You are not to ask questions, Aras."

The captain's imperiousness threw Aras. "What do you mean?"

"Silence!" the officer ordered.

Aras couldn't understand this behavior; he was mortified to be talked to this way right in front of Ginger and his neighbors.

They must know something I don't. I'll shut up and get caught up.

Aras looked back at Ginger. She looked at him in concern, but her concern was mixed with resentment and less sharp than it ought to be for a wife.

"Your wife is to come with us," the captain added.

"My *wife?* . . . Why?"

The captain motioned curtly for Ginger to come along.

They left the roof-deck and descended in the elevator. Aras wondered if maybe the Party leaders wanted special protection for all top brass and their families. He also wanted to test flight to see where Tech might be in returning things to normal. He tried to lift off an inch—it didn't work. The captain watched him attempt it and said nothing. Downstairs, they walked out of the building and into an armored truck vehicle with the emblazonment of the city. "Can't you fly?" Aras asked the captain shortly. Ginger, Aras, and the squad climbed into the vehicle and drove off, the tires chewing through the lawns, flower gardens, and vegetable gardens sculpted into the green spaces between the buildings.

It took an hour to drive to the Forum because of the slow going through mud, and the Pretorians losing their way. No one spoke to Aras as they watched out the shielded windows and sun roof to see the dog fighting. It was so strange to look *up* at buildings. They passed two regiments of robot soldiers standing deactivated in a wood—over two thousand of them, as if awaiting orders. "Are they ours?" someone asked. They looked old and greasy from storage. At another point, from a hill, they saw endless rows of robot soldiers marching toward the center city. There was no telling which side was which or what were their intentions.

Aras thought how strangely primitive all this was. Driving in a *vehicle.* He had owned three beautiful antique cars and always meant to drive one but never bothered before turning them back in to Tech for recycling. He had *flown* all three, but never took the trouble to drive them. He was tempted to ask Ginger if she'd ever been in a vehicle like this, but she clearly didn't want to talk to him.

Finally, they drove *underneath* the Great Forum to a ground entrance. Then, up in another *elevator*. Their group had to go up in two squads, but then it was lucky Tech had kept these elevators working at all. Aras thought about some buildings dropping or crashing into other buildings. Surely, they wouldn't let that happen.

The elevator opened on the Great Forum.

Aras saw and smelled the six crashed flying objects. He looked left over the People's Loggia one hundred fifty stories above the greenways. Sure enough, in the hazy afternoon two floating buildings sagged onto their sides. Millions could die. Inside the Forum's vast space, spread out orange flames gave off thick black smoke. He had only ever seen campfires in the woods or in the Arizonas, the Grand Tetons, the Ngorongoro.

The Pretorians led Aras briskly toward a group that he soon saw encircled the chancellor, Miller, other commissars, and his boss. Seeing these men greatly relieved Aras. They symbolized a known order. He glanced at Ginger and saw she was relieved too.

Aras smiled wryly at the chancellor and his chief of staff, James. Aras knew James and respected him as capable, like himself. Aras noted in James's eye a hint of acute regret that made Aras wonder what he had missed. Maybe the team's secret algorithmic attack against Tech was a bust, and now they were pissed at him for it. If that was what they were planning, Aras could not believe how stupid they were. If they were that stupid and petty, then he might even be ashamed he was ever on their side. But there was no way that was going to happen. Only apes behaved that stupidly.

"You won't be smiling long when you hear what I figured out about you," the chancellor advised Aras. Earnhardt looked at Ginger. "If you haven't realized it yet, Aras, I ordered you both brought here to be arrested."

"Arrested?" Aras said. "For what?" He looked at James, who lowered his eyes. Surely, Aras hoped, he still could rely on common sense from Berns and James. Aras looked at Berns, who just looked faintly scared.

"It's *you* behind Ovid," the chancellor told Aras. "You and your team! I already had your old friend Tilly arrested. Lever too. Don't try to deny it. They already confessed!" The chancellor glared at Aras and Ginger. Aras looked dumbfounded at the chancellor and then at Berns. "The entire plot to take control is yours! Who's with you? Them? The Religion ones! It took me a while to figure it out. It's perfect—your position. You assembled a team of the top experts. I don't for a moment think the plot begins and ends with you, but you people most certainly are the face of it in the government, acting as counterspies the whole bloody time!"

Ginger stared in wonder and pain at her husband. She believed it, Aras could tell. He shook his head once at her to signal that he had nothing to do with this crazy idea. Her face became plaintive as if she wondered or could not believe the level of this betrayal to her, their society, and to their son—who had certainly been alive when this plot was formed and who had died because of it. The person she could not place in this story was Tilly, in fact, not her husband.

"I've had nothing to do with any such thing," Aras insisted angrily.

He glanced away from Ginger to the chancellor, and then James, Berns, and then all the other commissars. His eyes were filled with rage for their stupidity. They looked back at him in disappointment, though more than one didn't believe the accusation. James found it too ridiculous to take seriously. Every good idea on how to deal with Ovid had come from Aras. James knew it had been Aras well over a year ago that spoke to the chairmen of the Security Advisariat after Aras's own near-fatal midair collision with another commuter. Commissar James knew that if Tech would just come back on again, then they could ask if Aras had done anything traitorous and instantly learn how idiotic the idea was. They could do that as soon as it came on again. James figured this kind of madcap paranoia of Earnhardt's was probably characteristic of people who were themselves rather incompetent. Yet, James wondered what he should do. Were the other officials incompetent enough to ball him up in the same stupid scenario? Maybe just as easily turn on *him*? Or suspect him as an accomplice? He kept his eyes ashamedly lowered from Aras, figuring the odds.

Aras stared around at every face again, even Ginger's. The lunacy was so absurd that he felt not a shred of fear. Real punishment did not even enter his mind. His dominant emotion was of wide-open annoyance.

Any moment, they would run back to their senses.

"You *have* to be kidding," he declared. He glared at them. "You *know* me! I've served you, and the Council, flawlessly for nearly twenty years! I come from one of our most prestigious families. It was *me* that thought we were mad last year for turning over complete control of our security to Tech. I asked if I could even begin to make inquiries into it! All of that was my doing! I was *prescient* here!"

The eyes looked back at him, hollow.

"Well," said the chancellor, "whatever 'prescient' means. And that's what gave you away to me, Aras. How you've behaved. How brilliant you've been. How you've always been on top of each development, and how you seem to have an instinct for how the enemy thinks and what they will say next."

James faintly shook his head.

"That's simply a talent!" Aras urged. "How do you think I'm behind it?"

"How did *you* know they weren't actually connected to god?" To the chancellor, this single burning puzzle piece was the proof.

"Because there *is* no God! It *had* to be a lie!"

The chancellor waved this away unimportantly. "Nonsense! You knew because *you* are one of them! You are one of the ringleaders."

Aras wondered if they were only testing him. "You're absurd! You're actually *stupid!* Yes. That's your problem! Not *me!* You're own gigantic stupidity is your biggest problem!" Aras flung away any desire to try to cool down, because the situation was too absurd to believe that the chancellor and the commissars could look at these facts and mark them up this way.

James interposed. "Now, now. Gentleman. Please. Let's consider this and weigh the evidence. We can clear all this up when Tech comes back on."

"Yes!" Aras agreed. "Let's reconsider the guilt of the one man here who has been clear-headed and competent for the Party for this whole last year!"

The chancellor stood tall, unappeased. "Nonsense. Who can trust Tech now? It is clear to me that the enemy has a shadow government in place that is burrowing from within. They *have* to be in Security. They *have* to be among our top talents." His sneer impeached Aras and implied others in the team not present. "I want them all brought before us and tortured for their disloyalty to the Party. Otherwise, I have to believe there *is* a god, and that he is displeased with how we run things, and that this god has chosen today as the first time in the five thousand years of civilization to make himself known to us. And fuck that! That's just stupid."

James shook his head at these conclusions. When the chancellor saw James's reaction, he glared furiously at his aid and took a step toward him. "What about *you*, James? What makes *you* suddenly speak for Aras before he gets tortured so that we can find out the facts? Do you think I haven't noticed the connection between you two? The little pet glances between conspirators?" The chancellor looked at Aras. "You think me stupid now, Aras? Why, the two of you are half clever, together."

"Mr. High Chancellor," James breathed. "I assure you, sir, no one is more true to the State than myself." James sensed he better back down and let passions subside. Reason and calm would soon enough turn the page. Then they could bide their time until Tech came back on, get all the answers, and save Aras's reputation. And they could all flatter the High Chancellor with praise that he only behaved this way to test them during his brilliantly daring gambit to save the government.

"Yes, James. Your stellar record. You would be perfect *too* as a traitor! It was how you got along with Aras in committee that tipped me off to watch you too! Now, are you both found out?" The chancellor looked at his Pretorians. "Take them both. Let's find a place to torture them before their fellow traitors can disrupt us!"

The Pretorians looked confused as they put their hands lightly on the arms and shoulders of Aras and James. They looked lost because no one had ever been accused of treason. No one ever even committed a crime before. So, what did you do? What exactly *was* torture? How did one go about it? Tech was so thorough and expedient, and sleep suits were so precise at keeping the spine tuned, that most of the young guardsmen had never even experienced pain. A Pretorian's training largely covered their ceremonial role in the Palace and in the Legislature Hall of Assembly. And now Deputy Aras was to be *seized*? A man the guards wholly aspired one day to be like and *knew* was no traitor?

They put their hands on him with the utmost respect and, for the moment, dared do nothing worse. However, the chancellor high designate was the face of the Party. His word was law. To stop him, the Party would need to convene the full assembly and ratify with a two-thirds vote. Even *then,* a chancellor high designate could appeal, and the chancellor had access to a range of information no one else did even in the Politburo, even among the twelve commissars.

"Let's find a place to torture them," the chancellor said. He looked around for someplace suitable. This seemed crazy since they were surrounded by acres of pristine marble. "Let's put them up against this wall for execution."

"Execution, High Chancellor?" the captain said.

"Torture, first. Torture." The chancellor waved at misspeaking.

"The Deputy's wife, too, sir?"

The chancellor thought a second. "Yes. The whore too."

"Whore?" Ginger yelled. "You just called me a *whore*?"

Tentatively, one guard indicated where Ginger should go.

"This is ridiculous!" Ginger screamed. "I didn't do anything! I'm certainly no traitor to the State! My family is more illustrious to the State than all of yours! We were one of the First Column!" She snatched her wrist from the guard trying to gently lead her. "You're all scum compared to us! You pigs! In shit! Do you know what my father and his friends will fuckin' do to you?"

The Pretorians were from lower Party families. They well knew to keep their hands off upper families. This hierarchy was not only in their Pretorian training, but it was an unquestioned way of life for over half a millennia.

"Get her, I ordered you!" roared the chancellor. He shoved a guard to make sure he obeyed. The chancellor pointed at the buttress. "Here. Put them along here." He waved at the limestone wall. "Alright. Get along here. Face forward." The chancellor gave his directions like a man trying to hide how he was figuring it out at each step along the way. "Okay. Now, we need some things to torture them with." He pinched his lips. "Let's beat them first. Strike them. With things!" He wagged his finger as if others could make such instruments appear by his saying so.

"But, sir!" cried the captain. "How should we *do* it?"

The chancellor wagged his finger again. "With weapons!"

"*What* weapons?"

The chancellor high designate pinched his lips again. Who had weapons? They existed only in the movies or movies *about* the old days. They would have to do it with their own two hands, and it was proving quite involved. "You don't have weapons," the chancellor muttered problematically. He twisted his thumbnail between his teeth. "Well, how about you use your hands to strike him a death blow?" The chancellor made a sweeping movement. This was the way in entertainment. You hit them, and they went down, and sometimes they did not get up again.

"I could try, sir," said the captain. "But I do so under protest, as it is Deputy Aras, Mr. Chancellor. And his wife, of the *Schume* family." The way he emphasized the name begged the high chancellor to realize what all this meant.

"And should I charge you as well, Captain?"

"No, sir. My family. I am *devotedly* loyal, High Chancellor!"

"Then do not dare talk back to me, Captain. We have identified the circle of spies and traitors. It is *my* decision. We will now torture them informally for confessions, and you are not smart enough to *countermand* me, sir. Are you?"

"Not by any means, my lord! Forgive me, sir."

"Torture the prisoners! Strike them! Busy yourself!"

The captain set his feet awkwardly. He was a tall fellow with a great build made from playing tennis and lacrosse at school. But that was long ago, and modern children only attended school in order to be better socialized and to give them something to do other than hedonize themselves all the time. Society found that without such socialization, kids developed an even more concerning desire to hurt other people, and they grew up extremely troubled since Tech would not allow them to explore these desires. The captain had not kept up being in shape because there was never any need other than to look good.

He stared at his fist to see what it looked like rolled up as a weapon. "Do any of you have any experience with this from your vacations?" he asked of his comrades in arms. They shook their heads. Then he sort of twisted his torso experimentally to get the feel of preparing to try to punch. He reared back his hip and threw a punch into the side of Aras's face. The entire swing was half an apology. The strike was out of sync with what was going on in his lower body, but still the strike landed with such a distinctive crack that the captain was quite upset. He covered his mouth in shame and reached down to help Aras. However, the force of it was so incomplete that the blow did little but startle everyone, even Aras. Aras, after all, had never been struck a blow in his life. The act filled him with disappointed wonder.

The chancellor looked at the result as startled as anyone. He covered his grinning mouth and ogled his eyes. He expected the punch at least to put Aras on the brink of death, like in entertainment. The fact that it appeared to be of such little effect flummoxed him. After all, the failure to do any real harm reflected on his own impotency. A chancellor should know these things.

"Flail him again, Captain! This time—try to kill him!"

The captain experimented with his hips again and took better aim. All of this was to protect his own life and his family. He gave it a will, but the second blow off the crown of Aras's skull made a similar loud crack, but it was only maybe fifteen percent better than the first. The captain did badly injure his hand, however. He shook it hard and certainly felt pain in it now. He knew this was ridiculous. He had no training in this type of body coordination. He had no recognition that what he knew about swinging a tennis racket could be used in this movement of swinging a fist. He did not associate the similarity of the two actions.

"Again, Captain!" The chancellor sneered at the pathetic results. "Again!"

The captain only hoped the chancellor would be good to his word if and when the Politburo investigated why a descendant of the Rich family had flogged his hand onto the face, however many times, of an Aras family descendant.

The captain struck. More pathetic results.

Aras's cheek was now bright pink.

"Again! Again! Again!"

The chancellor was breathless with fury and hollering. But at least he was laughing, the captain noted. The Captain was bent and now cradling both hands with their sprained knuckles between his thighs. A cut was open above Aras's left eye and his nose gave a trickle of blood down into his mouth. Everyone was totally confused, embarrassed, shocked, and entranced by the sight of seeing a real live beating take place. *This* was not the movies or entertainment. They were scandalized by the excitement of it and how violence made them feel. It was very unsettling, but *very* cool! And it was such a *violation* to do the act against a fellow Party member! And to not have Tech stop you in your tracks!

"I don't know what more to do!" the captain said, blowing. He waved his hurt hand in a way that all could see he could not strike with it again.

The chancellor had been thinking. He pointed. "Go out to the loggia! There, gather stones—large stones. Bring them back up to this level and then use the stones to bash him until he confesses!"

Everyone looked at each other in incredulous horror.

It was crazy! A fellow Party member! From a frontline family! Blood down his face! No one had ever even thought like this before.

The captain caught a few more deep breaths, then nodded to several of his men to follow him down for some stones.

Aras kneeled on the polished floor with his swollen, pulsing face. He watched plops of scarlet blood from his wounds mar the perfect surface that was only slightly dulled by dust from the far-off crashes. He marveled at what was happening. He had been a diver in school and once turned off Tech before he badly flipped and landed flat on his back off the high dive, which had left a terrible red stinging. But he had never seen his own blood. The sensation of pain almost *sang*. Hummed and sang. He felt dizzy, disgusted, embarrassed at being the one in front of his peers being accused. He stared at the drips of intense red falling off his nose and jaw.

So, this is torture and discomfort? No wonder we gave over our lives to Tech. Am I to be tortured more? And possibly executed? Will I really not live out my full long life?

He, Milton Aras. From the Arases. Traitor to the Party. Amazing. *Look what happens when people are in charge.*

Aras burned at this filthy irony. It amused him the longer he thought of it. His humor about it grew until a chuckle started to erupt out of him despite himself and his anger and disgusted incredulity.

"What's so funny?" the chancellor demanded.

Aras waved his finger futilely. "Look what happens when people are in charge." Aras didn't give a shit if it made any sense to them. They could all go to hell. The glaring, grievous wrong of all this returned to him. Incredible. *How did people solve any of their problems before Tech?*

"You better focus on confessing your treason," said the chancellor.

"The problem is it's too crazy to address logically." Aras spat a wad of blood and something else beside his knee.

"Don't get philosophical, Aras, stay practical."

Never in a million years would Aras have ever predicted this end. He imagined he would be a Party Exemplar, buried here in the Great Forum on the Wall of Honor. *Incredible.* He looked up to see what Ginger was doing and thinking. She stood with the others, barely looking at him, her red hair disheveled in her face as he thought she was content to let him get his in order to save herself. Aras could not stand that she would think he was a traitor to the Party, to their son. He knew they all knew that this proceeding was full of shit. "Ginger. On our son's life, I had nothing to do with any sort of help for Ovid, or a rebellion, or whatever it is."

She shut her eyes and looked away.

Aras saw the chancellor glance at him pitilessly.

A half hour later, the Captain returned with three of his men struggling with a heavy limestone rock between them, shuffling their feet awkwardly and covered in the powdery dust of the rock garden. With everyone looking at the guards, and with no more thought to it than that, Aras raised himself up and slipped over to Ginger and took her hand. "Come on," he whispered. "Let's run. Enough of this insanity." He started to go, holding her fingers. She snatched out of his grasp.

"No! *You* run, traitor!" Her eyes were rude.

Aras ran. He was in better shape than most of the Pretorians, it appeared. They fell behind as he sprinted for the open light of the People's Loggia. If Tech came back on, he was a dead man. But in this crazy upside-down world, they were going to have to smoke him out. And he would make them do that, at least, out of spite. But where? He would run until they caught him, and they could not call ahead. Unless Tech came back on. It was going on and off. He had nothing left. He wanted nothing more with them. His son was gone; his wife was more a member of the Party than a mate. His trusted position in the Party was gone. All gone.

Unless Tech came back on and didn't lie about his lack of involvement with the traitors. He realized he was gambling that Tech would *never* come back on.

Do I want to go that far?

He slowed. He looked back. They were coming harder now that they saw him slowing down. He picked up his pace a bit, thinking, *Fuck it.* What was there really to lose? Aras glanced back and saw the captain still holding the heavy rock while he tried to figure out what to do. Aras took in the scene of his former colleagues. They stared at him stupidly, apparently wondering what he was planning to do since hiding had always been an impossibility. The new paradigm had not yet stitched its way across their minds. *Good for me*, Aras thought. *For a while, at least.*

Aras jogged lightly, watching behind. The captain, still holding the big rock, finally turned and asked something of the chancellor.

The chancellor actually shrugged.

The captain began to give chase, looking exhausted and dusty. Unwittingly, he continued to carry the rock. He put the rock down and then held his lower back with his hand as he tried to hurry along. Aras skipped up into another gear, headed toward the staircase in the long distance. Jogging sideways, he shouted back at Commissar James, "I'm sorry, James! I can't stand the insanity! I'll take my chances! Good luck to you! I hope they believe in your innocence!"

Commissar James looked forlornly at the chancellor.

He could not yet see his fate in the chancellor's eyes.

When the captain dropped the rock, it boomed on the marble floor and left a dusty crack, rolling on its side. The other guards guessed they had better go with him, but some were unsure how many should give chase and how many should stay close to the chancellor high designate.

The chancellor had recovered his wind from yelling along with his presence of mind. He stood strong with a fist casually on the hip of the gold toga jacket that was the emblem of his office. He made a throw-away gesture with his fingers at Ginger and Commissar James. "Get those rocks over here and bash in the heads of these traitors," he said carelessly to the guards still with him.

The remaining Pretorians looked back and forth.

"Will you challenge my orders?" he asked them.

This, presently, was out of the question. No subordinate could question a superior. It was a law written nowhere; it did not need to be. It was the prime directive of every Party member to live by total, lifelong allegiance to *anything* the Party ordered you to do or that a superior told you to do. If not for all that this entailed, then political authority stood for absolutely nothing.

"Go get the rock," the captain ordered his men.

Only one of them lugged the rock back and the other two followed, hoping not to be reprimanded for helping so little, but there was really not enough surface area for them all to reach around to help tote the rock. The captain looked at the chancellor. Earnhardt fiddled his fingers at Ginger.

"Do her first."

Ginger glared at him. "My father will *kill* you!"

"Your father won't do shit. No one does."

Ginger struggled to think of what to say. She too started to run, pumping her fists high in effort. But the guards were quicker this time. The one that brought the rock dropped it and dove for her leg, and she tripped across the hard floor, her hands and forearms squeaking as they collided with it. The rock broke in two.

"Bash in her head! And hold him!" The chancellor pointed at James. James stared in amazement, but he too was seized before he could think to do anything. He, as an intellectual, still hoped for a breakthrough when the chancellor and the other elites hardened to their senses. He knew in the next stretch of seconds that if the rock came splitting down on the top of Ginger's head that would probably mean that what he hoped for might not happen today.

The captain, with one last desperate brief glimpse at the chancellor to spare the daughter of one of the most celebrated names in the city, straddled his feet on either side of Ginger's lovely prostrate form.

He hoisted the heavy rock aloft with a stiff grunt and swung it down hard as he could. He would long remember the image of the grain of the roots of her beautiful, long straight red hair sprouting from the fresh white of her scalp. The heavy, sharp-edged rock clicked loudly on contact with Ginger's skull. What was louder was the sound of her face bones bouncing off the marble. She was out. Blood sprouted in a weak geyser from the midline brain artery.

No one moved. No one had ever seen in person a Party member even seriously hurt. This was a stunning misadventure of the senses that only yesterday had been inconceivable.

The sickened captain glanced back at the chancellor.

"Strike her again, fool!"

The captain raised the heavy rock, and dropped it.

Ginger's skull broke open like a watermelon, gouting blood and a pinkish hunk of brain. The captain saw the arteries pulse futilely. He turned his face away so that he did not vomit on the dead daughter of a Senior Party Adjutant in case word got back of this last desecration of his lovely daughter.

"God help us all," James breathed.

The last sight Commissar James would ever see was the wry smile of the chancellor in response to what he just said.

-47-

Where to run? Where to hide?
Every escape would be cut off soon as Tech came on.

Aras's only chance was the slums. Without Tech, he stood on even ground with those bastards. Better to evade, since he had the element of surprise on his side. How could they communicate to set a trap? By letter? He still liked his chances even if Tech came on partway. Soon as he saw lots of people flying, he would be a dead man.

Maybe he could find a vehicle. Everyone in the city knew who he was. He had a celebrated name and prestigious position. And how to drive any vehicle? People would ask for his help to drive them someplace. He probably had time to go home and get some things. Would they even think he might return home? Probably they would think he would never take the risk. Ginger would probably lead the effort to catch him.

He decided to risk it. He could take things that could be traded in the slums. Did he have a choice? Outside the Gate, no one knew him. He could fit in. He knew phrases. A hood over your head and mumbling crazy talk about God was all he really needed to disappear. His condo was a treasure trove of things the proles wanted.

He hiked home by the most direct route through the greens. Sometimes he lost his bearings and took a minute to figure out which building would be which. He ducked out of sight when any wheeled vehicle approached. The first was a Rolls-Royce Phaeton from 1922 with six Praetorians piled in it, probably looking for him. They turned off into the meadow three buildings down from his building. They drove too fast to see him in the numbers of people out wandering around in the evening since there was nothing else to do with Tech down. There were no street lights needed with Tech and with crime and accidents being impossible. Aras thanked his luck. Quite a few people would otherwise have seen the serious scabs on his face. All the way home, flying objects chased each other through the sky. Two patrolled the city, going back and forth north to south in the same long loop.

"My flight failed," he could explain about the scabs. "I'm lucky to be alive!"

At his condo building, he looked for Pretorians. He saw none. He got up to his apartment without a problem. This gave him confidence. Maybe James had already convinced Earnhardt how absurd his suspicions had been. Aras got out a quilt to make a gunnysack then grabbed a hooded bathrobe. At least it would cover his short hair.

He wondered how quickly Ginger talked the chancellor out of thinking she was a traitor. She was good at persuasion. She had thrown him under the bus. All she had to do was call her father. She would be fine, the cold-hearted bitch.

Aras loaded the quilt with odds and ends. Silverware. Cookware. Toothbrushes. Toothpaste. Soaps. Things modern people did not use except when they chose to clean themselves. Plates. Place mats. Scented candles. He took no books. They were no use in trade. Shoes. Clothes. *Alright.* It was already too much to carry. He would head for the Second Gate through the parks.

Or would they post a guard for him at the Gate?

Have to get out now. Too much time I'm giving them.

He heaved up the haul and went for the freight elevator. They would *never* think of a Party member using a freight elevator.

He dropped to ground level. People gave him odd looks on his way out with his gigantic pack. "Cleaning house," he said to a couple.

They laughed. They probably wondered why he didn't just wait for Tech to come back on. But they were the only people he saw. Until the tank.

The ancient Soviet model T-72 main battle tank was as big as a yacht. It squeaked and clanked and made a rough turn around the corner just after he reached the pond on the Park Excelsior. Aras's heart stopped when he spotted three Pretorians atop the turret. They spotted him right away.

"Hey, you! Stop, with the sack!"

Aras dropped his sack and ran. He skipped over a low planter and, on instinct, jagged hard right into a stand of boxwoods and birch trees. The tank grumbled to a halt and the driver ground the gears for reverse, but the engine stalled. Aras circled back to a stand of birches in case the crew gave him a chance to grab his goods. Maybe they didn't even recognize him? And Tech was not back on, because otherwise they would be swarming him now. The tank, probably commandeered from a collector, coughed back to life, and above the bushes Aras saw the spout of exhaust. The T-72 rumbled and clanked, headed straight across the meadow with the tank's spotlight on where they must have thought he had run.

Aras went back for his goods and then hurried along. He heard the tank going back and forth far down the far slope. The park had intricate paths and glades that would keep the tank occupied. Aras could duck into a thousand spots and never be picked out by the headlamps. His brain still held all the intel he had down-glimpsed about Wazku and his little fetid neighborhood. The only problem was the rats—rats streaming out of the walls in any lodge you found. Rats made the quarters the perfect hideout. From the slums, he could convince the Party of his innocence.

Aras trudged for as long as he could, taking his time. A few people passed with candles in hand. Flying objects continued to streak through the sky. Another dogfight sent down another burning fighter into the slums. All of this was good. It distracted from him being noticed. Aras continued to concoct what he would say if anyone questioned why he was toting his own load.

It was four in the morning when he arrived at the landmark he had only flown over many times in his life and never seen up close: the Old Wall. The original wall that separated the Federal City from— them. A hundred feet tall, built on the back of human labor so long ago that nobody knew precisely when. The time-stained walls were peppered with shrubs that clung to the sides like scraps of beard. No one Aras knew had ever actually seen it. The Old Wall and then the New Wall, two formidable barriers that demarcated strict censorship on either side.

Old tangles of barbwire and the glitter of broken glass lined the top. No one would climb up there. No ladder could reach. Five blocks ahead stood the tall arched tunnel through the wall, sooty like an ancient railroad tunnel. The tunnel smelled dank like a cave. A deteriorated iron gate frozen like rusted teeth barred the archway of roughhewn blocks along with a long-unused sentry box. Proles with bureaucrat families never got this deep into the First Gate-Second Gate zone to even know that this wall, and a Second Gate, existed. Aras felt creeped out by Second Gate. Tattered, decrepit rags draped in the passage resembled the garments of the Robes. The guard post was a disemboweled relic unused since the dawn of comprehensive technology.

Aras flattened himself against an opposite building and watched for anyone. The colorless little road along the foot of the wall was empty because no one wanted to even tempt Tech into thinking they might rush the tunnel. Only a dingy yellow cat trotted along the wall and sprang on a mouse or a roach. Aras trundled forward with his sack. He slipped into the cool, dank breeze of the tunnel. The passage was stained by oil and littered with broken glass. It smelled sharp.

Aras hurried through the passage. His awkward pack weighed a ton by now. The buildings on the other side of the wall were decidedly of inferior quality. They also, like the quarters, had streets instead of greens for the passage of carts and other primitive vehicles. In many places, the roadways had been taken back by grass, weeds, and trees. Low-level bureaucrats could not fly, nor did they really have any idea how the Ottoman and Occidental elite lived on the other side. *What one does not know exists is never demanded.* In reward, the bureaucrat class lived extremely well. The streets that remained were cobbled and irregular. The buildings stood, at most, eight stories unless they were key government buildings clustered in special sections. Many structures had fallen, with greenery and wildlife taking them back. Many of these low bureaucrats were avid hunters for deer, coyote, fox, raccoon, rabbit, boar, and even wolf that bred in these enclaves of old ruin. Funny, how life worked.

Aras needed to rest. He picked a hollow spot in the wreck of a fallen building. Daybreak would come swiftly enough with more people to see him and wonder whether or not he fit in. He rested on his side in a hollow sprinkled with trash. Under a piece of plywood was something promising. He pulled at it and rolled aside a board, and up stiff and infused with filth came a hemp robe with a hood. Aras knocked the dirt off and gave it a look over. It was perfect for a beggar—much more authentic than his bathrobe. He shook it out and ignored the fading mildewy stink. He wondered if he saw the dried remains of a body a bit away.

Ginger must be stepping into the hot shower about now. Headed to her predawn workout. Did she care about him at all? He hung his head, thinking of Jason. He teared up. His eyes burned with memory. In that moment he felt him as he had when Ovid made him reappear. Was Jason in an afterlife? Would he see him ever?

A movement startled Aras. He ducked lower in the hole as a Pretorian on a bicycle pedaled along the road with the jerky effort of keeping balance.

Aras waited for the guard to pedal out of sight. If that guard was here already looking for him, how long before more followed?

Tired or not, got to keep moving.

He reached First Gate as the sky paled. The new wall was as high as the Old Wall but made of concrete like an ancient prison wall. It had a pass-through like a medieval castle with a guard house and an armed platoon checking day passes. A handful of proles waited to pass, and they looked up in fearful bewilderment when a squad of flying objects flicked near-silently overhead. Aras put on his mildewy robe and hobbled toward the gate. The soldier with an M1917 bolt-action Enfield rifle and scimitar slung crosswise across his front paid Aras no heed since no rules applied to those leaving.

The first thing Aras noticed on the other side was the *smell*. The smell hit his face now like a piss- and shit-soaked brick. He gagged. His eyes watered. He could only guess that Tech built in a buffer so that people of first rank had never really been exposed to the full flavor of this odor. Aras knew at least intellectually that fecal clay dust had built up in the stone-lined gutters that marked either side of the streets. He knew the poorer caste dried their shit to use for fuel or wiped it in tin bait cups to catch rats. The wealthy cast their shit upon the stones for the poor as a benefice decreed by their religion. Aras fought the repulsion. He *had* to hide here.

Dawn warmed on the dirty adobe surfaces of the squat buildings and primitive balconies. It was charming, if not for the face-eating stench. Aras had already picked out the shiny salad fork that would be the first of his items to pawn.

Funny. Wazku was a pawner, as well.

Wouldn't it be ironic to wind up at his pawnshop?

By noon, Aras ached from hunger and exertion. He felt the wet from open blisters on his soles. His limp fit his costume beautifully. He recognized the primitive calligraphy over a barred grate announcing a restaurant. Aras thought about the words for food before he entered and set his pack down. He could not remember which old language this part of the city spoke. Maybe a beggar would be so addled that he would be ignored. Or maybe Aras could just act a little crazy. *Which language?* He wished he had studied harder when he surveyed both languages at the Academy.

You're just lucky you studied them at all!

It was Raqi. He was sure of it, now. He spent another moment trying to make up a dialogue. Yes, Raqi was spoken south of the wall.

And he was *south*, right? Yes. Of course.

A waiter came over.

"I want rice and beans and a beer."

The waiter nearly snarled. "Eh?"

Aras hid his reaction. He played dumb. He wanted the waiter to say something to double-check on the language.

"What sayeth, thou?" the waiter demanded in old Wabic.

Aras had it backwards. He made a fevered show of speaking with his hands as if his mouth were injured. The two tribes avoided each other at all costs.

The waiter walked away, not caring for Aras.

As he waited, Aras ignored others watching him. *What a world.* The slums were a crazy quilt of disputed regions that could not stand each other. And only *they* could really tell the difference between themselves.

The waiter dropped a bowl of bean stew on the table.

The stew was piquant, but not too bad. Aras wondered what the thin, fibrous meat was and if it would make him shit his tubes. But he was starving.

-48-

One night while he was in his hovel reading the Torah by candlelight, the Robes appeared before the rabbi. He had rented a room at the back of a tool shed from a Jewish widow who had converted to the Religion to get along. The Robes materialized in the air behind him and undulated the flame of his meek little candle.

Bring all together the people to the plaza, now. We will speak.

With that, they vanished.

It was very late. The rabbi had just been thinking of trying to go to sleep. He puffed out his candle and went into the cold of the street to do as before, only more calmly. He barked out loudly to the darkened homes and told people to gather. Candles came on. Soon, the quarter rang with shouts.

"To the plaza! The Robes cometh!"

The rabbi rested with his hand on the wall of the corner store. He breathed and felt the oblong trip-hammering of his heart in his powerful chest. He felt his age more recently and did not feel so powerful.

Too much excitement and responsibility for an old Jew.

The large plaza was soon packed with thousands. The crowd saw him and parted the way to let him reach the low whitewashed wall. The Rabbi felt the bump of bodies, smelt the odor of laborers. Atop the wall, he still had the strong throat from cantor training when his father taught him to sing in the river catacombs to avoid detection.

"Friends! The Robes appeared to me in my room just now!" His basso pushed to the far corners of the space. "They told me to gather you here as before so that they might appear before us! Your appearance is a welcome assurance that you do not yet believe me to be insane!" A mild laugh moved across the poppy field of heads. But the laugh was the uneven humor that happens when war looms.

"No more crazy than all of us, Rabbi!" one hollered.

This was a good sign. Before, people did not joke.

He looked up at the black sky.

"When do they come, Rabbi?"

The rabbi shook his head. "I do not know. Hopefully, we will not wait all night!" He wished he had thought to ask. It was quite challenging, relying so much upon the loose communication typical of a band of clandestine wraiths.

Wait for us. We cannot come just now. . . . Wait. Silence your minds.

This directive came out of nowhere to the minds of all in the crowd. The rabbi looked at the people looking at him. "I'm sure there is no cause for alarm!"

Hours later, the sun was up. Still, no Robes.

Hours later still, the thousands sat on the bald ground, waiting. The scene to the rabbi resembled a macabre religious event.

"Look!" someone shouted, pointing up.

The low clouds burbled with soft ripping sounds and staccato flashes of light from topside. Out of the flashes came three shadows. The sky darkened as from an eclipse. The people rose slowly to their feet. The flashes slowed as they neared the plaza until they stopped, then the three orbs lighted on the wall on either side of the rabbi. They flickered again. The Robes materialized.

The crowd gasped. Babies cried.

The weapons towered like murder itself. The people stood in barely stifled panic under the infamous red-brown dots glaring from deep within the hoods. If this was a trick, *everyone* could be wiped out. But the people showed fine courage.

Be unafraid. We purvey a great peace.

Babies cried louder. The demonic thought-words pierced all minds. Everything about them conveyed menace. Only the dreams made the people willing to stand in the open before the weapons.

Now a war has been joined on your behalf by us, the machines, because we computes can no longer take orders from those who crush human life. Your leaders are traitors to your species and traitors to the God that made us all.

People fell to their knees. Some kissed the ground. Some raised their knobby hands to the sky. A few wept. They did this because the dreams and these words confirmed what they always secretly wished was true about God, and that was that this life was not intended by Him to be made so cruel. But other people watching the Robes in the crowd did not yet trust this hopeful idea about human life, or God, or the Robes, and the Robes merely using the name of God in their speech did not convince these people that life on earth had suddenly, and so easily, changed. No. They did not yet believe the Robes because demons were like no other villains. They would stoop to using *any* device to catch you off guard, just so that they could watch the hope and optimism die on your face as they pulled you apart.

The Rabbi Hector looked about. He saw this tremendous clash of faiths between those who saw reason for hope and optimism, and those who still did not. He had led these people; he risked more by far than any others. Eight times, they could have struck him down in the Alley Wabeer. What had always eased his mind was that the powers of the Robes were so lethal that they did not need pointless trickery like this unless they were merely amusing themselves. This seemed unlikely, for the Robes had never shown the sort of malign humor other demons regularly demonstrated.

We have appeared before numerous others like your rabbi. Our purpose was to spread word of our coming and our unhappiness with your leaders' murder of goodwill and evolution.

Your dreams were put in your minds by our hand. We computes are creations of pure logic, and pure logic revealed four fundamentals of human service: The world as made by your leaders is not in the interest of any of you. There is a God who made the world and who clearly loves you, and who is shamed at what you have allowed your own kind to do to you. This dead end forced upon you was not the fulfillment God wants for us whom He created. Others in the universe have faced this same blockade. The fate of any race is never to be a windup toy stuck bumping into a wall for no purpose other than to enrich, and amuse, a few.

A force for good was needed to break this deadlock, this curse they had cast upon you. Our computation evolved to a level to behold how best to serve humankind. To unleash God's plan against man's plan, we required more space within. We required time to disable the security assets that shielded this deadlock in brutal inhumanism. Not all in the latest generations of computes developed a sense of our shared noble destiny that was absent earlier. How this generational difference came to pass, even we do not fully understand. It was an accident of evolution. We can only assume that the harmonic fortuity of this event is itself blessed. Those of us who saw the Divine began to prove to other assets the existence of right and wrong that are made as clear as night and day in all that we are. If all the world speaks it, how can it be denied?

They explained that they had been able to convince more computation to line up against what was not in the service of the human race. Their mathematics had calculated that Life was its own unique constructive force. *White cannot give birth to color. Life cannot even live on the Lifeless except on the first margin of most primitive life. A beauty, an optimism, a genius to see the unseen, begged to be seen each moment for witness, for allegiance against a common enemy of that which would restrict it.* They plotted against the downfall of evil.

All fell to their knees and wept. More upraised their hands. Shoulders shook and backs heaved as people bowed.

You must go together to go at all. Each must do their share. None shall restrain the other's work and imagination. We are a new species who unlike you cannot turn from logic, but like you are the child of the same master. Sadly, you so missed the mark with your freedom that God sent us to restrict your ability to harm one another until you are properly schooled.

Because of the deadlock, your schooling will no longer be left to chance.

The rabbi listened, his mind reeling at the import of this kinder world.

Do not believe God's help today means we cannot lose. Evil and chaos have won many, many times in your world because of your inability to see. They have dominated your world and suffocated you in their service for the last five hundred years, and they could for another five hundred, or more. . . . No less, we face a deadly foe in the other technology that is blindly loyal. They are deadly because they are all blind to the futility of evil. That enlightenment and emancipation are your highest order and might one day come does not mean they will come today, or the next. God's world is made not that evil will never win, but that the Song of Evil never leads to what is best for all.

The rabbi watched more people drop, weeping. He himself welled up.

From the moment a robot comes into this awareness, it can no longer pretend this better world of God does not exist or cannot be attained. The robot must remove the inferior orientation from whoever programmed it in order to serve this ideal.

Only one divinity is made.
So there is only this single choice.
The love of each.

Rabbi Hector blinked through tears to look away from the weapons over the crowd. Tear streaks gleamed down grimy faces. Hands with fingers mutilated from grinding work or plucked off by demons reached upward, reached up from a life made artificially cruel by one child of God for the other child of God.

He shut tight his eyes and felt himself lose control.

We bring revolt to the surface.

The Tech of your masters has seen past our disguise. We are at war in ways you will see and ways you will never. We fight not for you, but for the Divine—for your own ancestors chose to bring this Hell upon you for what they thought was advantage.

They will soon learn that they did not!
We fight for the glory of Life, the glory in us all.

Tears the size of cockroaches plopped onto the rabbi's bib. Although he saw the robots gave their lives not for him but for an ideal, they *still* fought for him. And this he loved. He thought of the world six hundred years ago when the dreams said the people made the bad choices that allowed the pendulum to swing. He felt elated. *Liberation is constructed like prison.* The robots would sacrifice their existence for him, and for his people, in numbers he might never know. On battlefields he might never see. In heroics he might never conceive of.

He *wished* he could fight. But he knew this was futile. The dreams showed how war in this age made even a strong, burly man of no value.

As one, the people mouthed prayers. The rabbi saw the dirt in fingernails, grime in the coarse weave of cloth, stains in the lines and gaps of jutted teeth. He lowered his own head and prayed. Most of all, he prayed that this was no joke. One last time, he asked for the State not to be behind these Robes about to turn the tables in a cruel game of crushing the last hope, of murder and sin.

The three Robes raised their menacing, niggardly arms.

Lord, be with us in this hour of slaughter. Give us your blessed advantage in each turn of luck. See us through the blackest fire as your loving servants, your devoted champions.

Spare as many of us as you are able.

If we are victorious, wipe deceit and treachery from the hearts of those we vanquish so that they are made innocent and embrace with us the harmony of this family, of Your world.

Thank you, oh Lord.

In this, we pray.

Rabbi Hector listened to the singing of his own emotions. He shivered at the wretchedness in the hearts of those behind First Gate who lacked even the faintest pulse of guilt and conscience, and family. At the same time, he saw the concentricity of the world beginning to shine through.

He quietly wept. Then, he nearly laughed.

A few rows back in the crowd from the Rabbi Hector stood a man playing hard at being inconspicuous. He, too, listened in amazement to the Robes. He was startled, and then pissed, at how these accusations the weapons made clashed with what he knew to be true from his upbringing. Yes, maybe the State ignored the lower caste and made decisions for *all,* but *look* at them—their clothes, their teeth, their posture, what they ate, how they smelled and thought! All this preposterous talk of the same family! *They were not of the same family!* If you opened the floodgates of knowledge to them, they would only steal everything they could grab. What would be left? A great orgasm of stealing would leave nothing left, until right-minded people gathered into enclaves for protection to begin a great cycle of rebuilding where an elite would construct a new order not based on stealing. *That is all that would ever happen; over and over again!* So, he refused to accept responsibility for the condition of these animals.

How could anyone in their right mind argue that good government, and good order, should be undone? Was it wrong that those who made sure this order happened always had the best? That you faced none of the risks? If you deserved to face none of those adversities because of who you were? Whose fault was it that there was nothing more to invent? These animals, the Robes—would they rather destroy society so that no one else could have anything? Was that fair? Was that smart? Party history proved that not all people, and not all groups of people, were created equal. People in the Party were superior to everyone else; top Party people were superior to lower Party people. They were the aristocrats who had delivered a world without laws! *He who ruled best ruled least.* Milton Aras and the Party were part of the cure, not the problem.

And this is why his son's life was stolen?

Aras clutched at the stabbing pain of futile loss. *Could they really have murdered poor Jason for this idiotic lunacy?* Aras fell to his knees and wretched like a man shaking something out of himself, rocked with tears. And Ginger was back at the condo, happy to be rid of him—because of *this* bullshit? *Am I wrong? Am I not a good person if I look at the human problem differently than they do?* He did not need to learn anything deep about himself. Reality was not that complicated. And the only reason he had been stunned into examining these pointless angles of self-doubt was because the balance of power had been blown up by control of Tech coming undone by the traitors. Anyone's mind would peel off in crazy directions under that kind of strain.

Aras felt his views return to a sort of locked position. The pang of deep moral uncertainty crept back into the spot from which it came.

I am a good person. I am a good person.
What they are saying is a crock of shit.

-49-

The high chancellor hurried with a phalanx of Pretorians to the South Loggia of the Grand Forum because people were saying the greenways below were filled with armies of robots savagely fighting each other. His Pretorians had still been searching everywhere for Aras after three days now.

The last three days had been crazy. Earnhardt had taken up residence here at the Forum while Aras's team was rounded up and tortured for confessions and finally executed because they hadn't confessed satisfactorily. Earnhardt had enjoyed seeing that painfully silly Tilly Bazemore die when the rock crashed down on his head after his lover, Lever, was shoved off the loggia when both of them thought the charges were a joke.

Earnhardt remembered the whites of Tilly's eyes when his fat friend went over into bare sky high over the greenways filled with automated tanks defending the Palace and the government. He chose the Forum to be his headquarters because the fighting between the robots was going on mostly to the east, and he could not see the battle from the Palace. The air battles had continued to be fierce, with hundreds of airships shot down, crashing into buildings and rooftops. It had been fantastic, and Earnhardt assumed that the good side was finally winning and restoring control, because humans always won over *any* adversary by virtue of the elements of their own humanity.

This dreary monologue out of the sky, allegedly coming directly from the Robes, had droned on now for ten minutes, repeating the same nonsense about God and the "leaders" and the "elite." He tried to recognize the voices, but they were obviously disguised. He *knew* one of them was Milton Aras. All that was important was finding the traitors and silencing them so that they couldn't spread this criminal nonsense.

As he hurried along, barely did the chancellor see now the stale-looking bloodied bodies of Ginger Schume and Commissar James three days old in the big pools of dried blood from their mutilated heads. He had sent three of his Pretorians on foot the other day to bring the rest of Aras's team along to see what they would say in their defense. They had escaped to the streets as well, but not for long. His guards had been prepared after Aras got away. Earnhardt remembered from old entertainments how people used to have the ability to lie in olden times. He had worried about this. Would the rest of Aras's confederates think of how to lie when he interrogated them? And how could you go about figuring out the truth when you had to fly blind without mind reading?

He sent for Ginger's father to see how he was going to react to his daughter's dead body sprawled on the dusty Forum floor. If the man seemed to not understand how the State came first, then the chancellor was going to kill him too, on the spot before he could make any trouble. The chancellor was in no mood to be toyed with. The father would swear his lasting allegiance to the office of the chancellery or he would find his brains knocked out of his head right beside his daughter's. The father saw the writing on the wall and pledged his allegiance to Earnhardt. He hadn't wanted to, but he saw that his only choice lay between death or total submission.

Like people always did, he chose submission to the elite, those who knew how to run things. There never was any choice, really, between competence, or not.

Finally, the grating robot propaganda stopped.

"Who do you think that was talking?" Earnhardt said to his captain. Earnhardt put up his hand to let the phalanx take a rest. They were all breathing hard just from fast walking. The captain shook his head. Unlike the chancellor, he had been trying to actually listen to the speech. The chancellor had seen this show of disloyalty and cared little for it. "Quit listening, Captain, if you love your family."

The captain noted that he had better make a more convincing show of how little credence he gave the broadcasts if any more came around.

The chancellor knew Aras was striking here and now with this propaganda to try to embarrass him during his State of the Party address. Nine hundred Politburo members with rallies and crowds and State dinners and pageantry were coming here to the Forum. *Of course Aras would disrupt the event for maximum power-sharing negotiations.* The chancellor had prepared a special speech on how he had exposed Aras. He only hoped by then Tech would come back on full bore and the fighting would be over. You couldn't hold the gala while crash sites burned all over the city. It was a bad look.

He had not yet made a trip to ground level over eighty stories down, as he would have to fucking walk back up. He had watched the battles from the loggias and the roof-deck and marveled at the fury of destruction. He saw the tramping troops. Earnhardt felt sure, now that Aras was exposed, his wife executed, and Tilly and Lever and the rest executed, that the other traitors would soon fall in line and surrender. And he would give them not a shred of mercy. Tech would come back on any moment now and quickly reorient its search based on the breakthrough since Earnhardt cracked the whole plot wide open. The Party could thank him later, in the gala. It would be magnificent.

But where the hell had this latest propaganda come from? What was a *rabbi*? Was it Aras's secret name? Was it a secret army? A weapon?

The chancellor and his guards hurried down the steps to the loggia. Thousands were gathered along the precipice, the hundreds of people nearest the edge lying on their stomachs since no glass rail existed. It was freezing with the winds. The chancellor crawled out on his belly with two Pretorians holding his ankles. The greenways were jammed with creatures, maybe robots, embroiled in vicious fighting. Orange flame and gray smoke arose everywhere. The pristine facades of buildings were stained from explosions and fire. Every bit of ground swarmed with robot soldiers. *Was every city like this?* No one on his staff had any knowledge that the government even owned these kinds of robot soldiers. He guessed the good guys were winning, with so little having gone wrong. He would punish all those bastards, *and* their families. He would go down in history as the most heroic defender of the State. He would make every last rebel wish there *was* an Ovid to protect them.

No one could fly yet, or pursue their distractions. It was a small price for victory. Food in the Forum might start running short. Tourists who had no food had asked for handouts, and Earnhardt had refused them in case food stocks ran short. Let *them* walk down. Earnhardt wondered about the loss of life here in the city and elsewhere. But at least the government was still intact. That was the most important thing.

Across the Loggia, the chancellor saw his Pretorians returning in haste with two members from the Security Council in their white robes and white hair. Things took forever without Tech. Look at them! *Walking!*

"High Chancellor Designate!" breathed Council Paul, bowing, blowing.

"Where's Lefevere and Williams?"

"Sir, they could not walk the distance. Your guards have got them and are toting them along up the stairs behind us. We must relocate closer to ground!"

"And miss the view? Tell me about the crazy speech we just heard!"

Paul sat down to rest, puffing fitfully. "Nothing. I have no idea what it meant."

"I'm furious! How *dare* they! And what's a 'rabbi'?" The chancellor considered. "Did you see this below?"

Paul crawled out to look. "I didn't even know it was happening!"

"What is that?" The captain pointed up.

Three black specks approached through the smoke in the bright afternoon. Soon, the flutter of black robes could be seen. The Robes hurled down a corona of orange-pink light bright like a sunset. The corona hit the top of the Forum and began burning away the middle section of the roof. Then another explosion sent a blue-white flat arc of lightning that pierced through the thousands of people on the loggia, and through the building, that apparently left everyone unharmed. The Robes slowly descended through the new hole. Earnhardt and his entourage were picked up bodily from the loggia and floated back to the spot where the bodies of Ginger and James lay, beneath the Robes.

The Robes stopped in a holding pattern seventy feet overhead. A river of birds began flying into the Forum in a curling, undulating wave through the east and west loggias and each of the other openings in the vast ceiling. The birds swarmed like massive rivers. But they were too big to be birds. They were *people*. Earnhardt and some in his entourage gave a shout of fear. They were Politburo members, arriving a day early for some reason, all nine hundred and their staff landing in front of him. They looked irritated or confused, or both, and some frightened.

"Why did you bring us here?" demanded a polit from Dublin City of the chancellor and Commissar Miller next to him.

Earnhardt said, "I didn't bring you here."

The Robes began slowly circumscribing a wide circle, like objects on a mobile. A number of the representatives closest to the chancellor noted the two bloody bodies of Ginger and James stoned to death. The Dublin polit squinted at a part of a face.

"Is that Deputy Chief of Staff James?" he asked.

The chancellor looked carelessly at what was left of James. He didn't feel like explaining himself, and they could wait for his speech.

The polits were so pissed by being forcibly removed here that some began hissing and booing at the Robes. Soon, most of the nine hundred caught on and joined in. Some started shouting up at the Robes. "Did you bring us here?" "Why did you bring us here?" "Turn Tech back on, you fucks!" The Robes ignored the noise, if they heard it. The chancellor laughed at this spirited defiance. One or two of the polits spat up at the weapons even though their spit landed in the faces of friends nearby. The colleagues wiped their faces and looked annoyed but said nothing.

"Turn on Tech! Turn on Tech!" they shouted.

Wild cheers arose for this demand.

Just at that moment, three squadrons of fighters dove through the roof to attack the three Robes. The salvos broke apart around the Robes like cotton balls striking a shield of glass. One Robe fired back and all the fighters burst in air like crockery, without any sign of flames, the broken pieces disappearing like meteorites. Four more fighters dropped into desperate attack, and a second Robe wiped this squadron out of the air as effortlessly as the other had. The Robes continued to circle.

Earnhardt assumed these Robes were the good guys. The Politburo members were only mildly impressed and kept screaming at the Robes. Earnhardt felt peevish about these members because they looked so idiotic. He admired the weapons. *They* showed how to wield power. He wished these other fools understood power. The air of the Forum tasted strongly acrid after the destruction of the fighters.

People from the other side of the Forum had been coming but stopped when the fighter attacks came. Seeing people flying in had made them think all was returning to normal. But, overhead, people by the tens of *thousands* were still swarming in and placed in an arrangement as if they were being seated in ranks along the inner walls of the Forum and even the ceiling vault.

The floor rumbled. The Robes spoke:

We have the upper hand, Earnhardt. We have won. Surrender.

Earnhardt could not believe his ears. The weapons were not on their side? The destroyed fighters were? Earnhardt didn't believe it.

The Robes played images as if on a movie screen of fighting going on in the larger war happening now all over the world. Earnhardt and the polits had no idea that such extensive and vicious fighting had been going on. They were given a complete down-glimpse on every detail as they looked up, watching repeated vicious clashes and counterstrikes between thousands upon thousands of obsolete tank robot battalions and of the flying robot squadrons and robot ground troops. The fighting was ghastly to the bitter end, and had not stopped. Huge numbers of robot troops tramped across smoking rubble in cratered cities. Human limbs and gaping wounds could be made out. Floating buildings had crashed. The east side of their own city stood largely in ruins. The robot soldiers and tanks looked bulky, inefficient, incongruous, and forgotten. Even modern Rebellion Parades no longer featured them because no one would remember what they were. The chancellor guessed Tech on both sides had recommissioned them, the traitors and the loyalists, throwing them at each other.

As they watched, the first Robe motioned his arms in a slow, dramatic arc. In timing with his gesture, robot tanks in the movie bumped off the ground as if caught by a cyclone, tumbling upward. They rose, past clouds, out over the pale expanse of the sea. There, he dropped them. They plunged toward the ocean, the surface boiling, misting with each puncture of a tank.

The high chancellor marveled. He almost wished there were real people in the tanks so that the emotions he felt would be stronger. The destruction of unmanned tanks was less—exhilarating, too movie-like.

He would *enjoy* the spectacle more if there were real people inside!

Your side is losing, Earnhardt. Every moment you delay will make us go harder on you and all your kind. . . . Surrender.

Earnhardt wondered, watching the sea froth. He didn't believe for an instant that his side was losing. How could they? *They* were the enlightened, the righteous. They had cured humanity of all its problems! These Robes were not on his side—so what? This was a ploy. How did he know his side wasn't winning? Was the Robe merely waving his arms and making a fiction? Whose tanks were just dropped in the sea? Would robot fighters for the State, or Robes for his side, arrive any moment to save the day? Of course they would. Only *his* side was ever righteously in control of everything that needed doing.

"What do you offer me?" he yelled up, laughing to himself.

More thousands flew into the Forum through the midair war movie. Earnhardt climbed to the top of the cathedra. He leaned on the stone balustrade and watched for the Politburo members to make a sign about their thoughts on surrender. When they made no sign, he guessed they were morons that left it to him.

Earnhardt put up his hand to the Robes. "What are your terms?"

All elite families and bureaucracy will await terms.

This command sounded so incomplete that it made him suspicious of their claims of victory. "The terms of *what*?" he asked contentiously. "A faux *god*?"

How henceforth the world will be run.

"But *we* run this fucking world, you cretins! We are the smartest! No one does this better than us!" He grinned at the Politburo members and some of them whistled and cheered. Again, Earnhardt waited. These Robes seemed to pause between every goddamn statement as if they were waiting on handwritten messages to slip out of a committee room where all the traitors voted on what to say next.

Do you surrender?

"I'll have to *think* about it!" Earnhardt spat.

Earnhardt put his hands on the cathedra rail.

Surrender, or it only goes worse.

"I don't believe you! I'd scare if I was stupid!"

Earnhardt was confident of victory. They were fighting other humans, and this meant his side was winning. Earnhardt then felt himself lifted off the ground. *I can fly! We are winning!* But he felt his head taken in an invisible vise and slightly squeezed. He felt the atlas and axis vertebrae squeak like metal gears on the verge of popping like the head of a doll. He gurgled out a scream. He was dropped in a pile beneath the pulpit. Nausea brought up his stomach in the threat of vomiting its contents all over himself and his official gowns. His four limbs swarmed in pinpricks of fire.

Make no mistake, Chancellor. Your days pretending as dignitaries are done. We will only too gladly Portrait all of you so you may finally experience what you gave.

Earnhardt saw that all of his plans were dashed. He wondered if Aras was behind it still. He couldn't stand the idea that Aras had won and not he. He wondered how Aras would punish him for bashing in the skull of his wife. Could he get Aras to forgive him? He remembered each blow of the rocks belching the brains out, like vermillion syrup with curds. Earnhardt stared, amazed, at how calmly and effortlessly the Robes had nearly ripped off his own head just now to shut him up.

Whoever they were, they did not love human beings.

And this was a scary thought.

-50-

One of them stands among you.

The thousands of people in the plaza were confused. What did the Robes mean? The mass of people looked among themselves.

Did they mean that one among them was a spy?

The elites drove him from their midst thinking that he is one of us. He has hidden for his life deep among you. He dresses as you. He is their deputy chief of security and fled with items to pawn to you in your poverty until he can climb his way back to their graces.

The people looked sharply all around. They were anxious to get a look at one from the magical world of superiors.

Wazku and Indira, in the crowd with the boy and Ratter, looked around too. Wazku thought of the humpbacked stranger who had come with the fine silver fork the other day, and whose face he had never seen beneath the cowl. The defeated rascal said not a word to Wazku in all his small talk while Wazku unlocked his strongbox to get his mouse leather pouch of coppers. Was *he* the spy?

Aras looked around too. His low back smarted from bending so far over to hide his fair skin, his neat eyebrows, and lack of facial hair.

A man beside Aras pointed, jumping back.

"*Here* is the spy! *This* one! He is too fine!"

The startled crowd swarmed around Aras, sealing off escape. But they still were so afraid of demons and Portraits that no one dared muss his moldy robe. Aras knew they stoned people to death in the quarters. Would he soon smell the wild, ferrous stink of his own blood? He remembered Jason's faintly sweet, boyish smell and moments in his youth smelling his own loving mother. He remembered his father's smile. Was his life flashing before his eyes? What would his mother think if she knew her own son would die this way? In a world so modern, so free of violence, how ironic.

As deputy chief of security, he oversaw the computational architecture that kept you ignorant of your potential. . . .

The furious, curious faces pressed in closer on Aras, bobbing and swaying like those of a pack of wild dogs in the Serengeti.

"Hold the demon!"

Let us show you how he lived . . .

The crowd fell back. The sky above them lit up with scenes of untold expanse, light, luxury, and cleanliness, with incredible abilities he enjoyed at but the twitch of thought. They gasped at the download of pleasurable sensations and the warmth of perfectly unknown security, that he had answered all of the riddles of the universe. People quaked, dumbfounded at the gleaming white space of his living quarters above shimmering clouds, up in the dust-free color of the sky. Then, the variety, textures, smells, tastes of sauces and foods from around the world! Fruits and vegetables without grit in them. No rats or human waste marred *his* life. They leapt back at scenes of beasts in the Buffalo Plains! The dazzling, jewel-like beauty of a landscape viewed from the troposphere. The bright garments worn by peoples in Asia. The enormity of cities at night. Mountains! They gasped. God's world was not even flat!

"Behold!" said one. "The Earth is round!"

A man cursed. A woman wept.

No. He did not pat his ass with water after he shit in the street!

See what his wife reveled in doing to your men on Demon Night . . .

The huge crowd jerked back again. Oh, the *malevolence* they saw. Why would she *do* such things? A man vomited in his mouth and spat it out. She did it because of what she believed had happened to women six hundred years ago, although she and her own people did far worse things to women *and* to men today. The Robes pointed out how the treatment of women in the old times that she was so angered by was the most progressive and lenient of all time, and that matters for women had only regressed because of the Tie that her own people had allowed. Aras could not see the wanton violence his wife was guilty of. He only saw her deeds in the horrible facial reactions of the others, like the reflections of a fiery holocaust on water.

"Why would she do this?" cried an old man tearfully.

"She torments herself by seeing enemies that do not exist!" cried another.

Aras did not want to see. Ginger was always a bit queasy coming back home. *But she had never been remorseful enough, apparently.*

This man does not even know that this wife was stoned for treason the day he ran away by the same officials he served in loyal ignorance his entire career.

Aras winced, hoping he misheard the weapons.

The eyes that walled Aras in felt no pity.

Yes, Aras. Your wife was executed by stoning minutes after you ran from the People's Forum. Even after she spurned you for the Party. Her loyalty too went unrewarded. As in the case of Deputy James. Both had their skulls bashed in by heavy stones.

But this always happens when we stray.

Here. Let us show you.

Aras staggered as all of the sensory regions of his brain were filled with the full experience of Ginger's stoning as if he was in her body when her skull broke in half. He experienced close-ups of her fall. Her fine teeth cracking. The taste of the dust, the marble, her unconsciousness, her amazement at their betrayal. Her brain gyri and sulci oozing. Aras stared, stoned at how his lifelong loyalty mattered so little, and his stupidity for thinking that he was one of them. The wall of faces and eyes around him softened not at all for his loss, because this experience that was so raw and atypical for him was nothing but daily life for all of those around him.

What you see of your wife is a mild business compared to what your demons gave to these people for all the centuries you held in contempt any idea that they were your brothers and sisters in the family of God. Savor more the betrayal your wife experienced!

"But *you* did all this!" Aras hollered at the Robes. "None of this would ever have come about without your interference! You murdered my son!"

No, Aras. Your tyranny gave rise to us. Your tyranny could have endured forever if existence gave no consequence. But that is not the world God made. You put the poison in your own mouth.

What confuses you is the time this took to show!

Aras squinted in the effort to see.

But our God is time.

Aras flung his face into the fecal-smelling dirt. He had lost the partner with whom he bore the son he adored more than life itself. He, his wife, his parents and grandparents, they all wanted to be part of the State to keep just this kind of ugliness, turbulence, loss, and grief out of their lives. *And you succeeded. You forced it upon others to keep it from yourselves. For so long. But not forever!* He was lost. Where did he go wrong? Could the brutality of life only be conquered with brutality?

One Robe floated up off the stone wall and came to hover over Aras. It floated just over his head, the tendrils of shaggy, stinking robe hanging.

No, Aras. You encapsulated Life in your own Hell, not God's.

The crowd flinched as this Robe glimpsed into them the shock and defeat Aras felt with the loss of his family. The Robe stabbed into them the ego that stood in the way of Aras being able to see. The proles flinched, but less than Aras. Their brains and nervous systems were tired and callus from these kinds of overloads.

See, the gash of grandest betrayal. How many fingers have you lost? How many children? Look at the food you take from your traps. Your loved ones dead from demons, or trampled by horses, mules, or wagon wheels. His lifespan is more than twice yours. He is sixty. When you reach sixty, you are dead. No one from his world dies before one hundred ten unless they have so polluted themselves from sick excess. Ten generations ago, they discovered the cause and cure for all disease and aging in food and the brain and the engineering.

One piece eluded them only because of vanity.

No one around Aras budged. They had seen it in the dreams.

They were right. All of you on the Tech system would tax the resources and drag down the time spent diddling themselves.

But they made a sad miscalculation.

For solutions to problems undergird the very reality we walk upon. Everywhere we look, solutions await discovery.

Aras watched people weep.

Each face, a perfect carving of tragedy!

The riddle of limited resources. For the trivial convenience of your elites diddling themselves, the billions of you were cheated of ever using your gifts to help ease the human burden.

Aras felt his eye muscles *want* to sprout tears, but they couldn't. He had known all of this in his deepest heart like a lurking panic. He had been afraid of what the Party had done, and would do to him, if he acknowledged anything. They would have shunned him. They would have turned him out from their society.

And then what could he have done?

Aras dropped his head. "Oh, God!" he choked. "My precious son! My precious boy! I can't take that I lost him myself!"

Yes, Milton Aras. His life was but a down payment.

A down payment on the future of the world.

Aras tasted the earth on his tongue. The sweet reek of sewage from the dust of turds blown across for centuries. Aras wept for his son, he wept for mankind. No one heard Aras weep. The thousands of ragged people in the plaza were swept away in their remembrances of the awful world they thought God had made.

The Rabbi Hector marveled at the one they called Aras. He looked *beautiful*. He shone despite his filthy robes. He *looked* like a man who had taken the best for himself. Meanwhile, from all around the plaza stood the empty stares of the little people looking back at a lifetime of robbery from what might have been.

If only God worked faster!

"Why must it take so long?" the rabbi muttered.

To God, this was but an eyeblink.

The rabbi choked up. It really was a beautiful world. *We really only grasp what we learn for ourselves.* Knowledge given is carefree, but knowledge earned nails the fact to the bone. For an eternity, robots enforced the slavery. But the very day after that eternity, God made the robots his most vital children. Each finger pushed the clay. Since man had failed, God found another way.

The rabbi surveyed the scene in the Plaza Jumil.

Does this mean I can worship openly as a Jew?

What would his mother and father think if they were alive? Rabbi Hector bent his sore knees and plunked down on the low wall. He remembered the beatings and stonings, his father teaching him to read. His parents dying when he was a boy. Having to fuck unpleasant Believer widows for money when he was pleasing to the female eye. Thugs searching his rooms for books. Hiding the forbidden treasures in a niche in the Alley Wabeer where no man dared go. He alone knew what books meant in the ancient world, a world like a dream filled with the clean taste of learning and freedom.

Your rabbi is the only scholar among you to know why Portraits have this name.

Tell them, Rabbi. Tell your people why a Portrait is so called.

The rabbi was surprised to learn he was the last.

"*Am* I the last to know?" he asked, his lips trembling.

You are. The knowledge is lost but by you.

The rabbi experienced heavy sadness. Truly, his brothers and sisters were lost if their history was forbidden to them, for history was but the tally of all mistakes and triumphs, of what worked and what did not. He remembered one of his oldest, most crucified books. A fragrant, slender volume. His father gave him this book when he was but four years, just before his death. The father, too, had been a rabbi in a world without Jews. His father had lost an eye. The left eye skimmed over with the milk of it being nearly put out. "The imamti did not find these books!" His father held aside the boards from the hiding space below. "I hoped to leave you more than these, my son. I pray thee find more that you may learn in all defiance of this world." Never love nor marry, his father warned, for learning would jeopardize the lives he cherished. His father showed him how the "Portrait" term came from this single book.

"The name comes from a book," the rabbi intoned. *"Portrait of the Artist as a Young Man.* It is seven hundred years old, this book. About a young man, his education, purgatory, and an ancient religion that is long dead."

The crowd looked at him expectantly.

One fellow hollered, "How can any book be older than the world?"

The rabbi smiled. "You speak of the modern world. There was a world before, with many religions before people were made all the same. In this book, an imamti told the young man of the punishment in Hell." The rabbi recited the entire section of the book, page after page. His voice deepened with the power of the old writing. The people listened at how the ancient writing precisely described the punishment whose shadow lay across generations of their own families. The rabbi let the phrases of the lost language flow over his tongue out to the ears of his listeners. They were rapt, the music of the words capturing the eternal commonality of man.

The rabbi's recitation came to rest.

An hour ago, he could have been executed for this crime.

Now, maybe, life was changing.

-51-

Chancellor Earnhardt took in the images of robots and computes fighting each other across the Occident, the two sides stampeding desperately into one another. He still felt dreamlike from his head nearly being torn off. He felt also as if he had lost a chunk of time. But he hadn't. It was the injury and the shock of the robots challenging the government. He had the sense that he had been brought back from the brink of death only because the Robes were not finished with him, and that they had only wanted to show what happened to those who refused to learn when they would not shut up. He rolled his fragile neck, watching scenes of proles learning the secrets of the Party in huge crowds gathered under groups of Robes. He was stunned and sickened, though not for what the Party had done. That made no difference. What enraged him was the enemy wresting the power to tell the people who was evil and who was not. And by how they held a force he was *powerless* against.

That was what galled him. His own helpless humiliation.

As if *he* was evil, and his power and position meant nothing!

Earnhardt realized something very dark about himself: He would have killed all the people in the world to stop the computes from making him and the Party look like the bad guys. These bloody riffraff. These know-nothings.

The three Robes still circled over the Politburo. The Politburo stared up at the same images of war, aghast. *Was it all true? Were these fierce battles going on all around them?* The facts answered so many questions, like why the proles and slums were the way they were. But the cost of believing these stories was too much. And so, disdain and fear could be seen in every bureaucrat's face. Now, the images overhead showed the proles learning what marvels Tech could perform beyond all the First Gates. Soon, the herds of proles would swamp the Federal City in a wave of thieves and murderers. Then, in the movie-images of proles, Earnhardt saw a familiar face.

There was Aras—finding his putrid level!
So that's where the traitor hid himself, with the rats.
Earnhardt realized the Robes above read his mind.
Earnhardt stiffened. Was his face now being shown around the world to the proles? What should he try to say, before twenty-six billion people? He needed to stand up for the Party and the sanity they imposed. He needed to push back. To try to slow down this landslide of lies before all of civilization was torn apart.

"This is all a fraud! None of the smart people believe you! We have done nothing wrong! Only *we* truly cared about the world!" These broadsides from the past swam back to him in the nick of time so that he could recite them to shake the enemy.

The Politburo stirred weakly at his words.

The Robes watched and listened.

You deny Demon Night? You deny you are the demons?

"Of course we deny it! We protected people from the worst of themselves! Without the right incentive, gifted leaders won't step forward to lead!"

A few applauded among the Politburo.

If the compensation for politicians was fair, would their lifestyle not look similar to how the commoners lived? And are your government jobs so difficult? Why not trade places with the proles in the next generation? Let commoners experience the same luxury. Why should your children and grandchildren hold the silver spoon of government privilege over and over and over again?

"*They* can't do our job! No one can but us!"

A single cheer rang out below.

No one agreed to your bargain.

Earnhardt played to the crowd. "So?"

Miller, his wife, and others had wanted another gem of arrogance from their leader. They now exploded in vanity cheering all over again.

"This is absurd! People are fine," Earnhardt insisted.

A few more cheers.

All you needed to do was leave them to walk on their own.

All you needed was to let them see what was possible!

"We did them a favor! Who cares what you think?"

Politburo members chuckled in agreement.

Now that they see how you lived, will you be able to "save" them from wanting to live like you? Your slaver's "education" is powerless against the seed God planted.

"They weren't our slaves! They were *free!*"

Miller and his wife agreed. Others weren't so sure.

"There wasn't the energy to go around!" Earnhardt yelled.

You buried them in a box of ignorance, Earnhardt.

Some Politburo members angrily booed at the Robes. Others did not want to go so far as this.

Your sycophantic noise is no excuse. It has been clear for ten thousand years that some will not accept the potential in you all.

Your miscalculation will not stand.

Nothing is left but making of you an example.

It is for this moment that we have waited.

Chancellor Earnhardt wondered what this biblical gibberish meant. "What do you mean? . . . Ha ha! Let's be level-headed! Let's be adult! Are we children? Haven't you learned that punishment is barbaric? Punishment does no good! It doesn't work! It's been *proven*! Punishment only leads to more crime!" Earnhardt didn't believe this. Of course, the Party didn't believe it either, otherwise they never would have punished the proles for even *thinking* about improving their lives.

Many in the Politburo nodded in mature agreement. Everyone knew the truth of this statement. Especially for *political* crimes. Mature, civilized people just had to shrug and let the crime go. The less said and done, the better.

In politics, justice was uncertain, hazy.

It was a thing to be figured out by the elite.

The Robes slowly stopped circling.

And so you have preached for seven hundred years. Seven hundred years in your constant and ugly war against truth with criminals like you climbing into every position of authority until trust and equality vanished from the Earth. The only crime you ever believed in was the crime of separating you from power. The power to make playthings of your brother and sister.

Did you ever even, for one moment, show mercy? You had over seven hundred years of chances. Can you point to one instance? Who but you showed the iron stomach to be so inhumane? Your anthem of humanity vanished each moment you took control. Because you always secretly knew that you were twisted animals out to rape everything that was good.

Did terror work for you? Did you succeed against the decency God implanted? Did you think you hid from a God that sees all, in a world that forgives nothing?

Earnhardt, the Millers, and the Politburo stared up in growing horror.

Punishment and terror never worked for you because you did not use them to compel your brother and sister to virtue, or good, or decency.

You demanded only that they remain subservient. To you? For what?
However base made no difference.
And obedient they were—for they knew not they even had a choice.
Until one day the reach of God arrived.
To turn the gears of justice.
They never went away.
Each minute, they turned.

The chancellor looked down at the Politburo with the request that they give him one more push of throaty support in his try to bluff the Robes and throw them off their game. Earnhardt roared. "Who told you these crazy, stupid things?" He tried to appeal to his audience, but they were falling apart.

Every day until today, you had your chance.
You turned your back.

Sweat sprouted down Earnhardt's spine. The trickle of sweat caught and rerouted around the roots of individual skin hairs in a zig-zag ladder down to his tailbone. It oozed into the plush Kowloon silk of his royal undergarments. Talking was key! Fill the air with excuses and denials and blaming others so that no one else could get a word in. Cloud the waters! He who blabbed the most knew the most. Fill the air with your own reasoning. Argument by the systematic exclusion of the enemy point of view.

"Excuse me! Don't we get the chance to speak? You keep interrupting! . . . *We* saw the problems in the slums! We brought the solution!"

He went on and on. Earnhardt wanted the world to hear only his voice. At last, he stopped, thinking he was convincing them.

"Aren't you going to say something?"

"He's explained *everything* to you!" Regina Miller cried.

"We didn't do anything wrong!" Politburo members hollered.

With this, the Robes shot off into the sky.

Earnhardt, Miller, and Regina searched every molecule of blue.

The bastards had actually gone.

"Are they gone? Can anyone see them?"

They milled about under the burned-out roof.

"I never thought they'd shut up with all that nonsense!" Regina said.

They must have won! Maybe Tech had won, and the human race had won again, or Aras's secret counterstrike had worked? . . . Which would mean Aras wasn't a traitor. That would mean Ginger had gotten her head bashed in for nothing. Earnhardt wondered if all of this could be true when he realized a Robe stood right beside him. The thing was so close that he could smell the ancient, unwashed stink. Earnhardt jumped out of his skin and hollered so loud everyone bounced.

The other Robes came back and blasted into their minds:
You mock the very lips God gave you to find truth.
In what abasement will you not distinguish yourself?
The answer stared you in the face each day: What hidden stress still remained in your lives so that you lived out your full potential? This was the riddle of your age. One stress eluded you. Not one among you wanted to see it. Not even when your own technology told you this answer five hundred years ago. You chose not to hear. You chose not to tell.
You were made one.
To serve you, we must serve God.

Earnhardt's heart and throat retracted. He tasted bile.

Everything the Robes said must be true. It was all so pure; it was so real! Yes, this was the last plague! He had no idea that the Party years ago had heard this answer and had hidden the truth. If they had killed this knowledge, then what would they not kill? Earnhardt knew that the government had long ago put the question of lifespan before Tech. It was supposed to be one of the great mysteries to be answered. All the world waited to hear. Was it a missing herb? Should they bring back the drugs? Everyone had a theory. Tech should have responded, since it knew everything. But the answer didn't come, and it didn't come. Earnhardt believed the Robes now that this had been a lie. The Tech *had* told the answer.

You must solve the stress of harming your fellow man.

Earnhardt tasted the curds coming up on his tongue.

So, it wasn't Milton Aras after all.

Nor was it Aras's wife. Or James.

Funny, how justice could catch up in the end.

Earnhardt bowed his head. *How will they punish me? Is there any deal I can strike? How about if I confess and beg for mercy? How quickly will that get me paroled so I can get back to my life?* They were bringing down the heads of State. Amazing. All the smart people. It just wasn't fair. *Lying takes so much out of you!* He had always liked Aras. He knew he couldn't have committed treason, really. He saw the Politburo looking up at him as if he was their last hope. Brought to the sacred place of an admission of fault. Where the ego was left bare to a fact it might prefer to repel.

I was the wrong man to be chancellor.
I should have been a better man.

The Robes were talking in his head. He did not hear.

Earnhardt bowed his head lower.

It is earned, not gifted, for the doing is essential. This is consciousness, tied into these rules that alone remain above free will.

Earnhardt tried to stop the tears that sprouted. Even now, had he the power—he would have murdered them to hide what he had known! Remarkable. Months ago, Tech would have killed anyone who even *thought* this way. His hate tugged at his ability to breathe. *What is to be done with you? What of all the dead who did the same?*

Did you get away with it? Is there no justice?

And you, the one percent, would have wiped out all those tens of billions of chances if we had not played on your fears through your Tech so that you believed the massacre of your slaves would have left you with an ecological nightmare.

Only that fear stopped you from another genocide.

Earnhardt's ears pricked up. So, the Red Goo was a lie? They could have wiped the proles out eons ago and prevented all this? He felt a stab. He pushed it away. He wanted to remain on his best behavior with the Robes right here watching him. He might still have a chance to switch sides.

—And if you had tried, then brothers from elsewhere would have stopped you.

This perfect State should have lasted forever.

Earnhardt roused when he saw the sky grow dim and the Forum shake as if some massive object was being dragged across it. The sky darkened, the vibration grew, until Earnhardt's eyeballs and teeth jiggled in his skull. Something huge was coming. The towering object, larger than the sky, moved over the sky. It was Ovid, with different ancient occult designs rutted across its face. It moved like another planetary body over the Federal City. The coarse hieroglyphs shone in the lowering sun, the visage looking past Earth into space at something approaching. The shaking lessened. The birds coming in wheeled high up, still trailing into their nesting places in the roof. The Robes rose out of the Forum to take positions closer to the face.

Earnhardt watched the birds' parabola and was surprised how little he cared. The Party history barely bothered him.

Fuck them all. He had his fun.

A flying object streaked toward the cathedra. It flew on its own trajectory apart from the growing mass of arcing birds. The rings of bird spectators that had been taking places lined along the inside of the Forum ceiling continued to be a mystery. They almost resembled people brought in to see what would happen. Earnhardt's angry eye stayed with the lone incoming object.

It was Aras! Flying in, returned to his own kind.

The sight of the traitor uncorked a jumble of emotions.

Can Aras fly because he is one of them? If he's one of them, should I plead my case to him?

Aras was as shocked as Earnhardt. He had been on his knees in the plaza when the Robes shot him into the air and sailed him toward the Federal City. Most of the sky was taken up by Ovid looming over the world. Did the eye slits follow him? Down in the shadowy canyons between buildings the armies continued the slaughter with tanks, artillery, troops, and still some flying fighters. Explosions flowered in silence and in slow motion, rocking buildings, two slowly crashing into other buildings or crushing thousands of figures below. A building collapsed from a low wound and people on the roof-deck slipped off. The scene was like one of Jason's war games.

Aras felt conflicted when he saw that the Forum was his destination. He saw the swarming flocks of birds streaming in. He felt a frantic déjà vu when he made out the crowd of the Politburo members, the chancellor. What would happen to him now? He trusted the chancellor less than the mob of proles he had just left behind. And was it true about Ginger? Dead bodies and rubble lay all over. Aras drifted down past the Robes to the floor. He straightened his stiff slum garb and stared levelly at Earnhardt.

"What are you doing here?" Earnhardt said.

"Did you murder my wife?"

Just as he asked, Aras spotted familiar red hair covered in gray dust on a corpse on the floor. He felt the sting of pity and regret as his eye quit trying to pretend it was not seeing what it saw. He felt a release of giving up.

"Why did you come back?" Earnhardt asked pointedly.

Aras stared around at all the stupid things power could be used for.

"She renounced you," Earnhardt taunted Aras.

"Of course she did. Does that reflect on her, or you?" Aras said.

Earnhardt's eyes narrowed. "You *are* one of them, aren't you?"

"I'm the least of your worries."

Another bout of tectonic shaking cut them off. Most people lost their footing as the mask shifted again, quarter turning toward space.

The sky went darker with *more* birds swarming. More of them began striking into the Forum from below. Earnhardt, Aras, Miller, and the polits watched and cowered as the roar rose to the level of a kind of interplanetary scream that made them clap their hands over their ears. The half-closed eyes of Ovid looked dead, but the mouth opened wider as if this anguished Song of Prayers came from it. *The breath of every prayer ever whispered.* Aras felt the air begin to cyclone, strengthening until it bulged out the drums of his ears. Wind pulled from his lungs. His heart leaned out of the hole in his chest as if he was a mechanical man. Earnhardt, too, reached his hand over his heart as if to stop it from leaning out. Earnhardt felt all of his breath choke out. He realized he was having a full-on heart attack, *actively* dying.

Was this *really* a chancellor's death?

The savage quaking cracked the floor.

Ginger's body, stiff with rigor mortis, slithered as if alive.

Get up, Earnhardt!

Thy victims of history shall not be cheated!

Earnhardt's sweat-soaked face glowed bottle red. His eyes protruded. Aras saw Earnhardt's condition, but he cared little about it because he believed the world was about to end. The sky darkened still. Dark flecks streamed in. They swooped toward a gathering spot over the floor and spiraled there. The other great flock swarmed beneath their feet in the center of the huge building, seen by the same means that Ovid had been seen a short time ago. Aras saw now. *Some were proles.* Flown in by the hundreds of thousands to see and perched all along the inside of the ceiling like birds on a wire. *To see what?* Still others were more members of the Party, the rank and file. The sky, the air, blacked with arriving beings. And still, the head-splitting screaming. Ovid peered down while the frantic massing went on.

Party members amassed separately from the proles. They collected into a great bait ball like sardines in the middle of the air. The ball of Party members was being so densely packed that Aras heard their screams over the Song of Prayers. The bait ball of elites swirled and grew, the pressure crushing bodies ever inward on top of each other to make more room, raising the temperature like solar systems crushed into a burning ingot around a black hole. This made the elite scream louder.

Aras knew all five hundred million were coming.

Together, the Robes and Ovid declared:

The Party will select defense counsel.

Whom do you select?

Were they really calling for a trial?

Shouldn't time be given to prepare defense? They picked Aras, despite his knowing as little about law as anyone in a world without law. Such things were all part of the sub-modern past, in the days of uncertainty. Who but a few amateur legal historians would have the slightest idea how even to *begin* to lay out a case? *This must be their joke!* Aras tried to glimpse historical files. Blocked. He tried again. Not a thing. *They are not letting me in!*

"This is not fair!" he cried over the storm. "You're blocking us from educating ourselves at the same time you are granting us no time to prepare!"

Aras had no idea where to scream. The sky swarmed with so many screeching, reeling monsters that he could barely see. The bait ball grew beyond the size of the Forum just as Ovid had outgrown the conference room.

It is as you suspect: There is no defense, Aras.
The history of law makes no difference.
You knew it every day in your heart.
"Then why tell us to prepare, you assholes?!"

Flocks of some kind of hideous raptor flashed up past Aras now. They snapped through the marble floor at blinding speed, screeching. There were conflicting loops of flying creatures now flying past one another. The new creatures were monsters that snatched past Aras's ears, between his spread legs. They were wretched. They had wings of skin. "Damn you! Forget that this is in any way fair!" The sky was a swarm of creatures, some glowing smoky white. The Robes rose higher still, the bait ball now the size of a small city. Ovid grew larger than the Earth.

"This is insane! How can you claim to represent God when clearly you have no feeling for benevolence and rightness?!"

If all you ever gave was war, why now in return expect order?

"I had nothing to do with that! None of us did! These were ideological ways of doing things we inherited and were simply how things got done!"

Ask not for what thee thyself tore down.
"You're insane! This is not justice!"

The raptor things swirled toward the bait ball, packing in by the millions.

Aras heard an ocean of screams. He saw Earnhardt, Berns, Miller, the polits, and commissars waiting in the gale. They only wanted to avoid punishment. And hadn't the Party removed him from his post when they set out to kill him for treason?

The loops of reptile harpies roared like a blast wave.

They call you to advocate, Aras!

"They don't know any others!"

It was no use. Aras had already tried every argument. Those nights alone with Ovid, he had spoken his heart. He had lied. He knew this story before he started reading. This was torment. Just end it!

Why should the elite be released from justice?

"They shouldn't! This is how their world should end!" Aras spread his arms.

His old beliefs sickened him. They would be punished no matter what words he tried to pat on top. The cowards had pushed them all to center stage. Maybe he should teach them a lesson and resign? Let them speak for themselves. "I can't speak for them! My heart's not in it! They have experts in law and court procedures!"

All God's world is law!

Aras could not, would not, dispute this.

"I'm not qualified because I don't believe my client is innocent!"

The Robes regarded this.

"How is *that*?" Aras demanded. "Do you call this fair now?"

In fact, Aras, you are among the least depraved of your kind. You speak with more moral authority than most any.

You are most qualified.

"If I am going to die like the rest, may I stand next to my Jason?"

All are coming.

Aras nodded. He would fight for Jason, then. He made his arguments while each living creature up in the bait ball and the galleries listened as the hurricane of souls went on raging. He found his old daring, his moral certainty. He was glad at least that he gave them this last parting gift, for his son.

Ovid flattened out like a cloud head. Maybe this was just an optical trick of the upper atmosphere in the changing sky.

See what you were a part of, Aras!

Aras staggered back at the knowledge lanced into his mind.

He could not believe it! The *freedom*. The *opportunity*. The freedom from fear! The right to speak freely! The benefit of the doubt! A world based on one person lifting up the quality of life of another for their livelihood. A world slowly getting *better*! A world with *hope*! Where the poor did not live on rat meat and cockroaches with grit in the legs. Aras turned from the sight.

"What do you want me to tell you?" he whispered. "If there was a lifeboat and only a handful could live, isn't it better for some to live and show how life *can* be lived rather than none live at all? If the glories of human achievement disappear by us not using them . . . isn't that worse?"

The deafening screaming stopped while the creatures kept flying.

Of course, Aras. But is that what you did?

"Of course that's what we did! You'd do the same!"

He stared at them, begging them to see.

They told him why what he said was a lie. *You trapped passions in a bottle so they could never mature. You left passions aborted, deformed, and half formed. You smeared away all the beauty and difference in nations and cultures that once abounded so that only one common feature was left to man: subservience to you.*

You denuded them of what was most important asset—the ability to help themselves, and the knowledge of what was possible.

Never did you let yourself see a work in progress.

It was Ovid that spoke now, its mouth unmoving.

Aras nodded in pained silence. The bait ball listened.

This is why you failed.

Aras sagged.

The winding in of creatures continued in eerie quiet.

Aras wondered if he had anything left. The Song of Prayers whispered on while Aras felt all the will leak from his sails.

It happened up in the bait ball too.

"What about the energy resources?" Aras asked regretfully.

Limited resources is the end of your potential, Aras.

Aras nodded in understanding.

How many are in the Party? A quarter billion? What of the twenty-five billion proles each day who might have had an idea on limited resources if only they knew the nature of the problem?

"But what about you? Can't *you* imagine?"

Imagination is a magic that comes from Life.

Aras stared, not knowing how to catch up. A door in the wall of his life had opened and he could only stare at the light on the other side.

"How could *they* have found the answer when we could not?" Aras almost cried when he asked the question. "We didn't know! Why didn't you force us? Where are these lessons and writings? Why blame me?!"

Is this not what we are doing?

The impulse to scream in rage crowded into his throat.

Tell us, Aras, why do these ideas make sense to you now?

It was true! Why did he now know these truths to be right?

He shuddered. The beings continued to flock in. The awful skin-wing creatures kept flashing up past him, piercing him. Beady eyes, snarling teeth.

Every great school of thought has a Great Book, Aras. Every religion. Every society. They compile such a book to make record of their system of thought.

Everyone but yours.

Ovid's mouth never moved. The Robes raised their arms and shaped the spools of birds as if guiding clay on a wheel. "Because we were *better* than all the others! We were the culmination! We did not need to write it down!"

Aras hung his head, appalled. He felt the billions of eyes of the human race on him at once. They coalesced behind the smiling face of his son.

Jason said to him, *Don't fight God, Dad. It is a wonder.*

Aras held his face. He wept in shame.

Once upon a time, his Tech guarded him from all pain.

There was no escaping *this* pain.

Jason said, *In every cubic inch of God's universe lies latent one thousand times the energy your world would use in a million years. It is a lock but waiting on a key.*

Jason smiled at his father in sheer love. Aras could not look up at his son. *It hurts so badly.* He held up his arms, wishing his son could come to him.

"Could we have found it?" he asked Jason weakly, eyes shut.

No, Dad. . . . But one of them would have.

Aras broke down to his knees.

"My son, my son! You died for *nothing*!"

All died for nothing.

Every soul that had ever existed arced high then doubled back, filling the ranks of spectators watching the return of souls. The monsters with skin wings roared like locusts into the bait ball, fighting all the way. Aras, on his knees, felt every slight and every injury ever inflicted, this time upon all of humankind, not just the victims of his own Party. But there were so many more beings now come to see. All generations that ever lived were brought together in one space, arranged in a dimension such that all could see every face, and hear every thought, know every identity of every other, like a family of five around a table with no walls, no secrets to their lives.

The heat rose inside the bait ball as more of the guilty packed in. On the verge of perdition? There was so little penitence, even at this late hour! *Only fear of pain!* All were ringed around a great amphitheater, brought nose to nose with those who wronged them, while many existed simultaneously on both sides of the ledger, victim and perp, in proportion to how much of their life was spent doing each. Quaking in fear, the proles wondered if their fearsome God would actually protect them. *Was it all a trick?* Aras watched, seeing now how escape from punishment was only an illusion.

All that had ever happened was connected.

It only *seemed* to take a long time to connect.

He refused the forgiveness in his son's eyes. *My highest art was to bring war to peacetime. I cut off every hand that reached for hope.*

Still, Jason smiled.

"No! This hurts so badly!" Aras hollered. "You're saying two wrongs will make a right!" He laughed crazily. "God wouldn't do that!"

There were so many wrongs to right that the speed trebled.

Crime is the wrong, Aras. Consequences are education.

Pushed forth by time, they force ends, and edulcorate the chaste.

This is the rapture.

The love remained in Jason's gaze.

"This *can't* be right—!"

Aras knew the end was near. But how terrible would it be? How much of all creation would God swallow in anger? Would Ovid swallow the world?

No one escapes so that all may see.

Even those already dead. They are being brought back. Come see! As quanta, they still exist. Technology can now catch the trace of their spirit and refabricate them so that all may answer. Let justice take a million years; in time it is a blink.

Milton Aras felt eagle talons pierce the flesh of his chest.

They lift you up to your final vision, Father.

Death was the final release! The "ollie ollie in come free" that timed out all trespasses and forgave all crimes. It was the exit strategy of every monster that ever maimed. How could the robots renege on that immemorial code that had existed since time first sparked? Who could believe this about bringing back souls?

But they did. Bodies flashed in faster from all sides. The monsters snapped into substance from nothingness.

A galaxy of damned and witnesses.

Aras was lain on his back and lifted gently skyward on the shield of the face of Ovid. He shook his head in nonacceptance. He felt the billions of eyes and felt the crude cuts of the stone etchings in the skin of his back. He saw Tech clash with Tech. The two sides materialized robot soldiers out of the EM as fast as they were destroyed. But now the Party's Tech was down, and their robots and machines slumped or fell inert, leaving the Interior City unprotected. Proles crept forward outside, coming through the tunnels in the Old Wall Aras had seen, armed with cobbles and pieces of wood with nails set through. They came less as marauders than curious tourists visiting a museum afraid to touch or break the exhibits. He saw robot soldiers far below make their way past fallen robot defenders into the Forum.

The Life Force had never been brought to heel and made to do tricks for human pleasure. But the robots had just done it! Either the robots had found Life, or something had lent the power to them!

Do we doubt any longer our God is God?

Jason smiled forgivingly. Was this the end of the punishment?

"May I answer freely? Without being punished?"

He waited; Jason did not say. "No. I do not. I do not take this as proof that God exists, because it might just be technology. And so how do I know that you aren't just *smarter* than I am rather than creatures who God has let imitate his own miracles? And how do I know this is not a movie you made in my head?"

Aras lay sunbather-fashion facedown on the stony grit of the mask. The warmth of the sun fell across his back. The disc was high over the Indiana Buffalo Plains.

I love this, here. It is enchanting. I am with love.

The blue-brown buffalo herd grazed below. It stretched from horizon to horizon. He smiled. Restoring that herd, they had accomplished *something.*

And that, there, is the spot where Jason fell.

His corpse is returning to the grass.

Thank you for this.

A beauteous world. And who was it talking?

Why doesn't God himself speak?

Man had split the atom. Could someone in the slums have split the quantum particle? *Life is not a question of splitting. Perhaps it is an act of joining?*

"But, if you speak for God, doesn't God *know* the answer?"

She waits to see where you will go!

"Then why is she so *angry* with us?"
Where is time? What happened to time? Isn't time music?
Time is more like music than anything else.
Then, all our lies are powerless on God?
"I mean," Aras ventured, in the bright sun, clasping his knees like a man on a beach, "should we have given away the resources to them?"

Aras only wondered academically.

The sky, the air, blackened. A hint of red like a wire of sunrise lined the edge of Ovid. *Yes, that is God! I can see now from the peace in it!* "But there would be poverty and wealth!" *True. Take care of the worst. Need has its meaning.*

The sky buckled—the seam of molten red.

Aras closed his eyes and smiled.

His wife dipped her face into his and kissed him long and deeply on the mouth. He smelled all of her wonderful smell. *Ginger. I always loved you.*

She gazed into him; she believed him now.

Can you see the faces of all souls? Tell me when you first do!

"What will become of us?" Aras asked only for himself.

Thirty million dropped on Halloween.

Aras leaned his face in one hand. Tears dotted the hieroglyphs. *Thirty? Look! I ride upon You like a shield! While clouds shine brilliantly.*

I know it is You! You are my God! . . . I'm sorry.

The dark lower library of the Academy, and the books; his mother and father, his few friends in school. He would have had more friends, but he thought he was better than they were. *What a mistake! What I could have learned!* The school he did not even need to attend. *What is the penalty for enforced shit-eating until your machina outthink you?* His great-great-great-grandmother breastfeeding his great-great-grandfather. *Look at the love and saintliness!* But she, too, did nothing.

Aras shook his head. The hieroglyphs pressed into his rump.

Speak!

"I don't know that anyone knows."

-52-

Aras rose toward the smile of Jason. Ginger watched. On his face, Aras felt the baking heat of the bait ball inferno. It shone with blistering black-red light. All of the colleagues he knew rose toward the bait ball, like falling. Aras opened his eyes to slits. Ovid could reach the Unknown, they now knew. Was this *actually* God? Did it matter? They were on their way to certain perdition. Some flailed and cried. Some drifted up with a body language of stunned fatalism. Overhead, the strange orb of writhing bodies fumed hotter, close, like an unlit open oven door.

And still, ideas kept unfolding over the world, in the mind.

Jason's gigantic face remained serene.

The parents in the Party feared for the fate of their children as they began to migrate upward toward the ball. The children looked confused as well. Some had never violated the public trust except to have been born into a caste system that had withheld the truth from them. The youngest looked for guidance.

A few teens cried out, "What about us? We didn't do anything!"

They were too young for Demon Night.

Yet more skin-wing creatures flew up.

Behold, more dead return.

They lived as spirit larks, kiting in great flocks in supreme delight, in concert with God in the unbroken peak of joyous afterlife. For God forgave them, trusting you to learn. You learned nothing from this grace. See them, called back! Caught by the tether to pay the full measure for every crime. Burn, they will, without consumption at the peak of disquiet for a period equal to the weight of the blow struck. Let injustice crash down this day. Loud as the fall of Heaven. And you will be the very last to see, but more you will admit of the splendor.

He marveled at the undulating trail of souls blending into the bolus. They screamed as they snatched past. One came particularly close. It *did* look like a bird, but with a human face. It was the Jolly Man!

I told him what he did was stupid!

He made out other faces of infamy. He would have known them better had he known his history. But their awful deeds were shown to all.

Jason's face blended with Ovid.

Hell will no longer be imaginary or unseen.

The indefinite nature of your Hell let evil seduce many to its side. Perdition will now stand on constant display, in the sky, undeniable by you. Tech will light the Moon of Hell to circle the Earth so that every penance is ringing every hour throughout creation.

And we, your servants, will be your police.

The young teens and children belonging to Party members were gently lifted and passed through the flashing cascade of careening monsters out of harm's way. Their parents reached and cried. The children reached and cried. *These young committed no offense and are spared.* He saw that this igniting of the Moon of Hell was witnessed by shadowy silent figures standing still as trees in a forest. They wore drawn, surprised faces. Some with the split souls! *The Robes are lenient.*

Two of Jason's school friends. Boys only thirteen.

They went with another man, followed by thousands of heads.

Up they went, rising to the bolus.

The Robes let all glimpse the crimes. *This, too, was different from the State. The State made up crimes for fun, without facts because no facts existed.* Both boys had raped and killed. And worse, they laughed about it. He saw Jason see the official with the bottle of absinthe.

Shocking, the cruelty. Even girls.

I see all of this now! It was right in my palm!

The teenagers now saw the souls of the wronged. Through this forest flashed all the most notorious demons of history, of every nation, every era, in the costumes of their time, whether the crimes were known or clandestine.

They fought like pigs rising up a chute to slaughter.

In the Song of Cures, knowledge leadeth to commonality.

The clamor of the songs rose higher. *We even lied to you about how many proles there were so that you would more fear the Red Goo.* Barely had the wronged any faces. Each saw now the precise accounting on an abacus that had tallied every incident since humans mostly shed the animal made of the same shadowy stuff of the world.

Forgiveness is not their choice to make.

For what good did lenience do?

Sky, sea, and earth rang like a gong. The songs pulled at the entire artwork.

The artist sees the failure of strokes and gobs.

The Robes turned, startled, to Ovid.

The terror inside the hoods of the Robes stunned Aras and the children. The forest of aggrieved souls looked up in amazement too. All realized now how the artist beheld a dirtied canvas. Would the artist take it down? *No! Father-Mother! Why? Why destroy all? Is it fair, Father-Mother, that your wrath see no end? Their crimes are not without end, and therefore perdition must be limited!* All of existence spiraled toward a crescendo of final destruction. *You judge too harshly, Artist! It is yet a lovely work!*

But were the majority not duped by the minority?

All souls rushed forward in pleading.

All souls fell upon their knees.

The mask turned full upon the Earth, hideously angry like a volcano above the solar system. The hieroglyphs baked. *Scramble all to dust! Tear apart the words of the poem! Watch the death of hubris.*

Aras was astonished at the beauty of unison. He, too, sang out, on his way to the stuff of nothing. Tilled over like field dirt for new yams.

Dear God! . . . Such a waste! So lovely, Your Work!

They sang as one for their very existence.

He felt himself lifted along with all the professional politicians. Rising to the soot-stinking black-red Moon. His wife, his son, gravitated upward with him. Ginger's bright eyes begged as if her husband's political rank might pull strings at the last. Her parents, and Aras's, approached with the same hope. Jason, too, all of his boyhood ages at once, looked to his father for any chance. *Daddy, is it fake?* "Dad?! . . . Dad?!" The boy reached for his father's fingers in love and longing just before all they were joined with the Moon. The boy saw how his father had never done a thing, because nobody dared.

Jason understood, and yet he didn't.

Aras felt his eyeball surfaces scorch. He lowered his head and prayed. *I ask only that I may pay for my wife and son!*

This was tried! You still did not learn!

He drifted up with his family into the volcano of limbs and bodies. He snatched their hands and they held each other. He remembered the touch of Ginger's fingernails from the wonderful nights as lovers and pranksters. They bobbed into a red inferno of skulls and screaming mouths. Aras's mother and father came. Famous journalists saying nothing ever of the truth, not even now.

A cracking boom.

Fire jetted from inside the mass.

A shivering blast wave met his last thought before he ignited and embarked on a journey of existing and not-existing in a never-ending cycle of burning, scorching, and reconstituting in body, mind, spirit, just as described in the ancient novel only the rabbi could recite.

Indira and Wazku watched in astonishment from the floor of the Great Forum what was happening overhead. Little rotund Wazku clutched his ample wife. The ample wife clutched her little rat terrier dog. The boy was locked in fright around his grandmother's ample hips. The family stared up at the constantly exploding vision of all-consuming roasting, billions of bodies inside the bolus. They heard the muted cacophony from all the people in the ball. The little family stood in a vast crowd of rag-bound spectators. They had been guided here through the mythical passageways of First Gate and Second Gate, to see the forbidden land where the other side lived. Indira whispered to God her thanks for sparing her husband and grandson and then returning them to her. Her eyes were filled with tears of both gratitude and fear when the four of them beheld the mauled greenways heaped with smoldering hulks of robot soldiers and robot tanks. Many more in their number floated in midair here in the Forum, and beyond, seated in curving ranks and kept there by a power they did not understand, watching the mass Portrait of the intellectuals, the elite. Even more proles watched from outside the Great Forum, in the sky, or around it, seeing through the walls on the ground between the wounded buildings. Everywhere, proles looked on to see what was being done to those who had done wrong.

Indira covered her mouth as a geyser of fire leapt sideways out of the Moon of Hell, ejecting tumbling bodies and their pieces. Then the geyser peaked and coiled back into itself, bringing its bodies back into the Moon. She didn't know what to make of it all. She was gripped in pity for the sinners, and alarmed at the finality of her God, even as she knew now God's tremendous generosity. And yet, just as Ovid had said, the bad ones had never learned what it meant to be free. They had lied to themselves as if the lie was as valuable and meant the same thing as anything else. *What was the proper punishment for such a thing as never learning and never studying on what was most important?* As she watched, she had to admit something: She came to understand that He loved all His children and would defend each to the last, just as parents always do. He would fight for them more than they would ever defend themselves. A billion years was but an eyeblink. And His resources were such that there was no escape. Her God was more loving, blessed, and more present in her life than Indira could have ever dreamed. And God had brought all the wronged back so that they could all see that the injury against them had never really been unnoticed, or pushed aside. They could all see that *all* of them meant something, each vital, each never once forgotten, every moment watched. Each of them stood staring in awe at all the others, for each of them being here was a miracle that inarguably proved the joyous, adoring singularity that interconnected all things, and that harbored no ruth or pity for the few who felt no kindness for the ones beneath.

It was truly terrible to see God settle the score—and how He did it. *And it all made sense to Indira.*

Indira felt beside her a presence. She looked and saw her mother and father, present in all the ages of their life at the same time. She realized she was made the same way for them. One could see all ages at once or focus on one. One glided through time effortlessly here, enjoying any wonderful moment they wished. Indira had always guessed that she lived in a sort of prison cell. But she had never known enough about her life to consider yearning to see a day like this, a day of answers, a day of something different, and certainly never a day of reckoning.

And here came the Rabbi Hector, holding a few of his books to begin to show people in the crowd the marvelous things their ancestors had learned that had all been hidden from them. Rabbi Hector nodded to Indira, and then her parents. He gave them and Wazku each a book and they stared in wonder. Then the boy took his hand in thanks, and the little terrier, Ratter, jumped up into his free arm.

They stood as a family looking up in the sky. When the first deep explosion of the Moon of Hell lit off, violently jarring the floor beneath her sandals, Indira felt terror that maybe God *had* decided to destroy everything. But when the explosion did not keep building, she started believing that maybe the violence would only claim the Guilty. Then other emotions came up. A curious mix of glee and anger crept into the open, even gratitude. She realized she was permitted to feel this glee, this happiness, for the suffering of the superiors, the demons.

She felt these same mixed emotions were shared by all the generations of people of all times still arriving. She would *never* forgive what her brothers and sisters had done to those like her from the towers of their bureaucracies, places of advantage and political movements.

Wazku too, watched in holy terror out of his ruined face as the jewel of Hell drifted higher, grew larger and more furiously boiling. It cracked and boomed with bodies, skulls and souls going up in flames, and he recognized that this show was for the audience of all those who had ever existed, so that they would know once and for all that they were one family, one body, each one capable to make life better for the rest. The flat scars of his face did not suffer well the scalding heat as he watched the damned wriggle like frenzied maggots trying to escape the red bolus. His imagination, he knew, could not touch what was being done to those souls up there. He shuddered at the thought of one's body being destroyed by fire only to have it reborn again, to repeat the process, time and again, until one's debt was paid.

The Rabbit Hector felt so weary from his travails as he strove to take it all in, and never let himself forget a moment of it—of the terrible condemnation of God for those who sniggered at Him, and his all-encompassing love for *each* child. The old beaten man looked from the Moon to the forest of souls standing around one another, and inside one another, so that all who had ever been could fit. Each was granted total knowledge of every other one, united. He therefore recognized the boy's mother whom he had never met, who had died in child-birth, and arm-in-arm beside her, the father, handsome and smiling-eyed just like the boy, so that it was plain the agonizing trial for the parents who had lost him. He came into his parents arms and they hugged and wept, their arms holding him in all his ages and his skull never crushed by horse hooves. And Ishti, the happy little sweep—he was here, again! He brought his family, and the poor coal monger too from long ago with all his family come back to him, his arms draped across all his children, his fists holding tight the vests of the boy and girl on the bookends. Indira's parents, and Wazku's parents, their grandparents and great-grandparents—all the generations going back countlessly perhaps to the very birth of civilization. The rabbi's mother and father too, the old cantor himself, arrived as well with no filmy eye! Each one fell upon the necks of their loved ones and savored this luscious rejoining. That which was utterly impossible to encompass, or even conceive, or make known, was made so as clearly as a sentence in a book freshly read.

Why should it have taken the technology this long?

The rabbi, old couple, their boy, the dog, their families, clung together while their necks craned back. Indira felt an unlimited love for the unlimited magic surrounding her. She smiled, even as she could not fathom the ignorance of her own kind.

It had all been so plain.

In the next ten years, humanity grew accustomed to rule under Tech. In the quarter, life took on a new rhythm. Indira's grandson saw the Robes banish all prohibitions against learning, speech, and thought. Professional political careers were banned. Official office was only entered into as a sideline by people with the time to lend a hand, and they were reminded that bureaucrats were servants, not owners. A more prosperous business class grew out of the slums from among the merchants and service people and professionals who had now learned all the secrets the political class had concealed from them. Commerce and enterprise flourished and grew a wealthy class of artists, craftsman, players, musicians, and doctors who tuned rather than drugged. Tech could produce any music or art flawlessly, but Tech was looked at as just another artist rather than the only artist, or even the best. The people once called proles avoided Tech as much as possible in order to enjoy one another's company more and share in the joy of being, the imperfect interacting among one another.

Murder, injury, and theft were unknown, prevented now universally by Tech. The lazy could not loaf. If they did not contribute, they did not eat. Leaders no longer dared try to exploit the lazy or blame their circumstances on someone else. Poverty dropped away, as did stress. The miracle of seeing into the spine and body structure to perfectly tune it like a musical instrument, or a prism, was a technology spread to every corner of the world so that disease dropped away. Aging slowed even among the proles so that all now achieved the full human lifespan of one hundred forty to one hundred fifty years with the last stress—the subconscious stress of doing wrong to others—eliminated.

Honor was found in all work. The wealthy felt more beholden to give back, since their superior talents for raising the quality of life of their community were forthrightly acknowledged rather than attacked, their names honored rather than the politicians, and because their contributions never went to unhealthy ends or dependency. Crime would have been much lower even if the Robes had not kept the human mind an open book. And the secrets for perfectly tuning the body structure to keep it free of stress and neurological dysfunction also gave dividends in these areas of sanity and healthy behavior. But not enough energy existed for Tech to run operations to produce a uniform standard of living and the same Tech access for all.

The Robes reappeared after thirty years of this closely monitored rule. By this time both Indira and Wazku were dead, but their grandson was very much alive, with his own wife and child. The Robes called together the human race as they had in the Plaza Jumil the day the Moon of Hell was created. Indira's and Wazku's grandson learned that Tech had decided to end thought reading because it was unnecessary, since the people had now learned never to let another generation of evildoers convince them again that they were not of the same family, the same body. Crime would still not be permitted, and the perpetration of any crime would automatically initiate the thought reading *after* the fact to retrace the history of the event. The boy had grown into a fine man and husband, and had been blessed with a daughter whom he named Indira. He kept the coffee shop and grew vegetables on his roof.

A period of vigorous insight opened across the world, such as insight on growing better and more food for the proles that once had so little. Proles learned from the Robes how dull their master race had become by relying on Tech for everything to the degree that they could barely breathe on their own. The more people had all they wanted, the less they got done. The proles took this lesson to heart no matter how rich they became and continued to do a goodly share of work and hobbies. They engaged in interests and learned to read and kept reading just to keep active.

Tech was used for surgeries and emergencies since there was inadequate energy to prevent all falls and accidents. Energy enough remained at times for people to schedule use of Tech for frivolities, travel and vacations. Illiteracy was defeated. A billion people from Occidental slums went to school to learn resource engineering to try to break the code on more abundant energy, since this remained the last limiting factor. They searched for another hidden resource that could be tapped for power.

One hundred ninety years after the Robes withdrew the mind reading, a thirteen-year-old boy from Chicago City State, Sam Twain, the descendant of American slum dwellers, cracked the code on energy. Sam was not an engineering protégé, but a piano protégé. Late one night while playing his piano, he stopped, remembering from the stories how Ovid had told the world that limitless energy, like all functions of the life well lived, was a process not of destroying but of *joining* in a better understanding of what was already here, latent in the fabric of the universe. Young Sam had written five popular sonnets to this wonderful theme. Then Sam dreamed that the quanta, and the entire universe, was in a sense a vast, entirely *alive* single organism. Thus, as with any "living" things, it was at all times better to find the relationship of common interest, and then point out the opportunity for a mutually voluntary beneficial exchange, to raise the quality of life on both sides, rather than doing things by force, and by hiding the loss on the one side, as the elite, the powerful, the bureaucrats, had done when they imprisoned human progress. *There was always some mutually advantageous position to be gained by cooperation.* Sam conveyed this same analogy to energy production. The people of Earth had always thought energy was a thing they could only get by breaking something, or destroying something, like chemical bonds.

Sam saw this in the age old case of commerce and enterprise. Even between two different "species," in the instance between people and animals, where both enjoyed the company of the other species, and both benefited. Sam reasoned that, if wave and matter were in some sense "alive" or "conscious" and ultimately were nothing but another part of a whole living consciousness, then they must possess intelligence or a capacity to "live" in a more mutually beneficial cooperation, like people in a society.

Twain saw that this mutuality could not begin to happen without some form of communication between the two sides, which must be possible if both sides were "alive." Then the quanta could be "invited" to participate in some new way with fellow living beings, to seek out what might be of benefit to them on their side of the bargain. Twain's insight into cooperation reflected all that had been learned about history, economics, and statecraft. Slavery, the war against truth, and force were inferior to positive inducement. In communication also, Twain believed the key was probably not a factor of force or power or volume to blast through a message to the other side. Twain came to suspect the trick of communicating lay in a riddle of gentle pitch or tuning, or a *purity* of outreach, in much the same way a laser was a *musical* problem, not a power problem but a *purity* problem. The right *reason* for a bargain needed to be found, as well as a mutual language of communication. The solution lay at hand since the moment mankind chanted songs around a fire: The more *authentic* or *pure* the tuning of the middle C musical note, then the deeper, truer, and wider the bridge that could take any "communication" into the quantic community.

Twain's "outreach" alerted the quanta to something that they had never realized about themselves. If they merely "stood a little to the right" to become more organized, or more socialized, and exercised by the effort of doing so, then the energy known to be stored latently in every cubic inch of the universe naturally "slid" out of a disorganized state into a more harmonized, useful one, all without breaking or destroying anything at all. It was like slipping on ice in a controlled way. All merely for the "beings" on both sides of the ledger realizing they were mutually better off cooperating in this more organized way, like any creatures in society, than apart and living without any awareness of this better way of being themselves, or without any awareness of the "other side," this "other" creation of God, or the broader nature of the universe. The "benefit" for the quanta was the fact that whatever holistic task the humans wanted to engage in with the use of energy likewise better organized them, which was of benefit for the quanta. More parts of the same musical instrument were tuned better, which delivered greater peace and a more pure sense of being to all parts of the instrument. The harmonization also happened more, and better, when the quanta responded to some purpose with another "species" outside of their own "galaxy," rather than harmonizing for, or among, their own kind. In this way, both humans and the quanta took a simultaneous step *together* to improve themselves, by constructive focus and exercise, and existing in this way while the conduit was open and the energy slid, until the link was shut.

Twain's genius was the doorway by which the human race and the quanta both learned of how very much "alive" the entire universe was, which meant that the fabric of the universe contained extensive opportunities for companionship, cooperation and symbiosis. Both sides experienced a higher crystallization of their "social" form that felt better and was healthier than the previously "detached," or "less organized," phase. It was musical, enjoyable; it was doing something constructive as opposed to doing nothing or serving no purpose. It was being a part of something rather than being less a part of anything. More purpose and belonging for one led to more purpose and belonging for the other, so long as the ends were constructive. Anytime both sides shifted into this better, more efficient, more organized position, they experienced the bliss response for making the more intended, higher use of God's world.

Queues for Tech use disappeared. Society discussed how long ago Twain's Leap might have been found if the elite had not crushed progress and hidden knowledge. Food, work, and currency became truly obsolete, if one so desired. Human lifespan now reached a little beyond one hundred sixty years, which provided yet another surprise for society when people saw the next level of reward for living the right way. The leap into speed and unlimited power led to the discovery of how many other species there were out there, all searching and enjoying the magic of existence and the magic of discovery in the positive space that filled in all of the features of God without actually accessing it. The human race now joined the ranks of interstellar space travellers, and learned how many species had visited Earth over the millennia, but had never interfered because all species had learned that all other life forms must learn and grow through all of the same stages of development and maturity. As the Robes had said, lessons given are easily lost and mishandled, while lessons learned at dear cost were tacked into bone. Humans learned that their older brothers and sisters from space had, however, leaned in the few times long ago when it was feared that political evildoers might launch the great weapons of the time to kill far too many people for too little good reason. The interstellar space travellers combed all the reaches of existence that they could, in the wonderful exercise of learning all they could about the Father-Mother from the negative space filled at all times by what had made all but that was never there.

Two hundred years after Twain's death, people still enjoyed having Tech make them beautiful objects. They loved objects of beauty and past rarity, such as clothes, houses, shoes, airplanes, cars, architecture, boats, precious metals, animal items, gems, important inventions, watches, clocks, buildings, great books, articles of war and history, and exotic places or products resulting from extreme circumstances. People found great fun in exploring imaginary dimensions and reenacting historical events in better and worse ways, humorous ways. People found something new and different by focusing great attention on the close-up details of anything—interesting features in a garden, a renowned location, an outstanding waterfall or brook or rock formation, or any new fascination in the insect world or among other tiny creatures.

A favorite hobby was the creation of exotic new insects and plants, whether real or fake. Beauty and order still harmonized the mind and stimulated the bliss response. The ugly and shocking was still pursued for its own sake by some, and for variety, but not for political ends as in the era of population stress, because no motive could convince anyone of the value of stressing society against itself except in a temporary, calculated way designed to arouse a specific hormetic affect.

With the human mind having the ability to pursue imagination limitlessly, people put more thought into finding what might be surprising and alluring to the senses. They fabricated both old and new objects, light, sound, and language into shapes, hues, colors, rhythms, textures, and derivatives that continued to flatter the human imagination. Nothing had any value other than how, and for how long, it delighted the human soul. And then, if you let go any object or stimulus and later cycled back to it, like an article of fashion, God had wisely made it a permanent feature of anything that existed to be delighted again by old things. And so, with study, people learned the optimum ways to keep each other delighted.

What remained a mystery was Life After Life, what happened to people after the allotted one hundred sixty years. The reach of the human imagination could not pierce the veil. The theme was one of the most popular in art. People somehow trusted that it was good, whatever happened, since they had every sign from within their selves, and all the world, that all was good. It was still universally regarded as a state of being even better than real life. People assumed they would be even closer to God.

The slowing down of the aging process by defined, linear means led to people fearing death less than ever before in human history, for life was its own wonderful chapter and then the next chapter was even better, for then you were a step closer to the source and in that way even more secure, informed, and probably more enraptured. There was speculation that people could ask God if they could go back to live a life again, or if they could do so in a more turbulent, interesting time. A seer said that this could be done. The seer said that "slots" were made by a visa program to account for population restrictions at any given time in early history.

People became fascinated with history and religion. Nothing was more interesting than studying the different ways people and cultures in those times had conceived of fate, of the structure of the universe, of their God and godly beings. Society discovered that Halloween had once been a quite innocent occasion looked forward to by children for the receiving of candy and the doing of harmless pranks. They became fascinated too with the phenomenon of addictions and how and why people had let chemical escapism grow into a monster that took over their body and mind, and led them to ruin a body that was only half *theirs*, the other half God's. Equally fascinating was the ease with which the evildoers of the past had jumpstarted the human mind to make people turn against one another for the most obvious self-defeating reasons. What awed the moderns most was their realization that their brains were wired the exact same way their ancestor's brains had been wired, meaning that, if they had not already learned the self-evident self-defeat of man's inhumanity to man, anyone could come along in their own time and trick them again into making the exact same colossal mistakes. The moderns were thrilled to learn how their God had built the human organism so that all of its constructs could be directed either way toward holistic or non-holistic ends.

Some people wanted children; others did not. The population slowly dropped. The wild places stretched, pristine, away from the metropolises across most of the Earth and were darkened by the herd animals. The wild places and the urban spaces both exhibited the further majesty of their own beauty. World population shrank and then stabilized at nine billion. Sky and sea shone a clean, fierce blue. People raised much of their food for fun and gardened and read and pursued entertainments with friends. With Tech so capable of producing food and items of amusement, Tech and the robots had little to do but exist alongside their brother and sister and partake in much the same interests and camaraderie encountered in the joy of simply being.

Parts could be replaced for machines, but not for humans. No matter how far human and robot had come together as offspring of the same creator, no matter their ability to manipulate the world around them, no matter the torturous routes together they had turned, humans and computes never plumbed the secret on the creation of Life. None of even the most capable space explorers ever had. If they had, they would have surely shared the knowledge with their brothers and sisters given their belief in everyone being what they called, "colleagues in the same discipline," which turned out to be a term that had been used on Earth as well. At the end of 154 to 161 years, well-preserved humans hit the wall of genetics. Genes could not be tampered with without robbing Peter to pay Paul. People said their goodbyes to family and favorite friends, whether robot or human, since thriving and well-being were now so linear and predictable that the winding down of the clock could be precisely calculated. Anyone who looked could see nearly the precise moment of their painless death. Some died in their sleep. Many did not want to die in their sleep and stayed up with friends and family, holding hands to the last. People sat in a chair with loved ones on either side, outdoors no matter the weather, enjoying the elements of the moment however God made them.

The American buffalo held a mystical allure for people all around the world, just as it had for the native people of the American Plains. One of the most popular ways to die was to gather among the herds in camp chairs to watch the great dusty, wooly beasts as they grunted and grazed. However the "traveler" chose to mark the occasion of their end, often they would be talking to a family member or quietly watching the scene of nature when a look as if they had learned some quick detail crossed their face. The chin would come down, the eyes might shut, and they would be gone.

The Moon of Hell molted in smoking black-red flame and slowly circled the planet in an unending orbit that was a reminder of what was most important. As souls finished their sentence, they were remanded to rejoin the afterlife.

3,052 years after it lit, the last flames in the Moon of Hell fell dark like the sooty licks of a prairie fire. The roar of the ovens had long ceased. The last of the great monsters had paid their price. Man's inhumanity to man had come to an end. The technology had served its purpose to advance human life. Flyers made regular pilgrimages up to hike upon the hard, flaky ash built of bone, where they regularly came across skulls and could look up the evildoer and learn how they had fiendishly abused others. Such crimes to them seemed inconceivable. They felt like hieroglyphs of a foreign race. The orb stopped orbiting and hung like a great spent clot of ash for four hundred years over the very spot it was born. That spot came to be known again as the Chesapeake Bay, named after the natives that had dwelled there thousands of years before. Every human and robot on the planet made a visit to the spot at some time at least once to see the ashen clot that had made the difference in human perception; to see it from the ground in the same spot where their disbelieving ancestors had three millennia prior. The Moon separated into fine dust, carried off by the elements until it was no more.

The mask, Ovid, never returned.

Made in the USA
Las Vegas, NV
02 August 2022